We hope you enjoy this book. Please return or renew it by the due date.

You can renew it at www.norfolk.gov.uk/libraries or by using our free library app.

Otherwise you can phone 0344 800 8020 - please have your library card and PIN ready.

You can sign up for email reminders too.

NORFOLK ITEM

30129 083 514 266

A Lawless Place

DAVID DONACHIE

Allison & Busby Limited
11 Wardour Mews
London W1F 8AN
allisonandbusby.com

First published in Great Britain by Allison & Busby in 2018.
This paperback edition published by Allison & Busby in 2019.

Copyright © 2018 by DAVID DONACHIE

A CIP catalogue record for this book is available from
the British Library.

10 9 8 7 6 5 4 3 2 1

ISBN 978-0-7490-2116-0

Typeset in 11/16 pt Adobe Garamond Pro by
Allison & Busby Ltd.

The paper used for this Allison & Busby publication
has been produced from trees that have been legally sourced
from well-managed and credibly certified forests.

Printed and bound by
CPI Group (UK) Ltd, Croydon, CR0 4YY

To Benji & Cate
who have certainly
raised the tone of the
Lower Valley Road

CHAPTER ONE

It was the sound of loud snoring that woke Betsey Langridge. The next thing to register was a splitting headache, soon followed by the realisation she had no memory of how she had got to her bedroom, indeed no recall at all of the night before. After several seconds of confusion, Betsey was also wondering why she was fully clothed, and that included her outdoor shoes. Having hauled herself upright, she staggered round to the vacant side of the bed to find there a total stranger, a young fellow with corn-coloured hair, crumpled in a sort of foetal position, clutching an empty brandy bottle and snoring steadily.

There was a pool of bile close to his mouth, the stench of which had her swoon, the supports of the four-poster enabling her to endure the wave of nausea without falling. Betsey tried to make sense of what she was seeing, coming slowly to the conclusion there was none. Looking towards the bedroom door, it seemed not to be fixed; indeed the whole room, the walls, the fireplace and the floor appeared to be moving in and out of focus, which made the move towards it otherworldly. Each step was an effort, accompanied by a feeling that, at any moment, her legs could give way.

Opening the door revealed a house in darkness, as well as silence. The light from a near-full moon was coming through the large landing window, throwing forward a shaft strong enough to bathe everything in a slivery glow. Tempted to go back into the room, to ring the bell by the fireplace and summon a servant, she reasoned it cruel to drag them from their beds. Betsey was also worried about stability, which made the newel post at the head of the stairs a better bet for an outstretched hand.

What followed was a slow and cautious downward progress, one step at a time, both hands on the bannister, until she made the ground floor. The same shaft of moonlight bounced off the highly polished boards, providing enough of a gleam to make further progress possible. Not that she could move on immediately; Betsey had to stop and gather herself, eyes tight shut, for, given her exertions, she felt close to a faint. Only after several deep breaths could she raise her head, opening them to look around.

Familiarity identified the outlines of the various items of furnishing in the spacious hallway: the twin settles and, in the centre of the circular table, a great silver and light-reflecting bowl, which prompted a memory. At the social gathering she had organised weeks before, it had served as a receptacle for a popular rum punch, too much so for some of the guests.

There had been gaiety, laughter, with melancholy Cottington Court and its grounds turned into a place of pleasure, brought on by numerous guests and games, a gathering of old friends and acquaintances, followed by a splendid dinner in a specially erected marquee to round off a wonderful day. How long ago that now seemed, like another world.

It was slow to dawn on Betsey, as more slivers of memory intruded. She should not be here in this house, a place she had been determined to flee. Or was that a dream? Was Edward Brazier, who had promised to come and take her to freedom and much more besides, an illusion?

A faint strip of light coming from her brother's study, leaking out from under the door, caught her eye. It needed the support of both her hands on the wainscot to make progress towards it and, once outside, turning the handle also required effort. The catch released, she fell forward, which threw the door open, leaving her hanging on to the brass knob as her knees nearly gave way.

A multi-branch candlestick sat on Henry's desk, all the wax stems guttering and not far off vanishing. He was asleep in a chair before the fireplace, his long, spindly legs stretched out, crossed at the feet, shoes almost in the grate, hands folded corpse-like on his chest. There was little but ash now, with the odd faint hint of red, where the last of the embers retained some heat.

Hauling herself upright, Betsey made the distance between the door and Henry's huge desk to stand, hands pressed down, wondering at the disorder, highly unusual for a man so fussy about everything being orderly. There were two empty champagne bottles, used glasses and, once she turned her head, in another chair, the wild, pepper-and-salt hair of the Reverend Joshua Moyle. He lay, crown to one side, with tongue lolling out, also sound asleep.

'Elisabeth?'

Reacting too speedily to what was an urgent whisper nearly unbalanced her. One hand, clutching the edge of the desk, was required to stop her from sinking to her knees. Her Aunt Sarah stood in the doorway, looking anxious and making frantic gestures for both silence and that she should come away. Slow-witted, Betsey failed to respond, so her aunt closed the space between them, took her arm and led her back out into the hallway, softly pulling the door shut behind her.

'What is happening? I scarce know where I am.'

'My poor dear,' was all Sarah Lovell could say in response, this imparted in a voice full of misery. 'I never realised Henry could be so wicked.'

'Why? What has he done?'

'Best sit, Elisabeth,' was the reply, as Betsey was eased onto one of the hallway settles.

The scream, which rent the air a few minutes later, was enough to wake the dead, if not those too drunk to hear it. It stirred Henry Tulkington, who shuddered slightly at the unpleasant feeling of being chilled. For a moment he, too, was left to wonder where he was and why. What did register was the fur on his tongue, as well as the sour taste of stale wine on his breath.

Rising, his legs stiff from discomfort until fully erect, he laid his hands on the mantle to stare into the embers as the events of the last few hours came back to him, bringing forth a feeling of satisfaction. The crash of his door being thrown open, so violently it hit the wall, had him spin round. There stood his younger sister, glaring at him, her hands stretched out to hold herself steady on the frame. Even with a slightly woolly head, and knowing he was in for a tongue lashing, Henry forced himself to smile.

'Elisabeth, my dear—'

'You utter swine.'

'What a lack of gratitude. I must profess myself shocked.'

'I will not let this stand.'

'Really? I don't see how you can do anything to alter it.'

'What did you put in that champagne?'

Henry picked up one of the bottles to examine it, as though it was an article unknown to him. 'The means to make you compliant, which I see as being in the service of your best interests, as well as my own.'

A snuffling sound had Henry look towards Moyle, whose head had slipped off the back of the chair to leave him, hand outstretched towards the floor, suspended over the padded arm. 'And here was the means to make it so.'

'No, never . . .'

Henry moved a couple of feet towards the desk, to look down at a large open ledger, on to which he laid and drew a finger, followed by a quick glance at the wall clock. When he spoke, he did so in a voice full of faux wonder.

'Dated yesterday, Elisabeth. Mr Harry Spafford, Groom, was joined in holy matrimony to Mrs Elisabeth Langridge, widow, service conducted by the Reverend Doctor Joshua Moyle, Vicar of the Parish of Cottington, witnessed by myself and your Aunt Sarah.'

The tone changed to icy disdain as he looked at her shaking head and heard her muttered denials.

'You sought to defy me, Elisabeth, and that was bad enough. Yet worse was being interrogated on matters which were none of your concern. I must have failed to satisfy you, given you sank to the point of acting the spy.'

Her headshaking became more pronounced, accompanied by a tearful whimper.

'Do you think me a fool? Did I not find you in this very room, when you thought I was absent? What were you seeking in here, something damaging to pass on to your naval captain?' The finger jabbed the ledger. 'You put his interests before that of your own family. This is payment for your duplicity.'

The tone lightened again, becoming almost jocose. 'You will not be aware of it, but Brazier came for you, I suspect by arrangement, and he was not alone. Was it to help you to elope, to run away and bring disgrace upon the family? He and his band of ruffians were stood outside yonder window, just after your nuptials. I confess, I was tempted to ask him in, so he could act as an extra witness, but I doubt he would have seen the delicious irony.'

'He will kill you.'

'No, Sister,' was a malevolent hiss. 'Unless he wants to swing in Newgate. Even now, I could have him arrested, given that, in front of a crowd of witnesses, he aimed a pistol at my head. I shall pen a note to your admirer and advise him, since his purpose in coming to Deal is no longer capable of being realised, it would be best for all if he departed and went back to whichever rock he crawled from under.

'Well, well,' was all he said, as Betsey fainted away, to crumple in the doorway.

A bell was rung to rouse out the servants and, once they had responded, Henry Tulkington gave them their instructions. 'Take Mrs Spafford to her bedroom.'

Faced with a blank look at the use of the name, he shouted, which was past unusual for a man ever in tight control of his emotions, 'That is her name now and, by damn, I hope she has good cause to regret it.'

It had taken time and eight strong arms to get Edward Brazier back to Deal, which came with many an admonishment telling him it would be impossible, whatever he thought, to bring on immediate redress. The odds they had faced, some two dozen of Tulkington's hard and armed bargains, were too great to contest with. Even if they had shot a couple, and it had been considered, it would have ended in a beating and possibly much worse.

All five had got away from Cottington Court, exiting through the same hidden postern gate by which, with such high hopes, they had entered an hour before. They took with them, for security, the unsteady figure of one John Hawker, he being Henry Tulkington's right-hand man and a nasty bastard to boot. Belting him had provided one of the few bright spots of an otherwise disastrous night.

The blow had been delivered by Tom 'Dutchy' Holland, who was more than a match in size for most men and could land a punch enough to fell an ox. When in service aboard the frigate HMS *Diomede*, he had served as coxswain to Edward Brazier. It was he who had taken the lead in getting his one-time captain away, not that he could have succeeded on his own: it had required the combined efforts of all of his erstwhile shipmates, both physical and verbal, to move him.

Peddler Palmer had prised Brazier's pistol from him lest, given his mood of uncontrolled fury, he shot Hawker out of hand. Every time he turned to go back and 'sort out that bastard Tulkington', Dutchy had required the help of Peddler, as well as Cocky Logan and Brazier's servant, Joe Lascelles, to both restrain him and keep the head of his horse pointed in the right direction.

It was a slow ride back to Deal, made so by both the gloom and their prisoner: he was hauled along on foot, to be dragged along the ground when he fell. Hawker had been dumped as soon as they felt they were far enough off from Cottington to be secure, thrown into a muddy ditch and left to make his own way back, no mercy being shown to a man devoid of that quality in his own disreputable life.

It was a town, long asleep, to which they returned, with barely a lantern still burning in a window: even the numerous places of entertainment were closed, though a few of their customers were still about and ambulant, if barely so. Brazier was pushed through the door of his rented home as Peddler took the reins of the horses, leading them towards the nearby Navy Yard, where they would be stabled for the remainder of the night.

'Get a fire going, Joe,' Dutchy asked. 'Don't see us gettin' much sleep with the captain in such a state.'

Cocky Logan was quick to add his opinion, delivered in his strong Scots brogue. 'If we did, one ay us would have tae lay against the front door. Ye ken what the Turk's like when his dander's up.'

The use of Brazier's soubriquet got sage nods from the others. Given to him as a fresh-faced midshipman, many years previously, it had stuck. It went with his saturnine looks as well as his temperament, that of a fighting sailor ever eager for action; one – man or boy – who would bear no condescension from anyone.

Right now, he was sat in the parlour, staring at an empty inglenook, lost in his own thoughts. All of them were circled around ways to reverse what had occurred, for he had no doubt the claimed 'marriage' of Betsey Langridge to this Spafford creature was illegal. Even as he ruminated on this, he could not bring himself to believe Henry Tulkington had gone so far to prevent him marrying his sister.

He had only known of the man for a number of weeks, but to say they had not hit it off, on first meeting, was an understatement. At first, Brazier could not pin down a reason. Tulkington, for no discernible motive, seemed dead set against his widowed sister remarrying anyone and that extended especially to him. He had sought deflection by implying Brazier was a fortune-hunter, given that Betsey, over two years widowed, was in possession of several highly profitable sugar plantations.

That was easy to prove as nonsense: a successful post captain in King George's Navy, Edward Brazier was prosperous in his own right. In addition to his rank and pay, he had, in the Caribbean, taken a Spanish vessel carrying a cargo of silver. The Spaniard having been captured and in French possession for over two days, it could legitimately be claimed as a prize when the French privateer was sunk. Madrid had complained vigorously, only to be ignored by Whitehall.

Both ship and cargo had been bought in through the Prize Court, and that included head and gun money for the crew and the armaments, the proceeds to be distributed to the crew of HMS *Diomede*. As the ship's captain, he had been in receipt of an eighth of the money, with a further tranche of the same size coming to him as the senior officer on a station which, due to an untimely death, lacked a commanding admiral.

The truth had finally emerged when he had been told of Tulkington's true colours, which were dark and menacing. Far from merely being a highly successful man of business, he had control of smuggling on the East Kent coast, near to an industry, as well as a firm grip on the trade in the town of Deal, where he was feared and admired in equal measure.

The prospect of an upright naval officer as a brother-in-law seriously alarmed him. This was enough to take an apparent disinclination to approve of his intentions on to a violent reaction. The severe beating to which Brazier had been subjected, mystifying at the time and within days of his arrival in Deal, stemmed from that source. Unaware of the cause at that point, and given a misleading name to chew on, had caused Brazier to send for some old shipmates to guard against repetition.

Joe Lascelles apart, the trio of Dutchy, Peddler and Cocky were all handy in a fight. They had been the reliable men of his barge crew, always by his side when action was called for. Often they formed a boarding party, seeking to get a foothold on an opposed deck, with never a hesitation at the prospect of hurt. With them around, he felt his back was safe from the still-mysterious threat. When the truth about Tulkington emerged, he was doubly grateful for their presence.

'I fetched a bottle of brandy, your honour. Thought you might need it.'

Brazier glanced up at Dutchy, a man who could look down on him stood upright. The bottle in his hand appeared tiny, the crystal goblet even more so. Joe Lascelles slipped by, flashing one of those smiles that always lit up his dark-skinned face, his arms laden with kindling with which to get going the fire.

'What I need right now, Dutchy, is the whole of the crew of *Diomede*, armed and ready for a cutting out.'

'Wouldn't serve, your honour.'

'It would serve to satisfy me.'

Holland gave no reply; he knew himself to be right, just as he knew Brazier would see the sense when his mind cleared. This was not like being at sea in wartime, contesting control of the oceans with the French and Spaniards, or dealing with ex-colonists running contraband into the sugar islands from America. It was on land, at a time of peace, and there was the law to contend with.

'I can't let it go.'

'Didn't reckon you could.'

'Did you see her, Dutchy?'

'Not as plain as you, Capt'n.'

Brazier was back at the large sash window of Henry Tulkington's study. With John Hawker's men threatening his back and the well-lit room before him, Betsey's brother had come to and opened the window. He stood grinning as he looked down the barrel of Brazier's pistol, no doubt reckoning the man his sister had planned to run away with would not shoot. He had no idea how close he had come to being mistaken.

'Betsey was looking straight at me, Dutchy, but with no recognition in her eyes. It was as if I was not there. The priest was drunk and so was what I assume to be the one named Harry Spafford.'

Brazier recalled Betsey's aunt as well, her eyes red with weeping while clutching a handkerchief, which looked as if it had been much employed. Sarah Lovell had never given any indication of liking him, obvious from the first time he had come across her in Jamaica. As Betsey's chaperone, sent out by her nephew after her being widowed, it had been her task to ward off the attentions of eager suitors and, given her niece's evident beauty added to her known affluence, they had been many. But there had been real sadness when their eyes met. Surely she would not have just stood by and let this happen?

'Your lady is likely a fighter, Capt'n, and will sort matters out, without you go seekin' blood. Happen things will look better once you've had a chance to pass a word with her.'

'I hope you're right, Dutchy. And since you brought that brandy, you'd best fetch another four goblets. I have no desire, this night, to drink alone.'

CHAPTER TWO

John Hawker waited 'til the slow clip-clop of the hooves fell away to silence before he lifted himself up, not without pain, to clamber back onto the rutted dirt road. If he was murderously furious, Hawker also knew nothing could be done about it at this time. He needed to get back home to clean himself up, as well as to examine the scrapes and scratches with which he reckoned himself to be covered. He had spent as much time being dragged as he had staggering on the end of a rope.

His clothing was torn, both coat and breeches in many places, which mattered little, as long as he was not seen in such a state. A man who revelled in his fearsome reputation, this had him, as cloud cover obscured the moon, bless the darkness, even if it made progress difficult. Normally, night or day, John Hawker walked in dread of no man in these parts, very much the reverse. People made way for him to pass and, if some made to ignore him, it was from fear of catching his eye.

Progressing unsteadily, sometimes stumbling, both from his still muzzy condition and the uneven ground, he eventually put aside the curses and visions of revenge he would later rain down on Brazier, as well as the Jack tar bastards he led. Instead he concentrated on Henry Tulkington, for it was clear, this night, it could be imputed he had let his employer down.

It would have taken a man with the powers of a saint to foresee that two problems, the trespass of Dan Spafford's smuggling gang, coinciding with the arrival of Brazier, would merge into one. But that might not count with a man who could be capricious. Any reckoning there would have to wait as well, but he could not avoid concern, for he had sensed recently the bond that held him and Tulkington together, to the profit of both, was not as secure as it needed to be.

It had been a long, solitary walk back to Worth for Jaleel 'Daisy' Trotter, one in which he had tried and utterly failed to make head or tail of that which he had just witnessed. Everything was in a state of flux, yet such had been true of these last weeks as Dan Spafford had sought a way to bring down Henry Tulkington, or at least secure a profitable hold on his own smuggling operations.

In terms of size, it was the Tulkington whale versus the Spafford minnow. Now the country was at peace, profits were cut so far to the bone that Dan was close to giving up the game altogether. His only alternative was to somehow even matters up between him and the man who controlled nearly all the running of contraband on this stretch of coast.

The first attempt, contrived by Daisy, to trick their rival into a dubious alliance had failed. But there had followed, for a brief window, a feeling of matters levelling up, this coming as they stole Tulkington's recently landed goods, carried out in a manner that denied him certainty the Spafford gang were the culprits. Thanks to Dan's useless son Harry, the deception had collapsed. He had given chapter and verse of what his pa had been up to.

Spafford Junior was a whoremonger and drunk, as well as a constant disappointment to his overindulgent sire. He had fallen into the hands of John Hawker, with foreseeable results, for the boy was weak. Daisy, who had known Harry since the day he was spawned, could well imagine how little of a threat to his person would have to be mooted to get from him a full admission of what he knew.

'You should have left the little sod to rot, Dan,' was not spoken silently, it being cried to the heavens, for there was real anger in the sentiment. 'Or let Hawker feed him to the pigs, instead of seeking to bargain for him.'

Daisy became distraught when he thought on what might have happened to Dan, a man he had known, loved and served since they were both nippers sailing trading ships on the Baltic route. Dan had gone to treat with Tulkington for his boy, ostensibly going to the meeting alone. In truth, not trusting the bastard, he had arranged for his gang to sneak into Cottington Court, available to free Harry by force if necessary.

The ploy had been anticipated and, in a night of utter confusion, Spafford's men had been outwitted and were now prisoners. Daisy, who had managed, in the darkness and confusion, to hide from everyone, his own mates included, was adrift in wondering how to right matters. If Dan was still alive, and that not a certainty, a way had to be found to get him free, which raised many insurmountable difficulties. He could see no way to achieve it, especially on his own.

Once he made a cot in which sleep would come eventually, one name overheard kept coming to mind, to repeat itself endlessly in his brain until the sky lightened to herald the approach of a new day. There had been a third lot in the chaotic brawl Daisy had witnessed, which had made what was bewildering enough even more confusing. He could clearly recall the name Henry Tulkington had used for what was clearly another adversary, a fellow who had aimed a pistol at Tulkington and looked set to pull the trigger?

Who in creation was this Captain Brazier?

Sarah Lovell found Henry alone and eating breakfast, informing her nephew of the comatose, drunken figure lying beside his sister's bed, to suggest that, at the very least, the mess he had made be cleaned up. In doing so, she underlined for him the fact that he too had fallen asleep at a time when he should not have done so.

His aunt also reminded him of a factor to which he had given insufficient attention in his haste to thwart his sister: what would be expected to happen after a normal marriage, which this was most assuredly not. Much as Elisabeth had enraged him and brought upon herself the present fate, he had no notion that being wedded to a slug like Harry Spafford should proceed to anything like consummation. What might emerge from that was too horrible to contemplate.

'Have the servants move Spafford to another room.'

'Henry . . .'

Looking at Sarah Lovell, Henry would have had to be blind not to note her anxiety.

'I acted as I did because Elisabeth gave me no choice.' There came to him a wheedling tone, as he sought to cast himself as the victim in the affair, not an unusual way to for him to behave. 'I tried to reason with her, but would she listen? No: as ever, she was headstrong and selfish.'

'I believe she became strongly attracted to Captain Brazier, even more so than she showed in Jamaica.'

The response was cutting. 'Something I sent you to the West Indies to stop.'

Sarah Lovell wanted to reply that no one could overcome such feelings, but held her tongue. She depended on Henry for the very food she ate and the bed she slept in. Given what he had just done to his own sister, there could be little doubt he would cast her out of his house if she failed to please him, and she was penniless. Her eyes dropped to avoid being seen to be defiant when faced with a challenging look.

'I do hope I can rely on you, Aunt Sarah?'

'Of course, Nephew.'

'I will not have Elisabeth suffer any more than is necessary, you have my word upon it.'

Given he had dropped his head as he said this, to concentrate on his food, she was far from sure it was safe to believe him, but there was no room for a rebuttal. Best to change the subject. 'The Reverend has gone, I take it?'

'Home, yes.' That was followed by a chortle. Henry Tulkington was not a man much given to laughter, very much the reverse. But Moyle, so distant from what he should be when it came to both honesty, divinity and behaviour, always seemed to amuse him. 'No doubt to a thorough and well-deserved wigging from his good lady wife.'

She was tempted to speak once more, to say he would benefit from such a thing, both the consort and the berating. That too was supressed, but she did manage a slight barb. 'I will go and see to your fine addition to the household.'

The sarcasm flew right over Henry's bowed head.

Two grooms had to be fetched from the stables, men who would have no trouble in bodily lifting Spafford, not true of the indoor servants. Her next command was to fetch hot water to Betsey's bedroom, with cloths to clean up the vomit. Only then did she go to the room itself, to stand by her niece, taking and holding her hand as her instructions were obeyed.

Subjected to many a curious glance, all were studiously ignored. The servants would be full of inquisitiveness as to what had happened, both the night before and what was being undertaken now. With the level of hullabaloo, at least some must have overheard things happening in the twilight hours. Let them wonder and gossip, they would hear nothing from her lips.

Once the room was clear and cleaned, a fire laid and burning, she went to the door and closed it, turned the key in the lock, removed and pocketed it. Back at the bedside she gazed at a sleeping Elisabeth, reprising the depressing events of the last few hours, before moving to take a chair by the fireplace, to wonder at what the future would hold.

Henry lay back in a leather chair, the razor his manservant was wielding gently scraping the light growth off his face. Eyes on the ceiling, he sought to formulate a way to proceed, for what had occurred these last forty-eight hours – the coming together of a whole set of disparate problems – had left no time for contemplation of outcomes, indeed the possibilities had been too numerous.

There was no feeling that he had overreacted. As the heir to his position, both legal and questionable, he had seen it as vital to protect his inheritance. In addition, he valued his standing both locally and in other parts of the country; the prospect of a sister neither beholden to him nor under his control, and one who, in her intended misalliance with Brazier, might bring everything crashing down, was too dangerous to contemplate.

Not wishing to dwell on that, he turned his thinking to the one thing that was certain, an outcome that brought much satisfaction. He had smashed the Spafford gang, who had been an irritant for years. He could, of course, have brought that on at any time of his own choosing, but sense dictated it could very likely not be done without public violence.

In the smuggling game, it never served to attract attention, which open conflicts, or too aggressive a way of behaving, tended to produce. The Revenue Service, poorly paid and badly provided for, was inactive enough to suit the Tulkington purpose. To this was added the occasional sprat John Hawker threw their way, normally a group of souls operating off Deal Beach who had forewarned a man they trusted of their intentions.

Start a war, with possible public bloodshed, and it would bring in the army, as it had, three decades past, with the Hawkhurst Gang. Many of that crew had either been killed by the soldiers or had been captured to swing for their crimes, and that was not a fate to contemplate. So, much as they had irritated him and, in truth, their activities barely dented his own, Tulkington had let Spafford operate.

But stealing his goods went beyond tolerance and good fortune, which he saw almost as his due, and had delivered them into his hands. Spafford senior was chained in his cellar, the younger one upstairs, probably still snoring his head off. The other gang members had been sent off with Hawker's men, instructions being given to make for the Deal slaughterhouse-cum-tannery, where he reckoned they would rejoin Hawker himself, once that swine Brazier released him.

Not that he was entirely clear of their baleful presence. The father presented more of a problem than the son, for he was a cussed individual, typical of the coast, rough of manner and speech, with a stubbornness that seemed to characterise the lower classes of East Kent. The original notion, of absorbing Spafford into his own operations, might appear a solution, but it was not necessarily a secure one.

Henry Tulkington was careful to keep his activities clandestine and his involvement in the actual act of smuggling at arm's length; indeed, even having the men he employed come to Cottington had broken a rule. Everything locally went through Hawker, only financing and the arrangements for disposal were overseen by him. Spafford, who knew too much and could not necessarily be relied on to hold his tongue, might jeopardise that.

Still, in the presence of his worthless son, Henry held the same high card that had led to his capture. Threaten to harm the boy, and his father would do as he was told. Harry was easy to deal with, given the slightest threat to his person rendered him a wreck. He reasoned that as long as he was provided with the means to buy drink and entertain whores, and with the prospect of a sound thrashing always in the background, young Spafford would give him little trouble.

That accepted, other problems arose, like his lack of discretion, really a tongue too easily loosened. To have him carousing in Deal, and at his usual haunts, risked what had just happened at Cottington Court being talked about around the town and that was anathema. He considered the possibility of sending both Spafford and his sister off to the West Indies, to take charge of her plantations.

They had come to Elisabeth after the death of Stephen Langridge and would now devolve to the control of Spafford as her new spouse. The prospect of him in possession of the income from those properties, while many months distant from any oversight, did not bear thinking about. He would either ruin them through mismanagement or drink away the income they generated.

His face was being towelled when a footman entered with an unsealed and scribbled note, which simply said his presence would be appreciated, appended with the letters JH. There was no need to mention a location; that was a commonplace. He would comply, but first he had to allow himself the pleasure of a gloat, which took him to the cellar to face the cause of one half of his present concerns.

He was about to ask Grady, his senior servant-cum-valet and the man who had just shaved him, for the key to the cellar, only to recall he had demanded the man surrender it the day before. If it was given up swiftly, it had been impossible not to notice it had been done with little grace, which reprised a thought often considered: retainers had to be continually reminded of their place, especially long-serving ones, lest they get ideas above their station.

Dan Spafford was sat on the floor, seemingly half-asleep, the chain and padlock, with which John Hawker had restrained him, set to keep him well away from any of the bottles in the racks that lined the walls. The sound of Tulkington's footsteps had him look up to see his nemesis moving towards him, slowly and carefully, pulling bottle after bottle from the racks and examining the labels.

'It is reckoned to be one of the best cellars in Kent, Spafford, did you know that? You have slept surrounded by wines of a quality to which you could never aspire or appreciate. Not that "quality" is a word anyone would apply to you.'

'The boy?' Dan Spafford demanded.

'Is alive,' was stated without a hint of feeling.

Towering over his captive, Tulkington looked down into the square, red-skinned face, showing, as it did, evidence of poor stock, added to a life spent either at sea or on an exposed shoreline. The expression returned was not one of supplication; Spafford probably expected his fate to be terminal, yet he was not going to beg that it should be otherwise. The gaze was steady, taking in the tall, slim figure with the slightly hollow chest and the habitual, haughty expression.

'There's alive and barely so.'

'Your progeny is, if you excuse what will be a sore morning head, in better health than you could imagine.'

'Don't mock me, Tulkington.'

'While it would give me great pleasure to do so, I am not. But I am wondering what to do about you.'

'I expect your worst.'

Henry put a finger and thumb to his chin, as if in deep contemplation. 'That might be a solution.'

'Not that your hand will be employed, whatever you have in mind. That will be left to Hawker. You see yourself as too much the gent to soil them, not that it's true. A man can be as much a shit in silk as in sackcloth.'

That broke the studied Tulkington reserve. With a furious expression, he lashed out with a foot to kick Spafford's knee. When his victim declined to react with a squeal of justified pain, he repeated the blow, to then make a great effort to contain himself.

'I will not let you rile me, Spafford, for you are unworthy of my anger.'

The Spafford jaw was set tight when he replied; if he was determined not to show pain, it did not mean he felt none. 'Unchain me and I'll stand against you with any weapon you choose – pistol, sword or knife.'

'What?' Tulkington sneered, his manner of equanimity restored. 'Grant you the attributes of a gentleman? Fists are more your station.'

'I ask for fair, nothing more.'

'You may ask, but it is I who dispose. It may please you to learn I have yet to decide what to do with you, so you will have to rest where you are until I do. I might even feed you, to show that I am not the ogre you imagine.'

'The condemned man eats a hearty meal?'

'It will not, I assure you, be hearty. You warrant no more than bread and water.'

'Bastard,' was the Spafford response, as Henry Tulkington walked away and up the cellar steps.

Halfway to the ground floor it dawned on him. He could not ask a servant to take even bread and water to Spafford. Despite what had happened, it was a tenet that nothing of his illicit activities was allowed to infiltrate the walls of Cottington Court. So he would be required to undertake that duty himself, a thought that came near to being nauseating.

It was a small leap then to the conclusion that the man would have to wait. In the hallway, the cellar locked behind him and about to call for his coach, he paused. Given the excitements of the last twelve hours, he felt a strong need for carnal gratification. The means of that, as well as the location, was not something to share with anyone, least of all a couple of gossipy coachmen.

'Tell the grooms to get my horse ready.'

Twenty minutes later, wrapped in a heavy coat, with a muffler to protect his neck and a hat pulled low over his head, Henry Tulkington emerged from his front door to find his horse saddled and waiting. Not an eye met his, which was as it should be. Likewise, no brow was raised at his attire, excessive for a mild day, in which Upton, the head groom, was stood, and happily so, in a sleeveless smock and a leather apron.

His master, a man known to be ever careful of his well-being, was convinced every wind that blew, or drop of rain that fell, was designed to bring on to his being all manner of afflictions.

* * *

When Betsey came back to wakefulness, it was to find a fire in the grate and her aunt dozing beside it. She lay still, gazing at the silken bed canopy, as the enormity of what had happened assailed her. That quickly shifted to remedies, which led to how to conjure up the means to secure an annulment. Yet even as pressing as that seemed, her mind kept wandering to Edward Brazier. He had obviously kept his word and come for her, only to be thwarted.

It was with a sense of horror that she wondered at his reaction. Did he think her complicit? Was it that which had made him angry enough to threaten Henry with a loaded pistol? Surely not, but since she had no recollection herself, any number of disturbing notions were free to play out in her imagination and none of them brought comfort.

Slowly Betsey raised herself up and, feet on the floor, pushing upright, she tested her balance, pleased to find it restored. There were no shoes now, they had been removed, so it was with silent, stockinged feet that she crept round the bed, pleased to see her unwanted visitor and his puke had been removed.

Creeping up to the chair in which sat her aunt, she looked into a face which, in repose, showed all the lines of her age, as well as her temperament. The jaw hung slightly, which exposed both teeth and a lolling tongue. The lines on either side of her nose, as well as those running down from lower lip to jaw, seemed much more pronounced than when animated, if one excused her expression – too frequently one of disapproval.

Turning away, Betsey went to the door for, if there was to be a solution to the predicament Henry had placed her in, it would not be found in her bedchamber. She was put out to find the key missing and it could only be her Aunt Sarah who had removed it, which led to speculation as regards to motive. Henry's sneering words, spoken in his study, came back to her, more than any the fact that the parish register he had alluded to contained Sarah Lovell's signature as a witness. Could that really be true? Could her aunt have colluded in this farrago? Was she being confined as part of that?

'Reluctantly' Henry had said. What did that mean? Had she been coerced? In frustration, Betsey grabbed the door handle and tugged at it, which created just enough noise to bring Sarah Lovell out of her slumbers, she too looking confused as she came into wakefulness. Then she turned towards the door and her niece, her face carrying the same expression of sadness with which she had greeted her earlier.

'How could you?' Betsey said softly.

'I tried to dissuade him, you must believe that, Elisabeth.'

'Not hard enough,' was bitterly delivered. 'You could have refused to witness.'

Sarah Lovell bit her lower lip. It was obvious she was seeking words to explain and finding none, or at least not any that would serve as justification.

'Why did you lock the door and remove the key?'

'To keep out the servants and—'

'Henry, or that slug I found by my bedside earlier. Perhaps it was to keep me in and supine?'

'That is cruel, Elisabeth.'

Betsey came closer with her riposte, to stand menacingly over her aunt. 'You have the effrontery to use such a word to me?'

'I am on your side.' There was a significant pause before she added. 'As much as I can be.'

A hand came out. 'Then oblige me with the key.'

It was produced and handed over, with an admonishment to be careful, ignored as Betsey unlocked the door, adding a parting shot. 'What do I have to fear, Aunt Sarah, now Henry has done his worst?'

She left behind a relative unsure that her niece had spoken the truth.

CHAPTER THREE

If it was seen as eccentric behaviour to swim in the sea of a morning, indeed at any time of the day by most folk of sense, it was even more peculiar that it was done in the company of a trio of armed and tough-looking companions sporting cutlasses slung over their shoulders. There was, as well, a servant of African extraction bearing an armful of towels who waited right by the shoreline. On this morning Edward Brazier had a sore head to contend with, the result of imbibing far too much brandy, as well as what he would have found hard to admit to: a damaged heart. The shock of the water, close to ice-cold, was welcomed as a distraction from his troubled thoughts, but not for long.

In a vain attempt to keep from reflection, he put extra effort into striking out against the current, one which left a swimmer feeling a total lack of any progress when measured against any object on the shore. If he emerged bodily refreshed, it did not long extend to his reminiscences, including those more distant than the events of the previous night. His attraction to, and pursuit of, Betsey Langridge had been challenging from the very start.

Now, wrapped in towels and on his way back to Quebec House, he reprised their relationship from the very first meeting at the Governor's Ball in Jamaica, given in honour of the King's birthday, one it would have been impolitic to miss. A gaggle of naval inferiors had been present, with whom he could have easily conversed, as well as the soldier types, not least the governor's aide-de-camp, a young fresh-faced fellow who had been delightfully indiscreet on the subject of inter-service rivalries.

The bulk of the guests had been civilians discussing, as always, at least in the case of the menfolk, the concerns that animated them: the price of sugar and, given they were a profligate lot when in funds, the cost of borrowing to plant a new season's crop. He being a man of healthy appetites, and spotting a decidedly attractive female across a crowded room, had prompted questions as to her identity from the governor's wife, the best source possible, which got him a typically sharp response.

'You will face a challenge boarding that particular deck, Captain Brazier.'

This opinion had been presented in her habitual direct manner and to that had been added a particularly telling gleam in her eye, which hinted at something more. The leading light of local society, Kitty Clarke stood at the centre of everything, including gossip. Not much, it was said, escaped her attention in matters relating to the lives, loves and endemic indebtedness of those who lived on the island, whatever their gender.

'I think what you allude to a trifle premature, Lady Clarke,' had been his less than candid reply. 'I merely wish to lay myself alongside such a charming creature and exchange pleasantries.'

By holding to the naval metaphor, the Brazier riposte had engendered a soft cackle. Kitty Clarke was direct in her opinions, not least in the matter of dalliance and its inevitable aim of conquest, which was much lauded by some and heartily disapproved of by others, to which she was said to give not a fig.

Brazier had liked her on first acquaintance for her utter lack of hypocrisy, added to which she came with something of a racy reputation. As a young woman, she had caused a huge scandal by eloping to Holland with the Earl of Pembroke, despite the fact he was already married and had sired an heir. Even more scandalously, Kitty had gone on to bear Pembroke a son, though it was a boy he acknowledged and supported, as well as one she was openly proud of.

'A pursuit has to begin with a sighting, sir,' had come with a vigorous wave of her fan. 'And you will have observed, you are not alone in your interest. There are vultures circling.'

That had been true; in the short time since first spotting this unknown beauty, several men had managed to enter the orbit of her attention. But none, he had also noted, succeeded in staying there for long.

'Again,' he had insisted, 'you're ahead of my purpose.'

'Stuff it, Brazier,' was what he had got in a brisk reply. 'You're a man and she's a woman, as well as a rare beauty, ripe for the plucking, I'll hazard. What's the point of all your enquiries, if it's not to plan an approach and, at the back of your mind, a great deal more?'

It had been time to move matters on from something he had no desire to discuss in detail, even with someone so lacking in tact. 'While I am forced to respect your opinion, Lady Clarke, I find, while you've been erroneously dissecting my purpose, you have yet to impart anything of interest about the lady.'

'Elisabeth Langridge is her name, though she goes by the diminutive of Betsey. She's a widow and a wealthy one to boot. If I were you, Brazier, I would set course soon, or you'll find her prize to another.'

There being no point in seeking to deflect her low opinion of his intentions, he had listened as more was conveyed about this Betsey Langridge: how long she had been in the West Indies and the several properties she now owned. Kitty Clarke alluded to the sad fate of a husband, ill-equipped to ward off the endemic diseases of the tropics, what an attractive couple they had been, given they were of the same age and clearly much smitten with each other.

'The death of her husband badly affected her. She's scarce been seen these twelve months, such was her grief. This may well be the first occasion on which she has ventured to cross her threshold, and rumour has it she may be returning to England. The lady beside her is an aunt, sent to fetch her and, by all accounts, an immovable object to anyone seeking to engage in conversation.'

Informed and fascinated, Brazier then set out to manoeuvre himself into a position that made polite exchange inevitable, only to be forced to contend with the presence of said aunt. She being a woman of pinched expression and a very steely determination, to the point of being downright rude, had made normal banter impossible. Yet, brief and constrained as it had been talking to Betsey, he had sensed a spark of interest, prior to a requirement to move on. That, of course, had come with the caveat of wishful thinking.

The circles in which Edward Brazier had moved in the West Indies, if you excluded those purely to do with naval service, had been small, consisting of plantation owners, government officials and factors engaged in the sugar trade, which included the importation and auctioning of slaves, an activity of which he had heartily and vocally disapproved.

Normally he had tended to avoid too many of these gatherings at which he regularly met the same people, albeit as the second most senior naval officer on the station he was ever in receipt of an invite. Added to his other reservations had been the presence of his superior, Admiral Hassall, he a constant attendee at both these soirées and the inevitable punch bowl spiced with rum.

Since they had not seen eye to eye on certain matters, disputes that would surface when Hassall was inebriated, meeting him outside official necessity had been best avoided. The governor's annual garden party, held in the grounds of his official residence, had demanded attendance, where it had been interesting to see how many people had avoided engaging with him.

Edward Brazier had naturally been held in some regard for his rank as a senior post captain. In terms of reputation locally, that had become somewhat muted by his activities. As the commanding officer of the 32-gun frigate, HMS *Diomede*, he had been assiduous, many said too much so, and that included Admiral Hassall, in pursuit of those seeking to break the embargo of the Navigation Acts.

These stated that no produce could be imported into the Crown-owned colonies that was not carried in British vessels.

In essence, this meant it had to come from home ports such as Bristol. Prior to the American War, much of what was required for comfort had been brought in, albeit illegally, from their fellow colonists to the north, with a blind eye being turned to the trade by officialdom. But not any more: the newly minted United States, if not quite enemies, were nevertheless not seen by Albion as friends to indulge.

Fetching every one of the necessities for both comfort and business over three thousand miles of ocean added significantly to the cost, which was much resented by those faced with the bill. The Carolinas, North and South, upped their game now they were independent, the blind eye having not entirely gone away. If it was no longer officialdom winking, it was maintained by a planter society that had, with the Americans, a shared interest.

The task of King George's Navy was to stop it, not that his commanding admiral rated it as a priority. This had formed the bone of contention with his superior, over which they had argued with some passion and perhaps too loudly for good sense. Brazier needed to know where, and if, he was officially supported. It had thus become politic to engage Kitty Clarke at the social events he had chosen to attend, which had nothing to do with an interest in gossip or attractive females.

It had emerged there was a plan by a group of planters and tradesfolk to sue him for their losses. Given the judges in the local courts were closer to a tolerance of their point of view than his own, it seemed possible they could well succeed, which might have seen him locked up, and worse, made personally liable for damages to cover their costs.

'I take it Hassall is equivocating?' Kitty Clarke had enquired, met with a flick of his eyebrows for raising the subject. Outright condemnation was unwise, even with her.

'I'm far from sure I have his full backing.'

There had been an implied question in his response; what would keep his detractors at bay, what was the attitude of the governor and, while he baulked at the notion of asking the man himself – too direct a query might produce too definitive a negative answer – he had seen no problem in aiming a hint at his wife.

'My husband will hold them off, Brazier.'

'Can I be sure of that?'

Kitty Clarke had been a stunning beauty as a young woman and there was much evidence of it still. But it was not an attribute to survive any trace of exasperation. Emotion changed her countenance in a remarkable way and it had done so then; she had gone from faded attractiveness to termagant in a split second.

'He will answer to me if he fails to do so. The King's law must be upheld.'

'You have no idea how reassuring I find that to be.'

Which had contained a touch of sophistry; it had been common knowledge the governor, Colonel Alured Clarke, doted on Kitty and was wont to seek her advice on matters of contention. Not that he was weak in any way; he was, after all, a much-lauded soldier as well as a royal favourite. But his position on the island rendered him isolated when it came to advice, so he was given to relying on his forthright and brutally honest wife as a sounding board.

Her attention had wandered as her angry expression relaxed, the fan waving once more, even under a parasol in place to ward off the heat. 'Do I see a certain lady arriving, Brazier, one I recall of some interest to you?'

The pointed fan had shown Betsey Langridge descending from a covered carriage, her parasol opening at once, for the sun was strong and the normally cooling breeze slight. He had managed to talk to her on two other occasions, though it could not have been said to extend to much more than exchanged pleasantries. The presence of Sarah Lovell had posed a constant barrier to anything more, which did not apply just to him.

It had even extended to a royal prince, albeit the one in question – William – deserved every rebuff he encountered and he got a very public one from Betsey Langridge. She was far from alone: touring the Caribbean in command of his frigate, Prince William had, given his boorish behaviour, left behind a bad odour in every island he visited.

Especially outré in drink, this rendered no woman safe from his outrageous sallies and salacious suggestiveness, like the pleasure and kudos to be had from bedding a blood royal. More than one husband had required to be dissuaded from calling him out, a task that often fell to Edward Brazier, and they had crossed swords in another context.

Admiral Hassall, whose responsibility it should have been, had declined to haul William up with a round turn for his want of decent manners, no doubt for fear of the latter's father and the effect it might have on his career. Then came William's martinet behaviour aboard ship, where he had publicly humiliated his first lieutenant, delivered in such a manner as to leave the poor fellow no choice but to demand a court martial to adjudicate on his competence, a court at which Brazier had been obliged to act as the senior adjudicator. The verdict, which he was called on to deliver, had come close to being a public rebuke to Prince William. That, troubling as it was to recall, had soon ceased to be a matter to dwell upon.

His eye and mind had turned to Betsey Langridge and to the problems posed by the continuous presence and blatant disapproval of her aunt, one he felt was not shared by her charge. Attraction is not necessarily demonstrated in words, however few, and he had seen in her expression, in particular in her eyes, that his attentions were not unwelcome. Once more thinking of how to surmount the Lovell barrier, Kitty Clarke had put her finger on the matter.

'Time to be bold, Brazier. Rumour has it she has booked passage and will be off back to England soon. Time and tide, sir.'

Thinking on that, and stood naked in the backyard of Quebec House as Joe Lascelles doused him with warm water to wash off the salt of the sea, he recalled those words, which had led to a determination not to be deflected. He had headed straight for Betsey, ignoring the fact she was in conversation with another possible suitor, to quite rudely cut in on their conversation in a way that had forced the poor soul to retreat.

'I'm told you are shortly to leave us, Mrs Langridge.'

'Is that of any interest to you, sir?' came from Sarah Lovell. Betsey, on the other hand, had smiled and nodded in a way that indicated a measure of regret.

Emboldened he had replied, 'It is surely so, when the island will be much diminished by the loss, as will I.'

Lovell's parasol spun furiously. 'By the Lord, sir, you are overbold.'

Brazier had ignored her and looked hard at Betsey, but with a care to keep his voice soft. The smile he had aimed at her was meant as both a message and one he wished to be taken as utterly genuine. 'I cannot feel we have had enough time to properly acquaint ourselves.'

'And you would wish that altered, Captain?'

'I would most certainly like it to be so.'

'Elisabeth, I see the governor looking in our direction. I do believe he wishes our presence.'

That had been responded to with a sweet smile, even if the words were outright rejection. 'He has any number of people who want his attention, Aunt Sarah, so I do not fear he will miss ours. If you wish to engage with him, please feel free to do so.'

The intake of breath was audible, but Lovell had not moved, as Brazier used a shoulder to partially cut her off.

'Is it true, you're leaving?' A nod. 'To return to?'

'Deal in Kent, to my family home.'

'Which is?

'Cottington Court, just outside the town. It overlooks the anchorage.'

'It is a part of the world with which I'm unfamiliar,' had seemed a banal rejoinder. 'I have touched at the Downs, of course, but spent no time there.'

Another sweet and engaging smile. 'Then you may find much of interest should you do so.'

The sound coming from her aunt's throat then would not have

shamed a person dying from the bloody flux, being half-cough and half-groan. But her charge was not going to be deflected.

'But I do not leave before Race Day, so perhaps we will come across each other there.'

'Would I be allowed to ask for a commitment to that?'

'You most certainly would not,' Sarah Lovell had snapped.

The look on Betsey's face, especially the twinkle in her eyes, had stated the precise opposite. 'Perhaps you will enter and race, Captain?'

'I am a man at home on the deck of a ship, Mrs Langridge, not the back of a horse.'

'Quite daring in that milieu, I'm informed.' So she had been asking about him. 'I suspect you would be audacious mounted, if you were more familiar with horses.'

'Audacity would scarce keep me in the saddle, Mrs Langridge. But in other things, besides horsemanship, I might be seen to be foolhardy.'

'Elisabeth, I fear I am suffering from too much heat.'

They had both so nearly laughed, not at the excuse being made but at a connection between them, the sharing of a similar thought. If heat was being generated, it was in the look exchanged, or perhaps in the palpitations of the Lovell concerns. Tight control had been necessary for Edward Brazier to keep a straight face: it had been impossible to miss the tightness of Betsey's jaw, as she fought a similar affliction.

'Perhaps a cooling drink, Aunt Sarah.'

'Allow me to escort you to the marquee.'

'That would be most kind, Captain Brazier.'

His intention to take Betsey's arm had been thwarted by

determination: Sarah Lovell got between them to ensure it could not be, which left him with a dilemma. Did he take her arm, this being something her niece alluded to with a mischievous grin?

'I'm sure my aunt would welcome your support, Captain.'

'Given willingly,' he had said, to have it rudely refused.

If mutual attraction had finally been cemented, it had happened at the Race Day, even if it was all in gesture and gentle innuendo. With crowds occasionally surging to watch the horses speed by, added to the sound of thudding hooves, Sarah Lovell's immediate presence and her ability to overhear had become severely curtailed.

When he gently put his hand on Betsey's back, to edge her towards the approaching runners, she had offered no resistance, which was reassuring while, with the crowd closing behind them, her aunt had become marooned. Even more telling was the slight frisson he had felt running up his arm on contact, like a current of electricity. Did she feel it too? It was not a question he could ask.

'Would you be offended, if I was to say I will miss you?'

'How could anyone be put out by such a compliment?'

'I am forced to wonder what it is you're going back to.'

'Just my brother and my home.'

'I've never commiserated with you for your loss. I have a feeling I would have liked your late husband.'

'He was a man easy to like, Captain Brazier.'

'Would that be a hard condition to replicate?'

He had felt her tense then and he knew why, for that was very close to a step too far. The mounts had sped by at the same time, their hooves throwing up clods of the heavily watered earth, one heading straight for Betsey's face. As she had recoiled into his hand, he had held her firmly, reaching out with the other to catch it in mid-air. With an exaggerated bow, he then presented it to her.

'A souvenir to remember the day by, Mrs Langridge, and perhaps to remember me also.'

Passage might have been booked, but the ship in which she would travel had yet to arrive, such things being seasonal. Much in the nature of duty happened in the meantime, which had kept Brazier from any further pursuit. There was the sudden and mysterious death of Admiral Hassall while he was on patrol, immediately after which, HMS *Diomede* had put to sea a second time for a cruise that saw the deceased admiral buried with fitting ceremony.

That was only one part of his purpose. Remaining at sea, having been supplied with intelligence as to where it would be intercepted, Brazier had gone on to capture and bring back to Kingston Harbour the Spanish plate ship he had set off to intercept. He had also brought in prisoners from the French privateer to which the *Santa Clara* had fallen, their ship having been sent to the bottom of the sea.

This had added much to the general talk of a colony in which one day tended to meld into another, with little in the way of incident. Hassall's untimely demise, the subject of curious speculation, soon faded from the gossip, in favour of conjecture on how much Brazier and his crew had earned from their Spanish prize. If fabulous figures had been bandied about, there was no doubt in anyone's mind the gains were substantial.

He had met Betsey one more time, at a ball given by Kitty Clarke to celebrate his good fortune, one more occasion when every indication he could detect pointed towards a mutual magnetism. He could recall clearly, as he dressed himself, Sarah Lovell's parting shot when it had been time to depart, as well as the pinched expression that accompanied it.

'Goodbye, Captain Brazier, I doubt we shall meet again.'

He had looked at Betsey then, hoping she would counter the sentiment, but she had merely dropped her gaze, to leave him in excruciating limbo.

CHAPTER FOUR

Henry Tulkington could scarce avoid noticing the heavy blackening round John Hawker's right eye. With no desire to be caught staring, he turned away, as he often did, to stand by the stove, removing his gloves and warming his hands over the bowl of herbs sat on top. They were placed to take away the noxious, all-pervading odours of the slaughterhouse and tannery. The noise of dying animals, when slaughter was in progress, was harder to disguise.

The bruise was large, blueish going yellow at the edges, which did nothing for a countenance far from flattering to begin with. With his large head and pockmarked face, as well as a nose that showed evidence of many a thump, Hawker would have struggled to claim allure. He also had a rough gravel voice, allied to an expression which, as it implied a threat of violence, rendered him generally disagreeable.

That said, Hawker always addressed Henry Tulkington with respect, even if on this day he was in dispute with a proposal. 'I won't say I is happy with havin' any of Spafford's lot getting involved in our affairs.'

'Why?' was delivered in a level tone, with a back still turned.

'They're a mouthy lot and tavern boasters, who we can't keep locked away forever. Let loose, they're not like to keep quiet 'bout last night either, regardless of threat. It'll be all over Deal an' beyond in a week. Might be, anyway, since we missed Daisy Trotter.'

'He's on his own and, from what you tell me, no great shakes in the fighting line?'

'Skin and bone, and ugly with it, but handy with a blade. Happen he wasn't there last night, for it would have suited him to stab someone in the dark. If he causes trouble, I know where to find him.'

'Last night?' Tulkington said enigmatically, raising his head to look at the roof beams: the thought of Trotter free did not seem to trouble him. 'Do we need to examine that, John? All that mayhem was far from as it should have been.'

'Would have been safe if it'd been just the Spafford lot,' Hawker protested, stung by the criticism. 'Could have seen to them without too much trouble. The others, well . . .'

The implied question was left hanging, and with it John Hawker's curiosity about what he would dearly love to know. Had the near-simultaneous arrival of Brazier and his tars been a coincidence or was it anticipated? If the latter, he should have been forewarned so it could have been dealt with, possibly before they even got into the grounds.

His recollection was vague on what happened after the discovery of their presence, due to the incapacitating clout he took in the dark from one of their number. Tempted to enquire, he held his tongue; any question there did not appear welcome and he would probably whistle for an answer. This thought increased the feeling that had been growing on him these last few days: that things did not feel right between him and Tulkington.

This disquiet he could date back to the first meeting, in a hilltop coach, he and Daisy Trotter had brokered between his employer and Dan Spafford. It had taken weeks to arrange, due to deep mutual suspicion, with no indication of distrust having been eased when it ended. Not that he had been told anything; it was only later he found out things had been said, not agreements but telling facts, of which he should not have been kept in ignorance.

Prior to that day, John Hawker had felt himself trusted completely within the remit of his responsibilities, happily accepting there were areas of the whole to which he was not privy. The feeling of things not being as they were rendered him unhappy, but it was not his sole concern. To his mind, and he had stated it before the events of the night, the way he had been asked to deal with the Spafford lot was all wrong.

Putting a cap on their thieving of his contraband had been the primary aim. Presenting them a chance to invade Cottington Court and taking them prisoner created a whole set of other problems. To his way of thinking, this made things worse not better. His solution would have been to beard them on their own patch, with superior numbers, and mete out a sound beating, applied especially to their leader and his useless son. A good hiding was not something to go around boasting about, very much the opposite: it would be a matter of shame.

Tulkington, who had denied him the opportunity to do that, turned and faced Hawker, his expression giving nothing away, to ask about the men captured and where they were now.

'Locked up, chained together and under guard in the smaller cowshed.'

'That eye of yours, it's bound to cause comment.'

'None of which will reach my ears.'

The abrupt change of subject had thrown Hawker and, if the reply was stated with certainty, he was not about to put off his main concern. 'Can I reckon, from your mood, gettin' rid of Spafford's lot, permanent like, is not favoured?'

The response was terse, as if the notion was foolish. 'That means over a dozen bodies and too many questions. They are all men known in the town and, if they disappear . . .'

'Been known for a smuggling lugger to founder often enough,' Hawker persisted, 'all hands going down.'

The nod was an acknowledgement of a fact, but it did not extend to agreement. 'Why are you so sure you can't trust them?'

'What I'm sure of, Mr Tulkington, is I don't want to have to.'

He might as well have said, for fear of blame, if they proved to be unreliable. Hawker was sure Tulkington got the point but he did not do what was wanted, which was for him to accept responsibility.

'Best you speak to them as a first step.'

'To say?'

'It might help to reassure them, whatever happens, they're not going to end up in a pork barrel.'

51

This was a rumour, given he ran the slaughterhouse, which fed into Hawker's reputation. It wasn't true that some of his victims ended up as cut and salted meat, food sent aboard departing ships, where the barrels would not be opened for months. Nor did he sell on the skins of his victims, to be made into the softest of saddles and other high-value artefacts. But it suited him to allow the story of such a fate to circulate; the thought induced a terrible fear in people who might be tempted to cross him.

'For now, keep them fed until I decide what to do. And send a couple of your most reliable men up to Cottington with a covered cart tonight, the kind who know how to keep their mouths shut. They are to ask for me in person. I can't keep Dan Spafford in my cellar forever, so it's best he too is brought here, with due discretion, but kept separate.'

'He, of all, should disappear.'

'Perhaps?' was the enigmatic reply. Tulkington then pulled a letter from his pocket and handed it over, prior to putting on his gloves, a sure sign that, for him, at this moment, the matter was dealt with. 'I need you to see that delivered, John. It is an invitation to Brazier that he depart Deal.'

'Ain't paid much attention afore.'

That was occasion for a thin smile and, finally, an explanation of what had taken place while Hawker was too groggy to register anything around him. It was one listened to impassively, though it as good as told him Brazier had been expected. He had been kept in ignorance of the possibility and paid the price in both pain and pride. If he was seething inwardly, he could let nothing show on his face.

Not that Tulkington noticed, he being too busy gloating. 'Once it's delivered, the house has to be watched for signs he has heeded my instruction.'

'And if not?'

'Then pressure will have to be applied.'

Hawker pointed a finger to his bruised face. 'I need to get even for this.'

A touch of exasperation came with the response. 'There's a greater purpose at stake, man. I need him gone, so matters can settle. My wish is that, hopes dashed, he will just go.'

Your purpose, Hawker was thinking, *not mine*.

Edward Brazier sat at his writing desk, quill in hand, though yet to be dipped in ink, given he was wondering what to say. At the back of his mind was a nagging doubt, the thought that, somehow, Betsey had been complicit in what had occurred; irksome because, even if he did not really believe it, the thought would not go away. Normally a fluid penman – as a King's officer his rank involved endless correspondence – being stuck for an opening was uncomfortable.

He forced himself to write his address and the date, only to realise that could be unwise. The letter, taken in by a servant, could be opened prior to being handed to Betsey. This engendered another even more depressing possibility: she might not get anything he sent to her at all. Yet he required certainty about what had happened and only she could provide it, which led to thoughts that an intermediary might be required, one who could carry his messages verbally, without them being intercepted.

It might provide a solution, yet it was far from an easy one to execute. He had been in Deal for weeks now, but that did not change his status much in what was a taut society. He was still a stranger and had few acquaintances locally who could bridge the divide between him and the woman he had set out to marry.

It was almost by its own volition that the quill moved, but it was not to write to her, but to the Admiralty, on a subject with which he was familiar; the composition of his request for command of a ship required no real thought. If what followed was more prevarication, the letters he penned to various people, it served a purpose: they took his mind off his most pressing concern.

There was one for his prize agent in London, requiring an update on his position financially, others to naval acquaintances with whom he regularly corresponded, not least his first captain, now Admiral Sir Eustace Pollock. This always ended with a commitment to call upon him when time permitted and that induced a pause. Pollock was not far away in the hamlet of Adisham. Would keeping such a promise be a way of keeping his mind off his present difficulties?

He felt very much the need to talk to someone, if only to pause the spin of speculation with which he was assailed. Much as he might seek to control his imagination and dismiss as absurd the more fanciful places to which his worries took him, he was failing, so the quill was thrown aside. Brazier stood up and made for the front door, grabbing his hat on the way. The slamming forced those who escorted him everywhere to rush to follow.

'Mood's not improved,' opined Cocky Logan, as he grabbed his weapons.

'Be a while, I reckon,' was Dutchy Holland's response. 'If ever.'

Peddler was the last to join them in the narrow street, just in time to see their captain disappear, turning left and heading towards the Lower Valley Road. He had in his hand the sheathed sword Brazier had left behind.

'Serve him right if he gets a sandbag round his earhole.'

Striding out, Edward Brazier had a look in his eye that tended to clear a path through anyone seeking to share his space, which, given his height and build, was not contained to begin with. For once, crossing the busy thoroughfare on which the town centred, the sweeper failed to get a coin for clearing the dust and dung. This had him stop and wonder, leaning on his broom, for the kindly Captain Brazier had never failed to tip him half a penny before.

Said captain's destination was the Old Playhouse, a theatre and tavern, where he hoped to find perhaps the one person to whom he could unburden himself without engendering useless pity. He didn't want sympathy, he wanted a way to proceed that did not involve skewering Henry Tulkington or putting a ball into his heart. That, as a solution, could not be, given he was dealing with a man, he was sure, who would refuse any challenge he issued.

Despite that knowledge, the image of fighting the bastard filled his thoughts. So mercurial was he in conjuring up scenarios, it extended to duelling with both swords and pistols, in all of which there was a most delicious point of triumph, in which Betsey's brother expired as they embraced above the body.

The thought could not be held, so by the time he went through the door of the Old Playhouse he was scowling again, to find the person he sought in her tiny den-cum-office, just off the card room. She was sat with a quill in her hand and a ledger open on what passed for a desk, one piled with bits of paper in various stacks, all bills.

Saoirse Riorden looked up at her visitor, a smile of greeting only halfway to completion when it faded; the glare with which Brazier was looking at her made that seem inappropriate, so it was replaced with one of open enquiry, added to a touch of annoyance.

'Well, you look to be in cheer of the day. I'd offer you a chair except I'm in want of one spare.'

'I need to talk to you,' came out through clenched teeth.

The woman he was addressing was not one to be trifled with, so his tone got what it deserved. 'Well, I'll be saying, if you do, that's not the manner likely to get you your wish.'

'It's important, Saoirse.'

'So is what I'm about, Edward. These figures will not do themselves and you know, though only the Lord knows why I trusted to let on to you, why I can't leave them to another.'

Brazier just shook his head, with a look in his eye that left little doubt he had no interest in her concerns, so she added, 'Hawker will be along later today and I must have them make sense.'

'If not truth?'

The quill was put down and she turned in her chair to look up at him, green eyes showing her clearly confused. 'Have you been at the bottle?'

His face lost the angry look, indeed it could have been said to fall. Saoirse was not thinking that had been caused by the words she'd used, indeed she was speculating here was a man who might benefit from a stiff drink, quickly offered.

'I reckon that to be the last thing I need.'

'Which leaves me wondering what is it you do want for.'

'Someone to talk to,' was delivered with a weary tone, 'who will help me make sense of what has happened, though I think it defies that commodity.'

It was a measure of her sagacity that Saoirse did not enquire; she waited for several seconds to allow him to gather his thoughts and nor did she interrupt as he told his tale. She was not aware it was filleted out, with no mention of Hawker and the presence of a whole host of other bodies. Brazier related it without holding her eye; in fact, he seemed to be talking to the shelves full of ledgers behind her head, which did allow Saoirse to display the shock she felt without him noticing. He stopped speaking eventually and did engage her, to find a slow shaking head. When she spoke, her Irish accent was more pronounced than normal.

'I can scarce believe it and, to be sure, I've heard some tales in my time.' Saoirse stood and held out a hand to take his, achieved without protest. 'We shall go upstairs.'

'These?' Brazier said, with a wave of his free hand towards the desk.

'Will wait,' was said softly.

Brazier followed her out to recall, as he reached the stairs to the upper floor, the last time he had ascended them. Or, to be nearer the truth, was half-carried up and in real pain from several bruises and a cracked rib. The blurred memory of the reason followed: the surprise of the assault as night was falling, not many yards from the Old Playhouse door. The way he had been dragged into an alley to be punched and kicked, with his own responses feeling more feeble in reverie than they had probably been in fact.

It was luck more than fighting ability that got him out into the street, where what was happening could be seen, even more so that the two toughs who guarded the door of the Old Playhouse came to his rescue. Had it been an act of charity on their behalf, or had Saoirse, for whom he had been idling while waiting, sent them to aid him? He'd never asked.

'Harriet,' Saoirse called before entering her parlour. 'Fetch your cloak. Go to Mr Hawker, you know where he is to be found. He will not yet be doing his rounds. Ask him if he can call tomorrow instead of today.

'I think you best sit,' she added, once she joined Brazier inside. 'Do you want anything to drink?'

'No.'

'Would it hurt you if I asked you to tell me a second time what happened? I'm struggling to make sense of it.'

'You're not alone.'

Brazier sat silently for some time before speaking and, as he reprised for her what he had gone over a hundred times already in his own mind, he felt a sense of futility and confusion.

'I cannot clear from my mind the interior of that damned room, Saoirse, and that bastard of a brother of hers. If you asked me now, I wish I had put a ball in his brain.'

The frown, if he'd seen it – his eyes were cast down – would have shown Brazier that Saoirse Riorden was at one with Dutchy in her view. She said nothing more until he was done.

'You're sure of the name Spafford?'

'Believe me, it is etched in my mind.'

'Well, I can tell you the drunken divine – not that he's ever sober – is called Moyle, and he is a disgrace to the cloth.'

'I know of him, Betsey told me. But his habits are of no consequence. He is a priest and has the right to marry?' Half-statement, half-question, it was acknowledged with a nod. 'And just who is this Spafford?'

'He's the son of a local smuggler.'

'Damn me, Saoirse,' came with real vehemence, 'is there a soul in Deal who is not?'

'Rare, I will grant, but the mystery to me is, why him?'

The look he gave her invited her to go on, which she did and what he heard affected both his anger as well as a sense of hopelessness. Had Tulkington deliberately chosen such a disreputable creature to send to him a message?

'Edward, the insult will be felt by your lady more than you. If Harry Spafford is not poxed to the eyeballs, it will be a miracle.'

'It must be set aside,' he hissed, with deep if frustrated passion. 'I need to know how it can be done.'

'Then you need to talk to a priest, for only one such will know how to go about it.' It took only a moment's thought before she added, 'The Reverend Benjamin, of St George's along the way, comes across as a decent man, able to nod to a papist like me without blushing or begging forgiveness.'

'Is he a discreet man, Saoirse, for this cannot be bandied about?'

'And how do you reckon it to be kept secret in a place like this? Sure, have I not already told you, Deal will invent a rumour if none already exists? You cannot but see this, sad as you find it, as a juicy tale.'

'Her reputation.'

'Will suffer, I cannot see how it will not.' She pursed her lips. 'It might be best to consult a lawyer before speaking to Mr Benjamin, though he is high church enough to respect the confessional.'

'Do you have a name? The man who contracted for my rental?'

'I'd caution against one local, not that we are overburdened. Henry Tulkington has too many in the town in thrall to him and I have no idea if one of them is the man I employ.' After a moment's thought she added. 'The matter is ecclesiastical, which minds me to say, find one in Canterbury.'

'I must find a way to communicate with Betsey, Saoirse.'

'There I doubt I can aid you. But I will put my mind to it.'

Brazier emerged from the Old Playhouse, to be greeted by the frown of those who had followed him and were waiting outside, while Dutchy Holland was not going to allow his rank to spare him a vocal complaint.

'That bastard Hawker is not going to forget how he got belted and, if I was the one who landed him one, he'll take it out on whoever he can find. So don't you go dashing off like that again, without you letting us know.'

It was a meek post captain in King George's Navy, a man that ruled like a monarch when at sea, who acknowledged the rightness of the reprimand. He did not know it, but it was that trait in his personality, the ability to admit he was not always right, which had helped to make him a popular commander. That and the obvious concern for the welfare of his men.

No one would, of course, tell him, to his face, such a thing.

CHAPTER FIVE

Daisy Trotter had woken up to an empty house, which was far from normal, though silence he was accustomed to. When they were not engaged in running or moving contraband, he was usually the first one abroad of a morning. He took responsibility for getting the fire going and the pots slung in the inglenook for hot water and breakfast. He took delivery of bread and milk brought from the local baker and the dairy farm, then raided the weekly stocked larder for ingredients, with the rest of the inhabitants called to attend when the food was ready.

The Spafford gang had not just smuggled together, they lived hugger-mugger in a ramshackle farmhouse on the western edge of the village of Worth. Maybe it was Dan Spafford's own less than happy experience with one woman, a liaison that had produced Harry, which dictated his policy of no females living in.

There were another couple of good reasons: loyalty to the group being uppermost, and keeping quiet about what they were up to day by day. A trip across the Channel required to be planned well in advance, with those who took their goods called upon beforehand to list what they were prepared to shell out for. The actual crossing had to take account of the impending weather but could not then be overly delayed, lest impatience send those same customers looking elsewhere.

That involved guesswork in the reading of impending conditions, based on a deep collective knowledge of the waters on which they would sail. Added to that was an ability to understand the elements, both as they were and what they would become, much of it folk memory handed down through generations of coastal sailors.

Someone with no part in the importation and sale of contraband, or the profits from such, male or female, might gossip. If the men who followed and depended on Dan Spafford wanted comfort, they could get it in the fleshpots of Deal, where there was no shortage of places to take their ease, or whores willing to oblige their needs, many on the streets and willing to oblige for small copper.

One or two, Daisy knew, had formed more lasting partnerships, but these were kept discreet and as such posed no problems. Harry Spafford was the opposite: since he had reached maturity, he was ever to be found in one of said burrows, running up bills for women and drink his overindulgent pa was obliged to settle.

It was eerie padding over the cold flagstones, knowing there was no one else about: enough to bring on the creeps, and that was before he even thought more about what had happened and any way to proceed. It was easy to allow imagination to run riot, conjuring up images of what Hawker might do to the lads who, only yesterday, had bustled about the place, yawning, scratching, exchanging jesting insults, all well-worn, to be taken with mock offence and general laughter.

'No laughter now, Daisy,' he murmured, as he cleared the grate of the previous day's ash.

The act of laying dry kindling and small logs was carried out automatically; likewise, he supposed, the next act: lighting the taper from the oil lamp on the mantle. It was one normally never allowed to go out, being topped up as the last thing carried out at the end of the day. Not last night – he had been too preoccupied to see to it on his return. That it was so just drove home his isolation and left him looking for flint and steel to get the necessary spark, as well as some dried grass.

The latter was doused in turpentine, so took quickly. When he got a proper flame, he stood back in contemplation and watched it spread to the kindling, then heard the cracks as the wooden logs began to heat and finally burn. A blaze going, he added thicker wood, but there was only one hanging of a pot, that for water.

Why bother with the others, given no one was here to eat anything? So he just remained staring into the fire. His brown study was broken by the door knocker, so he went to take delivery of the bread, bringing in, as well, the large earthenware jug of milk and block of butter and fresh eggs the farmer had left on the stoop.

Chewing bread still warm, spread with butter and a cherry preserve he had made himself, washed down with creamy milk, he literally sat and chewed the cud. The priority was to try to find out what had happened to Dan and the lads. Then, if what he feared had come to pass – indeed, regardless – he must find and have words with this Captain Brazier.

First he had some with himself. 'Might come to owt, Daisy, but who's to know 'til it's attempted?'

Several ladles of water, now hot, were transferred to a bowl, to be taken into his room and placed under the looking glass. Gazing at the image brought little comfort, given he had a nose wider than normal, with black bruising either side. This rendered a face well off being handsome even more depressing. It brought to mind the joke often made by his mates, taken as a jest, which said he looked so rodent-like that satisfaction, if he sought it, could always be had behind the skirting boards.

It had been possible to forget he looked even worse now, like some kind of ogre, as it had been possible to bury the cause of these afflictions, none other than Harry Spafford. His pa had dragged him home from the company of two whores and drink to be locked in a room to sober him up, as well as keep him away from further debauchery.

The gang were about to steal some of Tulkington's goods and Dan wanted his boy along, not that Harry showed any sign of being keen to go. No one else but his father had been allowed into the locked room, even down to taking in his meals and fetching away the empties, night soil included. It had begun to have an effect, though some of the screams that came from within on the first night spoke of the depth of Harry's demons, which would ease as time and abstinence saw his dependence of drink exorcised.

When Dan and the lads went off on their raid, Daisy, not seen as robust enough for the task, was left in charge. The memory of what happened triggered a whole raft of reminiscence, going back all the way to when he and Dan had been but boys. It may never have been returned in a way he would have wished, but he loved the man.

Daisy had extended something of the same feelings to Harry, acting like a surrogate parent, a replacement for his absent mother, which saw him looking at the image of a fool in the looking glass. It had been Harry who had headbutted Daisy and given him his bruising, to then skip past him and escape.

But it was the manner in which he had soft-soaped him beforehand, playing on his affections and suppressed desires, which hurt the most. The pricking of the eyes he tried to dismiss and fight off, but within seconds Daisy Trotter was weeping, his head in his hands, his shoulders racked, at the feeling of a life wasted.

Edward Brazier came home to find Quebec House smelling of freshly brewed coffee and Vincent Flaherty sat in his parlour. Much as he esteemed the horse dealer – if he had few friends in Deal, Flaherty could be said to be one – he was not really in the mood for his endemically cheerful presence and it showed, which led to a hurried excuse.

'Joe insisted I take coffee.'

'He would.'

This was delivered with little grace, which unsettled a guest accustomed, if you excused the odd lapse, to good humour. He didn't respond as Dutchy and the others, with a fair amount of clatter, relieved themselves of their cutlasses and pistols. Flaherty waited 'til they had passed down the hallway and the parlour door, before posing an obvious question, with some degree of pique.

'You're out of sorts, I can tell. Am I to be afforded a reason?'

'You do not think it might be a private matter?'

'If that is what you will say it is, so be it.'

Brazier turned to look out of the window, not that he could see much, no more than the warm brick wall and windows of the house opposite, across a street so narrow two carts would struggle to pass.

'If I'm not welcome, Edward . . .'

'Forgive me,' was said with a back still turned. 'I am somewhat in shock.'

Flaherty, near to being the first person Brazier had dealings with since he arrived in Deal, had become intimate enough to know of his reason for being here. Both being men who made friends easily, he and Brazier had bonded. The Irishman had even acted as a sort of spy, seeking to find out who had been responsible for his beating, the clue being that those assaulting him had, more than once, when driving home a verbal threat to go with their blows, used the mysterious name of Daisy.

Vincent could give him no clue to Daisy's identity so had been despatched to roam through the taverns of the town, given everything in Deal revolved around such places. His task was to seek out the identity of this lady, someone who Brazier had so unknowingly offended. Not that information had been readily forthcoming until very recently, when Daisy had turned out not to be a woman, but a man called Jaleel Trotter. He was said to be an expert at the silent knife, a fellow who had gained his soubriquet from his sexual proclivities.

'Do I sense Mrs Langridge is at the centre of this shock?' Vincent asked softly. The turn was slow and the look on Brazier's face enough to confirm to Flaherty he had the right of it. 'She's changed her mind?'

'Worse, Vincent, much worse.'

When Betsey called for outdoor clothing, suitable for walking, nothing was said. Yet Grady had about him an air that was beyond odd. It was common that a retainer would not directly catch the eye of the master of the house, for very sound reasons given his crabbed personality. But that had never applied to Betsey: she had grown from child to woman under this very roof and had been both as charming, entertaining and sulky as a girl going through adolescence could be.

Being married, albeit only for a short time, had made no difference and neither had it been so when she came home from Jamaica as a widow. Her relations with the servants had always been good, utterly at odds with that of her sombre and humourless sibling. She longed to ask Grady for his thoughts, but that was, of course, debarred by their differing stations.

The whole house must be abuzz with speculation on this sudden marriage: it would have been even more so on a subject she had managed to keep secret. They knew of Edward Brazier and his attentions, but not what had been planned for them both the previous night. What would they have said, if they had known of the plan to elope?

The thought was interrupted by her aunt appearing on the stairway 'Where are you going, Elisabeth?'

'For a walk,' was delivered in a biting riposte. 'I assume I can still do that?'

'If you wait, I will accompany you.'

'No!'

Betsey, by her acid tone added to the glare with which it was accompanied, might as well have said that was the last thing she desired. This had Sarah Lovell redden slightly, being in receipt of what sounded very much like a reproof, one delivered in front of a servant making it so much worse. Her niece did not wait to give her a chance to respond; pulling on her gloves, she rushed out of the front door before Grady could open it for her.

'Does madam require anything?' he then asked, looking up at the stony-faced older woman.

'No, Grady, nothing. But the young man we had moved, what of him?'

'He sent down for a tray of food and some wine, madam, and demanded a bath be fetched and filled. All have been attended to.'

Grady was well practised in the art of disguising disapproval, yet the way he used the word 'demanded' spoke volumes. Harry Spafford had, by his peremptory call, wasted no time in making himself unpopular with those below stairs. Sarah Lovell, with an air of resignation, nodded and retreated back up towards the first-floor landing.

The walk took Betsey on a familiar route, one she had traversed many times since childhood, with both friends, as well as her future husband, Stephen, who had been one of them. That was long before either even contemplated they might one day marry. But affection had grown between them to the point where nothing could have seemed more natural.

It was a bitter reflection that Henry had objected to that too, seeking, with their father dead, to act as if he had the right to decide. The arguments that ensued did not entirely replicate those she'd had over Edward; it was more about their youth and the unsuitability of a young man with few prospects. That had abruptly changed when, following on from the death of an uncle, Stephen Langridge had inherited his plantations.

The path led from the side gate of the formal garden, down a treelined track, to wind its way round the lake. Betsey decided, once she reached that, just in case she was being observed, to go round the left-hand side. It was a longer route which would, in time, bring her to the place she had so many times met Edward Brazier in secret. It was also the place where he had eventually become more than a mere suitor.

This engendered another memory, for it was on this very ground they had quarrelled about Henry, as Edward had told her of his nefarious activities, accusations that she refused to countenance as true. It was also the spot, once the scales had fallen from her eyes, where they had decided on marriage and planned her escape.

Before she approached the bushes, which hid from view the old postern door by which Edward had come and gone, she made great play of picking some wild daffodils, which allowed her to look about and make sure she was alone. Sure she was safe, Betsey pushed her way through the bushes, to haul on the dilapidated gate, seeking to get it open, her hopes fading very swiftly. It would not budge an inch, even with strenuous effort.

She laid her head on the remains of what paint was yet to peel off, knowing her intention to escape was impossible to achieve. Henry had forestalled her by having the gate sealed, which told her he must have known the purpose to which it had been put before last night, maybe as far back as the first time it had been used for her 'secret' trysts.

An image came to mind of him laughing, as usual, with little in the way of humour, sarcasm being his habit. He would be saying, 'My dear Elisabeth, what an obvious creature you are.'

It was a dispirited sister who made her way to the main carriage driveway, which ran up to the house from the road to Canterbury. She suspected Tanner, who manned the outer gate, would have been instructed to deny her exit and Betsey did not even have to pose the question: an exchanged look told her that was the case at several yards' distance, so she wearily retraced her steps.

Back at the house, and divested of her cloak and outdoor shoes, Betsey went in search of her aunt, finding her in the drawing room. She made no attempt to moderate her fury, or to keep it from other ears by shutting the door. Sarah Lovell tried to get past her, but Betsey physically blocked her path, spittle coming from her lips as she screamed at her.

'How could you allow yourself to become complicit in this crime?'

'I was not complicit.'

'You witnessed the parish register.'

If the older woman had set out to be defiant, it could not last in the face of her own self-censure. The expression crumpled and the voice turned to a plea. 'What choice do I have, Elisabeth?'

'So you will just obey Henry, regardless of the dishonesty of his actions. Do you know what that makes you?'

Sarah Lovell's chin was near to her chest and her voice was low, but there was a sting in her response. 'It makes me what I have to be, for I have never been in receipt of the advantages you have enjoyed.'

'Advantages?'

It was an unwise response, which Betsey knew it to be as soon as the word was uttered. She was soon given a list of those, from a woman who clearly harboured and had kept hidden a whole raft of resentments. Betsey had been doted on by her father, even before the death of her mother, Sarah Lovell's sister, but no one had ever bothered to enquire whether she, bereft of a husband who had gone out one day and never returned, was happy to step into those shoes.

'How do you think everyone in this house sees me? As one of the family? No, and that extends and always has, even to the servants. They do my bidding for fear of my nephew, not out of respect for me. And Henry is content to have his home run for him by someone who is bound to Cottington Court, not by love or affection, but by the need to keep body and soul together.'

'You have never intimated before that you were unhappy.'

'What good would it have done if I had? What could I have said? Did it ever occur to you that I might petition to have my Samuel declared dead after all these years, for which, by the way, I would have had to plead for the funds to make the case? That I might want to seek happiness elsewhere, just like you?'

Betsey's anger had abated somewhat in the face of these revelations, emotions that labelled her as being as insensitive as Henry, which was an uncomfortable thought. But she was not prepared to back down completely.

'I still cannot forgive that in which you were a participant.'

'Would it surprise you to know that I, too, cannot forgive myself?'

The glance over Betsey's shoulder, added to the look that accompanied it, had her spin round, to find standing in the doorway the person she had last seen lying drunk by her bed, in his pool of vomit. In a flash she was past her Aunt Sarah and by the fire, where she grabbed and began to brandish a long brass poker, her face contorted with fury.

'Don't you dare come near me.'

A sneer appeared on the slightly puffy face. 'Is that the way a new bride addresses her husband?'

'You are not my husband,' came out with spit and several forward paces, the poker waving menacingly. 'So you may disabuse yourself of the thought that you might enforce any rights you suppose you have. Come near me and I will brain you.'

Harry Spafford had taken a couple of backward steps, his eye on the poker. Sure he was well out of the arc of possible harm, the sneer disappeared to be replaced by a snarl, which rendered ugly what could have been, without the excess puffy flesh, a quite becoming countenance.

'I think you may rest in peace on that score. As meat you will be too refined for my tastes. Mind you, perhaps I should recount that in which I take pleasure. It may excite you and have you begging me to share your bed.'

Betsey rushed at him, poker held high, but it was only to drive him backwards so she could slam the drawing room door and lock it. She leant a hand against the waxed pine and dropped her head, her words near a whisper, but enough to carry to Sarah Lovell.

'You have to help me, Aunt Sarah – without you I have no one else.'

With Vincent Flaherty gone, Brazier continued to brood through the remainder of the day, writing plans before discarding them into scrunched-up balls. Suddenly deciding he needed air, this took him, plus his escort, at a striding pace, south and over the open country towards and past Walmer Castle. It was on his way back he recalled something that required to be remedied, instructions issued as soon as he was through the door.

'Joe, I need you to go to the Three Kings. Tell Mr Garlick I will no longer require the room I bespoke yesterday. Take enough money to settle for the lack of occupancy last night and for tonight, if he feels dunned.'

It took stiff resolve to say this without showing his dejection. The room had been booked for Betsey, given – he suspected even if he had hoped otherwise – she would have baulked, for the sake of her reputation, at staying in Quebec House. That said, he had to have a care with the owner of the hotel, the place he had stayed on first arriving in Deal and the lasting impression thus gained.

A picture of Garlick came to mind, that long face with its purple imbiber's nose framed by those long side whiskers, running down from a bald dome. But it was not his appearance, unprepossessing as it was, that struck him so much as the man's quite shameless inquisitiveness.

'Garlick will seek a reason, Joe, for I've rarely met a man whose nose is so steeped in curiosity regarding the affairs of others. Ensure you give nothing away.'

CHAPTER SIX

Henry Tulkington was not a fellow for a fiery mount, quite the reverse, so, in the late afternoon as he made his way back from his assignation with both pain and carnal pleasure, he could relax, stinging back aside. The sinking sun was shining and, with summer on the way, there was warmth to be had from its glow, though that was often cut off by the overhanging trees coming to full leaf to dapple the roadway before him.

Nothing more was required of his steady mare than an occasional tug on the reins to alter her direction, which gave him ample time for contemplation. Having come to the point where he had sight of the gates to Cottington Court, he had mulled over possible ways to proceed on several fronts, not least on Hawker's desire to take one of Spafford's luggers out to sea and sink it with him and his men tied up in the hold.

A man to whom haste was anathema, Henry Tulkington hated to be pushed into too rapid a conclusion, as he had been over Elisabeth's inquisitiveness allied to her intentions regarding Brazier. Yet, even in a relaxed mood, he had to acknowledge time was not on his side; decisions required to be made on other matters in which he had been forced to act with unaccustomed rapidity.

He was only too aware of the constraints on any arrangements mooted, for, if the few who knew anything of his affairs reckoned him omnipotent, he knew it to be far from the case. Having inherited the contraband trade from his father, he could all too easily recall the admonishments from his sire on how it should be overseen. Care was as necessary as activity and being too greedy, or too threatening to the body politic, could result in exposure and fatal retribution.

A balance required to be struck between profit and the survival of the family enterprise, the latter taking primacy. Over three generations, the Tulkingtons had gone from being of no consequence to the eminence he now enjoyed, that achieved with a degree of circumspection. The ability to operate depended, first of all, on the endemic blind eye of the coastal community to the smuggling trade, which extended from the meanest beach hoveller to the very pillars of the community, all of whom were avid purchasers of run and untaxed goods.

Ultimately, it rested on the fact that such an attitude was widespread throughout the land: everyone who could buy goods free of duty did so, which had provided the opportunity for those who had preceded him to prosper by consolidation, gathering into their hands smaller operations, to create a greater and more viable, steadily profitable whole.

No longer was it necessary for a family member to put to sea, nor was he required to carry to the Continent gold to purchase supplies. Monies to pay for cargoes were now transferred from the City of London by Jewish bankers, the goods bought transported in hired and foreign-registered vessels, so ownership of hull or cargo could not be traced.

The landings, now overseen by Hawker, who had also inherited the role, having proved himself reliable to Henry's father, had no other connection to the son than his need to advise when and where to deploy his men. Then he did get involved, but only to ensure nothing imported was being purloined or missing, a necessary precaution. Those employed in movement were likely to be light-fingered, where no complaint regarding theft could be officially noted. Such a thing, if found, fell to John Hawker to deal with.

Distribution was arranged by intermediaries – so high were the profits, it appeared as a minimal expense – and it was carried out by men unconnected to Hawker. Again he was free of involvement, if you left out the subtle manipulation of the local magistrates and the overworked and underpaid functionary who oversaw the Revenue Service. Bribery was too strong a word for how Henry treated with him. Best to say, gifts were welcome to a fellow who actually did not hold the office and was poorly rewarded by the man who did.

So the concerns on which Henry Tulkington ruminated were much closer to the present, and number one was Dan Spafford. He would never fit in with John Hawker, too accustomed to being the man giving the orders to take them from another. Yet disposal was dangerous, given he was so well known. Wagging tongues were not to be encouraged.

Deprived of his men, he would find it near impossible to operate as a smuggler. But, in order to ensure no resurgence, Henry Tulkington could demand he give up his two luggers, for a sum to be paid over time. This, dissipated by the expenditure needed to keep body and soul together, would deny him the chance to fund replacements. That he would agree was scarce in doubt, once he was told what the alternative could be.

His wastrel son could not be allowed to take control of Elisabeth's plantations, even at a distance. Sending him or both to the West Indies had been abandoned as too risky on several counts. But Spafford was the titular person in control of the income of Elisabeth's estates on the conclusion of the marriage.

Papers would have to be drawn up assigning such monies to Henry, which would at least see them properly run by a manager he would engage to take charge of the overseers already in place. Harry Spafford would be granted a stipend, which would allow him to pay for his pursuits, with added demand to stay away from his titular wife.

Elisabeth presented the greatest problem, for her brother had no illusions regarding her now seeking to have the marriage annulled. It was not a subject on which he had expert knowledge, but he was as aware, as any educated person would be, of the grounds required to obtain such a decree. Consanguinity, lunacy or evidence of violent force.

Spafford was not in any way related to the Tulkington family, though given the extent and regularities of his debaucheries, a case could perhaps be made questioning his mental abilities. Force formed the grounds on which she would seek to apply and Elisabeth would have a case, barring one pertinent fact: to gain an annulment on such grounds, she required a witness or witnesses to swear, on her behalf, that the ceremony was not voluntary.

Spafford would not so swear and neither would Joshua Moyle, for fear of being deprived of his living, which had been under Tulkington family control since Henry's grandfather's day. It belonged to Cottington Court and could be taken from him in the unlikely event he had an attack of conscience. Sarah Lovell was the only one who might so swear but Henry was sure she would not do so.

She had, with great reluctance, tearfully signed the parish register, seeing her own needs as transcending those of her niece and nothing in her station had altered; she was still utterly dependent on him and as poor as a church mouse. It would also require money to bring such a case and Elisabeth now had none of her own. So it was a reasonably satisfied Henry Tulkington who made his front gate, to be greeted by the fellow who manned and lived in the gatehouse.

'Tried, Mr Tulkington,' Tanner said as he pulled the gate open, 'as you said she would, but I reckon my look was enough to give pause.'

'She will do so again, Tanner, so mark my instructions.'

'Not allowed out, except on your command.'

'And at all times escorted, Tanner, recall that too.'

'It will be so, your honour, night and day.'

A nod and a kick of the heels set his mare in motion, with Tulkington thinking that was not an entirely sustainable solution. Keeping his sister a prisoner would be problematic, giving rise to questions from neighbours and friends, people she had shown an inclination to call upon. There were occasional visits to St Leonard's Church in Upper Deal, where local society gathered. Such excursions would have to be indulged, but would also have to be carefully managed.

Would it be enough? Elisabeth was a determined creature, which she had proved on the matter of marrying Brazier against his wishes. Indeed, she had been like that since childhood. As he approached the house he was recalling, and not fondly, the way she had manipulated their father. First it had been with childish pleas, then later with feminine wiles, twisting him round her finger, this at the same time as he was in receipt of harsh parental discipline and rigid control.

Time was an ally. Matters would ease once Brazier was gone, either willingly or by force. Until then, the gardeners would be required to lock away the ladders needed for their tasks, for if the estate was walled, they were not insurmountable. The head groom must ensure no horse was made available without his permission, which would allow him to assign an escort. Elisabeth could go where she wished as long as it had his approval, and for a time yet to be determined, that did not apply to Lower Deal.

Close now, he took in, as he often did, the pleasing features of his house. Its warm red brick took the sun well and the features, which dated from the time of the Merry Monarch, in some way seemed to reflect the gaiety of his reign, especially when set against the more recent squared-off piety of the Hanoverian Georges.

Cottington boasted several examples of elaborate, cross-angled brickwork, which showed the skill in design of those overseeing the laying. To break up its frontage, twin bays boasted mullioned windows, though topped with expressions of the stonemason's art, and the main door, wide and solid, gleamed with the gloss of thick layers of paint.

The ornamental gates swung open to admit him to the parterre, the head gardener stopping his weeding to doff a hat at his arrival. Likewise, a lad rushed out from the stables to take his reins and hold them, leading the animal to the mounting block, where he alighted with ease. Like his sister had speculated earlier, he wondered at the level of gossip that must have greeted what had occurred, as well as how those who served him would see it.

Not that it worried him unduly. Every one of them depended on him for their bed and board. They would do his bidding, without comment, or face his wrath, which did not only extend to dismissal. Henry Tulkington knew himself as a man to be cautious of, if not downright respected. Any servitor sent away from Cottington Court would, once he had made plain and spread his displeasure, want for employment in the locality.

'Grady, ask Mrs Lovell to attend upon me.'

Divested of his outer garments, Henry made his way to his study where there was a good fire in the grate, making the room as warm as he liked it to be. When his aunt arrived, he noted her reaction to the heat: the pulling of a face before shutting the door, which he found annoying. Why was it that people could not comprehend how careful he had to be of his health?

'Elisabeth?'

'Is distraught, Nephew.'

'She must learn to live with the consequences of her actions, not something to which she has ever been accustomed. I look to you to help persuade her that, having brought this on herself, it would be best to accept the way she has carried herself up 'til now will no longer serve.'

'I am obliged to ask what will.'

The tenor of her response did not please him and he frowned to show it was so. But, for once, Sarah Lovell felt on safe ground. Henry required an interlocutor with Elisabeth and she was the only one who could fulfil the role. His sister would never be reconciled with what he had done and she needed to know what plans he had, if any. As usual, Henry took defence in his sense of persecution.

'I was master in my own house before you brought her back from Jamaica, but how long did it take until I was left to feel as if it was no longer so, filling the place with all and sundry, and dragging me round like a prize exhibit in a marriage auction?'

That had happened at the fete Elisabeth had arranged, inviting everyone she knew to a day of outdoor games, archery, bowls and the like, followed by a sumptuous evening meal in a special marquee.

'She was seeking to give the estate a more cheering aspect.'

It would not have been politic to add that she also believed he required a wife and, if he never entertained and rarely went to those thrown by his neighbours, such a thing was unlikely to come about.

'Do I detect, in the way you say that, an agreement that such an aspect is required?'

'I do not see it as my place to do so.'

'Quite right. You may tell Elisabeth that she need have no fear of being troubled by Harry Spafford, but there are bound to be restrictions on her movements. Also, I will be overseeing the management of her Caribbean estates and its revenues.'

'So they will not be sold, as she intended?'

'No, and given their profitability, and I told her so, it would have been madness to do so.'

'Even if I could not see myself agreeing with her, she had her reasons, Nephew.'

'I dislike the tone of that remark,' he snapped.

She knew she had overplayed her hand, so it was not a good idea to elaborate on those reasons, which, as Sarah Lovell had said and truthfully, she was unsure she concurred with. Elisabeth had, many times, both in Jamaica and on the voyage back to England, expressed her distaste for the institution of slavery, having witnessed it on her late husband's estates. This had led her to contemplate their disposal, so as to be no longer personally involved.

'The Good Lord,' Henry responded, in a very sententious way, 'has seen fit to order that some should rule and some should labour. It is not for us mere humans to gainsay a divine dispensation.'

Sarah sought to regain lost ground, speaking meekly in order to do so, 'I merely pointed out, Nephew, that such news will not be welcome. I wonder if, given where we are—'

'I must act,' he interrupted, 'I have no time to consider Elisabeth's feelings on the matter. Where is Spafford?'

'I have no idea.'

'Get him found.'

'Do you have anything you wish me to say to Elisabeth?'

'I leave it to you to tell her what you will.'

The direct look was a dismissal, quickly taken as such. Instructions given to the servants, Sarah Lovell ascended the stairs, to stand outside Elisabeth's bedroom. This she had retired to as soon as she was sure it was safe to do so, with Harry Spafford nowhere to be seen. A slow turn of the handle and a push established it was locked, which came as no surprise, unlike the soft knock, which was ignored.

Inside, Betsey heard the sound and saw the handle move, so assumed it was her aunt. She had no desire to see her, especially now, while she was composing a letter to be sent to the canonical authorities in Canterbury, detailing her reasons for seeking an annulment. Well aware of the rarity of such things, she was under no illusions as to the difficulties. Whereas Henry had seen no one prepared to witness for her – which she would have acknowledged had she known – she was relying on discomfort, which would come from any committed Christian swearing and perjuring themselves on a Bible. The problem was to get to that point.

The blocked-off postern and the look she'd got from Tanner established she was virtually a prisoner, and one at risk of being ravaged. This could occur if she ever allowed herself to be alone with the spouse who had been forced upon her, with no route to either objection or appeal: a husband had rights in law, which he was at liberty to exercise at will.

At all costs she must avoid consummation, which would add another reason to her case, though she had a vague feeling it was a papist issue and might not be one acknowledged in the Anglican faith. That had her scratching the quill once more, on many bits of paper, scarred by deletions, until she had a full statement with which she was satisfied.

Already written in tiny writing, folded into as small a size as possible, as well as hidden away, was a letter to Edward Brazier, explaining what Betsey was sure had occurred. She also begged he forgive her for being so naive, in not originally believing him when he told her the truth about her brother. Everything that had happened stemmed from that lack of faith.

Harry Spafford was ushered into Tulkington's study, it immediately registering that he had been at the bottle. Not drunk exactly, but with that swaggering air of alcohol-induced confidence. The grin was too fulsome, the eyes displaying a bent towards masculine humour, which was singularly inappropriate. This left his newly minted brother-in-law off balance, given, to him, the fellow should be cringing.

'You and I need to talk and establish certain facts for which the events of last night did not allow time.'

'I'm yours to command, Henry.' This came with lifted arms and exposed palms, like Christ addressing his flock.

The rejoinder was bitingly sharp. 'I do not think that we have yet progressed to such familiarity.'

The speed with which the air of easy assurance evaporated was palpable and immediate, driving home a reminder, as if any were needed, just what a supine creature Harry Spafford was. This pleased Henry, who had required and now had a malleable creature to play upon.

'Sit,' was an abrupt command, obeyed in the manner of a schoolboy anticipating a roasting. 'I wish you to know that the ceremony, last night, allows you no liberties with my sister.'

'She threatened to crown me with a poker.'

'Be assured, Spafford, displease me and you will wish for such light retribution. And I do not think I have to elaborate.'

The face lost all blood as the young man's imagination took over. Tulkington guessed he was harking back to the threats, relayed to him by John Hawker, when he had held young Spafford in the slaughterhouse. That had included the pork barrel, which he had taken as so believable he'd betrayed his father and revealed the truth of the theft and his future plans. This was to the good: Tulkington required the weakling to be in a state of terror.

'Provision will be made for you, so you may take your pleasures, but not in Deal, where you are too well known.' There followed a pause to allow that unwelcome news to sink in. 'Given your appetites, I suggest any of the Medway naval towns will serve you well.'

'I ain't to live here?' was plaintive and ignored.

'The other matter will have to be settled as soon as I can have the paperwork drawn up.' A hint of curiosity arose, quickly supressed in the face of a glare. 'You are, by law, now in control of my sister's property, which is substantial.'

As Henry described the plantations, their extent and income, he could see an intimation of obstinacy, as if Spafford was calculating that he might have the power to bargain. Legally he had that right, but morally, in any sense of the word, including fibre, he had none.

'The stipend you will be allowed takes cognisance of the income from those estates. The actual running of the plantations, as well as their management, you will sign over to me.'

Emboldened by a possibility of a negotiation, he asked. 'And if what you offer ain't enough, Mr Tulkington?'

'You will take what you're given and be thankful. If it is

not enough, you can spend your time thinking on it in the Marshalsea with all the others who have found poverty. I'm not your father and I will not settle your debts.'

'Where is my pa?'

Henry sneered. 'If I did not know you better, I would wonder if that was concern. As of now he is safe and, perhaps, his continued good health will be contingent on how you behave.'

'Can I see him?'

'What purpose would that serve? Until matters are resolved, I insist you stay in the room with which you have been provided. Sleep there, take your meals there and, for all I care, get stupidly drunk there.'

'Sounds like prison,' he protested, as ever with no real resolve to back up the complaint.

'More comfort than you deserve, Spafford. Take from this arrangement what you are gifted. Ask for more and I might hand you back to Hawker. I think I have nothing more to say, do you?'

Spafford came out of the chair slowly and, if he stood, it was not to his full height. He was like a just-whipped hound and Henry felt a surge of pleasure course through him. He had been subjected to domination earlier and enjoyed both it and the subsequent, short coupling, excellent value for his guinea. To be handing out something very similar was equally gratifying.

Having eaten a solitary dinner, his aunt having declined to join him, he was back in his study, in the process of writing to his Uncle Dirley in London to say he was intending to visit. Grady knocked and entered to inform him of the arrival of a covered wagon at the gate to the house, and two fellows with it.

'Let them in, Grady, and ask that they wait for me before alighting. That done, send the servants to bed, including yourself.' Faced with a look of poorly disguised curiosity, he added, 'I am seen to for the night, as will be everything else.'

He waited some twenty minutes before making his way out through the front door, where he called upon Hawker's men to follow him to the cellar. Dan Spafford was asleep, but the sound of movement brought him round just before a sack was placed over his head. It was a muffled voice that protested as the padlock holding his chains was undone.

'You will find out where you are going when you get there, Spafford.' Henry could not resist the barb and with it the implication. 'Of one thing you can be sure, it will not have pearly gates.'

A nod and he was dragged away. Once he had been loaded, which came with several blows to subdue him, and the cart was back through the gates and crunching its way down the drive, Tulkington went back to his letter, which concluded with the statement that he would be visiting London shortly, to finalise certain matters.

CHAPTER SEVEN

The early morning knocking took Joe Lascelles away from his daily chores to the door of Quebec House to be asked to take delivery of a letter in an unmarked cover. It was sealed with plain and unadorned red wax and to be given into the hand of Captain Edward Brazier. This was espoused by a grubby urchin, who was determined not to hand it over unpaid and, when challenged, not prepared to say from where it had come. That, he hinted, with a sly look, could be the subject of an extra coin.

Lacking a written address, Joe could not be sure it was genuine. Brazier was absent with the others, so it was for him to decide and he refused, not least for the quality of the hand doing the delivering.

'Capt'n ain't here and I ain't shelling out for what might be just a bit of paper, so you might as well sling your hook.'

Expecting protest, he was surprised when the ragamuffin just shrugged, smirked, then gave him a 'Suit yourself' look, before wandering off. Rounding the corner by the Navy Yard, the lad met John Hawker and a questioning look, quickly responded to with a nod and a smile.

'Blackamoor servant wouldn't take it, Mr Hawker. Said your captain was away and refused to pay.'

Hawker fetched out a small silver coin and handed it over. 'Here. Sixpence for your trouble. You know what to say if anyone asks. Good for a few flasks of gin and enough there to treat your mates.'

The urchin still had teeth with which to bite the coin, which made Hawker pull something close to a smile, to think the lad would suspect it forged. 'Share it? No fear, Mr Hawker, it'll be kept for me.'

'Keep your head clear, I might need you again this day.'

As he ran off, the plain seal was broken, so the unmarked paper could be removed to show Henry Tulkington's original superscription, which went into Hawker's pocket. As he strode back down towards the Lower Valley Road, he was unaware that what had just happened, including the exchange, had been spotted by Jaleel Trotter, obliged to slip into the recess of a doorway to avoid being seen.

It was natural to wonder at what he had just witnessed and just as natural for Daisy to conclude he would never know. Besides, his mind was set on finding a way to make contact with this Brazier fellow. He had been told by a crossing sweeper, always a mine of local knowledge, where his man could be found.

Right now, all he could do, once Hawker was out of sight, was saunter past the dark-blue door he had been told to look out for. This gave him no indication of how to proceed, for Daisy had a notion that just making himself known would not serve. He was not of the standing to just go calling on a naval captain, even more so with a broken nose and two black eyes.

The recollection of Hawker taking the letter from the urchin hinted at a way, so, not being lettered himself, he set out for Basil the Bulgar's Molly-house along Middle Street where he was sure he would find someone who was, it being a calling place for all sorts: sailors, rough diamonds, as well as the educated.

Brazier had set out for Canterbury just after dawn with Dutchy Holland, Cocky and Peddler in attendance. The last of that trio of lifelong sailors was deeply unhappy to be astride a horse, even one as tame as the plodding and elderly mare provided by Vincent Flaherty. He was not a joyful man when mounted, made worse by a buffeting and gusting north-east wind, which, he complained, was enough on its own to unseat him.

'Sure, she's short enough,' Flaherty had insisted when getting him seated. 'Not more'n sixteen hands, so if you come off, you won't break anything bar your pride.'

The Irishman had said that to reassure him; the man paying for the hire was less charitable. Brazier had sworn as they left the paddocks at barely a trot, the use of his one-time crewman's last name an indication of his exasperation.

'Damn me, Palmer, having you along is like escorting a merchant convoy.'

'Speed 'o the most lubberly,' added Cocky. 'I can recall you were minded to give them a gun, Capt'n, tae hurry them up.'

'Good idea, Cocky,' was Brazier's response. 'Is your pistol primed?'

'Happy to go home, Capt'n,' was Peddler's opinion, delivered with a wince, to indicate his pained haunches. 'Joe might need lookin' after as much as you.'

The proposal was ignored and, having passed through Upper Deal, their route brought them within sight of the gates of Cottington Court. Brazier set his mare to a canter and closed the distance, reining in his mare, Bonnie, to sit staring at the elaborate ironwork of the gate. Behind lay the long, straight, gravel drive which led to the house, hidden behind trees but for its chimneys and far enough off to be invisible. He did not need to see it: his thoughts, anxieties and uncontrollable imaginings were more on what might be happening within the walls.

Tanner emerged from the gatehouse to glare at him, tugging at the rope lead and encouraging his mutt to snarl menacingly, which pleased the object. He was sure his presence would be reported to Tulkington, which would send to him a signal that matters were not going to be allowed to rest. He sat there until the others caught up, he and Tanner glowering silently at each other, before hauling Bonnie's head round and trotting off up the road.

'Yon cully looked a cheery soul,' called Cocky.

'He works for Tulkington,' was all that was required by way of an explanation.

Brazier was set on killing two birds with one stone by journeying through Adisham, where he could call on Admiral Pollock to break what would, for the mounts as well as the riders, be a long journey in a single day. If the old man agreed, he could leave his escorts there and travel on alone, given he could not envisage any threat once he was away from Deal.

Leaving the coast behind, the wind eased, yet it still whistled through the treetops, to make them sway in a manner that had all four eye them for the danger of a falling branch. The route took them through a string of quiet villages and, there being no conversation to distract him from his own concerns, Brazier began to wonder what the others were thinking.

This in time led to thoughts of past events, not least the ritual of sailing a ship of war, endless days in which routine was sovereign, to the very occasional times action was called for. Over the course of a commission, he had got to know every member of his crew, their level of ability, as well as their foibles and ailments, even their superstitions. But none came closer to him than those who rowed his barge.

That duty had been mostly peaceful and repetitive, calling ashore at the various islands in the West Indies where he was required to pay his compliments to the local hierarchy. The presence of his ship was there to remind them of the laws he was tasked to uphold, the same ones he was sure they would be trying to evade.

The reception ashore was always polite and a dinner in his honour was seen as mandatory. Any resentments were held in check, even after copious amounts of rum punch, glasses of wine followed by decanters of port, lest it invite this pest of a naval officer to pay too much attention to what was being illegally imported into their speck of terra firma.

The times of excitement might be rare, but they stood out more starkly in memory. The sighting from the tops of a strange sail, which, once HMS *Diomede* had been identified, would close if friendly and legitimate to exchange news. Others would run if not, so then came the excitement of a chase, which given the sailing ability of American schooners and the competence of their crews, could last for days, with subterfuge being shown once darkness fell to put him off, which sometimes worked.

On other occasions, dawn would find him off their beam with his guns run out, but just as often the chase ended in daylight and he could then let fly a warning shot across their bows. If that failed to get them to haul their wind, it would become necessary to take to the boats and seek to board. No value came from the sinking of a contraband vessel; success was calculated in capture, the sale price of the goods it carried added to the value of the hull in which it was stored.

The Jonathans rarely gave up without a fight, so boarding would be opposed. It was in those situations where the likes of Cocky, Peddler, but most of all his coxswain, Dutchy, the man in command of his barge, showed their mettle. *Diomede*'s boats had to contend with the Caribbean swell, and so did the deck on which they were trying to gain a foothold. That could be rising and falling ten feet or more, full of men with weapons, determined to drive off these damned Limeys.

'I was just thinking, Dutchy, of some of our Caribbean adventures,' Brazier said, to break the silence.

Tom Holland was riding alongside him, head down and seemingly half-asleep, with Cocky and Pedder behind, he muttering an endless string of complaints and woes. The mount Dutchy rode was the biggest Flaherty possessed, not far off a ploughing beast, which was a good thing, given the size and weight of the man astride him. It was also a very steady platform, which allowed for conversation when Dutchy came to life.

The names of vessels *Diomede* had taken tripped off Dutchy's tongue, to be responded to by his one-time captain, as they both recalled the particulars of the ensuing fights: first musket balls that cracked by their ears, fried by the adversaries, others coming from their own marines. The combined yelling of insults and threats after *Diomede*'s trio of boats had split up to attack bow, stern and beam.

Then came the clang of their cutlasses as they met those of the fellows seeking to drive them off. It never ended well for the Americans, or the few British prepared to chance the trade. He had a crew just short of three hundred men, a high percentage willing fighters. They sailed sometimes with a contingent as low as a tenth of that number. For them, speed and evasion was the key to success, not manpower.

'Not as many captures as there should have been, Capt'n.' This was said with a bit of a bite, evidence of lasting bitterness. 'Too many times we was in the wrong place, were we not?'

Brazier's response was guarded. 'Don't recall ever having said that, Dutchy.'

'Didn't have to say it, such were plain on your chops. Then there was all that pacing to and fro and under-your-breath cursing.'

'That obvious?' came with a smile.

'To anyone who knows you, your honour, which I have to tell you now was near the whole muster.'

'Claimed to know me, Dutchy.'

'There weren't much left that were hidden.'

He could recall the frustration Dutchy was alluding to, with a barren seascape all around him and not a smuggler in sight, despite what he had been told in Kingston. Too many times they had returned from a cruise empty-handed, when they'd set out with high hopes and seemingly solid information. He could not tell his old coxswain now how that had become the case.

Interception depended a great deal on intelligence, which came from spies, usually one-time loyalists in the Carolina ports. If they espoused a hatred of Perfidious Albion, there were people who secretly longed for King George to recover the colonies he had so recently lost. Traitors to the majority of their fellow Americans, the information they provided was vital. But it would not serve to tell even Dutchy, whom he trusted implicitly, that the man in command of the station, Admiral Hassall, had been dishonest to the point of treachery, both to his sovereign and the service of which he was part, brought on by excessive greed.

The period of silence no doubt told Dutchy he was not going to be gifted an explanation, for he changed the drift of the conversation, recalling the taking of the *Santa Clara*, with one recollection advanced with real feeling.

'I'm glad we didn't try to board that French bugger. I thank 'e for that.'

'It would have been too bloody. They had a full buccaneer crew, maybe as many as a hundred and fifty men, all of them determined to fight to the death. If they lived, they were down to hang for piracy.'

Having caught up with the privateer and its Spanish capture, Brazier had stood off the former and battered the Frenchmen into submission with a level of cannon fire they could not match. Once subdued, he had manoeuvred across their stern, triple-shotted his guns and fired a salvo through her casements, knowing it would go right along the deck all the way to the very forepeak and kill or maim anyone who stood in its path.

He had never been sure, in retrospect, if he had carried out so bloody an action through necessity, or as a riposte to the actions of his commanding admiral and this, his French collaborator. Hassall had been dealing with them over many months, passing on the intelligence he should have shared with his own officers. He was deliberately depriving them of prize money, while lining his own purse with a half-share of the proceeds, instead of the eighth that would have normally come his way.

'I never asked, Dutchy,' Brazier asked, as a way of evading the subject, 'what did you do with your share of the *Santa Clara* prize money?'

'Got to recall, Capt'n, it weren't within a mile of what you got. My rating didn't run to a country estate and a coach and four.'

'For which I will not say sorry.'

''Tis the way of things, sure enough, that those who need the most suck the hind tit.'

That was delivered with a wry smile, which also implied it was not necessarily right.

'But there was monies owing for me being at sea when I was paid off, schooling for my nippers, rent and the like. Then there was family, large an' all in need.'

The over-the-shoulder shout, posing the same question to the others, got from Cocky the fact that he'd lived like a king for three months and found how easy it was to make friends with a full purse, and how quick they disappeared when it was empty.

'Peddler?'

'Same, Capt'n. Think I married more than one wench in my

cups. Right now, I'm wishing I'd bought a dog cart or a spare arse.'

'Spare head would suit you better,' hooted Dutchy. 'The one God gave you has never been right.'

'Happen your head was so big, there was nowt left for decent folk.'

The banter, once begun, continued, their one-time commander aware it was not something in which he could participate, even in the situation in which they now found themselves. It was like that on board ship, where his rank cut him off from the easy friendliness of his nature, even with his inferior officers.

It came with being in command, which brought on a degree of loneliness. He was the sole occupant of his cabin, a place where everyone deferred to him, even when he invited them to dine. With that in his thoughts, a wave of melancholy swept over him, so it was a blessing they soon entered Adisham.

The quartet turned up the lane that led to the home of Admiral Sir Eustace Pollock, to whom Brazier was still, and always would be, that blasted nuisance of a thirteen-year-old midshipman, known throughout the ship as 'the Turk'. The soubriquet had been earned by his behaviour in fighting any fellow mid, whatever their size, if he felt insulted or abused.

Pollock was delighted to see him, given he lived a lonely existence when it came to naval callers. A meal was ordered and cooking before the horses had finished their feed. Pollock would have respect locally and probably a lot of friends, for he was of the nature to be liked and admired, but to a man who spent all his years at sea, the lack of salty visitors hurt as much as the lack of employment.

At peace, the navy had too many officers and too few ships to give them all employment. So dozens of admirals, hundreds of captains and probably over a thousand lieutenants were beached from want of the kind of interest, a powerful politico or a peer of the realm, who would act on their behalf to ensure them a place.

None of this was alluded to as they shared the dining board, Dutchy, Peddler and Cocky eating with the servants in the kitchen. It was all naval gossip and seaboard reminiscence going all the way back to HMS *Magnanime*, Brazier's first ship. Various reputations were trashed and a few praised, which was the way of the service, while the politicians who refused to vote enough funds to keep up to strength the Wooden Walls of England were roundly cursed.

'France won't stir, Brazier,' Pollock opined through his chewing. 'Rumour has it King Louis has not a brass farthing to his name after fighting for the Americans.'

'We cannot, in all conscience, sir, pray for another war.'

'No, but we can say that war is when the likes of you and I prosper. Not that you're in need in that department. Happen you could lend the Bourbons a *sou* or two.'

Was there a barb in that? Brazier was unsure. Pollock was not beyond such things, even with someone he claimed to hold in admiration. The thought was dismissed; having known him for so long, and he being so much older, as well as a superior officer, Pollock had earned the right to be tetchy.

'So what brings you by?'

'Will not a chance to share your company suffice?' came with a quizzical smile.

100

'Don't bait me, Brazier,' was a faux irritated response, the good humour badly disguised. 'I've had occasion to put a birch to your backside afore and I can do it again.'

'I'm on my way to Canterbury to find a legal cove, well versed in Canon Law.'

'One to fire a forty-two-pounder ball of a suit, no doubt?'

'Very droll, sir.' Once the chortling at his own pun had subsided, the 'why' from the admiral was inevitable. 'A friend of mine has been forced into an unsuitable marriage. I'm on my way to seek out what can be done to get it set aside.'

'A friend?' was posed with a degree of suspicion.

'A very close one, sir.'

'I take it to be a lady. It would be damned uncommon for a man to be subject to such a misfortune.'

'Of course.'

'This lady is merely an acquaintance?'

'My plan is to carry on to Canterbury and, if I can, leave my men here with you until tomorrow. And their horses of course.'

That got Brazier a very direct look from a man who knew that such an abrupt change of subject usually emanated from a fellow dodging an uncomfortable truth. It would take no genius, Brazier realised, to fix the nature of the avoidance. He realised, as he was aware of the slight heat in his face, he might as well have just told the truth. It was to be thanked that, whatever he had concluded, Pollock chose to respect his reservations.

'That would be good, Brazier, as long as I can set your men to do some late pollarding of some of my trees. Getting too old for it myself.'

It was odd, given his coming purpose, to be ruminating on a retaliatory pun, on how to fashion one from the connection between Pollock and pollarding. But it would not come, so he was left to lamely reply, 'I'm sure they'd be delighted to assist you, sir.'

'As for you and your purpose, it would be best if you stay the night. I will send out to some of my local friends to get a name for you, a lawyer to whom you can take your case. Otherwise you will be obliged to wander Canterbury to find one suitable and, I have to tell you, there are many rogues in the legal profession.'

'Thank you, sir.'

'Excellent, and over dinner you can tell me of your exploits at Trincomalee. If it was worthy of your step to post rank, it must have been remarkable. I know from my own experience, Brazier, that raising a man to a captaincy requires some outstanding act of both bravery and skill, one which, to have confirmed, must equally impress their Lordships of the Admiralty.'

The response was made with a smile, as it had to be, but it was less than enthusiastic.

CHAPTER EIGHT

It annoyed Henry Tulkington that Brazier had been outside his gates and belligerent, even if Tanner assured him no words were exchanged. This was made worse when he met with John Hawker, unusually for the second day in a row, to be told his letter had been rejected. He was not, of course, told the truth of the circumstances, how it had been delivered, or that it had not been rejected by Brazier in person but one of his tars. He was also with someone keen to drive home the nail.

'My guess, Mr Tulkington, is that in seeing it were from you, he reckoned to know the content.' In the face of a questioning look, Hawker added, 'Well, you weren't likely to wish him good health, was you?'

'I want him out of Deal,' was said with a hint of petulance.

'An' if he don't choose to go?'

'Then he must be made to.'

Hawker's sense of satisfaction had to be hidden under an air of concern.

'Won't be easy, an' I feel bound to add, he might not be one to sit quiet and wait for whatever it is you would like to do.'

That was acknowledged with a sharp nod, and Hawker drove home another point. 'What if he recruits more of his tars, in numbers to take us on? There's no shortage with England being at peace.'

'Which cannot be allowed, and I say that not from any sense of dread. Public disorder is bad for business, John, which I have had occasion to point out to you before.'

The tone was annoying, like a schoolmaster-type admonishing a pupil. Hawker had been in receipt of that from the fellow who'd taught him letters and numbers. At the latter he had shown a natural ability, the skill that had originally made him valuable to the Tulkington family. The fellow teaching had found, even barely breeched, that John Hawker had fists of which to be wary.

'Can we find out what his plans are?'

'I can ask, don't say I'll get an answer. He has kept himself to himself these last weeks, outside of visits to the Navy Yard, which is only to be expected. That apart, he ain't done much in the mixing line.'

Again, there was pleasure to be had in withholding information. Henry Tulkington knew nothing of the likes of Saoirse Riorden or the Irish horse dealer, Flaherty. He had no idea who did the Quebec House laundry or who supplied their meat and drink, their candles and firewood. He was the master of the enterprise in which they were both engaged and had to be deferred to because of it. But John Hawker had never accepted, in his mind, that it was one of outright master and servant.

For all his power, Tulkington depended on him. In their arrangement, all matters to do with smuggling or impositions on the town were supposed to be kept away from Cottington Court. If it had been breached the other night, that was an exception. Thus Tulkington could keep up the facade of an upright and successful man of business, with his string of tenant farmers, this slaughterhouse-cum-tannery, added to his control of most of the water mills which surrounded the town, giving him control in the grinding of flour.

'Perhaps on your rounds, John, someone will reveal what you seek.'

'My thoughts too.'

In addition to all his other affairs, Henry Tulkington held the sinecure for tax gathering on the sale and purchase of commodities in the Deal area. In common with most holders of such profitable positions he employed someone else to carry out the actual work, none other than John Hawker, creating a beautiful symmetry.

Hawker called upon the local tradesfolk to assess from their ledgers what was due to the government. This he carried out assiduously, as did Tulkington in his returns to the Treasury in London. No hint of monies missing, and the enquiries which would ensue, could be allowed. Since the entire stipend that went with the office was passed on in full, it gave Hawker an enviable income.

He performed another task on his rounds, informing those interested of what was about to be smuggled in, which allowed him to compile a list of what they wished to buy and at what price. The third strand, first introduced by Tulkington's father, took care of income needed to keep the men Hawker led in funds.

It explained why he was hated and feared in equal measure, while also ensuring no trace of his men being employed by the owner of Cottington Court was visible. It was made plain to the good folk of Deal that if they wished to carry on their trade without trouble, it was wise to pay a small regular sum to ensure none came their way.

'Spafford's men and the sod hisself? What are we to do there?'

John Hawker had long ago realised it was a Tulkington habit to always turn away when deep in thought and, as ever, he placed himself close to the stove. Likewise, it was necessary to let him think, for he was ever in fear of anything which smacked of a rush. If their contraband game was hugely successful, it also had ramifications of which Hawker was unware and these had to be protected.

'Does it occur to you, John, that we might need them?'

'For what?' was too harshly delivered, obvious by the terse nature of the response.

'Have we been talking in riddles, man? If Brazier has to be forced to depart, much as I might deplore it, I doubt it can be done without a risk of violence. Perhaps a threat will not suffice and, in this, I would not wish you or your men to be involved for several reasons. Exposure is only one, the need to concentrate on what is, after all, their job is another, for we have cargoes due in the coming week. But Spafford's louts . . .'

'It's a thought,' was delivered with indecision.

'The uncertainty stems, as you have told me, from an inability to know which of them may be reliable and which are not.' The solution fully arrived at in his mind, Tulkington spun round. 'Let us set them on Brazier and see who holds true.'

'None to my mind.'

'You may not have heard of the Sage of Lichfield, Doctor Samuel Johnson, who was wont to say that the prospect of hanging wonderfully concentrates a man's mind. If it is made plain survival depends on a good outcome with Brazier, we will find out their mettle which, if you feel so disinclined, I will propose to Dan Spafford myself.'

'And after?'

If the chin was dropped to the chest to imply deep consideration, John Hawker had the less than comfortable feeling he was about to hear something already arrived at.

'Their activities prior to recent times posed us no real problems, even if Spafford was deluded enough to think so. It also gave us more than a sprat to offer up to the Revenue if the need arose. One day, those you finger on Deal Beach may not suffice.'

'You're willing to let them go back to running goods?'

'As a quid pro quo, for the departure of that swine Brazier, bruised and bloodied as he deserves to be, yes.'

The man being discussed was now with the Canterbury lawyer Pollock had pointed him towards, one Ebenezer Moat. Tall, overweight, with a sharp cast to a pair of blue eyes sunk in fleshy jowls, he was, like most of his trade, not at ease when asked for an unequivocal answer to Brazier's enquiry. This having been posed in a general sense, Moat took refuge in long perorations on the possible grounds for annulment, added to the manifest difficulty of establishing such grounds as fact.

'Then I find I must lay out the case as I see it.'

'Which would be most helpful, Captain Brazier, as would a glass of wine, which aids clarification.'

A bell was rung, the article ordered and the subject of the interview held in abeyance with general chat about the state of the world, frustrating for the supplicant, who resumed his case when the wine was delivered, poured and tasted with a smacking of the lips from Moat.

'The lady on whose behalf I am enquiring was, I believe, put in some state of stupor for a ceremony carried out against her wishes.'

'Your relationship to this lady?'

'Does that matter?'

'It is very much the case that it matters. Are you a relative, for instance?'

'No.'

The long fingers were spread. 'Then the connection is . . .'

'We had an understanding.'

'A formal one, acknowledged, banns read, ceremonies arranged?' The headshake was slow. 'So the "understanding", as you call it, would it be possible to say, was merely verbal?'

'It was more than merely, sir, I assure you.' The look Brazier was getting told him he would have to be open, there was no other way to proceed. 'The lady is a widow of independent means.'

'Forgive me for asking, Captain, but are those independent means germane to your pursuit?'

'No,' he growled, 'but her brother seemed convinced it was so.'

A querying eyebrow obliged him to tell Moat of his good fortune, which led to a topping up of his glass. 'Captain

Brazier, if I'm to advise you at all, I fear you must relate to me all the details from the beginning, even if some feel uncomfortable in explanation.'

There was no choice but to agree, so he went back to meeting Betsey in Jamaica, then his pursuit of her to Deal and what had occurred subsequently, mostly Henry Tulkington's attitude, left mysterious, since he was not going to mention his true colours. He related the vision he had witnessed of the unknown groom, as drunk as the minister who had no doubt conducted the ceremony; Betsey comatose and utterly failing to recognise or acknowledge him, as well as the distraught Aunt Sarah. He felt it would not be politic to mention pistols pointed at her nephew's head, or the presence of several dozen other men, some bearing weapons, others seemingly cowed and disarmed, or the fact of his departure with a dazed hostage.

The scenario had been repeatedly rehashed in his mind on the way from Adisham, yet it did not come out as smoothly as it had on reflection. Indeed, Brazier felt he was making a less than comprehensive case. That said, Moat listened in silence, this only interrupted when he reached for a quill to jot down a quick note, having thrown a quick glance at the gently ticking clock on the wall behind Brazier.

'What you describe seems to be in the nature of a crime, Captain. I wonder, am I the proper person to be telling this to?'

The temptation was to say, 'You would not be, if I were telling you everything.' But that could not happen, for having thought it through, he reckoned the difficulties were close to insurmountable and the dangers unquantifiable. These were conclusions reached at his own hearth, on the very night in question, staring at the flickering flames of his fire and drinking too much brandy.

Not long after his arrival in Deal, at the Three Kings where he was staying, he had met William Pitt, the King's First Minister, who resided at Walmer Castle. An invitation to dinner had followed, in which Pitt had sought to inveigle him, by a combination of flattery, inducement and an implied threat, into searching for the source of what he contended was local and highly organised smuggling.

This was a subject on which Pitt was passionate, so much so that, in frustration at the loss of revenue to the Exchequer, he had, two years previously, ordered the burning by the army of every boat on Deal Beach. Would telling him achieve the arrest of the man who gathered taxes for the government and was, in Pitt's own words, lauded as scrupulously honest? Could he make case enough to get the King's First Minister to bring to bear the power of government?

For several reasons he had decided it would not serve. First, all he had was rumour and hearsay that Tulkington was the man behind the trade Pitt was desperate to curtail. He had no direct evidence that what had been told to him, in confidence, by Saoirse Riorden, was true. To bring any kind of case he would need multiple witnesses and he possessed no great faith there were locals in Deal willing to denounce a man they apparently feared. Certainly Saoirse had made it plain she would not.

Nor, according to her, did Tulkington actually participate in the running of contraband. To bring a case that would hold water required irrefutable proof of his involvement. That could only be achieved by either catching him in the act, impossible if he did not actively get involved, or finding some record of his actions, accounts and papers that only a fool would compile and keep where they could be found.

Several other reasons why Brazier felt he could not take that course had surfaced, one being his own actions in entering Cottington Court uninvited and armed, then threatening Tulkington with a ball through his skull. The other and most telling was Betsey herself. While there was no notion of her being involved in her brother's alleged activities, would she be caught up in any action against him? They lived and had been raised in the same house: could she credibly plead ignorance? Would a brother who had already proved to be ruthless and spiteful, knowing Brazier as the instigator of any investigation, incriminate her as an act of revenge?

Saoirse had intimated Tulkington probably had the local magistrates in his pocket, and surely any jury formed to judge him would be made up of people whom he knew. Would any of them believe he led a double life of which they knew nothing? Or if they did know, would they admit to prior knowledge? In the end his reflections had come down to one point: what was his object?

Unlike in the Caribbean, where it had been a duty, the suppression of smuggling on the East Coast had nothing to do with him or the navy. The Admiralty was adamant it was none of their concern; let the Revenue Service wear out their vessels trying to interdict the trade. The King's Navy had other fish to cast for, like meeting and defeating the nation's enemies in a world where a new conflict with France or Spain was ever on the horizon.

Brazier was not even sure he disapproved of smuggling, for it was common knowledge the trade supported communities that might otherwise struggle to exist. Likewise, the purchase of untaxed goods was so widespread in society, it was not seen as a crime or even kept discreet: people boasted of their acquisitions.

His object had brought him to this office. He wanted Betsey free from what he was certain was an illegal coupling, so that he could, himself, lead her up the altar both legally and contentedly. Everything else was of no consequence in comparison so, as he had previously, he dismissed the notion of using any other legal means than those provided by the Church of England.

'I see it is the subject of much consideration,' Moat said, the quill moving once more.

'No, it is not.'

'Annulment?'

'Nothing less.'

'Then I must bring to your attention certain facts, Captain Brazier, the first being that you are in no position to bring any kind of case. You are not a relative of the person you say has been so affected and you have admitted the connection to be tenuous.' Seeing the thunderous look that engendered, Moat added quickly, 'And even a blood relative would struggle, without there being witnesses to the act of enforcement.'

'Which you could have told me some time ago.'

'Captain, you asked for advice. I am giving you the best and most truthful I can, based on a comprehensive knowledge of the circumstances. It would be remiss to raise your hopes on a matter I suspect is very close to you heart.'

The look adopted was pensive, though time was allowed for Moat's quill to make another note.

'To bring a case, such as the one you outline, well? Parting the Red Sea would be easier. It requires first a written complaint from the person suffering the imposed act. Further to that, you would need depositions from some of those actually present, people who would be willing to attend a Canonical Court, to swear in person to their written evidence. Then there is the priest who conducted the ceremony . . .'

'Whom, I would guess, was a full party to the wrongdoing.'

Moat was shocked and it showed. 'That is a most telling accusation, sir, which I must warn you, might on its own have the whole case refused. The Church does not take kindly any accusation of laxity in its ecclesiastics.'

It would have been pointless for Brazier to say that, given some of the divines he had met, mostly ship's chaplains, the Church would do well to examine its stock. For every one who was genuinely God-fearing and upright, there were twice as many who were drunkards, possible sodomites with a penchant for youth, as well as people whose lack of faith was palpable.

'Is there any way I can proceed?'

'Not that I can see. Bring me evidence and witnesses, drop all accusations against the priest, whom thankfully you have not named, and I would be prepared to approach the Canterbury diocese with a plea to enter a case. Lacking that, I fear you would be wasting your money.'

Which induced another silent thought. This was costing money by every word uttered. Brazier thanked Moat, even though he was unsure if he meant it. There was no point in

113

upsetting a man who, unlikely as it seemed, he might need in the future. So he stood to take his farewell and it was at that point he found out the reasons for the quill jottings.

'Might I suggest,' Moat, said, handing over a sheet of paper, 'that you take this to my clerk. You will find at the bottom of the page my fee for the work I have carried out on your behalf today. I would suggest, in the circumstances, given the complications of the case you laid out before me, it would be best settled.'

Moat did not actually say he was wasting his time, but it was implicit in both words and expression. Looking at the figure, Edward Brazier was inclined to suggest that most villains had missed their vocation. They should have taken to the law, not crime.

He might have been less censorious if he had known that Moat, who knew every divine in East Kent, wondered if it might be an idea to raise the matter with the Bishop of Dover's chaplain, lest it turn out to be true. If it was, the case would be an extremely profitable one.

CHAPTER NINE

The information that Betsey wanted to visit her friend Annabel Colpoys, who lived nearby, was greeted by Sarah Lovell with some reservations.

'That can only be granted by Henry.'

'Then you must ask him on my behalf.'

'Which I will do, when he returns.' Betsey saw her aunt bite her lip, before adding, 'It is my impression that, should you go out from Cottington Court, you will, at all times, be escorted.'

'By you,' was said with some bitterness.

'I think Henry intends that his coachman, or some such others, should act as escorts, in case of any unpleasantness. I doubt he will allow you a horse.'

There was little doubt on the meaning of that and, even if tempted to challenge the assumption that Edward Brazier could be labelled as unpleasantness, Betsey decided there was no point. But there was another that had to be nailed.

'And when we get to where I wish to go?'

'Naturally, I would be required to chaperone you.'

'Closely so?' That got a determined nod. 'In other words, I am not to be left alone with anyone.'

'I suspect that would chime with Henry's wishes.'

'What a strange definition you have, Aunt Sarah, on the meaning of the word "chaperone". Gaoler would seem more apposite.'

'I think we have covered this ground previously, Elisabeth. I know you find the present situation both confusing and unpleasant, but at least I have ensured that you are married in name only, which I fought for at some risk to my own position. Henry was all for throwing you at Spafford's feet, but I managed to dissuade him, so a degree of gratitude might be appropriate. Now if you excuse me, I have matters to attend to. This house does not run itself.'

Betsey said no more, allowing Sarah Lovell to depart without the barbs she wanted to aim in her direction. What she must concentrate on now was a way to get into Annabel Colpoys' hands the letter she needed delivered. If she could, Betsey had some confidence her friend would comply: she had delivered a note to Quebec House before.

Annabel lived, if not in dread of her husband Roger's temper, then in great trepidation of his approbation, which was not forthcoming when it came to anything that might upset Henry Tulkington. Annabel had as good as admitted her certainty that Roger, in dispute with Henry over a land boundary, had fallen foul of him to the point of being in receipt of a beating, which left him bruised and bleeding in a ditch.

Whatever Annabel's attitude, the attempt had to be made. The note she had composed would be folded to be small enough to fit in her glove, an article that she would try to leave behind, if she could not find a way to pass it over by normal means. The wording was sparse, as it had to be, no more than an assurance her marriage was a sham, added to her feeling of affection.

The latter had been the hardest to write, to put in words – without being too effusive – her feelings towards him. Betsey Langridge, as she still saw herself, was well enough raised to find difficulty in penning words of open adoration to anyone, let alone a man. Her prior attempts had ended up in the fire, to be consumed lest they be found. Some had gone to a burning, which matched the embarrassment she had felt in their composition.

There was some consideration to be put to what she was going to say regarding her sham marriage to the likes of Annabel. With Aunt Sarah witnessing every word exchanged, Betsey had to assume everything she said would be reported back to Henry. If it was condemnatory of him, the consequence would be curtailment of any excursions at all. She would, indeed, become a prisoner.

That the notion would trouble other people she had to take with a serious doubt. If she'd never personally come across the fact, it was commonly held that women were often locked away from society, the usual reason given being a weakness of the mind. Legally, until it could be overturned, this Spafford slug had the power of a husband in law, which was absolute. Outside murder, he could do what he wished, though given what had been imparted to her by her aunt, it would emanate from Henry.

Sitting down and reflecting on the past, it was necessary to acknowledge she had often been less than kind to him and had encouraged her friends to act likewise. Betsey refused to see what had been no more than teasing as cruel, yet he had thrown it in her face as a part justification for his behaviour. It was an excuse, of course, and a feeble one.

He had always been a bit of a misanthrope, even as a young man – the endless teasing came from his stiff reserve in the face of the youthful gaiety of her and her companions. How could she not have noted what had become a trait of character, to which she was only seemingly the latest victim? Her years away in the West Indies scarce provided a reason not to have seen what he was like. And to think she had badgered him about his lack of a wife and sought to encourage engagement with the eligible females she had invited to Cottington Court.

'God forbid that any woman should be saddled with such a husband,' was whispered to the sea coals pulsating in the fireplace.

Was it the gap in age between them that had helped mould his behaviour towards her? Betsey could recall clearly now, even if it had not occurred to her at the time, how her father had treated them very differently: stern with him, indulgent with her. Henry had been sent away to school, from which he evidently took no pleasure, judging by his moods in the holidays. She had been educated at home by an indulgent governess, until Sarah Lovell took over on her father's death, but that had lasted only a couple of years. This difference in upbringing Betsey had taken as the way of raising boys, as opposed to girls.

It was rare her thinking went back as far as this house when her father was alive; too much had happened since he passed away, albeit he was frequently absent on business. But it had been then what it was not now: a place of warmth, even if he was a widower. That was thrown into stark relief when she returned from Jamaica to find Henry even more miserable a creature than he had been previously.

Endless thoughts whirled through her mind, one concern or recollection replacing another, only to resurface minutes later to be examined once more and gnawed upon. Even if she determined the way Henry had treated her, as well as the methods he employed in his dealings with others, was and would remain a mystery, she could not avoid continued and fruitless speculation.

A change of location was the only answer, so Betsey left the room, locking the door behind her, to make her way to the hall and ring for her outdoor garments. She required air and, judging by the whistling of the wind from outside the windows, it was going to be given to her in abundance. Leaving the house, she had no doubt now, given what her aunt had said, she would be followed by someone. There was nothing that could be done about it, so Betsey took comfort from one fact. She might be unable to keep secret her movements, but no one could see what was in her mind.

Henry was just departing the slaughterhouse when his sister passed through the gate to the formal garden. The wind whipping at her cloak was just as strong in the town, welcome in her case, the cause of a tightly drawn muffler and discomfort for him. Even sure he was in danger of a chill, he could still be reasonably satisfied with the outcome of his talk with Dan Spafford, added to his subsequent instructions to John Hawker.

As usual, the former had been larded with mutual denigration, but Henry saw that as water off a duck's back. To be held in low esteem by the likes of Dan Spafford was, to him, a badge of respectability. It only mattered that the sod had, after much equivocation, accepted the bargain proposed: the release of him and his men for the burning out of Edward Brazier and his tars.

'And it will not be you who will bear the blame,' Tulkington had imparted with what he thought was a sly look, one which Spafford took as sneering and superior. 'Hawker will engineer a disturbance of which you will take advantage. Once the house he is renting is ablaze, you and your men can melt away.'

'What's he done to you?' Spafford had asked.

'None of your damned affair,' had come out as more vehement than was required. It had seriously annoyed Tulkington the way Spafford had grinned at his outburst, no doubt delighted at the thought of someone getting so far under his enemy's skin as to knock him off balance. 'Just take it as a warning of what could happen to you.'

'Will it get my Harry free?'

'Spafford, your Harry is in no danger.'

'How do I know you're telling the truth?'

'You don't.'

'Whoever this Brazier is, he will blame you.'

'How can he, when I will be far away from Deal?'

Back in the upstairs office, Tulkington had explained what he wanted done, which met with some satisfaction from his man. Yet it was not entirely the case: Hawker wanted personal retribution for both the blow he had taken and the humiliation he had suffered, and made the mistake of saying so.

'You're to stay well away, John,' had been the snapped response. 'Do not go near Brazier's dwelling. Just get things moving with the mob.'

'Speaking of the mob, what's to stir them?'

'I suggest a rumour that Brazier has come to Deal to put a cap on smuggling. That, spread along the beach, should suffice to get our hovellers and wherrymen fired up. He visited Pitt at Walmer Castle, you told me, so adding that much-hated name to the tale will pay dividends.'

'I'll spread he's Pitt's secret agent, hiding his true purpose for taking a house here.'

'That will do nicely. He will struggle to get out alive if the mob thinks it the case.'

'Need a day or two to sow the story.'

'Maybe more will be required. I wish to be well away from Cottington when this happens. Besides, you must prepare for the next cargo.'

Hawker was curious as to where Tulkington would be. It was past unusual for him to be absent with a load coming in. But he had not bothered to enquire, knowing it to be a waste of time.

Edward Brazier, having collected his companions from Admiral Pollock's, had returned to Deal from what he considered to be a waste of his time. Once the horses had been accommodated in the stables he joined the others in the parlour, Joe Lascelles handing over a folded and sealed letter, bearing only a last name, with no rank and no identifying design on the wax.

'This one came second, Capt'n. Leastways, the lad delivering it didn't demand it be paid for.'

The questioning look had Joe continue, describing the scruffy ragamuffin who had demanded money for a previous missive, as against the good-mannered and good-looking young cove who brought the second.

'Stank of attar too, that one,' Joe sniffed.

Within his explanation, there was a bit of hesitation; Joe was wondering if he had done right. Brazier was considering the same question, until he reasoned, though doubt was not entirely banished, Betsey would not have employed a street urchin as a messenger.

'Well, let us see what this one says.'

Opened, it revealed a very high standard of writing and composition, with several flowery phrases hailing his personality and standing, before it got to the purpose. This was to tell him the sender had observed, without any details, what occurred at Cottington Court and might prove an ally if he wished to confound Henry Tulkington.

'Signed Jaleel Trotter,' he said, having explained the contents to his quartet of supporters.

'Is he not the one you was weeks looking for?' asked Dutchy. 'Went by the name of Daisy.'

'Well remembered,' added Peddler, who had looked confused at the name. 'But what does the cove mean by confounding Tulkington?'

'Are you daft? He means tae turn tables on the sod.'

'I ain't daft Cocky. I is probing.'

'You'll never guess where he's asked to meet me.' Brazier let the curiosity linger for a moment, before adding. 'That damned Molly-house along Middle Street.'

'Explains the messenger,' Peddler intoned.

'That's one you can go to alone,' Dutchy said, only half in jest.

'When?' demanded Cocky, which was more to the point.

'At my convenience. He will wait there to hear.' Brazier went to hover over the empty grate, head bowed. 'I have to meet him, for we're at a stand right now. Maybe he has nothing to offer . . .'

'And maybe it's a trap, Capt'n,' Dutchy suggested. 'That means we must all go with you, and armed.'

'Which might be a good way to scare him off. Besides, how can I be at risk from a fellow know as Daisy?'

'If ye dinna ken that, you're no' a sailor.'

Dutchy pitched in again. 'How about a note back, Capt'n, suggesting a meet at the Old Playhouse. If he's on the up, he'll be safe there and so might we.'

'Good thinking, I'll write to him now.'

'I'd suggest tomorrow,' said Joe. 'If he's got anything planned, we'll have a chance to look out for trouble before it arrives.'

Brazier nodded. 'It will also give me time to alert Saoirse too. If anything is not right, she'll smoke it well beforehand.'

'Gives us the whole day to keep a lookout.'

'Get the fire lit in the kitchen, Joe,' Peddler asked. 'And never worry what's happening on the morrow. That Admiral Pollock eats like an old man and so do his servants. I got a hole where my gut should be.'

'Who's going to deliver my reply?'

The reluctance of all four, as they looked at each other, made Brazier laugh, which was the first time he'd done so the whole day, and the one before it too.

* * *

Daisy Trotter hadn't spent the day in idleness, waiting for a response. Deal leaked like a sieve when it came to what was going on behind closed doors, though it was essential to be able to sort fact from rumour, the spreading of which was a favourite hobby. He saw John Hawker once more, on his tax-gathering rounds, the now-black eye very obvious and an object of much attention, if not comment.

The road past the slaughterhouse was busy enough to watch for a bit, without attracting too much attention. With folk coming and going, farmers arranging to have their stock butchered or traders exiting with leather hides over their shoulders, he got a chance to ask, in a chatty way, what was going on inside. There were a lot of people about, not involved in the function of the place, and that was unusual enough to remark upon, which indicated an original supposition had been correct.

It was not guesswork, really; Daisy, his letter penned and sent, mulling over a glass of Basil the Bulgar's sloe gin, put his mind to the problem. He could think of no other place where Hawker could do what was needed that would not be obvious enough to cause comment. The slaughterhouse was a location in which he had visited the sod before, in the opening moves to set up the first meeting between Tulkington and Dan.

So wandering in and past the killing floor could have been seen as natural; it was not and caused alarm. Hawker's men hustled him back out into the street, which they would only have done if they had something to hide. Satisfied in his own mind, he made his way back to Basil's to wait for a reply from Brazier. The time it took in coming drove him to distraction and, tired from lack of sleep and a day of worry, he retired to Basil's upstairs room to lay down.

'Daisy,' came with a hand shaking his shoulder, 'letter's come.'

He opened his eyes, to look into the face of the handsome young man who had penned his own letter and delivered it. Blonde curly hair, blue eyes, a soft enchanting voice and the slightly plump face of one not yet fully mature. A thing of beauty. However much Daisy wished it otherwise, he knew it was not for him.

There was a likeness to a younger, less debauched Harry Spafford there, which brought to mind the last encounter: he still had the shiners from the headbutt Harry had given him. But it was not that which was truly painful and pricked his eyes with tears, it was the betrayal of trust the resemblance brought back.

'Thank you, Barnaby.'

This was imparted in a croaked, just-woken tone of voice. Taking the letter with one hand, he wiped his damp eyes with the other sleeve. After a glance at what was no more than a jumble to him the letter was handed over.

'Need your skills once more, and I hope matters have been set in motion, as desired?'

CHAPTER TEN

Unbeknown to Edward Brazier, another difficulty was looming: what could be said as a chicken coming home to roost. This stemmed from the arrival, off the River Medway, of the 74-gun ship-of-the-line, HMS *Alcide*, fresh back from the West Indies, where she had served as flagship to whatever officer had charge of the Jamaica Station. This had included Brazier's old, late and troubling commander, Admiral Sir William Hassall.

His replacement having come out in another seventy-four, *Alcide* was returning home, after years abroad, to be assessed as fit for continued service. But she was definitely to be laid up in ordinary, anchored in the Nore roads, as surplus to peacetime requirements. This meant any stores she carried were stripped out of her holds, to be taken ashore, warehoused and checked for monetary value against the purser's account.

The same applied to the guns, great and small, hand weapons, powder, flintlocks, spare sails and cordage, while her standing rigging was taken down, her upper masts and yards likewise, to be laid along the deck leaving her floating under a trio of stunted and bare lower poles. Finally, all the necessary work completed, her crew was paid off, the last act of the captain being to hand over the ship to the boatswain, a standing officer, who would stay with her until she was recommissioned, putting the whole process into reverse.

The crew, much reduced from that which had set out a decade previously, albeit augmented by drafts sent out from England, came ashore, to disperse to the various places from which they hailed. Others would make for London, or the other seaports from which they might get a berth on a merchant vessel. Many, the less practical, lingered in Chatham, drinking and carousing, until the pay they had accumulated was spent, leaving them, as too often happened with men of the sea, destitute.

For Brazier, if he had known of it, his concerns would have extended to the captain of HMS *Alcide* and his lieutenants. They would be cast ashore with little prospect of future employment, to live on half-pay until the fleet expanded again, which would only happen with the outbreak of another war. Like him, they would expend every ounce of energy and plague every contact, however remote, to get themselves a new position.

They would, beached or not, gossip with their naval peers and civilian contacts and one of the subjects occasionally discussed would be the strange circumstances surrounding the untimely death of Admiral Hassall. An even more engaging topic, namely prize money, would frequently raise its head, for envy was paramount on a subject close to every serving officer's heart.

Part of that would relate to the outrageous good fortune that had attended upon Captain Edward Brazier and the crew of HMS *Diomede*, not long after Hassall's strange and disconcerting demise. That the two could be linked was tenuous, but that did nothing to damp speculation.

And to those inclined to dabble in conspiracy, it could mean a whole lot more.

Blissfully in ignorance of what this might portend, Brazier called upon Saoirse Riorden, to ask that a private space be made available for a meeting with Daisy Trotter that evening. She was not the kind to assent to anything of which she was not fully aware, which extracted from him an explanation, including the fact that Jaleel Trotter claimed to have been present at Cottington Court on the fateful night of the sham wedding.

This led to an admission that he had failed to tell her everything. Nothing about the whole host of men who had appeared as he was challenging Tulkington added to the impression he had, and he was too mentally shocked to think further on it, to consider that there had been some kind of fracas. It was with greater certainty he could talk of what had happened with Hawker.

'I saw the evidence this very morning, and I have to say the black eye was a beauty. He'll not forgive you that.'

'About which I do not care, given I feel I'm paying him back.'

'So – Trotter, what is it you're hoping for?'

'If only I could tell you. This Daisy has asked to meet with me on a subject, he claims, mutually beneficial and I have no great desire it should be where he suggested.'

'Which was?'

'The Molly-house in Middle Street. I suggested here would be best.'

The face pinched in a way Brazier had seen before, a sure sign of exasperation. 'Without asking beforehand. Is that not what would be known as a liberty?'

It was a slightly shamefaced Brazier who responded. 'I would prefer not to meet in a place where we could be observed, but if you cannot oblige . . .'

'Why not Quebec House?'

'Trotter didn't say so, but since he made no mention of that as a possibility, I reckon it's an invitation he would decline. He wants to meet somewhere public. I want to do so somewhere safe.'

'So, is it danger you're talking about?'

'Saoirse, I have no idea. But my lads will be with me as they are now, and I have the feeling he will be coming alone.'

'By reputation he is one for the quiet knife in the back, Edward, I told you that afore, I recall. Make sure he's not coming to skewer you.'

'I'm aware of it,' he replied, not willing to admit he'd forgotten.

'I take it you don't know Daisy Trotter is Dan Spafford's right-hand man.'

'That name again,' was spat out.

'Dan is Harry's father, though if he had any sense, he would have disowned the louse long past. Instead, he pays his debts to tavern and whores alike, which must strain his purse.'

The way Saoirse paused, which was lengthy, added to the look that crossed her face caused Brazier to wonder what was going through her mind. He had said she would know if anything was being planned that might cause him trouble, given she obviously knew a great deal of what was going on in the town. As the owner of a place of drinking and pleasure, people confided in Saoirse, but that did not necessarily mean she would tell him.

The proof of that had been in the guarded way she had related to him certain things about Henry Tulkington, matters she had hitherto kept to herself. Even when she opened up, it had come with reservations. Saoirse had a certain standing in Deal and made no secret of dealing in smuggled goods herself. This she did through John Hawker, buying fine wines and good brandy, dispensed to the better class of clients in her card room.

Brazier was aware that an initial fascination, for she was striking to look at and he was a red-blooded male, had moved to admiration. This was only partly shaped because she was an unmarried woman in charge of an establishment like the Old Playhouse, remarkable in itself. That she more than held her own in a place like Deal, which was rough and violent, like all the places where ships berthed and tars took their pleasure, made it doubly so.

First met in the company of Vincent Flaherty, it had become obvious the Irishman was infatuated, the impression given on introduction being that she liked him, but did not reciprocate his feelings. With her red hair and beguiling figure, Saoirse was one to take the eye of every man in a room. This she allied to the easy manner of a born hostess, able to indulge in banter, exercise a sharp wit, be flippant and, if required, rigidly firm.

Even before she took him in, after his beating, Brazier had sensed she liked him and it was mutual, which made their exchanges comfortable. But even with all the help she had afforded him, Saoirse Riorden was one to put her own needs first. He would never ask her to risk her livelihood, for the very simple reason he knew she would refuse. The question now posed was a way to jog her, to bring her back to his reason for calling, given he had the distinct impression she was holding something back.

'You say he's a smuggler, this Dan Spafford?'

The reply came after another lengthy pause for consideration. 'In a small way and at loggerheads with Hawker, which, if what is implied by gossip is true, then with Tulkington too.'

'Yet he has married the son, a wastrel you say, to Betsey.'

There was no need for either to remark it made no sense. Saoirse then proved, just as he had not told her about abducting a dazed Hawker, she too had held back on something she could have told him the day before, but had chosen not to, perhaps to spare his feelings.

'Not four days past, Harry Spafford was snatched off the street by John Hawker, dragged by his collar to the slaughterhouse, which is Hawker's place of business. It's not somewhere anyone of sense would want to be, even freely entered, what with the rumours of things that take place there. For a weakling like Harry Spafford . . .'

Brazier did not blench when told what he could have been threatened with; he had heard the same story too often to give it any credence. It was one related to the gullible by sailors in every port he had ever visited, as well as joked about in the wardrooms of the ships in which he had served. It was a common myth, though given the way Saoirse was describing it, he knew debunking it would be unwise.

'Dan Spafford would not take that well,' she concluded.

'Which perhaps tells me Trotter's purpose. An offer to join forces, perhaps?'

'Sure, I don't know the ins and outs, Edward, but Spafford is no match for what I reckon you're up against.'

'Which brings me back to my request.'

'Jesus,' she exclaimed, 'I could be sorry for the day you ever darkened my door.'

Which he knew was as good as a yes.

John Hawker never found it easy to pass along Beach Street with anything approaching haste; too many people wanted to catch his eye and engage his ear. A man who seemed to know the doings of the Revenue Service was a fellow with whom to be friendly. There was not a soul who made their living on the beach who had not, at some time, crossed to France to purchase and run contraband.

Always a swift dash, it was carried out when opportunity presented itself, with the wind and sea state favourable, added to a combination of men and funds put together for the purpose. Nor was it always under sail; men who rowed for a living, servicing the hundreds of vessels who used the Downs anchorage, had the muscles for over twenty miles of endurance and double that on a dark enough night.

On a calm sea, with the moon cloud obscured, they could cross the Goodwin Sands at high tide and get to the opposite shore in a matter of hours. Nothing heavy like brandy, which would weigh down the boat, would be purchased. The easiest, lightest and most profitable artefact to smuggle was tea. Thus, every man on an oar would be wearing a specially sewn oilskin waistcoat, which could hold thirty pounds of leaf.

On his perambulations, and because he was trusted, John Hawker often heard about the planned dash, while gentle enquiry usually told him at what point on the beach the galley would be coming ashore. It was necessary, once a landfall was made, in case the Revenue men were waiting, to disperse quickly and store the contraband in preordained places no search would uncover.

Hawker then had a choice: whether to alert the excisemen and tell them where to wait, or to direct them to another spot, far enough away from the proposed landing to foil interdiction, and how that was decided was his to make. He could give them a sprat of a collar, which kept them satisfied and away from the cargoes Tulkington had coming in by ship. Or he could enhance his reputation with the boatmen as the fellow who could fool the law and send them chasing shadows.

In spreading the rumour about Brazier, Hawker was too shrewd to accuse him of anything. All he did was hint at something to be found odd, in a town where the same people saw each other every day and where a stranger, of some presence and odd habits, stood out and was the subject of comment anyway.

'Full post captain an' full of hisself. Got to enquire, if he ain't got a ship, what's the bugger doin' here, don't you reckon?'

There was no need to use anything other than the name. A stranger this sailor sod might be, but he was one mad enough to swim in the sea of a morning, which was observed by some, to be then talked about by many. The boatmen of Deal, whatever their particular daily grind, saw immersion in the waters they lived by and from as close to insanity.

'I'm told he's been seen visiting Walmer Castle, as well, when Pitt was residing there. Hugger-mugger I heard they were.'

That was a name to set local blood boiling; these where the very men whose boats William Pitt had ordered burnt, with no hint that they might be compensated for their loss. It had thrown the whole community in debt, as new craft had to be built, though that had been partially alleviated by a collection of funds from the better heeled citizenry, not least Henry Tulkington, which came with a degree of self-interest.

The prosperity of the town depended on it being able to serve the ships that berthed offshore. The local traders supplied meat, ship's biscuit, fresh vegetables, small beer and spirits, as well as the thousands of articles a sailing ship required to be safe at sea and the only way to load those articles was by boat or hoy.

Suspicion planted, it only required the possibility of a revenue spy to spread – not hard since it was held, as a fact, that the town had hidden away such creatures already. It could never be accepted that smugglers interdicted and arrested had fallen to anything like bad luck. It had to be a loose tongue or malevolent and secret observation. So, seed planted, John Hawker could go about his affairs, knowing his task was complete.

The matter he thought hard on now was more complex: how to be a part of what would follow, without his presence being too obvious, this not made easy by his face being known to all. For a fellow who held himself in high esteem, the way he had been humiliated by Brazier and his tars could not be remedied by any other hand than his own, though he was obliged to admit he would need help, given their numbers.

Could he get himself and his men close enough to exact physical revenge before what would follow took place? There was little doubt it would be an ordeal by fire, for that was the way of the Deal mob of boatmen when feeling threatened. The very least a soul railing against smuggling could expect – and there were some, like the Methodists, Baptists and the Temperance League – was their meeting houses reduced to ash in the middle of the night.

The worst fear was that the torch-carrying multitude would set fire to such places when they were within, leaving them the choice to die in the flames or exit, which was inevitable, to face a sound beating. Magistrates could huff and puff in the following days and promise retribution and arrests, but finding anyone to swear against another was impossible.

It was also the case that such officials, men who lived in close proximity to the culprits, were shy of being too stern, their own safety and property being a toothsome target for revenge. So they could shake their heads and ask, had these evangelicals not brought down their fate upon their own heads? Another motive for laxity was easy to surmise: they benefited themselves from smuggling, and besides, King Canute had as much chance of reversing an incoming tide as they had of putting a stopper on the trade.

As Hawker made his way through the town, calling at the various enterprises to examine their accounts and collect the taxes due, he added to his rumour-mongering in those places where it would have an effect, all the while cogitating on his own concern. He reasoned he would have to get in to Quebec

House first, to exact what he needed, before the worked-up crowd got going.

This would take a few days, so the rumour gained force and resentment had time to fester, allowing the feeling of being threatened to grow until collective anger would begin to combust. Hawker reasoned it would happen once night fell, and enough drink had been consumed to take growing bitterness at a perceived injustice to action.

It would begin with a few of the more raucous and gullible souls, men who lived in a general state of the ever hard done by. As it left the taverns and coursed through the streets, it would, like a boulder rolling down a hill, gather other discontents, or the merely excitable, until the watchmen, poorly paid and few in number, would reckon on discretion and quietly melt away.

By that time, Hawker needed to have taken his personal revenge. Then he had to get Spafford and his men to the fore, so there could be no backsliding. They were tasked to lead the crowd, to throw the stones that would smash the windows, at which point they could melt away and return to their hovel in Worth.

There was always a chance he could catch Brazier when he was out of Quebec House, in which case he needed to be able to act swiftly. With that as a possibility he knew what he needed as well as where to find it. The urchins of Deal had several favoured spots where they would congregate to drink gin when they could afford it. That usually depended on a successful run of picking pockets in the bustle of the Lower Valley Road or Middle Street. The churchyard behind St George's Church was one of their chosen spots, where the gravestones provided a bit of shelter from the wind, if not the chill.

'Here,' he said, passing out a handful of copper. 'There's double that if I get what I needs.'

Knowing John Hawker as a man of his word and often inclined to be generous, as well as one to be afeared of if crossed, they were eager to do his bidding. So he was sure neither Brazier, or his tars, would be able to so much as twitch an eyebrow without him being told of it.

CHAPTER ELEVEN

Henry Tulkington had already seen off Harry Spafford, sent away in the dog cart with the funds to travel on to Chatham, as well as monies to fund his habits. He was now making his own preparations to depart for London, when the request that Elisabeth be allowed a visit to Annabel Colpoys was mooted. Even if he reckoned there was no choice but to agree, he made his aunt wait for a reply as he appeared to mull it over: he did not want her to think his acquiescence came without reservations.

'It cannot be today. I will be travelling to Dover to pick up the mail coach.'

'Henry, we are in possession of more than one conveyance.'

'I'm aware of that, but if Elisabeth goes off the estate, it will be in the Berlin and my coachmen will be with her.'

'So you're going to London?' was cover for her being at a loss to say anything else.

'Obviously.'

Sarah Lovell was tempted to say nothing was obvious where he was concerned, but took refuge in triviality, given Henry seemed to have no intention of enlightening her as to what he would be doing. She felt she needed to know.

'To visit your Uncle Dirley?'

'Why else?' came with a note of exasperation. 'There are many things that require to be resolved. I doubt I have to explain what they are.'

'Would I be allowed to point out again, since Elisabeth will not speak with you, I have become the link? In that situation it would help if I were to know what you had planned, so I can answer her enquiries.'

Henry's face showed how little he liked her tone.

'Please forgive me if I've been too direct, Nephew, but I feel the circumstances warrant it.'

He took a while to see the sense, even longer to respond, so his dignity was not punctured. 'I need proper legal documentation on various matters, not least the power of attorney to manage the West Indian plantations. Their value must be preserved and that can only be done if the persons supervising the estates are reporting to someone who can properly scrutinise their activities.'

'Can I at least tell Elisabeth there is no plan to send her back to Jamaica?'

She meant her and Harry Spafford, this a thought that horrified aunt as much as niece, with the added fear she might be sent with them. She recalled the West Indies with nothing approaching fondness and the journey even less so. It had been too often spent groaning in a cot in which she had been both sick and violently thrown out of by the state of the sea.

'None at present,' came with an arch look, which implied it could be a future possibility. 'I have, as you know, removed Spafford

139

from Cottington and he will be kept at a distance, unless . . .'

If it was necessary, because of the significant pause, to read between the lines – and there was ample space to do so – Harry Spafford would behave in whatever way Henry wished and that would include exercising his matrimonial rights. Confined to property, that was one thing, but how far would Henry go if Elisabeth sought to defy him? Judging by his actions already, there was no way to tell, but everything was possible.

'There are agreements Spafford will be required to sign, which I will see to on my way back.'

'You have yet to say where that will take place.'

'Why, Aunt Sarah, would you need to know that? As to the Colpoys' visit, I suggest, since I require the coach, Elisabeth pen a note asking to call, which I will see delivered. Perhaps tomorrow, if it's convenient to them.'

Henry went back to the papers he was no doubt preparing for London so, without any acknowledgment, she was able to stand and depart. The door closed on a man pondering on the instructions he would be required to issue to his coachmen when they were carrying his sister. One always carried a loaded and primed pistol in case of highwaymen, but perhaps it would be best if both were armed from now on, to protect against any attempt by Brazier to kidnap her.

Henry had no doubt, should it happen, it would involve weapons. The road leading to Cottington Court should be seen to be clear before Elisabeth went off the estate. The sod could have no prior knowledge of her movements, if any, so would be reduced to standing and watching in hope.

The note to Annabel Colpoys was sent down by Sarah

Lovell and he recognised Elisabeth's firm style with the quill. That, once read, went into a drawer, while he wrote another to Roger Colpoys. It was couched in very much the same vein, friendly, with the added point that since Roger did not see Henry's sister often, it might be a good idea for him to be present to entertain her.

Told his coach was waiting, he gave instructions, once it was sanded and sealed, for his note to be delivered. His next orders were given to the two men who attended him when travelling, his first words the far-from-surprising information his sister would use it to travel. But more followed.

'At whichever destination to which you take my sister, you're to stand guard at the entrance and allow no one past who is not connected to the household. Is that understood?'

The assent was murmured, for it was beyond curious. But clearly, it had been taken on board, as was his luggage and eventually himself, this after he had instructed Upton, his head groom, of another stricture. Prior to Elisabeth and his aunt departing the estate, a stable boy should be sent to survey the road outside for any sign of lurking strangers.

If it was true those who served Henry Tulkington were in dread of his poor opinion, and would obey whatever instructions he issued, that did not preclude quiet speculation, especially between the senior retainers. The cook was close to Lionel Upton, the head groom, neither being in the first flush of youth. They would have, if it had been possible, moved from affection to a more formal connection. This required the courage to ask their master for permission, talked about often and postponed every time. What if he said no?

Grady and Upton were, with the gardener, Creevy, the top trio of servitors. That said, the one who claimed green fingers was not trusted, given he was too often seen grovelling to Tulkington, even when it was not required. So when Grady and Upton had their quiet chats, he was always excluded. This was seen as even more essential now, given the speculation regarding what had occurred a few days past, matters that still lacked clarity.

It had been discussed on the morning of revelation, even if the task of making a logical deduction was impossible. It had to be, for there was no one it was safe to ask regarding clarification. The other servants, if they were curious, were keeping their thoughts to themselves. If the master kept rigid control, Sarah Lovell, who ran Cottington Court domestically, was not one to care if she was liked or hated.

Thus she ensured she was neither esteemed nor respected and, as a source of information, she was not one to be questioned. A hint of such a query might reach the ears of Tulkington, which could result in the offender being shown the gate.

Miss Elisabeth – the long-serving retainers could not bring themselves to think of her otherwise – had always been held to a different standard. This applied especially to Grady and Upton, men who had been working at Cottington, though not in their present elevated tasks, when she was a growing girl, with all the lack of decorum permitted by her age.

Even widowed and back at Cottington, she had held to her mode of address, which was not only respectful, but also hinted at an innate kindness, while showing none of the stiff reserve that characterised her relatives. So, as far as it was possible for a servant to esteem a family member, she was held in high regard.

'Rum do, Grady,' Upton moaned, easing himself into a chair. 'Said it t'other day and I do so again now.'

They always met in the storeroom, over which Grady ruled. Off to one side lay his sleeping quarters, that being a space no one entered without knocking first, Henry Tulkington being the sole exception. The stables were the opposite: open to all. Very recently, Miss Elisabeth had been a frequent visitor. She would engage one of the younger stable boys to take out a pony and run errands for her, carrying notes to destinations about which Upton did not enquire. It had become easy to guess subsequently, not that such information was vouchsafed to anyone, especially the master of the house.

'Lookout for strangers on the road,' Upton added, 'what the devil for?'

'Never been so hard to find out anything, Lionel. No one is even whispering in the corners.'

When it came to secrets, generally, the people they served had none. It seemed a common misconception of those who employed servants that they were deaf, dumb and blind, unable to hear, see or to make sense of overheard conversations. They acted as if their inferiors had no views worth consideration, nor had the sight to see the silent interactions and facial expressions, which imparted more of what was going between those they attended to than talk.

'T'was like me being put to tailing Miss Elisabeth from weeks past.'

That referred back to another discussion: Henry had ordered Upton to follow Betsey on her daily walks, so he had been obliged to admit to whom she met and how often. The fact that he disliked the duty, or relating the details of what he had seen, mattered little. Henry Tulkington, as ever, got what he wanted, which included the recent boarding up of the broken and hidden postern gate, by which Brazier had so many times effected entry.

'Her naval captain is at the seat of it, true enough,' Grady acknowledged.

Upton sighed, possibly for what he and the cook did not have. 'They were sweet and getting sweeter, from what I saw. I could have sworn there were to be bells a' ringing.'

'There were bells and we didn't hear, Lionel, for they were done without.'

'Can't believe she's really been wed off to that uppity young bugger?'

'The way her brother named her, as Mrs Spafford, makes it so. An' it can only have been done to thwart the cove you saw her kissing.'

'Hard to credit he'd go that far.'

'He'll do as he wishes. Did I not have another locked up in the cellar?'

By accident, not being expected to be about, Grady had seen some stocky, rough-looking cove taken through the cellar door. His key, by which he could stock the dining and drawing rooms, as well as his pantry, with wine and brandy, had been removed by Tulkington and only given back the day before, obviously once the detainee was gone.

'There's one I'd have liked to kick in the arse,' Grady added, there being no need to say whom; Spafford junior had got under his far-from-thick skin with his demands and the rude manner of delivery. 'If he'd asked me to shave him, I might have been tempted to slit his gullet.'

Upton knew that to be so much fancy. Grady was given to talking in a like manner in here, bellicose and hard. Outside, he was the sort who only opened his mouth when asked to do so. But they had common ground, for it was necessary they look after themselves and those over who they exercised supervision: footmen, maids and stable lads. If they cared for the quality of Cottington Court with due attention, their own well-being was of equal value.

'Nothing said by Miss Elisabeth?' Upton enquired. 'She ain't been near the stables.'

'Maids can't talk to her and enquire, though they told of how strange was her state the morning after all the shouting and bawling. Lovell was there to stop any talk and she's ever there now. If Miss Elisabeth rings down, she has to be told, it's for her to answer, not any of us. Can't ask to aid her, can we, but I'm dying to know what's what.'

Upton sat with him for a while in a state of silent study, before admitting something which had occurred to him. 'Goes for walks on her own, every day?'

Grady's keen look indicated he understood. He saw Miss Elisabeth in the hallway and the drawing room, which he held to be his patch. He was the one who fetched and helped her into her outdoor clothing. But that was no location in which to pose questions: you would never have known who could overhear before the present troubles. Now it was certain Lovell would do so.

'Be careful, Lionel, is all I would say.'

'One of the spare coach mares has been ailing with laminitis, but is coming back to fitness, so she has to be walked regular, a job I gave to one of my hands, normal like. What if I were to take it on myself? Timed right and on the path to the lake for a change, I could just run into her. What harm in asking how she is and what's goin' on then?'

'Even I know that's not your normal path.'

Upton chose to ignore that. 'She's fond of a horse too, always has been.'

A bell rang on the panel just outside the storeroom, so Grady hauled himself up and went out, intoning, 'No rest for the wicked.' His head soon came back through the door. 'Miss Elisabeth's bell, so I have sent for Lovell.'

He found Elisabeth in the hallway, with an expression-free Sarah Lovell in attendance. Given he knew her requirements, the garments necessary for outdoors – a thick cloak and a bonnet plus a muffler – were fetched to be put on. This was carried out without the need for words, the cloak placed round her shoulders so she could tie the cord herself.

By his face you would never have known it, but Grady was affected by memory just then, thinking back to what Miss Elisabeth had so recently been, in contrast to the dejected creature he was observing now. It was worse the further back his mind went, recalling the skipping and laughter that had characterised her as a girl.

She had also, and just as often, filled the house with dispute, for she argued with her father over any restraint. And it had to be noted with some glee, she had either carried the day by the sheer ferocity of her argument or, if that failed, by the kind of coquettish cheek afforded to daughters of strong-minded male parents.

Then came the proposed nuptials and, with Tulkington senior gone to meet his maker, the arguments that had ensued with Master Henry before matters were settled and harmony reigned once more. Grady had been present at her wedding and, even fully occupied in supervision, he had observed how happy she seemed, and took from it some pleasure of his own. Even her misery guts of a brother had found it possible to smile on that sunny day.

As Betsey went out the door, her aunt addressed Grady, to repeat a message previously delivered. 'Someone to keep a look out for my niece's return.'

The last part she did not bother to add: she was to be called as soon as Miss Elisabeth was spotted coming through the garden gate.

Just breathing the fresh air had a positive effect on Betsey. Despite Henry's restrictions, she would be getting out of Cottington Court come morning, with a chance she might affect her predicament. There was relief that he was gone, she having seen his coach pull away from her bedroom window. In itself this lifted a bit of weight; he was a baleful presence even unseen.

The wind, which had whipped at her cloak the day before, had moderated, the sky was as it should be in spring, a mixture of sunshine and billowing cloud, with the occasional fast-moving shadow obvious as it progressed over patches of open ground. Her thoughts were much the same, the bright hopes, so recently a warming vision, overborne by dark thoughts. They were as they had been from the moment she awoke in that drugged stupor: how could it be otherwise?

Having gone right round the lake, Betsey was on her way back to the house when she spotted Upton coming towards her, leading a horse. He being a man who had always behaved kindly towards her, keen to encourage her love of riding, the sight raised both questions and perhaps, though she was careful in her anticipation, possibilities. What did he know of those notes she had pressed his youngest stable lad to deliver?

He could not have been much in ignorance, if you excluded the contents. No one could take a pony out of the stables without his permission and he had never objected to the imposition, one as a family member she had a right to make. That accepted, it would have been more than curiosity could bear not to ask after the destination.

The realisation that Henry had never mentioned those notes came suddenly, along with a conviction. If he had been aware, he would not have passed up an opportunity to throw such knowledge in her face. Another thought occurred: the woods and the lake, outside an annual coppicing, pollarding and keeping down the rabbits, were held to be the preserve of the family, unlike the rest of the estate outside the walls, home to much activity.

She had played here as a child and young woman, keeping her and her friends away from the kind of prying eyes that might report on any mischief, not that such would extend beyond pranks. But the same had held in her meetings with Edward

Brazier, a knowledge it was unlikely they would be observed by servants or farm labourers.

'Ma'am,' emerged when Upton was close, his leather hat pulled off in respect.

'Mr Upton, it is unusual to see you hereabouts.'

These words induced in the groom a slight feeling of discomfort; he was more accustomed to being here than she knew. He had, however, his excuse prepared.

'Change of scenery, ma'am. My lads have been walking herself here for days now, an' it was time I saw how she's progressin' myself. Normally she's been taken round the farm fields and down to the main paddocks to have a sniff of the herd. But they are fresh ploughed now and the ground is wet. Thought if I went that way, we'd come in with a ton of mud on her feet, an' mine too.'

A short conversation ensued about laminitis and the need to keep a horse so affected in a stall, which might appear comfortable for a human, but tended to deny equines – herd and prey animals – the company they liked and in which they felt safe. It moved on to how unpleasant were the paths round the outer fields in such conditions, churned up by both the shire horses and indifferent ploughing.

While talking of this, Betsey's thinking was on another subject entirely. Upton, his grooms and stable lads, must be in and out of the enclosed part of the estate all the time, going to and from the well-stocked outer paddocks. Cottington was home to active horse breeding, providing a steady supply to the house, as well as a good source of revenue from the annual horse sales.

She could remember being taken down to the paddocks by her father, to choose her first pony, followed over the years by others as she grew out of them in succession, until finally it was a proper horse of eighteen hands and no shortage of spirit. The question she finally posed came with what she hoped was an air of innocence.

'You still come and go by the north gate, I assume?'

That was acknowledged. There should have been no need to refer to them being locked against poaching and the thieving of wood, but Betsey did so. Cottington Court consisted of a high-walled interior manor, containing the house, the parish church, this wood and lake, plus a number of barns for the storage of farming implements as well as Upton's stable block. Extensive cultivated fields and said paddocks lay on the outer fields, reached by several sets of double gates, through which traffic could pass. These were kept padlocked unless in use.

Betsey sank down on her haunches, feeling the lower leg for signs of heat and, finding none, smiled up at the head groom, who seemed taken by her concern. 'How long was she in a stall? Forgive me, I should surely ask her name.'

'This one's called Posy an' can be put to a coach when fit. Two weeks and ever a moan for hunger. Couldn't feed her as she wanted, for her weight.'

'Of course.'

Betsey was up now and by Posy's head, stroking her head and getting the gentle nudge of pleasure in return. More importantly, proximity to Upton allowed for quiet conversation and what might be construed as a tentative hint.

'You should come this way more often, Mr Upton, or

perhaps it is I who should vary my route? I could even walk the mare if you so desired.' A self-deprecating smile was necessary. 'Always assuming you trusted me to be firm.'

'She's not of the kind to seek to run off.'

Betsey was now at a loss as to what to say but that did not preclude thinking. Would it be wise to open up completely, to tell Upton of her problem? Hesitation was natural, for the mere fact of his being on this path, if no other. Was his change of scenery an excuse to follow her, in case she was looking for a way to escape? Would anything she said be reported back to her aunt, or worse, to Henry?

What did he know? Was it safe to ask? Upton was smilingly chatty and could be suggesting a route to freedom. Genuine or a ruse? She could ask to walk Posy the following day, or the one after, but suggest she'd need the key to the gate, which would gain her partial freedom, incomplete because she would have to get to somewhere safe.

Would the home of the Colpoys suffice? Annabel had helped her before, but she had declined on another occasion, being too afraid of her husband. Roger would most certainly not welcome her as a guest. According to Annabel, he would do nothing to upset Henry, given what had been visited upon him on one occasion when he did.

The only safe place was in Deal and not in rooms or the Three Kings, where she could be found and fetched back by force. Quebec House provided the only refuge that would serve. Edward would take her in and protect her. If her reputation was then shredded by taking up residence in the house of an unmarried man, so be it.

The possibilities Upton might afford her would have ended, had she known they were being observed. Creevy, the head gardener, had seen the groom heading out with his mare on an unfamiliar route and, prompted by curiosity, had followed him. He was now wondering what to do with the information he could see before him, Miss Elisabeth and Upton as chatty as old friends.

The pair were walking back towards both house and stables, conversing as they progressed, but it was nothing more than banal exchange. Betsey had decided she must hold her tongue and not succumb to the temptation to confide in Upton. The time might come when she would need to do so, but on the morrow, hopefully, she was going to visit her old friend.

There was a chance matters could begin to be altered there, which made it too risky to confide in him now. Only if her plans were thwarted could it be an avenue she must pursue. So as she talked, Betsey sought to create a positive rapport, this kept up until the time came for them to part company.

'I hope you will avail Posy of a walk round the lake again, Mr Upton. It is sometimes lonely when I'm out, so it is nice to have someone to talk to.'

The leather hat came off again. 'Nice of you to say so, ma'am, and I bid you good day while, like you, hoping for another chance encounter.'

I can trust him, was her thought, as she turned away, her smile hidden from him and soon from the world. Creevy was in the parterre when she came through the side gate, Betsey was treated to a half-bowed head and a toothless smile. This was returned automatically, albeit with no real warmth. He was not a person to whom she had ever taken, even if it would have to be admitted that his attendance to his duties, not least in this formal garden, was exemplary.

Sarah Lovell was waiting as she came through the door, Grady soon appearing to take her hat and cloak, this carried out in silence.

CHAPTER TWELVE

Face-to-face with Trotter, as he entered the parlour, Brazier knew immediately where he had seen him before. The too-large nose and a protruding lower lip, as well as the scrawny body, were printed on his memory, as was the wheezing, when he opened his mouth to speak. What was unprepossessing to begin with had not been improved by the swollen bridge of the nose and the bruises below the eyes, now yellow edged with purple.

He had first come across him at an inn on the road to Deal, where his hired coachman had stopped to change horses. Daisy had been in the company of John Hawker, though the name was, at that point, unknown. The attitude was not; he had come very close to a fight with Hawker over the most trivial of disputes, the ability to take a free chair in a crowded tavern.

'I've seen you afore,' was Trotter's opening gambit, his face screwed up in a state of enquiry. 'But it weren't just at Cottington. Can't place it, though.'

Would it serve to enlighten him? Brazier was far from sure and he knew why Trotter was confused. On the occasion just recalled, he had been in his uniform and had on his distinctive naval scraper. Now he was hatless and in civilian clothes, added to this being a very different setting, so it was only the face that partially registered.

'I think we'd best get to the object you wish to pursue, Trotter,' came with a gesture offering Daisy to sit.

'Happy standing,' was his reply.

That was followed by a worried look, which encompassed the room, as if there might be some danger lurking behind the chairs, settle or the velvet drapes. It was also clear he wished to stay near the door, his host suspecting so as to have a quick exit available. Choosing to stand himself might imply he was justified in his suspicions, so Brazier made a great play of not only taking a seat, but doing so in a manner designed to show he was at ease, sitting well back and crossing his legs. He was also well away from Trotter and he had a sword hidden by the far side of the settle, should that famed knife appear.

'So?'

'From what I saw at Cottington, you is not on good terms with Tulkington.'

'And if that's true?'

'If you looked about, you'd have seen why. All the lads with whom I berthed were captive and nursing bruises, having been given a thumping by John Hawker's lot. Did note he wasn't lookin' too chipper himself, mind.'

'Is that where you got your bruises?' The denial was vehement, changing an otherwise unthreatening face. In truth, if he had no desire to say where and when, it made no odds. 'I think it best if you tell me what happened.'

'You don't know?

The response to so stupid a question had to be delivered without sarcasm, which would not serve. 'If I did, I wouldn't ask, would I?'

'Not sure where to start.'

'The beginning is usually best,' said Brazier coldly.

Absurdly, he seemed to have to think about this, but it made so much sense Trotter had to accede and Brazier listened carefully, hoping that, in the explanation, there would be some gem that might give him grounds to seriously threaten Tulkington. It was the only way he could see to get Betsey free.

'What do you know of Dan Spafford?' Trotter asked.

'I know who he is and what he does.' It seemed unwise to mention the source of his information, or the wastrel son. 'Little more.'

Daisy went into a long and unnecessary tale regarding the way he and Spafford had met, as boys, and their adventures on the Baltic run, followed by the way they had been as close as brothers ever since, turning to smuggling.

'I was with Dan all the way, helping him when he needed thinkin' done.'

The temptation to tell him to get to the point had to be avoided; if there was something he could use, he had no idea where it might reside. He did interrupt the telling from time to time, for clarification. One point was the nature of the meeting between Tulkington and Spafford, which Daisy had been arranging when first espied in that inn.

'Can I take it, even if you told Tulkington it was so, your Dan is not at death's door?'

'Never. It were a ploy to suck Tulkington into an alliance,

156

on the grounds that Dan's boy Harry wouldn't last two shakes once he was gone. As it happens, that bit's likely true. Harry could never take over from his pa, being as he is one of Dan's own gang would have done for him within weeks. Keeping him whole was supposed to be the point, but it were really an attempt to come close to Tulkington, to get on the inside, so as to have a chance to topple the bugger.'

'From your tone, I can tell he didn't bite.'

Daisy had moved away from the door to hunch over the back of an armchair, his face becoming more animated as he related Spafford's real motive for wanting the meeting. There being peace between Britain and France, he was coming close to penury. It hardly needed to be said war was so much better for smugglers: a higher price could be placed on contraband when the risks seemed so much greater.

'Are they greater?' Brazier asked, this before he realised he didn't truly care.

'Not much. Frenchie wants to sell his produce, an' has no more respect for the law than we do. He jacks his price, mind.' Trotter moved on to Spafford twice pinching Tulkington's property, though it was noticeable he avoided any detail of how that had been done. 'More was planned, 'cause we knew it would make him spit, which were enough. Had no idea who was carryin' out the thieving. That was, 'til Harry was grabbed by Hawker and squawked.'

'Cottington?'

'Dan was invited to go alone and negotiate for Harry's release, maybe to give back to Tulkington what we'd pilfered, who knows? But he didn't go alone, an' that was foreseen.'

Brazier had wondered if the presence of so many other people had anything to do with what was happening to Betsey; now he know it was just coincidence.

'They was waiting for us,' came with a bitter tone, as if Tulkington had somehow broken an unwritten rule. 'Lads walked into a trap and were had up to a man, but I managed to hide.'

'Not get away?'

'I was there for Dan, not Harry, worrying on what Tulkington, or more like Hawker, would do to him. Wouldn't be the first time a soul has gone into the sea with a ball and chain to his ankle. I was on the ground not far off from where you was stood, hidden with it being dark outside the light from yon winder. I saw you aiming a pistol at Tulkington's head and callin' him all sorts. Have to admit I was hoping you'd pull the trigger.'

'Do you know why?' A headshake. 'It matters only that I had good reason, Trotter, but the odds that night did not favour me. Tulkington and I are sworn enemies, so how do you think anything you can do will aid me? Or is it the reverse, you looking for me to help you?'

'There's still no sign of Dan,' was not really an answer.

'What of the men you said you berthed with?'

'The way I was seen off, I reckon them to be locked up in Hawker's slaughterhouse. Get them out. With them and you combined . . .'

'We could effect a rescue?' was issued in a dry tone, which should have told Trotter, who was looking at him eagerly, he was whistling for the moon. 'How many men does Hawker have at his command?'

'Much as twenty, but he can call on more if they're needed. Lots of folk in Deal want to be right side of him.'

'And how many do you think I can muster?' A shrug. 'Three men who are fighters, four bodies at a pinch, and myself.'

'Got to do something,' was a plea. 'First we get the lads out of that damned slaughterhouse, then see about Dan.'

Brazier later concluded it was certainly not sympathy that prompted him to say he would think on it, more pragmatism. As an ally, Daisy Trotter did not much appeal and nor did Dan Spafford, even if he had been free. But there was no point in saying so; best leave the door open.

'I take it I can contact you at the place from which you wrote?' A nod. 'And you know where to find me. If I can think of a way we can combine to effect, I will be in touch. Likewise, if anything occurs at your end.'

Trotter nodded.

'Let me show you out.'

As luck or misfortune would have it – this dependant on the side of the argument one occupied – while John Hawker's planted seed was nurturing in the fertile soil of gossip, news came that William Pitt had arrived at Walmer Castle, this being the official residence of the Lord Warden of the Cinque Ports. The King's First Minister did not occupy the sinecure, but a member of his cabinet, who had no use for the castle, did. A lover of sea air, Pitt used it instead, as a retreat from the cares of office.

For Edward Brazier, this did not bode well. Given the rumours filtering through the taverns and gin shops about him, the coincidence of Pitt's arrival was not seen as such. Suspicions went up a notch, as speculation combined his presence with Brazier's purported purpose. Both were being tarred as sods who would see honest men starve. As ever the case, it was not seen as hypocrisy by those who held the law in contempt and broke it frequently.

Brazier came back to Quebec House, to find an invitation that he should call on Pitt at his earliest convenience, there being a matter of much interest of which he might wish to be appraised. Given his present preoccupations, he could only think of one notion that would pertain, so he sent Joe Lascelles back with a suggestion to call first thing in the morning, which was declined.

Instead Pitt suggested he would be eating at the Three Kings on the morrow and invited Brazier to join him there, happy to dine at the naval hour if that suited.

Rattling down the drive in the early morning, Betsey was astonished they were obliged to stop prior to the gate being opened and so was her Aunt Sarah. It was even more to wonder on that Tanner peered into the coach, to stare at them with what was seen as a want of respect before nodding silently. The gate was then opened and they could proceed.

'The effrontery of the fellow.'

Sarah Lovell felt compelled to complain, as she often did about the behaviour of servants, both indoors and out, though she had little to do with the latter. As her niece listened to her litany, she recalled her aunt had been a problem in the West Indies, treating the Langridge servants in a way Betsey had never sunk to, even if they were slaves.

It had been dear, sweet Stephen, always fair-minded, who had proposed a justification: Aunt Sarah had little and was so dependent at home, she would seek compensation by being overbearing with those who dare not answer back. There was no temptation from Betsey to make this opinion known: the fewer words exchanged suited her most. Besides she was dealing with nerves and speculations on that which was to come, for the permission to call on the Colpoys had come quickly and with seeming delight.

'Betsey, my dear,' Annabel cried from the front step, to be followed by a more sober, 'Mrs Lovell.'

Annabel's enthusiasm was not replicated. Betsey could see behind her, hovering in the doorway, the red hair and pugnacious rubicund face of her husband Roger. His presence had not been anticipated, she assuming that as the owner of a working farm, at this time of year especially with ploughing in progress, Roger would be out supervising his fields. But she had to respond with a smile when Annabel trilled that Roger had stayed behind today, especially because she was about to call.

There was a temptation to be churlish and point something out. The same Roger had instructed his wife and children to shun Betsey. Very recently they had ignored her before and after a divine Sunday service at St Leonard's Church. There would have been satisfaction in saying so but it had to be beaten back. That Annabel had obeyed the injunction hurt a great deal, as did the shy avoidance of the normally overboisterous Colpoys children.

Roger she cared not a fig about; he had always seemed to her, with his air of bluff pomposity, a bit of a caricature of John

Bull manners, a man Annabel, who had not been as favoured by nature as she, had married to avoid the shelf.

'Damn good to see you, Elisabeth,' he boomed, to get a frown from a wife who was ever upset by his coarse language, not that her disapproval ever had any effect. 'Been too long, far too long. Mrs Lovell, likewise.'

The three children were lined up in the hall, their unruly ginger hair combed and their clothing neat, which was in stark contrast to normality. When it came to being rowdy and finding dirt, few could hold a candle to them, evidence they took after their sire, not their mother. Betsey and Sarah Lovell were treated to a pair of regulation bows from the boys and a curtsy from the daughter, before they were sent upstairs to their schoolroom.

A servant materialised to take hats and cloaks, he instructed to tell the groom to see to the Tulkington coachmen, who would, no doubt, be grateful for some beer and a home-made pie.

'Mrs Colpoys has ordered tea, ladies,' Roger imparted, in a whisper, as they entered the drawing room. 'But I have decanted some very fine claret, if that is what you would prefer.'

'Tea will serve nicely, Mr Colpoys,' came from the aunt, with Betsey given a look that took for granted her compliance.

The nod in response was made in the abstract; Betsey was looking around a room she had been in often, wondering why it seemed so unfamiliar, until she realised it was not the place, but her gazing upon it differently. At no time in the past had she come here so intent on intrigue, looking for somewhere to surreptitiously leave her message. This made her aware that beneath the linen of her glove, her palm was sweating, which gave some concern that it would ruin the folded note she had tucked there.

Distraction came from everyone being invited to sit and, in doing so, engage in the normal concomitant of enquiries about health and references to the weather. Everyone talked of how happy they were winter was over and gave forth on being in good order. Only Roger, seeing the requirement to boom with an added thump on his chest, felt it necessary to say he had never felt better, that immediately followed by a deep gulp of wine.

'And how are things at Cottington?' Annabel asked, smiling at Betsey.

Posed with seeming innocence, it was larded with anything but. She knew her friend had been in dispute with Henry, knew about Edward Brazier and the burgeoning affection of which Betsey had made no secret. Annabel suspected it would surely lead to matrimony, as soon as her term of widowhood was seen as served.

Betsey's smile in response was forced, Sarah Lovell looking at her with a gimlet stare. Here was the test and she was wondering if her niece would pass it. Henry had insisted that matters of recent importance be treated with the utmost discretion. There was no need for Elisabeth to tell the world she was now Mrs Spafford; certainly she would pay dearly if she let out how such a union had come about.

In what was no more than a second, but felt like a lifetime, Betsey ranged over her fears, the consequences of what would flow from disobedience and not just confinement. At a whim,

Henry could fetch back Spafford and what would happen then? She so dreaded the consequences, it was safer to say, 'Much improved.'

'So Henry and you are—'

Annabel stopped, realising she had nearly said reconciled, which was wandering into territory best left alone and had been imparted without Lovell knowing. Betsey had previously alluded to differences with her brother, so they were not secret in this house, but that was best not aired. Roger, if it was even possible, seemed to have gone a deeper shade of red in his cheeks. Sarah Lovell was so rigid she looked like a waxwork. The name Brazier hung in the air like Banquo's Ghost.

'On the very best of terms, Annabel,' Betsey added, with an enthusiasm entirely manufactured. 'He is kindness itself.'

'Splendid,' boomed a relieved husband, allowing himself another gulp, this as the door opened, which allowed him to add with seeming relief, 'Ah! Tea!'

The unbuttoning of Betsey's right-hand glove was accomplished while the tea was being poured. Getting out the note was done by stages, as conversation moved on. With the subject of Cottington now safely out of the way, it turned to other acquaintances and, as parents, Annabel and Roger tended to relate a great deal to the activities of the children, only some as amusing as they supposed.

Having got to the point of no return, Betsey found it necessary to drop her tea cup, which broke on the wooden floor, sending the contents flying, as well as bits of crockery. In the confusion created, the note was taken out and concealed, all accompanied by her apologies and an insistence from Annabel that the loss of a piece of china did not matter in the least.

When the time came to depart, and kisses on the cheek were exchanged, Betsey got a chance to give Annabel a very brief message. 'Cushion, side of. Note.'

As the heads moved apart, it was obvious to Betsey that Annabel was alarmed. But it was only in her eyes, so no one else could see it.

CHAPTER THIRTEEN

Henry Tulkington entered Lincoln's Inn, which housed the chambers of his Uncle Dirley, in a good frame of mind. Things had been set in motion in Deal, which should see one problem removed. Once Brazier was out of the way, he could begin to repair relations with Elisabeth, not that he thought such a thing would be straightforward; it would take time and there was some hope she would be free of entanglements sooner than anticipated.

His impression of Harry Spafford was of a man who would very likely drink himself into an early grave. When it came to that, he would find in his brother-in-law a willing provider of funds. Not that he would use his own money; the income from the West Indies plantations would more than meet any bill.

A night in London, giving him access to the more refined carnal entertainments to which he was wedded, had left him feeling contented. There was also something energising about the bustle of the city, with its air of affluence, added to the constant transacting of business. It differed so markedly, when set against the sleepy, repetitive and parochial culture he was obliged to mix with at home.

He was calling on the man who had guided him in his affairs following the death of his father. Dirley Tulkington had been raised in the same part of the world as Henry, but years here allowed him to exude an air of metropolitan polish. In addition, his appearance, in a frame not short of burly, was so different from that of his tall and narrow-chested nephew that no one in ignorance of the name would have guessed they shared a bloodline.

With a full ruddy face, albeit with a trace of hairy shadow, Dirley sported flowing silver locks, to which was added a deep and attractive voice. With that went the manner of a man at ease in the world in which he moved: the higher reaches of London society, in which he maintained important connections. Acquainted with everybody of standing, he numbered among his close friends numerous people of real influence.

From modest beginnings, Dirley had risen to move with ease in the upper social layers of the capital. An illegitimate scion of the family, sired by Henry's grandfather, he had been put to learning the law, so as to be of use in a family concern intent on expansion. The dividend came when he, using his legal skills, a fine brain and growing social connections, helped take it from an enterprise fraught with risk to one of comparative security.

Working with his half-brother, Acton, they had polished what Dirley always referred to as a rough stone: running contraband might involve the need for violence at the sharp end, but he saw no need to have it run through to the marrow. He had taken over the financial and technical details of the purchase and transportation of goods, connections arranged long past and nurtured ever since.

No longer was the seeking of supplies haphazard. Goods were ordered as they would be in any normal commercial company, albeit placed by a private messaging system that operated in two directions. The commercial and diplomatic traffic between Calais and Dover was a constant – occasionally delayed by weather of course, but rarely for any extended length of time.

Dirley would take receipt of the information of when a cargo of goods ordered was due to sail, from a courier sent by his main contact in France, the same person presenting the bill for the previous deliveries. That was met by the relationships between two banks, one in Paris, one in London. The same fellow would take back across the Channel the requirements for the next load with the time limits in which it was required. If traffic was occasionally interrupted and made more difficult by war, there were still ways to do business, even with putative enemies. In peace, it was oiled close to perfection.

Nothing of that nature was entrusted to a commercial postal service, certainly not one between Britain and the Continent, thus keeping information from prying eyes. Indeed, Dirley and Henry, on their last meeting, had decided this would need to apply to England too, if William Pitt succeeded in his efforts to buy out the fellow who owned the franchise for the postal service. A courier might be needed to keep Henry abreast of the dates of delivery instead of an apparently innocent but coded postal notification.

The chambers themselves reeked of a legal practice that had been in existence for centuries, tiny rooms full of heavy tomes and shelves of red-ribboned briefs overlooking toiling junior lawyers and clerks. There were also clients waiting to see the various qualified lawyers and senior partners, but a blood relation to the head of chambers was not to be kept waiting. Sitting behind a substantial desk and having greeted his nephew, Dirley pointed to an elegant silver pot on a like salver.

'You will take coffee, I hope, before you look over the books?'

Prior to any discussion, it was a requirement that Henry examine the ledgers by which every aspect of their enterprise was listed, books that never left Dirley's chambers. Funds expended and monies received, debts yet to be collected, lists of goods ordered and purchased, set against those disbursed. It conformed, in every respect, to a legitimate commercial concern, if you excluded the fact that only two people had access to the figures. They also benefited, though not in equal measure, from the proceeds, Henry taking the lion's share.

'The tedium first, as ever, Uncle,' Henry sighed, taking a chair, knowing he was about to undertake a task he heartily disliked.

'Necessary, Henry,' was imparted with gravity. Dirley stood up and pulled a key from his waistcoat pocket, which he then used to unlock a large safe, his voice echoing from within the steel-lined chamber. 'I do, as you know, take my responsibilities very seriously.'

Was there, in that statement, a sly rebuke, as if to say his nephew, the superior beneficiary of the business, should do likewise? Tempted to issue a pointed rejoinder, Henry held back on such touchiness. Several thick ledgers were extracted to be placed before him, these looked upon with less than pleasant anticipation.

'I wonder sometimes, Uncle,' he said, tapping the leather cover of one, 'if you feel I don't trust you.'

'It would pain me to think you could ever entertain such a thought. The way to ensure you never do, is to have you fully share in everything I record, so I will leave you to your task. Ring the bell if you want anything and, of course, when you're finished. Then we can share a capital lunch. I have taken to dining at Mrs Gould's bagnio in Arlington Street.'

'A new venue for pleasure, Uncle?'

Dirley smiled for the first time. 'I bore easily, Henry.'

Once he had gone, and the first set of figures were exposed, Henry found it hard to concentrate. If he had not responded to Dirley's seeming reproach, it still rankled and this had him reflecting on the nature of their relationship. This went back several years, to when the older man had been very much the teacher to his pupil. Henry should have been inducted into the business by his father, but there had been a raw edge to their relationship, which precluded shared confidence.

With his avuncular air and determination to fully involve his nephew, Dirley had seemed like a surrogate replacement to the now departed, rough-mannered and short-tempered parent. The tolerance that he had demonstrated – welcome to begin with – had, in Henry's mind, evolved over time into something bordering on conceit. Just a moment ago, it had come across as more pointed.

There was no choice but to knuckle down to the task at hand, to check the figures of funds transferred to France through their London bankers. The names of the recipients were familiar, enterprises with whom Dirley had forged an excellent working relationship. They oversaw the rental of the cargo vessels, which would transport the contraband to the designated spot on the Kentish shore.

At the base of the income column of the balance sheet lay the profit, which came from a whole network of regular purchasers of smuggled goods both in Kent and London. In the metropolis it was gentleman's clubs and a selection of the higher-class bagnios of the type Dirley liked to frequent. Places of entertainment that used food and music to cover for what most saw as their core activity: the provision of young and pretty female companionship.

The business also supplied selective London taverns where the customers possessed the right degree of discretion, like Molly-houses, a habit forced on them by the nature of their clientele. Private individuals abounded, some members of the legislature, added to which there were aristocrats aplenty. Rich men could be just as concerned with saving money as the poor.

'I often wonder what such people would say if they knew their names were listed in our accounts, Uncle.' That was accompanied by a braying laugh. 'We could dun them for a fortune to keep it secret.'

Dirley, as he cut into the breast of the duck, which had followed the soup, could not avoid a frown. At the same time he was wondering if treating a nephew, one in possession of a light head, to a couple of bumpers of champagne had been a good idea. Well into the wine on the table now, he was talking as if he wanted to address the entire room.

The response was hushed. 'I share the notion they would be displeased, Henry, I baulk at blackmail. And can I ask that you lower your voice.'

Judging by Henry's expression this was taken as absurd and it could be said he had a point: Mrs Gould's dining room was full and noisy with conversation, backed up by the playing of a harpsichord. True, there were other diners close by, but he guessed them to be engaged in their own concerns, not those of their neighbours.

The pretty girls, in fetching garments and expressing encouraging smiles, moving between the tables, playing at being hostesses, were not eavesdropping. They were encouraging the clients to spend money and, no doubt, lining up possible customers for a high-priced and subsequent frolic.

'I advise you to employ the kind of care I never fail to observe, Henry,' came as an addition, as well as portentous with gravity. 'Do I have to remind you of the nature of our affairs?'

Henry, nose in the air, cast his eyes around the room with an air of disdain. 'I dare say we are surrounded by all sorts of chicanery. I would wager, if you scratched beneath the silk garments of our fellow diners, you would find all sorts of mischief.'

'Mischief does not compare. There are those who would wish to curtail what we do and such creatures do not advertise themselves, nor would I have a clue as to the extent of any knowledge they possess. They could be sitting at the next board and you'd never know. Might I remind you that the penalty is likely the gibbet?'

Henry, emptying his glass again, responded with what for him was close to levity, 'Can we not rely on your famed legal prowess to confound such a fate? Every report tells me you're a tiger at the bar, feared by the bench.'

Dirley was wondering at how the conversation had wandered, but it was best to indulge Henry with an answer, albeit one tinged with humour. 'It is a lawyer's principle to avoid, wherever possible and whatever the case, ending up in court.'

'Is that not where fame is generated?'

'No, Henry, it is where both reputation and liberty for a client, as well as his advocate, can be too easily lost. Much better to settle matters before the need to stand before a judge and jury.'

Henry was tempted to name some of the judges with whom Dirley traded, but he decided against it, given the previous rebuke. In the gap, Dirley, who had gone back to his duck, changed the subject to one more germane.

'You said you were going to outline to me some other matters, were you not?'

'Ah yes. Elisabeth's plantations.'

'She seems set on disposing of them, as I have told you. Fallen for the Wilberforce claptrap about slavery, of course.'

It was with a smug air, somewhat added to by the consumption of wine, that Henry responded, 'The matter is no longer hers to decide.'

That stopped the cutlery, as Dirley looked at him, deeply curious. Suddenly, slightly ill at ease, Henry picked up his goblet again and drank deeply. If he had mentally rehearsed this conversation, the actuality was harder than the realisation. Taking a deep breath, he then launched into a filleted explanation of what had happened to alter matters, as well as what needed to be done legally to finalise arrangements.

'Am I allowed to say that this alliance seems rather rushed? Elisabeth gave me no inkling of any impeding nuptials in her correspondence.'

'She can be impetuous, Uncle, take my word on it.'

That stated, the goblet was used once more, to hide continued unease, caused not by the lies he was telling but by the look he was getting from across the table.

'I would accede to the word forceful, Henry, but I have never, in my dealings with Elisabeth, found her to be reckless. And what is she doing getting wed, when she is still supposed to be . . . what's that expression culled from Hindi . . . in purdah?'

'She quite lost her wits for this Spafford fellow,' Henry exclaimed, so loud that heads turned at the next table. A gesture from Dirley ensured the continuance was toned down to a near whisper. 'Handsome cove, and one who could charm the birds from the trees. You do not know Elisabeth as I do, being something of an outsider in the family.'

It was not the right thing to say. Dirley was such a rare visitor to Cottington, he was almost invisible as a Tulkington. It could be counted on the fingers of one hand the number of times he had come down to East Kent since the death of Acton. That included the funeral and, of course, Elisabeth's wedding to Stephen Langridge. On both occasions, a normally highly sociable creature had felt it necessary to retire into the background and avoid staying around after the ceremonies were over.

Dirley might be a master of obfuscation, a necessity of his profession, but there was no hiding the way the allusion had upset him. The matter of his birth was never raised, so his nephew could not know, first how acutely embarrassed he was by his bastardy and secondly, how mention of it was avoided by his family in their own bailiwick. Never alluded to in London, not that most people would have cared, they knew it led to pointed fingers or eye avoidance in a rural and more puritanical setting. A suspicion his status was known throughout the locality rendered him a rare caller.

Henry was too insensitive a soul to consider the possibility there might be a degree of jealousy in the way he was regarded; he would not have noticed it anyway, that being too well concealed. But for an accident of birth, it would have been Dirley who'd inherited what Henry held by right. It rankled that he, much older and, he was sure, ten times wiser, was obliged to treat his nephew with a degree of respect, which, in his eyes, Henry often failed to warrant.

If the mask slipped, it was soon back in place, as was the interest in the revelation. 'Well, if Elisabeth has succumbed to this fellow's charms and married him, what legal matters require to be settled? As her husband, he acquires her property by statute. There is no entail, unless Stephen Langridge had one drawn up in Jamaica. I do think, if he had, Elisabeth would have told me in her letters.'

Having crossed the first hurdle, Henry felt on safer ground, so he responded with confidence. 'Charming he might be, but Harry Spafford openly admits to having no head for business. He finds the idea of the West Indies daunting and the management of plantations utterly unnerving. He has expressed a wish to pass that to me.'

'I deduce from what you say there's going to be no sale?'

'Perish the thought.'

The main dishes had gone, to be replaced by a bowl of fruit, another of nuts as well as a decanter of port and a syllabub, which was tasted before Henry replied.

'Let us say, she has seen sense. Or perhaps her Harry has persuaded her that talk of freeing slaves is poppycock. I mentioned his silver tongue, did I not?'

'But surely,' Dirley replied, clearly mystified, 'if they are to be retained, it would be best if Elisabeth and this Spafford fellow went back out to Jamaica? Much easier to manage close at hand than from across the ocean, even for one shy of the responsibility. And I am sure poor Stephen, who was equally not keen on the task, managed it well, for he inherited a competent overseer.'

'I sought to persuade Spafford, of course, but . . .'

The gesture of futility, waving hands, was supposed to settle matters, but there was concern across the board.

'So what are you asking of me?'

'Is it not obvious? That you draw up a document, by which Spafford can transfer oversight to me, which I will get him to sign.'

'It will require to be witnessed.'

'Which Elisabeth can do, surely?'

'Better another, Henry. A wife can cause complications in that area. I have known them to claim duress and the courts can be sympathetic.'

Though Henry didn't know it, the note of exasperation with which he responded was an error. So accustomed to getting his own way, he had allowed to atrophy the antennae which would have sensed his uncle's discomfort. A highly regarded barrister, Dirley had honed skills over the years that could sense dissimulation a mile off and he was smelling it now.

A spoon was dipped into the last of the syllabub and that was savoured before Dirley spoke again. 'Why do I have the feeling, Henry, there are things you are not telling me?'

'I cannot guess what you mean,' came with an arch expression and an injured tone, before a glass of port was sunk whole. 'I am giving you matters as they stand, and I require you oblige me with your help.'

In seeking to deflect, Henry only made things worse for, unbeknown to him, Dirley's hackles were twitching. With anyone else, he would have briskly stated his concerns but – and this seriously rankled – he had to be careful with his nephew. He had learnt long ago, he was very sensitive to anything approaching criticism.

'Surely,' Dirley continued, 'it would have been best to have Elisabeth and her new husband come to see me in person, in company with you, of course, if you so desired. Or at least she could have written to me and advised of their intentions. I have always had a soft spot for her. It would have been nice to have met this fellow who you say has swept her off her feet.'

'In a perfect world, Uncle Dirley,' Henry insisted, with a note of conceit, partly induced by drink, 'everything is possible. I have been asked to do this and it would please me to be obliged.'

'Of course, Henry,' was what Dirley said.

But he was thinking he would write to Elisabeth and ensure what was being asked for accorded with her wishes, an intention dashed by Henry's next demand.

'I will take it back to Cottington for signature, if you can have the required papers drawn up this afternoon.'

I'm not your damned clerk was on the tip of Dirley's tongue. It stayed there. 'That syllabub was rather fine. Help yourself to more port.'

'As sweet as some of the girls employed here, Uncle,' Henry said, looking round the room again and chortling, signalling that to him the matter was closed. 'I am trying to guess which ones you have sampled. And, after such a good lunch, I'm wondering what to do with my afternoon.'

'I had in mind that we might look over that investment in St Mary-le-Bone. The construction of the houses you've put money into is well under way.'

The yawn was for effect and it was irritating, as was the salacious grin. 'Bricks and mortar cannot compare with soft flesh.'

Dirley Tulkington left Arlington Street alone, hiring a hack to take him back to his chambers. Too mature to allow his anger to fester, he calmly put his mind to what had just occurred and quickly concluded it did not add up to a consistent whole. Elisabeth was not impetuous and from what he knew of her – less, he had to admit, than he would have liked – he was sure she cared for the social norms.

This meant she would have seen out her term of widowhood. Added to that, it would have been seen as a disgrace and would have led to social death had she married too soon after the conclusion of the accepted three years. Following that, a long period of courtship was mandatory. Accepting there were matters of concern was one thing; deciding what could be done about it was another problem entirely.

CHAPTER FOURTEEN

Edward Brazier entered the Three Kings at half past two on the clock, to be greeted, as ever, by the lugubrious countenance of the proprietor, Garlick, not that it stayed that way. With a gimlet eye for profit, plus an overbearing necessity to know the business of other people, the look changed to one of false indifference. The new arrival was not fooled: Garlick, if he did not know already of Brazier's purpose, would surely bend himself to finding out.

'Is Mr Pitt arrived yet?'

This demand was made to forestall him, only to realise it was a foolish question. The King's First Minister never went anywhere, in these parts, without an armed escort. If the man had been here, there would have been two musket-bearing soldiers outside. Soon, when he came, they would join Dutchy and the others, so Pitt would be safer than ever from the people of Deal.

'He's expected, your honour – expected but not yet with us.'

'I assume he has requested the private room?'

'He has.'

'Then I shall wait for him in there.'

'I'll fetch along refreshments, Captain Brazier.'

'For which I will pay.'

'As you wish, but Mr Pitt is fond of a particular claret, already decanted.'

As he told Garlick to fetch that, he could not help but wonder at its provenance. The quality of the wine in the Three Kings had surprised him when he first arrived in Deal. But he had come to realise, in very short order, this establishment was not the only one with a superior cellar. Saoirse and the Old Playhouse were equally blessed, while she had more or less told him they were contraband goods, as were those he had bought from the local vintner. Could it be, the man who so railed against smuggling was able to turn a blind eye as long as his discerning palate was indulged?

The private room, once entered, had a table set for two. It also had a view from the windows over the sloping pebble beach and a busy anchorage, full of merchant vessels, stopping here to take on crew and the final stores necessary for voyages to far-off places. Brazier went to stand by one, looking out, registering the dozens of boats rowing to and fro, carrying humans as cargo as well as said stores, hoys with barrels of meat and others ready to pump water into barrels being knocked up on deck by the ship's cooper.

Off the naval yard sat a brand-new seventy-four-gun ship of the line, HMS *Bellerophon*, in the final stages of fitting out. Having been a sailor since he was no more than a nipper, the sight induced a deep hankering to be off somewhere himself, one which never faded, it being in his blood. It was impossible to explain to those who had never experienced it the lure of the sea.

People wedded to the land saw it as a dangerous and unpredictable element, with demons or giant monsters for the most superstitious, or deadly storms for the more rational, hurricanes which regularly swallowed humans whole and unwitnessed, leaving behind nothing but a mystery which, in time, would fade from memory. It was a setting of hard work and foul conditions, worse when it came to naval service, where to those who did not know the reality, every captain was seen as a cat-wielding tyrant. Like all wild tales, there was an element of truth in it, not least because it was one spread by tars to guy eager listeners over a pot of ale.

There were commanders too fond of the cat, though many less than legend had it. Strict discipline was applied aboard a ship of war and accepted by all for a very good reason: no one could sail in safety without it. Missing from the landsman's image was the camaraderie that came from being part of a close-knit company. It was a place where everyone was required to know and be expert at the several tasks they were there to perform, living in close proximity with people of shared values, common humour and a language particular unto itself.

Then came excitement. How to explain the sheer delight of sailing a frigate on a brisk wind, with a full set of canvas drawing over a deck heeling like a pitched roof, perhaps with a ship ahead in the act of being overhauled. What of the prospect of battle, of being part of a fighting whole, trained to and expecting to win, with at the end of it a purse full of prize money? If there was much dreaming in there, who would want to live without such?

'I find you in a brown study, Captain.'

Brazier spun round to face his host, who had opened the door but not yet closed it, an act which carried no sound. Pitt stood framed in the doorway, wearing a smile that could be termed enigmatic, for previous encounters had established he was not boisterous in his humour. He was wearing a powdered wig, which tended to make his face appear more rounded than it truly was. But there was no mistaking the air of self-control, as well as the acumen emanating from a steady gaze.

'I was reflecting on the attraction of a life at sea.'

'Not one I would rush to share and, is it not true, you don't have to look beyond the Goodwin Sands for a reason to keep your feet dry? If I could dredge out the gold and valuables from the hundreds of ships that have foundered there, I could pay off the government debt.'

Before Brazier could respond Garlick appeared behind him. 'Brought you the decanter, your honour.'

'Thank you, Mr Garlick,' Pitt said, standing to one side. 'You may leave it on the table.'

What followed was a bit of a comedy. Garlick did as he was asked, but then seemed to hover, his large purple nose twitching as if there was an odour to trace. Pitt's smile went to fulsome as he addressed the proprietor to tell him 'that will be all for the moment'. It was with an air of disappointment the command was obeyed, Pitt adding, as the door was closed, 'I am often tempted to say, or should I put it as invent, something which would set in motion a lively bit of gossip.'

'He's the one to spread it, that's the truth,' was Brazier's mordant reply, while wondering if both he and Pitt might be dunned for the same decanter: Garlick was a sly cove with his bills.

'I find you well, I trust, Captain?'

There was no point in supplying a negative; his present concerns would not be aired at this table and he was sure Pitt was unaware of them. 'You do, and how do you fare?'

Pitt moved to the decanter to begin to fill two glasses. 'I bless the air, sir, as ever, and the walk from Walmer. After the stench of Whitehall, it clears the brain.' A glass was offered to his guest and taken, his own raised. 'To sea breezes.'

Brazier raised his glass to sip; Pitt's went to his mouth to be emptied, then refilled. 'Did I see some men outside, Captain, fellows who are, by their dress, sailors?'

'I have had some of my old barge crew join me.'

'Commendable. But I'm forced to enquire as to their being armed. Do I take it you anticipate trouble merely from the act of meeting with me?'

That was tricky; the last time he had seen Pitt was at Walmer Castle in the company of his heavily pregnant sister, Lady Harriot Eliot. Then it was he who had the black eyes, added to a cracked rib on the mend, it being not long after his beating in the Lower Valley Road. His contusions were explained away and dismissed by a fall from a horse. What could he say now that would not be too revealing?

'I have found Deal to have elements residing within its boundaries which make precautions wise. But in reality, these are men paid off from the service and in need of employment. As their old commander, I feel it's my duty to provide it.'

'Commendable, sir,' soon saw another empty glass.

A knock brought a servant and a tureen of fish soup, so they sat down while bowls were filled, silent until the girl disappeared.

'How is Lady Harriot? Has she come down to Walmer with you once more?'

The face fell. 'You do not know? My dear sister expired following the birth of her child.'

Brazier felt as if he could kick himself; it must have been in the journals that came down daily from London, newspapers he had been too preoccupied to read. 'My condolences, she had a fine spirit. The child?'

'A daughter. I fear my brother-in-law will want for recovery. He is distraught.'

Sir James Eliot was discussed, not as the broken reed Pitt said he had become, but as a leading light of the anti-slavery movement, a close confidant and supporter of William Wilberforce. Lady Harriot had been just as committed to the cause and it was one Brazier could subscribe to, as would any man who had intercepted and boarded a slaver in the Western Atlantic, leaving him with an image of degradation and human cruelty he could not erase from his mind.

Much as the mood had been depressed by the demise of his sister, conversation, by its very nature, moved on to less unpleasant topics as the various courses, and a second decanter of wine, were fetched to the table. One subject aired was the behaviour of the male royal offspring, all of King George's sons having, it seemed, a devilment aimed at upsetting their sire, with Pitt getting the backwash.

'He has tried cutting off their funds, but of course there are those who will queue up to be in the company of royal blood, and many of them are eager to act as princely bankers.'

'I take it Prince William is as badly behaved as the rest?'

'Your good friend,' was delivered with a wicked expression.

'I'm sure he speaks very highly of me,' was Brazier's sardonic response.

There was another feeling behind the words, for, if he was in want of a ship, a poor opinion in that quarter would be a serious impediment. William was commonly referred to as the Sailor Prince, while his being labelled a martinet was more likely to endear him to Admiralty than shame him. Pitt, on their last meeting, had told Brazier his name was known, and not esteemed, by William's father, which was worse.

His dining companion's face went down to his cheese, but it seemed a ploy to avoid Brazier's eye, given he delivered another poisoned arrow, not that you would know it from his even tone. 'Are you aware that HMS *Alcide* has come back from the Jamaica station?'

'Really?' was the word that covered a tightening of the chest.

'Paid off and laid up at the Nore.'

The head came up to pin Brazier with a direct look, which was met with a contrived air of complete indifference. If that is what showed, it was not what was felt, for he now knew, and it had been a question he had asked himself, why Pitt had invited him to dine. They had only met on two previous occasions and could hardly be said to be friends.

'I would have thought the dockyard more likely,' Brazier opined, as though it was a matter of indifference. 'She's been in warm waters for a long time and, notwithstanding her copper, the Caribbean worm is an active beast.'

'It does not concern you more than her hull, that there may be rumours flying around?'

'Having been resident here in Deal for weeks now, I have been rendered immune.'

Brazier knew he would have to ask, there was no choice. If stories were spreading of events in Jamaica, they would need to be countered. The way Admiral Hassall had expired was so unusual as to warrant all sorts of theories and the question asked was a valid one. How had a deadly, venomous snake, on an island that possessed none, get into his quarters to sink its fangs, plus its poison, into his neck?

It had happened while Brazier was at sea, so he could state, unequivocally, he had nothing with which to reproach himself. Except there were the words he had used in addressing his junior officers before he weighed, which had occurred after a furious and strident row with his superior in Admiralty House, which surely had been overheard: he having discovered and informed the other ships' captains of Hassall's depredations, saying something of the nature that he deserved to be strung up.

'It is telling, Captain, that you do not ask what the rumours might pertain to.'

'I assume it is the nonsense you alluded to previously, some rubbish contained in an unsigned and thus anonymous letter of accusation, when you sought to engage me in your crusade against smuggling.'

'By the lord, that's the right word for what is required.'

When first mooted, it seemed to make sense to Pitt that Brazier help him combat smuggling, on the grounds that he was a captain without a ship, with very little prospect of getting one. That was more certain if you counted the factors working against him: royal disfavour and a fleet being run down, not expanded. William Pitt hinted he was in a position to overcome all these barriers.

The point Pitt had made at Walmer Castle was telling: what at one time had been an opportunistic occupation for Deal boatmen was now, if you took the massive and steady losses to the public purse, being conducted on a near industrial scale. Even as the First Lord of the Treasury, he was at a stand when it came to clapping a stopper on it, for too many in parliament either didn't care, or saw it as beneficial to their own needs. The navy declined to patrol the channel and he had only managed to burn the boats on the strand previously by begging for a body of soldiers, as he put it, 'On my dammed knees, and they nearly failed to show.'

The effect of that conflagration had proved negligible: boats were rebuilt in short order and they had to be. But, in the interim, until they were fully restored in the required numbers, there had been no discernible fall off in the supply of untaxed goods. His informants told him everything previously available to buy was still being hawked.

Which led him to conclude there was some secret controlling interest and that was what he needed to find out. It was not put forward that Brazier should do anything dangerous. But Pitt had picked up, no doubt from Garlick, who was a damned nuisance and eager informant, of his connection to the Tulkingtons, one of the leading local families.

He would thus be certain to move in certain circles, where

a misplaced word or a sharp observation might produce a clue. This followed could reveal something about the organising cabal, which Pitt insisted had to exist, since no one man could oversee such depredations. Brazier had not been in the least bit tempted. He knew no one in the locality, if you excluded Betsey and her family. Given he was not on good terms with her brother, the so-called social whirl Pitt referred to was unlikely to materialise; not that he would have agreed regardless.

Could he be tempted now, when he was in possession of the kind of information Pitt had hoped he would come across? Under heavy scrutiny, his mind was spinning. Was it just that anonymous missive he had referred to before, which landed in England with his own despatch, in which doubts had been raised about the manner in which Hassall had died, probably naming it as a foul murder, not a tragic accident?

It would not take too febrile a mind to consider it possible. The admiral had gone to bed in good health, to be found in the morning by his servant, his face blackened by venom, his expression one of a terrible rictus and his heart stopped. Again he had to enquire, but it could not be posed as a question.

'If you are aware of more nonsense being spread, I would be interested to hear of it.'

'Would it suffice if I say this? Lady Hassall was favoured by a visit from the captain of HMS *Alcide*. In quizzing him, she concluded that all was not as it should be and has descended on the Admiralty demanding answers.'

'To what questions?'

Pitt shrugged. 'First how the snake got into her husband's quarters, one so intent on employing its fangs on a sleeping man.

It is falsehood, I am told, that snakes are aggressive creatures. Sir Joseph Banks, whom I mentioned to you previously, insists they are shy unless in the presence of their young, more inclined to hide than attack. As the world's foremost expert on the natural world, he should know.'

'I know little of the creatures. I was told it is what the French call a fer de lance, quite common in other parts of the Caribbean and on several islands within a day's sailing distance of Kingston. As I explained to you before, the plantation slaves import them for their barbaric religious ceremonies.'

'All of which I made sure was conveyed to Lady Hassall by the conduit of my brother, Chatham. I must tell you, she does not accept a word of it. And she again questions why her husband was buried at sea, with what she sees as undue haste, when he had expressed a definite wish to be brought home to his family plot. I do believe the decision was yours.'

This was leading to questions Brazier did not want to deal with; time to nail the purpose. 'I cannot but feel you are telling me all this so you can reprise your wish that I become your spy.'

'My eyes and ears, Captain, in a situation where I am at risk if I merely enter the middle of Deal without an armed escort. Ergo, no one will talk to me.'

Edward Brazier needed to think; perhaps Pitt was, albeit inadvertently, offering him a way to confound Henry Tulkington, but what would be the effect on Betsey? She was still legally wed to Harry Spafford. Getting her free of that entanglement must take precedence over trying to bring down her brother, which he suspected would not be a simple matter. Best out of it for the present, was his conclusion.

'I was about to thank you for dinner, Mr Pitt, but since I'm about to disappoint you once more, perhaps I should meet the bill.'

'My invitation means it is my tariff, sir.'

Brazier stood, to look him right in the eye. 'Then I bid you good day.'

There he was, as ever, by his hatch, with that look in his eye, one which was on the lookout for any snip of information by which he would grease the rumour mill.

'Off home, your honour?'

The grunt of a positive might have been less abrupt if he had heard Garlick, later on in the day, boasting he'd had William Pitt eating at his board, though given his audience of beach householders he was wont to add his temptation to poison the sod.

'Aye,' he said, drawing on his pipe. 'Entertained that Brazier cove, you know the navy fellow who has a dip of a mornin', an' not for the first time. An' very friendly they was too.'

CHAPTER FIFTEEN

Having found the note not long after her old friend had departed, Annabel Colpoys was in a quandary. Roger too was no longer present, he having gone off to his farming duties. As she read the tiny writing, so shocking were the words, Annabel wondered if Betsey had been struck with some affliction of the mind. The notion that Henry had deliberately drugged her and put her through a marriage ceremony, of which she recalled nothing, was simply too outrageous to be seen as true.

The plea to deliver it to Edward Brazier, with Betsey begging to be rescued, also induced mixed emotions. It spoke of an involvement that her husband had expressly forbidden, even if it was a stricture she had previously disobeyed. To help Betsey meet with the man she was intent on marrying, while simultaneously humbugging stiff-necked brother Henry, had proved too appealing. Roger, whose curiosity rarely rose above the plough and the decanter, proved easy to circumvent.

What was being ask for now posited a different order of

magnitude: if Betsey was telling the truth, there had been more than a breach of family harmony and an internal dispute. This bordered on a crime and spoke of an involvement that could extend beyond merely acting as a carrier of a message, one more difficult to keep concealed, while discovery would bring retribution. Her husband had gone so far as to mention the horsewhip if she disobeyed him. Was it worth the risk?

When she reflected on his motives it was impossible not to feel a slight sense of shame, this reinforced by the sounds from above her head as her trio of children rushed noisily across the wooden floorboards of the schoolroom until a shout came from their tutor, which also penetrated, for them to get back to their desks. The feeling that her man could not, or would not, stand up for himself was the cause.

It had become obvious at some time past that Roger, in dispute with Henry Tulkington over a boundary, had been subjected to a thrashing. It had never been established who was responsible; indeed, once the contusions had faded, it was not acknowledged as to have taken place at all. He had been drinking, it had happened and was put down to an unknown assailant.

But Annabel knew Betsey's brother was the source, even if it could not be openly referred to, just by the manner in which Roger's behaviour had altered. Always in something of a passion – it was in his nature and doubly relevant when fuelled by drink – he had abruptly ceased to curse the Tulkington name and his intention to issue a challenge, to become seemingly fearful of having it even pronounced in any negative sense within his own walls.

Which begged the question, where was his pride? Where was the protection he owed to her and their children? She had no doubt he knew who had done the deed and, if it was not Henry himself, it had been meted out on his instructions. She could see him now in her mind's eye, in times long past, the streak of melancholy that she, Betsey and their childhood friends had mercilessly guyed. Could cheerless Henry really have turned into a person capable of that which he stood accused?

Reading the note again, and Betsey's pleas, she wondered at what was being asked of Brazier. 'I know you came as promised, will you come again?' What did that mean? Did Betsey hope to be rescued by a raid on Cottington Court, or was the request he employ the law against her brother the real purpose? The resolve to act came and went, yet what finally made Annabel Colpoys decide upon delivery was not the needs of Betsey.

She would act for the sake of her own family pride: if the man of the house would not uphold it, then she must.

There was another letter on the subject, this one in the act of being written, it being of proper length and containing several carefully crafted queries. Dirley Tulkington had to be cautious; he did not know the circumstances of this sudden decision by Elisabeth to wed, only what Henry had imparted, though a recollection of his demand, delivered with confidence and supercilious manner, rendered him apprehensive.

Even if it made no sense to his logical and legal mind, he was aware infatuation could make a fool of anyone, leading them to chuck overboard the values by which they lived. It was a thing he had never succumbed to himself but had seen it too often to lightly dismiss. Thus he had to congratulate his niece, while expressing surprise at her actions.

When asking about her new spouse, it was necessary to act as if he was the silver-tongued paragon reported and one he was looking forward to meeting. This he penned while enquiring if he came with any assets of his own, property or investments, which Dirley would be happy, now he was a member of the family, to take care of.

Delicacy had to be employed in the matter of the West Indian plantations, an admission that, while he respected her original intentions, he did not necessarily agree with them. That said, he would be happy to comply with her wishes in the matter of disposal. If her new husband desired they should be retained and that Henry should take over management, that too was a properly exercised right. He would, if it was preferred, offer his own services in that regard.

Finally, it was necessary to express a wish the newly-weds should visit London, where it would be his pleasure to entertain them and to celebrate their nuptials for a second time. Though not stated, he trusted Elisabeth to see it would also provide an opportunity for her to discuss matters with him, free of the interlocution of her brother.

The point took him back to the legal document he had drawn up at Henry's request, for there was a clause in there that stipulated the arrangement was only at the discretion of the rightful proprietor. It could be revoked by that person at any time they chose. Instinct, and the mood of Henry just witnessed, told him his nephew would not like it, but he would defend it on the grounds of proper legality; no right could be given away in perpetuity, and it was made plain this was the client's wish. In this case, he was acting to protect Elisabeth should anything untoward happen to this Harry Spafford.

If the quill stopped occasionally, it was to reflect on the way he saw the family of which he was a tenuous part. Could he really consider himself as such? If he kept a distance from Cottington Court for his own reasons, he had often been put out by the seemingly reciprocal disinterest.

Apart from two occasions already recalled, invitations to visit were non-existent, by which he could only conclude that if he did not wish to be reminded of his bastard status, neither did they. Not that he would have accepted an invite; that was beside the point. It annoyed him never to have been afforded the opportunity to politely decline a request to visit a place of which he had few fond memories.

He had enjoyed a fairly happy childhood, running in the streets of Deal with his younger brothers, as mischievous as was natural, all of which ceased when the family moved to Cottington Court. His father he recalled as a rough diamond, but also an extremely active and successful runner of contraband. From that had come the funds, not only to buy the estate, but to raise it back to what it had once been, a grand manor house and a productive farm.

It had also paid for proper schooling, which came with an ever-ready birch, as well as the various attributes seen as necessary to claim to be a gentleman. So it had been goodbye to freedom and innocent fun. What mattered was a good seat on a horse plus an ability to wield a sword, a smattering of Greek and Latin, added to enough fluency in French to hold a conversation, this rounded off by training in rhetoric.

Out went the grabbing of food at will and at any time of the day. Proper dinner times were imposed and bad table manners earned a cuff round the ear. Then there came the need to be at ease with a multitude of servants whose manners seemed better than those who paid them. Not that mere possession of the estate, extensive restoration and the schooling of the next generation had conferred respectability.

To begin with, few, if any, of the local gentry had taken to the Tulkingtons as neighbours. But time and money provided the grease that broke down even the most intractable barriers. It had done so for the family, as it had for him in London. Working at arm's length with Acton, he had set up the systems that made their business secure. Dirley had thus profited from a double source of income, funds put to use in the metropolis to both enhance his standing and to protect the enterprise in which they were engaged.

He was a shrewd and successful card player, often up against people who were not, though woefully short on any realisation of their incapacities. This meant Dirley had, in his files, un-redeemed promissory notes meant to cover losses sustained by those against whom he played.

Many were people of power, members of both the Houses of Parliament who required a facade of wealth to maintain their dignity, even if it was, in truth, hollow. Never pressing for repayment allowed Dirley to apply subtle pressure on those who would struggle to settle, in order to ensure certain matters went his way.

As of this moment, and not mentioned to his nephew, he was manoeuvring to have appointed the right kind of person to the sinecure of the Riding Officer of Kent Customs. The present incumbent was elderly and showing signs of failing health, while Dirley was sure William Pitt would be seeking to replace him, should he expire, with someone willing to be active in the office.

This was the last thing required for the family enterprise. The post should be filled with someone like the fellow who held it now: disinclined to leave London, unless it was to go to his country estates, comfortable only in a carriage so never mounted, and unwilling to pay properly the person he contracted to carry out the duties.

The solution might lie, in many cases, if not exclusively, in those promissory notes. There were enough votes in parliament to stymie Pitt on a matter in which the requirement for personal prosperity would trump any sense of duty to the nation. That was a sentiment, in any case, not much prevalent on the Westminster benches.

Pitt was in the business of abolishing sinecures and the monies they earned to ease the burden on the public purse. For those who stood to gain from one of the many that existed, stopping the King's First Minister was both a duty and a financial necessity. A little discreet pressure on a few key votes should ensure the right outcome.

The letter to Elisabeth was reread, sanded, folded and sealed, to be handed over to a clerk to see posted, along with a bundle tied with a red ribbon.

'This you're to take to Nerot's Hotel, where my nephew is residing. There should be no need to wait for a reply.'

For Annabel Colpoys to go into Lower Deal was far from straightforward; it was necessary to invent an excuse to descend on a place rarely visited and it could not be done discreetly. Such a visit required the use of the carriage, a vehicle only taken out when going to church or visiting friends. It also involved harnessing two of the better horses, while taking from the stables a groom to act as coachman, as well as a young lad to ride postilion, both clad in decent livery. None of that could be done without Roger finding out.

She was relying on disinterest, for her husband was not one to over enquire when it came to matters domestic. It was she who saw to the employment and overseeing of servants, not that such was onerous, given those she possessed fulfilled their needs and had been with the Colpoys family for a long time. Annabel made sure the larder and the coal shed were stocked by regular deliveries and, wine being separate, it was she who wrote up the household accounts, though Roger, once he had examined the sums, disbursed the funds to pay.

The commands given and all arranged, the coach set off on the downward slope to the lower town, with various excuses being tried and tested, until the correct one surfaced. Roger maintained he was not a man to merely lay out the money required to keep the house in provender and candles. He claimed an eagle eye for an error, but an even sharper one for being overcharged. It was a little less than true: Annabel was ever able to supplement her pin money by slight exaggerations in the family budget, presenting Roger with the figures when he had consumed at least a bottle.

She took the coach to the fields at the rear of St George's Church and, leaving it there, made her way through the graveyard, past a knot of gin-drinking young ruffians, to enter the church by one of the side entrances. A few moments at a pew, hands clasped in prayer, were necessary before she made her way out of the front door.

In the bustling street, she had to wait 'til a gap appeared in the near endless line of horse-drawn carts, vans and the odd coach, one big enough to allow the crossing sweeper the chance to clear a path through the dung, also sufficient to cross without getting too much of the horse droppings on the pedestrian foot.

Quebec House she knew, having delivered a note previously, one that showed Brazier a way to discretely enter the grounds of Cottington Court to meet Betsey without using the main gate. Not that she had met him, merely handing it to his smiling servant, saying who it was from, before hurrying away. That, she felt, would not serve now.

'I am calling in the hope of speaking with Captain Edward Brazier.'

'Who should I say is calling, ma'am?' asked Joe Lascelles.

'Mrs Colpoys. I have reason to hope the name will be known to him.'

Seeing quality, Joe nodded. 'Will you enter please?'

It was a grateful Annabel who acceded; a public street was no place to stand and wait, which might give unseen eyes a reason to wonder why. Even with her anxieties, she entered the parlour as would any one of her sex, with an eye for the waxed pine panelling, the quality of the furniture, the drapes and the paintings that filled the walls, deciding it was very much the abode of someone masculine.

Likewise judged, when he entered the room, was Brazier. Annabel took in a height that obliged him to duck under the lintel of the door, as well as the build of a man not wanting for physical strength. Black hair tied back in a queue, he was dressed in a white linen shirt, which exaggerated what could be described as a saturnine visage. But he did not smile, which told Annabel he was unsure of the nature of the call.

'Mrs Colpoys, we meet at last. Betsey spoke of you and I believe I owe to you our ability to share time together.'

'Captain. I come to see you on behalf of our mutual friend.'

'I had hoped it was so when your name was passed to me.'

The fellow who had opened the front door came to hover just enough so his shoulder could be seen by Brazier, which probably prompted the offer of refreshments.

'Forgive me, Captain, but I cannot linger.' The note came out from her hand muffs. 'I bring you this from dear Betsey.'

It was taken eagerly, but Brazier paused. 'Do you wish me to read it while you're present?'

'It would please me to enquire on certain things, but I must warn you, there seems little possibility of a reply. This was not passed to me openly, but pressed under a cushion when Betsey came to call.'

'She can call?'

'The note will tell you, she suspects only in the company of her Aunt Sarah.'

'Please, sit.'

Which she did as Brazier went to the window, where there was more light, to open and read what Betsey had written. Watching him, Annabel saw the broad shoulders sag slightly and the head go forward, to rest on the cold glass of a pane.

'It is not easy to believe.'

Brazier came round slowly to reply, 'On the contrary, Mrs Colpoys, for if you say that, it tells me you do not know Henry Tulkington very well.'

'I've known him for many a year.'

'Time alone would not reveal his nature.' The note was waved. 'This does.'

'Can it be reversed?' Annabel asked, biting her lips, as if in fear of his reply.

'If it can, I'm at a loss to know how.'

He followed that with an explanation of the legal position as explained to him, added to the fact of no one to witness.

'Betsey intimates in her note that you were present. Is that the case?'

'I was, but not at the time that mattered.' As he explained, which was, of necessity, complex, he could see Annabel Colpoys fidgeting and glancing towards the hallway door. What else to say to her?

'If Betsey can get a note to you once, she may do so again.'

'Captain, I am taking a great risk in calling here.'

'I must be able to communicate with you in case she does.' The note was waved again. 'I also need to reply to this, if to do no more than offer some reassurance she is not alone. But I sense I have no time to compose anything, even on the off chance it will get into her hand.'

She was on her feet. 'I'm afraid, as much as I love Betsey, I cannot oblige you by becoming a go-between.'

'Am I permitted to ask why?'

'No, Captain, you are not, but you must just accept my word it is so. Now, if you will forgive me . . .'

'Of course. Do you require to be accompanied? I have men here who will do so.'

'No, an escort might set tongues wagging. Now I must bid you goodbye, though I admit it was good to put a face to the person Betsey so esteems.'

'Joe, show the lady out.'

As Annabel Colpoys exited Quebec House, Brazier dashed out to the back, to where Dutchy, Peddler and Cocky were sitting throwing dice and either crowing or cursing.

'Dutchy, the woman who's just leaving, I need her followed. If you move quickly you'll spot her before she gets to a corner.'

His old coxswain moved with a speed that belied his size, as Brazier called after him to tell of the colour of the cloak she was wearing, while ignoring the enquiring looks he was getting from the others. Then he went back into the parlour, to drag a chair to the window so he could reread Betsey's words.

He took in for the first time that the paper seemed stained, which led him to wonder if the cause was tears. But one thing was certain: he must find a way to communicate with her, and if Annabel Colpoys was reluctant to the point of a downright refusal, she looked like the only conduit available.

'Where the devil have you been? I've been going mad here waiting for you.'

The look that got was one of irritation from Dutchy Holland. 'You said follow the woman and I did.'

'Where? To the moon?'

'To where she resides,' Dutchy snapped, 'an' given that was well more'n a mile away, and with me having to trot to keep up with her damned coach, I hope you don't mind if I stopped on the way back for a pot of ale, to ease my thirst.'

CHAPTER SIXTEEN

John Hawker had laid his plans for Edward Brazier but had other work to do, and not only in the collection of taxes. With a shipment due it meant various measures had to be put in place. First, he had to extract some of his men from guarding the Spafford gang, to be sent to various places, with an eye being kept out for any unusual activity by the Revenue. As they operated out of Dover, any sight of their cutter being prepared for sea would be noted: better if it was secured to the jetty with no sign of it being manned.

The men who crewed it lived locally, so it was known where they ate and drank, not that they were in any way loved. Their talk, always loose and of interest, could often warn of any impending movements while at the same time various souls, the kind who ever seemed to know what was afoot, were pumped for information.

Not that the Excise being overly keen was a commonplace. If the fellow in charge in Dover was poorly paid, it was even more the case with the six inept underlings he oversaw. As a group, they were distant from Corcoran, the fellow placed in the centre of the county with overall authority. He might provide more men if information received warranted it, enough to watch over a goodly stretch of the shore. They would also need to be sufficient to take on and capture men who would not surrender lightly.

Corcoran was responsible for many miles of coastline, which ran from the shore opposite the City of London all the way to the mouth of the Thames, which took in such smuggling hotbeds as Gravesend, the Isles of Grain and Sheppey, Whitstable, Faversham, Margate and Ramsgate. Arcing round the North Foreland, his domain ran down past Dover and on to Folkestone, to meet the border with Sussex near Rye, itself overlooking the Romney Marshes, now used for running contraband by the successors to the murderous Hawkhurst Gang.

Kent had near the longest stretch of shore requiring to be patrolled in the whole of England. It was blessed, or cursed if you saw it that way, with miles of open beaches, many backed by marshland, with the added advantage, for many a villain, of being within a day's sailing distance of France and thus open to easy penetration.

The Tulkington operations were by far the most refined and required the involvement of many people. To completely unload a heavily laden cargo vessel in a few hours of darkness, as well as get the consignment to where it could be safely stored, took many hands. These were provided by men who made a meagre living by fishing, aided by a couple of dozen who worked as farm labourers or apprentices, creatures poorly enough rewarded in their daily toil to eagerly work through the night for a few pennies reward.

Hawker would alert the end of a grapevine which stretched throughout the surrounding area, a slow-burning fuse of whispers which would have people ready to combine when the final alert was issued. That depended on a whole raft of factors: a cloudless night might not serve, for even a dull eye could see for miles if the moon was full and bright. Neither would too rough a sea state: beaching a ship on a pebble shore, with crashing waves, risked serious damage to the hull. In addition, it could be driven too far ashore to float off again when empty.

Lastly, but in truth the first consideration, was the right kind of tide at a suitable time of day. It should be off its peak after nightfall and near to the end of falling when the vessel made its landfall. An anchor was always dropped off the stern on approach, one that could be used to haul the ship off on the capstan if it showed any signs of being stuck. A rising sea level was best when unloading was complete, one which would raise a very much lighter vessel naturally, so it floated away without outside agency.

Hawker rode out to St Margaret's Bay, a high-sided horseshoe of an inlet between Deal and Dover, surrounded by chalk cliffs, with a pebble strand that could only be reached by precipitous paths. Halfway down one of those sat a dilapidated hut, which would be occupied in the days before the cargo was due, with a command to keep an eye open for anything unusual. A trapdoor, set within the floor, provided access to a series of tunnels in the chalk, some of which went through large, carved-out storage chambers, to continue all the way down to just above shore level. Blocked off with gorse bush-covered shutters, the entrances had long ladder-like ramps by which to access the beach and the contraband.

Two others, narrow, with room enough for only one body, ran to a high point on each arm of the bay, open at the end. Visible only from the sea, they formed the points by which lights could be shone to signal it was safe to make a landfall. Those same lights would provide navigation points so the vessel would ground in the middle of the strand and well away from the sharp rocks on either edge.

Hawker's men were not there to carry cargo, but to provide the armed sentinels covering the cliff top pathways, there to warn of any approach by the Revenue men. That spotted, a prearranged plan of dispersal was followed using even more tunnels, longer ones running inland to take everyone well beyond the area of danger. It was necessary to check that all was in place and the various articles required were where they should be and functioning, also that no nosy sod had been sneaking around where they were not wanted.

Sure all was well and back at the top of the cliffs, where he had tethered his mount to a gorse bush, Hawker stood for a while to look around him. The day was clear enough, with no mid-Channel haze, which gave him a sight of the grey shore of France. To the south, the ground rose, a greensward above the white cliffs, the pathway leading to a point which overlooked Dover Harbour as well as the berth of that Revenue Cutter. To the north was gently sloping farming land which ran down to overlook the sea, crashing on to the rocks below at high tide. At its far end the hill dropped down to Kingsdown beach, another strand of pebbles, which ran uninterrupted for several miles, all the way to the Stour Estuary.

Hawker was stood overlooking a spot the Tulkington line had claimed, fought for and enforced as their own, and the Lord help anyone who challenged them. It was possible for him, and not for the first time, as he contemplated a perfect setting for the running of contraband, to allow himself a smile, brought on by a rare feeling. He could almost summon up sympathy for the poor sods of the Revenue: the task they had was impossible.

The man who employed John Hawker was coaching to the Medway, a busy route, as it led from London to one of the main bases of the Royal Navy. It was thus one much frequented by sea officers, two of whom, both post captains, were sharing the journey. One was young-looking, if you allowed for a face made ruddy by the wind, and he wore only a single epaulette, which indicated he was in that rank for less than three years. His companion was older and had two, as well as a face well battered by weather, he being clearly comfortable in his longer held rank.

The navy, being a community, allowed Henry to enquire if they were acquainted with a certain Captain Edward Brazier. He was immediately appraised, in some detail, of the luck that had attended that officer in the Caribbean. No attempt was made to disguise the feelings of envy at Brazier's good fortune. Nor did they hold back on the wish they too should be gifted something similar.

This led their fellow passenger to reflect that, for all the guff such men spouted about serving King and Country, most blue-coated salts, from midshipman to admiral, were more interested in making money than earning glory. Of course, if both could be combined, that added up to perfection. But a full purse took precedence over public acclaim.

As he listened to them enumerating all the things Brazier could buy with his fluke capture, it was comforting to sense their naked avarice. This reinforced a view long held: everyone who might disapprove of his way of making money would bite off his hand for the chance to do likewise. Pious hypocrisy abounded, and at least he could absolve himself of that sin.

'Rumours. What rumours?'

Lost in thought, he had only partially picked up what these fellows had moved on to, which obliged them to repeat the gossip doing the rounds in the service. This hinted Brazier might have come by his fortune less by fair means than foul. Asked to tell him more, it was frustrating the way they began to hedge. The older one of the pair even said openly that such accusations attended anyone who had taken a prize vessel of such value and shouldn't be given too much credence.

The younger captain, obviously just as eager to avoid bringing the service into disrepute, changed the subject by asking Henry the reasons for his own journey to Chatham, an enquiry easily swept aside by the mention of business. To the enquiring looks that engendered, on what business, he merely responded to with an enigmatic smile; why bother to concoct a lie for people who, to his mind, were unworthy of the effort?

Lapsing into silence, he tried to assess what he had gleaned, which, mostly due to his own inattention, was not much. There was, it appeared, some question hanging over Brazier's head and it involved the sudden death of his commanding officer. How did that chime with what had been previously imparted to him by his Uncle Dirley? That the sod was out of favour at Windsor Castle?

Idle speculation on a man he believed would soon be removed from his life occupied him until the coach topped the hill. This overlooked the broad valley of the River Medway, at which point his thinking turned to his forthcoming meeting and what he was about to demand. There was one clause in the agreement Dirley had drawn up about which he was unhappy: the one revoking his control, should misfortune strike Spafford. He had, of course, queried it, only to be left with the feeling his uncle, in quoting necessity, had fobbed him off in his response.

'Never mind, it will serve.'

'Sir?' the younger officer enquired, to get an annoyed shake of the head and something close to a glare, not for the query, but for Henry being made aware he had spoken out loud.

Nothing more was said until the coach pulled into the courtyard of the Angel Inn, at which point polite goodbyes saw the trio part company. Having bespoken a room in advance by letter – he would spend the night in Chatham, given that was where he had accommodated Spafford – Henry had one task only, and that was to find the sod.

His enquiry of the staff first told him he was not within, while the looks that went with the information indicated Spafford was seen as a less than perfect guest. Not that anyone was more forthcoming when he enquired on the matter, except to say there was no assurance he would rest his head here, as he was wont to sleep elsewhere.

'Then I require someone to go and find him.'

This request was taken to the proprietor, who undertook

to engage a couple of young lads to go in search, this being carried out while Henry had his dinner. With still no sign of Spafford on completion, he went to his room to write to Dirley and ask him to enquire about what other shadows might cloud Brazier's reputation. Even if he scarcely cared, the notion of throwing some diminishing facts in his sister's face was something to be sweetly anticipated.

Sarah Lovell made sure, with Henry absent, that all post not addressed to him came to her, so a letter that had gone off in the mail coach, before her nephew left London, arrived at Cottington Court before he did. The superscription told her it came from Lincoln's Inn, which she knew to be the address of Dirley Tulkington and there was not much surprise in that. The query lay in the name of the addressee. What was he writing to Elisabeth about?

The letter was put in a drawer to await Henry but, as she went about her daily tasks, chiding the servants for various failings, the fiend of curiosity ate away at her resolve. Surely Henry would wish her to check the contents in case it boded ill? Several times the missive was removed to be examined, the seal picked at by a fingernail and put back, until she finally succumbed.

Not that she did so in public; she chose Henry's study and made sure the door was closed, before using a knife to break the wax. It was read with an inbuilt prejudice, Dirley not being a creature of whom she approved given the circumstances of his birth, clearly a stain on the family name. But underneath and never admitted, there was jealousy, for Dirley lived independently and, unlike her, seemed not to be beholden to anyone.

She had only met him once, at Elisabeth's wedding to Stephen Langridge and, given her reservations about being seen in his company allied to his retiring nature – he had stayed well in the background – they had barely exchanged a proper greeting, which suited her fine. He had been a long-time resident in London prior to her arrival at Cottington and it was some time before she, and her husband, knew anything of his existence.

The thought of that day reddened her cheeks, for the feeling of shame at being such a supplicant had never faded. It was made worse by the way she had always condescended to her pregnant sister Margaret, not least for the feeling she had married beneath herself. In Sarah Lovell's eyes, it took more than a handsome estate to confer status, which had meant few visits prior to moving in, obliged by circumstances to throw themselves on the generosity of her brother-in-law.

Acton Tulkington had sent his coach to Canterbury to fetch them, for she and her husband, Samuel, were in such straightened circumstances they lacked the means to hire a conveyance large enough to carry them and their possessions to what was supposed to be a temporary stay. This had been occasioned by a series of stupidly unwise projections in which her husband had become involved, ventures that incurred losses that came close to seeing him carried off to the Marshalsea.

How different Samuel Lovell had turned out to be from the man she thought he was on marriage. The air of easy confidence, plus his looks and standing in the business community, had blinded her to his real character. But was that not true of every union? A woman entered into matrimony with no more than an impression of the man with whom she would share her life. If he had felt any shame at their altered circumstances, it had been well hidden.

Samuel set about ingratiating himself with Acton, unable to see what his wife observed in her brother-in-law's expression – that he was tolerated, no more, which made questionable his assertions confided to her when they were alone that they would soon be back on their feet. He never said how this was to come about, merely fobbing her off with vague allusions to some plan he was hatching, which would bring them the funds to get back both their Canterbury residence and their social standing.

He had been in a strange mood the day he disappeared, a sort of fidgeting impatience, which lasted until the sun was near to going down when, with Acton absent and Margaret resting, he had borrowed a horse and departed Cottington without saying where he was going.

That night she had lain in their marital bed, wondering where he had got to and when he would return and join her. But Sam never came to the bedroom and he was not around in the morning either. Despite enquiries all over the county, both he and the animal he had borrowed had not been seen since.

She forced herself to go back to the letter, in order to kill off these memories, to read that twice-blessed Dirley, a bastard, was calling Elisabeth his niece, which Sarah thought he had no right to claim. She had made her own feelings plain when he had come to Cottington, giving him no more than a frosty greeting and refusing to engage in conversation.

By repute he was clever, though she had never had any

dealing with him herself: Dirley dealt with money and property and she had none. So there was a certain degree of amusement to read he had fallen for the notion Elisabeth's wedding had been brought about by a *coup de foudre*. That she had fallen so hopelessly in love and all the social norms had been abandoned. No doubt he had been given that information by Henry.

'Come to London, indeed. I wish they would, so you could see what a low creature Spafford is, spawned out of the same foul muck heap as you.'

Henry meant to take over managing the plantations. Had that been his motive all along? He had been dead set against any sale, something his aunt concurred with, amazed that Elisabeth, whom she had considered sensible until the arrival of Brazier, had fallen for abolitionist claptrap.

It was very obvious Elisabeth should not read this letter; she did not need her nephew to tell her that. But it did require that she formulate a good reason for doing so herself. Before she could conjure up an excuse, the door opened and Elisabeth entered.

'I wonder if it would be possible to visit Annabel once more?'

'So soon? I do think Annabel might find it odd that you should call again after only a day.'

The response was bitter. 'Perhaps if I was to tell her that I am prisoner in my own house, she would make me welcome.'

'She's not your only friend, Elisabeth. Perhaps someone else. It's a while since you visited Stephen's mother. You do owe that to her as a widow.'

'Then, as a companion, you'd be more suited to Mrs Langridge than I.'

Elisabeth slammed the door as she left. Given what she had been reflecting upon, Sarah Lovell had no doubt about the meaning of those words; she was very likely a widow too. But what if she was not? There was another recurring and unsettling vision, which usually came to her in the hours of darkness, when sleep was difficult. Had Samuel Lovell really fallen to some accident never revealed? What if he had deserted her and had found himself another woman? What if there had been a mistress all along?

CHAPTER SEVENTEEN

Inevitably, Harry Spafford had been found in a whorehouse, drunk and with the proprietor refusing to let him leave until his bill was settled. This was something he'd never had to face in Deal, where everyone knew his father was there to provide the necessary. Henry, being of a more refined nature than the wastrel's parent, was obliged to enter the kind of low establishment he would have avoided like the plague, to then make his way through an assemblage of powdered and rouged trollops, each trying to engage his interest.

'You cannot have run out of funds already?' he barked when he finally reached the seat of the problem, a dishevelled youth sat in a chair with a brute of a landlord standing over him. 'How much does he owe?'

The sum mentioned had Henry look at Spafford for confirmation, only to judge by his vague expression he had no idea if it was accurate or inflated, for if he was not drunk now, he looked as if he was not fully sober, however meek his demeanour. With long experience of such situations, Spafford did abashed very well and, as ever, was ready with an excuse for his disreputable behaviour. With what Henry took to be a cock and bull story, he told of having most of his money stolen, a sideways and surreptitious glance at the owner hinting him as the probable culprit.

Looking into those sapphire blue eyes, pleading to be believed, with a wholly unconvincing verge-of-tears expression on his puffy face, it was possible for Henry to wonder if he had made a mistake in his calculations. That had to be set aside; he needed to get Spafford out of this den of iniquity and back to the Angel, which involved a payment of the tariff, followed by a furious and rapid walk through the streets of Chatham, with Spafford scurrying to keep up, alternating between further excuses and promises of better behaviour in the future.

'If I could find some occupation to fill my time, Mr Tulkington,' came as a plaintive cry. 'That would save me from the temptations of idleness.'

'The only skill you have is in mendacity,' was the response, 'and I cannot see how you can live off that, without you dun me for the means.'

'Happen I could be put to a trade. If you was to put up an apprentice bond.'

'I could set you up as a purveyor of useless excuses or idiotic suggestions.'

As they entered the Angel Inn, Henry called for some service, commanded the person who attended to see Spafford fed and clean him up, for if it was questionable as to what stained the front of his coat and shirt, there was no doubt it was filth of some kind.

'If he asks for drink it is not to be provided. When he is presentable, and only then, bring him to my room.'

It was a process that did not take very long, but that still left enough time for Henry to brood on the problem and to come to one conclusion. Leaving Spafford loose in a place like Chatham, with its manifest temptations, was only marginally more troublesome than having him at Cottington Court. That, as a solution, even with tight restrictions, had to be avoided. He would never come to any kind of concord with Elisabeth if the lout was present.

It was in reflecting on that, Henry realised what he wanted from his sister was not just peace, but understanding and acquiescence: he needed Elisabeth to acknowledge his authority. That given, he had no doubt they could possibly coexist, if not in some kind of harmony, then in mutual respect. Not that such would be easy in the same household for some time to come, where the memories of what had occurred were bound to be raw.

Elisabeth thought he was against her marrying, which was not the case; it was to whom she had chosen as a potential husband that had brought this on her head. Pick someone of whom he could approve and he would have been sweetness and light. Why could she not see that? Perhaps if she had been appraised of the family trade, as he had from his sixteenth year, she might not have been so obtuse.

'You were too soft on her by far, Father, too soft, and it is I who have to clean up the mess.'

The other mess knocked as he uttered these words, though it had to be admitted the people he had commanded to clean him up had done a reasonable job. Once through the door, he adopted the same attitude he had employed in Henry's study, that of a schoolboy sure he was about to be punished. As he sat down, slowly and cautiously, Henry appeared to be examining him closely.

In truth, he was thinking what he could do with the wretch, while being aware he knew practically nothing about Harry Spafford, something to severely limit what were already constrained possibilities. Was there an occupation to which he might be suited? Not one he could presently think of and his parentage did not inspire.

He did know his mother had been a whore, a Welsh woman of reputedly fiery temperament, who had fled from Dan Spafford not long after the baby was born. If he didn't mix in the same circles, Henry was nevertheless aware of what was common knowledge, as well as the subject of many a jest. What he had witnessed this very morning was standard behaviour as reported by gossip, a habit off which he would have to be weaned.

Henry turned to thinking that before him was a young fellow with a potentially loose tongue and one who might react badly to excessive restraint. If he had never, as far as was known, actively engaged in smuggling himself, he knew too much about the game and who was involved.

It was a deeply annoying train of thought, which encompassed the knowledge he had already castigated himself for. Matters had obliged him to act in haste and sitting before him, now with a truly concerned look on his face, was just one of the many consequences. His own expression, a scowl, being the suspected cause of Spafford's anxieties, Henry made an effort to relax his features, reasoning he was in the presence of a booby and that could be used to his advantage.

'It may be that I have judged you over harshly.'

If the reply was insincere, it did not appear as such and only a very mistrustful mind would have thought it so. The face went from worry to an expression of sad-eyed contrition, soon backed up by the words, delivered after a deep indrawn breath, designed to indicate shame.

'No, you have judged right. I fear I have let you down and I'm sat here wondering how it could be possible to make amends.'

Happy to play the game, Henry asked. 'You truly wish that to be the case?'

Had he been inclined to good humour, he might have found it impossible not to laugh at the bogus sincerity with which Spafford responded. He sat slightly forward, his expression now one of eager intention, his eyes bright with positive possibilities.

'My pa sent me to school in Canterbury, so I have letters and numbers. If I'm in ignorance of all your affairs, it would be a blind man who could not see they're extensive. Surely there is somewhere within that where I can be of use?'

The expression changed to one that could have been steely determination. 'I'm aware I have wasted my growing years in dissolution, just as I know there are those who think I have no ability to live in a different way.'

Like your father, Henry Tulkington was thinking, but it did not show in his face. If this sod could do insincerity, so could he. 'Harry, I do not know you well enough to be aware if that is true.'

'Then I ask that you get to know me better.'

Henry dropped his chin to chest to indicate he was thinking about that, but his mind was in a very different place as regards solutions. Not that it stayed there for long: papers required to be signed and these were produced, along with a carrot.

'Given what you have said, and should that prove to be the case, it might be that, in time, I will wish to send you to the West Indies.'

The expression was one of confusion now; Spafford was trying to work out where the idea came from and what it might portend.

'But I fear, not yet. I would want to be sure you could carry out the duties that are necessary and that can only be done by a period of domestic observation. I would need to see how you progress in other areas before entrusting you with such a burden. Until then, the estates my sister inherited have to be managed, and I think, Harry, you would be the first to acknowledge, you are not yet ready for such a task.'

'Estates?'

'Sugar plantations.'

It was telling that he did not respond immediately, for he must know the law as well as anyone. Putting himself in Spafford's place, Henry sought to read his thoughts, which would centre on the fact he was now the rightful owner of those plantations. He was also, no doubt, wondering if it would be wise to say so.

'I admit to being slightly confused, Mr Tulkington.'

'The management of such properties is complex and it is something I will encourage you to study. Until such time as

I think you ready, I will run them on behalf of yourself and my sister.'

'But—?' That didn't get far: Henry cut him off quickly.

'While ensuring you receive the bulk of the income, which is considerable.' Spafford didn't know what to say and was unable to disguise his confusion, so Henry added, 'That is, after the necessary investments have been made.'

'Investments?'

'Plantations require an injection of capital. A considerable sum has to be put down to purchase seed and, perhaps, the number of slaves will require to be increased. The people presently acting as overseers have to be paid also, so they will take care of the planting and, I hesitate to point this out, but you lack the means to provide it.'

'How are they provided for now?'

That got a snapped response; Henry Tulkington couldn't help himself and before continuing he had to work fast to return his tone to that which it had been previously, which he saw as paternal.

'Take it that arrangements are in place, for now. But they require to be updated. But we must look to the future. If you husband the earnings, and the crop is as good as it has been in the past, you will be in a position to fund your own purchases. That may become the time to think about being on the spot.'

Henry guessed the Spafford brain was still whirring, as his features went through a gamut of emotions and reflections.

'You must understand, Harry, I need to take care of my sister's well-being. Before I can entrust these assets to you, I have to be sure they will be safe in your hands. So it is my intention to manage them until that time.'

The deed Dirley had drawn up was rolled out as Henry fetched a quill and a pot of ink, the former dipped and handed over with an invitation to sign. The quill hovered for some time, but Spafford must know that, as of this moment, he was penniless and dependent on the man holding it. He had neither money, nor any access to credit.

'In truth, I have to look out for you both now, not just Elisabeth.' There was another wait before the quill dropped and scraped across the base of the deed, Henry saying, 'I will have my sister append her signature when I get home, which I must do, since I have pressing matters to attend to.'

'What do I do in the meantime?'

'Stay here, for a week or two, while I consider how you can be of use to me.' He did not have to mention money, they both knew it was germane. 'I cannot have you behaving as you have done until now, Harry.'

'Have I not convinced you of my intention to change my ways?'

'Let us say I'm prepared to allow you the opportunity.'

The relief was obvious, as was the quickly suppressed smile.

'I'll draw a sum for your immediate needs and will also make arrangements for you to draw a weekly tranche of money.' A heavy frown was necessary to underline the gravity of what followed. 'Enough to fund pleasure – but not excess. I do not intend that you should be left here long, but when you return to Deal, it must be with something in mind to occupy you. I doubt I have to explain, given your parentage, in what manner that might be.'

'John Hawker?' came out with a worried frown, as well as proof he got the drift. 'What will he say?'

'He will do as he is instructed by me. And it may be, with matters as they are, I will seek to alter or expand my operations. I doubt I am required to say more. Now, I suggest you go to the room you occupy and wait. I will have to draw some monies and make certain arrangements, those I alluded to just a moment ago.'

'I won't let you down, Mr Tulkington,' Harry Spafford insisted, as he stood to leave, again producing a look of deep sincerity. 'I promise you.'

'You have no idea how much I wish that to be true.'

His leaving was hesitant too, as if he wanted to add more lies. Or did he really believe what he had been saying about reforming? Maybe he did, but the man he was talking to was sure it would not last beyond the dipping of the sun. Many a fellow Henry knew had promised to foreswear drink of a morning; it rarely lasted past six in the evening.

Once he was gone, he left a pensive Henry Tulkington, who was revisiting a conclusion, one arrived at just before Harry Spafford had entered the room. He was a problem, with only one viable solution and that might apply to his equally unreliable sire.

Dan Spafford, locked up in the tannery with only shackled hands, was free to pace the room in which he was incarcerated, his reflections a constant. There were only two things on his mind, the first of which was what had happened to Harry. When that bone had been gnawed to a splinter, he would turn to the other.

There was no possibility of him working for Henry Tulkington, and certainly not under the instruction of John Hawker. If it was pride which made that so, then he had enough.

Then concern number one would tell him, pride or no, the bastard held his boy's fate in his hands. He also had no doubt Hawker would not cavil to slit his throat, or finish him off in one of the dozens of ways that could be conjured up. From time to time he would reprise the faces of those he had led, as well as their disguised looks of disgust at his indulgence of his boy. Sometimes he would admit to himself he was too soft.

How many times had he promised himself to cut Harry out of his life, to leave him to stew in his own juice? How much money had he wasted sending him to school and what a farce that had been, Harry thrown out for every sin imaginable and that before he was fully grown.

There had been a time when his boy looked to him and admired him, when he'd been a nipper, at a time when his pa determined for him a future better than the one life had gifted him. Not for Harry the risks of the contraband trade, or the company of the ruffians who made their way by it. Dan Spafford wanted his son a gentleman, with looks and manners to make it so, looks that had come from his mother.

Temper, no. Harry was not a thrower of plates, pots and pans, or one you felt the need to sleep beside with one eye open, for Welsh Mary was not one to let go of a grudge or be mollified by a confession of regret when she was in drink. Perhaps the lack of a mother was responsible for the way Harry had turned out: perhaps he had inherited Mary's drinking habit as well as her looks.

Daisy had been kindness to him when they were home, but he had not, too busy earning the monies necessary for the lad's future. He could not be around all the time and, with a war raging, thanks to the Jonathans across a whole ocean of water, and their drivel about liberty and not being taxed, the profits had been good.

It was hard to think how life had been only four years past. Tulkington too busy to care about his activities and profits high enough to justify his owning two luggers, as well as needing the numbers to crew them. And then the buggers signed a treaty and the war ended, which was no good to man nor beast.

Costs had stayed high, especially in the numbers depending on him, but profits had plummeted. Somehow he had to get back to his old ways, maybe with fewer souls needing to be fed and provided for. Thinking on that was the only thing that stopped him from tearing out his hair in frustration. Whatever it took he would get back to where he had once been and Henry Tulkington be damned.

CHAPTER EIGHTEEN

It was one thing to be advised of a sailing date for a cargo of contraband, another to be sure of its imminent arrival. Dirley Tulkington had worked out a system to cover that. The waters between the Continent and England were close to being probably the busiest trade route outside the Straits of Messina, full of ships passing through, travelling to and from the Thames Estuary and to any number of ports further north.

Every national flag was represented: Dutchmen, Danes and Swedes traded with their colonies or the Levant, added to any number of vessels from the Baltic ports of the old Hanseatic League. French and Italian ships carried legitimate cargoes of wine, spirits and luxuries to London, taking back manufactures, the whole dwarfed by the mercantile might of Britannia, pursuing commercial relations with the entire world.

A deep-laden cargo vessel, even one beating to and fro for a short period, would excite no comment, nor would the singular pennant that flew on the masthead, along with a fleur de lys. To send a boat out, weather permitting, to make contact within a very limited expanse of sea presented no difficulty. Having found them in the expected position, they could then pass on a message that it was safe to proceed when darkness fell.

Once the information was brought back to John Hawker, he could initiate things at his end. Word was spread for those who earned from porterage to assemble, the sentinels from his personal following despatched to watch the approaches. If anyone cared to notice, and few did, it would be observed that certain bodies were missing from their usual haunts, while the various tracks leading to St Margaret's Bay carried more than the normal level of traffic.

Daisy Trotter had been watching the slaughterhouse for two days now, sure his mates were inside, less so regarding Dan Spafford. On the occasions when he had moved away, it had been to tail some of Hawker's men as, singly or in pairs, they emerged to go about their various activities, usually collecting payments from the local traders. Hawker he never followed, indeed he made himself scarce on sight of a man who knew his face too well.

So when the same folk came out in numbers, he could be sure something was up. When they headed out of the town, he had a very clear idea of what that would be, the knowledge sending him hurrying back to the point where he could continue to observe. One thing was obvious; if Hawker's gang were busy overseeing the running of goods, they could not, at the same time, be guarding anyone they were holding.

On his own, knowing that did not provide any easy solutions. The only place he could look for support was not one that gave him much in the way of confidence. He had, many times, reprised his talk with Brazier and nothing he took from the memory indicated he would be willing to help. The gossip of him being in league with William Pitt he had picked up. It had even penetrated the doors of Basil the Bulgar's place, though, very few being boatmen, there seemed to be few who gave any indication they cared if it was true.

Daisy didn't know either, but if it was, did it explain his dispute with Tulkington? Would alerting Brazier get him the help he needed? It had to be tried, which saw another letter delivered to Quebec House, asking for another meeting at the same place, with no explanation as to why but with hints it might be to mutual advantage. It stated that Daisy would make his way to the Old Playhouse, once he had registered eight peals of the St George's bell.

Joe Lascelles took it from the same attar-scented messenger and agreed to give it to his captain when he returned, while one of the urchins paid by Hawker wondered what to say about this visitor. He knew Brazier was not home, just as he knew where he was. He could see the man's doorway and the entrance to the Navy Yard from the same spot.

Inside the headquarters, presently occupied by Rear Admiral Sir Clifton Braddock, Brazier, in full uniform, was in conversation with Elizabeth Carter. Now that the worst of the seasonal weather had passed, she was back in Deal where she had been born and maintained the house in which she was raised, sharing with William Pitt, in whose honour this soirée was being held, a love of sea air.

'I was raised with it, Captain, as well as the local gales, though I confess my old bones can no longer bear the chill of the winter months. Nor can they withstand the waters for sea bathing, in which I took much pleasure.'

'I also find it efficacious, Miss Carter. It is my habit to start the day with a swim.'

'I think you will find it remarked upon, sir, as I and my companions did when using the bathing machine. The natives hereabouts have a morbid fear of water of any kind, except perhaps when it is used to brew beer.'

'My habit has become so commonplace, people have ceased to stop and stare.'

He had known they were near neighbours, even if the Carter house had been empty when he took on Quebec House: how could he not, with such a distinguished soul? One of the so-called Bluestocking Circle, a loose assemblage of women writers, she was probably the most celebrated person on this coast, equally so in London and Bath, an acquaintance of every luminary of note.

A woman of high ability, she added to that a very superior intellect and, while he was no ignoramus, the notion of even reading, never mind undertaking the translation of the works of the ancient Greeks, was way beyond him. Brazier was determined the conversation would stay within the bounds in which a naval officer could cope. When it came to erudition, he was out of his league.

'I envy you sailors, sir, for your duty takes you to places I have longed to visit.'

The look of polite enquiry named these as the sights of the classical world, the ruined temples of Greece and Rome, which peppered the shores of the Mediterranean. He was too embarrassed to admit they held little interest for him, to say he was more interested in the future than the past.

'Ah, here is our guest of honour,' Miss Carter claimed, just before a voice naming her took her from his side.

William Pitt stood in the doorway looking at those assembled, until a bustling admiral approached to welcome him, which had Brazier wondering at the invitation, though he reckoned he could pin the reason. In previous conversations, he knew Braddock had mixed views of the man, not least for his desire that the navy should interdict smuggling. Added to that he had named his brother, the Earl of Chatham, a civilian, as First Lord of the Admiralty, when naval opinion was adamant it should go to a sailor.

It was all about the state of the public purse, of which a very large slice went on the naval estimates, to build new ships as well as maintain those in service. Pitt was a ferocious cost-cutter, having inherited, on taking office, a huge deficit caused by the cost of the American imbroglio, which had spread from an already costly effort to chastise rebellious colonists to a near ruinous war with France. Chatham was there to seek to put a cap on expenditure.

For all his feelings of exasperation, loudly proclaimed in private, Chatham was now a person of some influence when it came to the allocation of employment. Giving a reception for his younger brother, who was a man of much authority in his own right, might produce for Braddock an elevation away from what he saw as a backwater posting. Watching the two exchange apparent pleasantries took his mind to what such an appointment might encompass. There were plums to be had in abundance and any number of rivals seeking them because of it. His old commander, Admiral Hassall, had held one of them, for there was a fortune to be made on the West Indies stations, even if the country was at peace.

In wartime, such postings were, with an eighth of any prize money going to the commanding officer, worth the price, on return, of a country estate. That was what made Hassall's actions all the more reprehensible; they had gone beyond greed to unbridled avarice, which occupied Brazier's thoughts as he circled the room making polite if unengaging conversation.

This he did with a weather eye on Braddock and Pitt, who seemed to have become glued to each other, though it was suspected it was the former latching on to the latter. Nor could he miss the occasional glance in his direction, which made him wonder if he was the subject of their conversation and, if he was, what was the substance.

At the back of his thinking was the notion, arrived at after his meal with Pitt, that he might be required to defend himself from any accusation stemming from the death of Hassall. Not that such should worry him unduly, given his absence from Kingston on the night it occurred. Yet it could be suspected he gave the order for the deed, leaving others to carry it out.

His blistering row with the admiral, where he had openly accused him of perfidy, would not have been contained by the walls of Admiralty House, and even less by the open windows of what was a warm-weather posting. He could conjure up Sir Lowell Hassall clearly in recollection; the long face and the lugubrious expression, a man normally self-contained seeking, by a combination of his inherent authority plus bluff and countering insults, to deflect the accusations Brazier was making against him.

That his inferior had proof of his actions was waved away with accusations of ingratitude. But it had failed to convince, not least because the man, with his inability to meet Brazier's eye, had reeked of guilt. It was possible to question now if it had been wise to share the information with his contemporaries, all of whom had suffered in their purse. The notion of writing to the Admiralty with a denunciation had faltered, first on the lack of demonstrable proof, but even more so on the certain knowledge that even believed, their Lordships would move to cover up anything which might bring disgrace on the service. It was at that point Brazier said, without naming anything in particular, that another way to stop Hassall would have to be found.

A distraction from these thoughts would have been a relief, if the subject of a conversation he was having with the Reverend Benjamin had been one in which to take comfort. The Vicar of St George's was no less reassuring on the subject of annulments than the Canterbury lawyer, though he didn't smoke, as had Moat, that he had a personal interest in a matter being discussed in general terms.

Not being a formal dinner, food came in the form of a buffet – wine had been provided by sailors acting as waiters, a task carried out with a grace that failed to match their tough-looking faces. It was while filling a plate that he found himself next to William Pitt.

'Perhaps one day we will meet when food is not the cause, Captain Brazier.'

There was guying in that and the man so addressed wasn't playing. 'I can think of few other occasions when it would be appropriate, given we are limited in what we have in common.'

'Not even the public good?'

'I fear my horizons in that regard do not match your own, sir.'

'It may be that I have heard otherwise.'

Brazier stabbed a slice of ham so hard it nearly went through to crack the platter. What did the sod mean by that? Was he saying he was in possession of more information than previously suggested? What had that anonymous letter that came home at the same time as his despatch actually said? He'd never been told. Was it merely that the admiral's death was a cause for suspicion, or he was got rid of for a reason?

'I cannot think who might have told you such, Mr Pitt. Outside taking on our nation's enemies, my interests tend to stop at the bulwarks of my ship.'

'Can a man who cares so much for his crew members that he troubles his purse for their welfare, not have a care for the greater good?'

About to say that was prompted by loyalty, Brazier stopped himself; it would sound pious and boastful. 'I think you'll find it commonplace in the service to look after one's followers.'

'It was interesting talking to Sir Clifton, he was most illuminating on the ways of the navy. Or was it the needs?'

It was time to shift the focus, which Brazier did with brio. 'No doubt Admiral Braddock would give that advice to your brother as quickly as he would impart it to you.'

'Neither of us want for advice.'

'William, am I to take it you're avoiding me?'

Pitt was forced to turn away from Brazier to deal with Elizabeth Carter who, despite what seemed to be a stinging rebuke, was smiling. It was telling she could address him by his first name. Given her age, of course, and the circles in which she moved, she might have known him as a child.

'My dear lady,' came out smoothly, 'I sought to dispose of my duties to the other guests, so I would have time left to give you the attention you merit.'

'Nonsense, but I will not bat away your flattery.' She looked past him. 'Behold, Captain Brazier, a fellow with a silken tongue. No wonder he has risen so swiftly at such a young age.'

'I'm sure you're right, Miss Carter,' Brazier said, taking the opportunity to move away.

Pitt was probing, and discomfort came from the lack of knowledge of what information he was working from. Could it be anything other than supposition? He was a clever sod, of course, how could he not be to have become the King's First Minister, taking over as leader of the Tory faction in the House of Commons aged only twenty-four.

There was an absolute certainty that none of the captains who had met in the cabin of HMS *Diomede*, on the morning he returned to Kingston, would have said anything likely to endanger him and, even more so, them as a group. If they knew which one of their number had been responsible for the deed – perhaps it was all of them – it had not been vouchsafed to him and nor had Brazier asked.

It could not be reversed and Hassall, since he was unlikely to be brought down legally, deserved a rope from the yardarm. All Brazier could do, once he had seen the doctors and had the nature of his demise confirmed, was get back to sea and bury the cadaver, thus removing from prying eyes anything that might raise further questions. That thought almost produced an ironic laugh. It seemed there was a raft of enquiries, including one he had asked himself many times.

What had Hassall done with his ill-gotten gains? Remitting home the prize money that came his way was simple, but other funds would have required to be kept hidden from prying eyes. There had been no overflowing chest of the type reputedly beloved by pirates, and shipping it home as specie would have been risky.

It was with some determination he put the matter out of his mind to concentrate on being what he was, a guest at a soirée. So he set himself to move around the room, engaging in inconsequential conversations with various locals, male and female, who made up the higher strata of Deal society, while wondering how many of them were acquainted with Henry Tulkington. Evermore to the point, how many of them had an inkling of his true nature?

He was preparing to leave – others like William Pitt and Miss Carter had already departed or were making preparations to do so – when Braddock came bustling over to buttonhole him.

'Well, Brazier, anything to report?'

'What could I possibly have to report, sir?'

There was a twinkle in the admiral's eye as he responded. 'Saw you talking with Pitt.'

'As did you, sir.'

'True, and he was curious to find out from me what I knew about you. Had to confess that was limited to our recent meeting, added to having served under Commodore Johnstone when you were Premier of HMS *Hero*. Just wondering if he had anything to say to you about me?'

'Nothing, sir, and had he enquired I would have been obliged to say, like you, how limited was our acquaintance.'

'Stiff bugger, wouldn't you say? Not much in the humour line.'

'I daresay he is burdened with many cares.'

'Not alone there, Brazier, is he,' was imparted with a feeling of hurt. 'Damned politicos don't know what it's like to be in charge of a station like the Downs, or any other one for that matter, and a ship just as bad, with the grubby clerks of the Navy Office poring over everything sent in, looking for mistakes.'

'And hopefully finding none, sir.'

'Curious, though,' Braddock said with a pensive look, but no explanation, which forced Brazier to enquire. 'Wanted to know about the West Indies and your service out there and what sort of fellow Hassall was. What the devil could I tell him?'

'Curious indeed. Now, sir, if you'll forgive me. Thank you for today.'

Hat fetched, Brazier made his way back the short distance to Quebec House and was given, on entry, the note delivered by Daisy Trotter. Having read it and about to react in the negative, he stopped himself, feeling the need for the company of someone nowhere near naval. He called upon Dutchy and the others to follow him out.

'Where to, Capt'n?' Peddler enquired.

'The Old Playhouse and a spot of decent wine, which does not encompass what Admiral Braddock was dispensing today.'

CHAPTER NINETEEN

Dutchy, Peddler and Cocky were in the main part of the Playhouse, able to partake of food and ale, but knowing they must have a care given they were still required to carry out the duty for which they were being rewarded. But the fact that Vincent Flaherty was also in the Old Playhouse did not serve Daisy Trotter well. He was a man fond of his clarets in the company of Brazier, who preferred burgundies, and they had set themselves to sample some of the best of Saoirse Riorden's cellar.

This led to a quartet of bottles on the table and, given Brazier had spent the afternoon drinking at Braddock's reception, albeit a distinctly inferior brew, he was past being fully sober when the bells struck eight. With tongues loosened by wine, the two men could easily have fallen to discussing their various problems, like Flaherty being smitten with Saoirse.

Brazier, who previously acknowledged that she was more than worthy of admiration, would not have welcomed the mention of his friend's problem: he would only have been reminded of his own. By an unstated agreement, both subjects were avoided. But talk they did, which included general ribbing about the different views held by their fellow countrymen about each other.

'You Irish are seen as feckless, Vincent.'

'While you Englishman are tyrants to any Celt.'

'I was about to add that such a denigration of the Irish is lazy. I had a goodly number in my crew and they were generally cheerful and industrious. You need not take my word for it. There are others in the main hall who shared a ship with them, who would attest to the same. And they do love a fight.'

Flaherty raised his goblet. 'Especially when in drink.'

'That applies to all peoples. I always favoured giving my men a tot of rum before going into action.'

'And you?'

'The man in command must keep a clear head. The time to drink is afterwards, hopefully to toast success.'

There was a discussion about the loss of the American colonies, with Brazier admitting it had been a badly fought war, Flaherty claiming it was one that should not have been fought at all. 'And I would wish Ireland to be three thousand miles away by water, then we too might be free.'

Sensing a bit of Irish belligerence, Brazier picked up a bottle and refilled Flaherty's glass for the umpteenth time. 'Now that is a subject that does not sit well with such fine wine.'

Sat facing the door, Brazier saw Daisy Trotter not so much fill the doorway as slide into it, half-hugging the frame. By his dress and appearance, he knew the Card Room was not for the likes of him. Those in occupation, either playing or merely drinking and conversing, were people of substance, successful men of trade or merchant ship captains come ashore to take their ease.

Half-tempted to go to meet him, Brazier decided to hold his place; Trotter had requested this meeting and there was no intention to ask Saoirse for her parlour once more. Also, his mood was rather salty: not angry, but disinclined to consideration. It took a while before Daisy realised he was not going to be indulged, while it was a measure of his perceived station that he moved like a man more at home in the shadows than strong candlelight.

'Shall I leave you to it, Edward?' Flaherty asked, just before Daisy reached their table.

'Why allow yourself to be troubled? I can't see there will be much to concern me.'

Daisy's progress had attracted a certain degree of attention, even from the card players, and none of it was benign. Brazier compounded what he later saw as deliberate and pointless rudeness, by issuing no invitation to sit. It was Flaherty who moved to give the man space to slide into a chair.

'What is it I can do for you, Trotter?' The answer was some time in coming; Daisy was looking around the room, examining faces, his own showing apprehension, which got an exasperated response. 'You've nothing to be concerned about here, man.'

'That so?' was the sniffed response. 'Happen I know who might be a threat when you lack a clue, being a stranger. Just because folk are coated in silk don't make them honest, an' I could name one who fits that notion well.'

'Your business?'

'In heaven's name, Edward, offer the man a drink.'

'Do you take wine, Trotter?'

'Not by habit.'

Flaherty was on his feet to offer Trotter a drink, as Brazier pointedly emptied his goblet and refilled it, 'I'll have some porter sent over, if that serves.'

That acceded to, and the Irishman moving away, Brazier gave the now-seated Trotter a look that demanded he speak.

'There's a cargo of contraband coming in this night.'

'From what I've been told, barely a night goes by when that is not the case.'

'Tulkington's contraband.'

Without knowing it, Daisy had moved to become equated with William Pitt, and the mood Brazier was in, not good in any case, went down like a falling barometer registering a coming tempest. Another goblet of wine disappeared.

'How many times do I have to tell people hereabouts, I have no interest in smuggling? Both your kind—' Brazier stopped himself from naming Pitt but added, 'and the Revenue can go to the devil.'

Flaherty returned to place a pot of porter in front of Trotter. Then, looking at Brazier's stony expression, he picked up his goblet and departed again, murmuring an excuse so softy delivered it was missed.

'There we are. A convivial evening with a friend ruined.'

'Hawker and his lot have gone to see it safe in.'

'And what do you expect of me?'

Daisy was surprised at the question, clearly seeing the matter as obvious. 'If they is doin' that, there can't be too many left behind at the slaughterhouse. Happen there be a chance to get free whoever it is they is holding there.'

'You don't seriously expect me to help you rescue them?'

'Be to your advantage to have help, Captain Brazier, would it not?'

'Help to do what?'

The question was so obtuse, Daisy was thrown. From what he had heard about this naval cove, it had to be said mainly from the crossing sweeper who worked by St George's Passage, he was a kindly soul, considerate and never failing to smile and tip a coin. The man opposite now was nothing like that. If Daisy had never served in the navy, he had been aboard ship with hard and mean sods as owners or masters. That was what he was seeing now.

'You're suggesting I stir myself,' Brazier growled.

'And the men you have too,' Daisy replied, a plea in his tone.

'To get out of Hawker's slaughterhouse a lot who've already been given a drubbing by him and his men. And what happens then, Trotter? Who will Hawker come after?'

'He can be taken on, if we's combined.'

'I think you mistake my purpose.'

'You want to go up against Tulkington. You put a pistol to his head, did you not?'

'Even if I did, I cannot see how the notion of becoming involved in a confrontation between two smuggling gangs will serve my needs.'

If Trotter had hinted at a plea previously, there was no mistaking it now. His voice broke, as he insisted, 'I got to get my Dan out from Hawker's clutches.'

'Then I suggest you find another way, because I am not it.'

'I'm on my own,' came out as a loud, head-turning cry.

The looks aimed at the corner they were occupying went

from the mildly curious, through slightly alarmed, to the seriously put out when it came to the men at the card tables. It was not loud enough to bring Saoirse into the card room at precisely that moment, that had to be mere coincidence, but it did bring her to Brazier's table.

'Is everything as it should be?'

The reply came as the Brazier goblet was filled again. 'In my case, yes. Do I have to introduce you to Daisy Trotter?'

'I know the name and face, but have never made acquaintance.'

'Perhaps something to be thankful for.' That got a pained look from Daisy, which Brazier ignored by taking a gulp of wine, on which the look changed to one of alarm as he added, 'You would scarce believe what it is he's asking me to do. He wants me to go to Hawker's slaughterhouse and prize from that sod's grasp a bunch of useless creatures I wouldn't give a hammock to on any ship of which I had command.'

'They're good lads,' was the protest.

'I'd be asking you to keep your voice down,' Saoirse hissed. 'This room is quiet for a reason.'

'So you won't aid me?'

'I don't think that requires an answer.'

It was now Daisy conjuring up the name of William Pitt, as well as the rumours going around, that this bastard was in league with him. If he had heard the gossip it had been mixed with what folk saw as a remedy. With knowledge of that, Brazier might change his tune. As he explained, it did not look like it from the disbelieving expression.

'Me, conspiring with Pitt?' he cried. Now he got a look

from Saoirse that had him moderate the level of his own voice to an angry hiss. 'Whoever sold you that canard has too vivid an imagination.'

'You'se visited him, an' dined with him at the Three King's twice, or so I's been told.'

'God in heaven, this town.'

That came with a look or irritation aimed at Saoirse, not of condemnation, but a general disapproval of Deal. If he had expected any response from her it was denied: she had on her face a look that said 'I told you so'. There was a temptation, nothing to do with Daisy, more to do with her and enhanced by his drinking, to tell of Pitt's proposal and his refusal. He would also be open about the reason the idea had been floated in the first place, as well as the pressure to which Pitt hoped he would succumb. That was until he realised, having consumed way too much wine, the danger of allowing his tongue to run away with itself.

'Well you may go, Trotter, and tell the idiots spreading the rumour, they are wrong.'

'And the other?'

'I am not minded to repeat myself.'

He didn't move immediately. It was as if Daisy, looking into the tankard of a yet-to-be-touched porter, was racking his brain for a way to change Brazier's mind, words that would get him what he so desperately needed. The man opposite gave no indication such arguments existed, so Daisy eased himself out of his chair and wiped his nose with his sleeve, before nodding to Saoirse.

Brazier was not prepared to let him go without a parting

shot. 'I suspected the last time we met you were seeking to use me for your own ends, Trotter. Be aware, I am not fool enough to fall for it.'

That obviously stung, Daisy going from miserable reflection to anger in a flash, calling over his sloping shoulder as he left.

'You might be more fool than you know, matey.'

The deep-laden vessel drifting a mile off the shore could see the lights of Dover, the beacons that marked the harbour entrance and the glim of multiple pinpoints behind, which denoted occupied buildings. A look around the invisible horizon showed any number of other pinpoints, which marked the positions of vessels either hove to for safety or, for the more adventurous, those making their way through the Channel narrows despite it being a cloudy night. Right ahead, over the prow, beyond its own lanterns, was Stygian blackness.

A lantern, seemingly suspended in mid-air, flashed three times, the signal for which the French captain had been waiting. John Hawker, standing behind it, saw the return message, a lamp shaded and unshaded to tell him his message had been received. On the other arm of St Margaret's Bay, a second light appeared, by which time the sails on board the ship, which had been backed and were flapping loosely, were drawn tight to take what little wind there was, which set the timbers creaking as the vessel began to move.

On the wheel, the Frenchman kept those two lights in his sights as he bisected them with his bowsprit. Another lookout, placed aloft, was concentrating on the unseen higher ground. If anything shone from there, it would mean danger, which would see the cargo ship put up its helm and withdraw. On either beam, crew members with the sharpest eyes made sure nothing was approaching from north or south.

They were safe until the ship was close to making its landfall. In the cabin was a proper manifest of the cargo, with details of the goods carried and for whom they were destined. All were proper names of legitimate importers, so they could plead innocence, being off course if intercepted. Having made the crossing several times, the fellow in command knew, by his position relative to those shore lanterns, when to give the order to drop a stern anchor, this paid out on a stout cable as the ship inched in.

The rest of his crew had been travelling between holds and deck, first unlashing the cargo, chests and bales secured against the motion of the sea, then fetching part of what was uncovered on to the deck, this to save time. There was a solitary figure in the chains, casting a weighted line and seeking to calculate the depth of water under the keel. At a soft call from him, the movement of cargo was abandoned. The sweeps, laid along the deck, were slipped into the water through portholes, the sails under which they had been edging let loose again.

Now they were inside the arc of the bay, the prow was set at the well-lit mouth of the main tunnel. Figures could be seen descending ladders, to make their way down to the water's edge, one party waiting for a line, which would be thrown from the ship's stern once the prow had been very gently beached. This, and another from the bows, would be lashed off to the dolphins, to hold the craft in position.

From a virtually silent manoeuvre, the noise grew markedly; even whispers and low calls multiplied, if issued by dozens of throats. The extra-wide gangway was opened, the gangplank shoved out to be taken by willing hands, who moved at the landward end as far as possible to create a shallow slope. That done, unloading could begin, the holds needing to be stripped in very short order.

A line of bearers took the barrels, bolts and small bales, as well as wooden chests of tea, scrabbling over the shingle and then up the wide ladders into the tunnel. John Hawker had a very limited view of what was happening, but then he had no need to see something that happened a dozen times a year, only broken off when the midsummer months denied them the darkness in which to work.

Inside the tunnels, in single file, the bearers of the contraband trudged their way up the slight incline and into the tunnel, which led to the chambers hewn out of the stable chalk, where the cargo would be stored prior to distribution. Hawker appeared halfway through the unloading to make his way in the reverse direction and to clamber down to the beach.

He found the Frenchman at the base of the gangplank and a few words in his language, just about all Hawker knew, were exchanged. Then it was mainly silence, if you excluded the sounds of heavy breathing, displaced shingle and the odd curse when someone slipped.

Eventually the time came for Hawker to go aboard and check the holds were clear, to take from the Frenchman the manifest, accurate in all respects excluding the intended recipients. He passed over to the captain his fee, a leather pouch heavy with coin, before making his way back to the beach, watching while those of the crew on land went back aboard, the gangplank being drawn in.

At a soft call, the securing cables were loosened and hauled inboard, while men on the capstan dug their feet into the deck and leant on the poles, to pull the stern out into deeper water. As many as were available of Hawker's porters put their shoulders to the hull and pushed. Slowly the vessel refloated, to be hauled out to a point where sails could be reset, the yards having been hauled round to take enough wind to get way on a ship that would set course for its home port.

The ladders were withdrawn back into the tunnels, the entrances shuttered off, leaving the strand clear of humanity. At first light, a couple of Hawker's men would come to the beach to ensure no trace of the night's activities existed: items dropped or a coat discarded. Meanwhile the man who employed them ensured that all was properly stacked, his porters paid their copper and dispersed.

Out at sea, the three-times shading of a lantern told those on the cliff tops it was time to depart. Last to leave was John Hawker, who made his way back to the hut, to where he had left his horse munching on a hay net in the nearby bothy, sitting down to wait for daylight. When that arrived, he had to lead the animal up the steep path to the grassy leas, which ran to the cliff edge. There he could mount and ride home, free from any danger of inadvertently going over a cliff edge in darkness.

Henry Tulkington would come the other way, possibly tomorrow or the day after, with the manifest Hawker had in his pocket, to check it against the cargo and make sure nothing was missing that should not be. That established, he could alert the other half of the coastal enterprise, run by a man John Hawker had never met, to begin distribution of the contraband to his waiting customers.

CHAPTER TWENTY

The pressure of time obliged Henry Tulkington to hire a private coach to get him back home. He arrived in the early hours of the morning in a reasonably good mood, which for him meant no one got a frown for some perceived error, which lasted until he was presented with Dirley's letter. The mere fact of it having been written was enough to make him angry: that his aunt had read it doubled the feeling, which was awkward, since the emotion had to be concealed. It did not sit well with him, but he knew he needed Sarah Lovell too much to offend her for something that could not be undone.

Nor did he have time. He needed to go and see John Hawker, to check if the cargo had come in as arranged, that it conformed to what was expected, so any thoughts on what his uncle might be up to would have to wait. Once more it required the use of a horse, St Margaret's Bay being another place he could not risk being seen by the prying eyes of curious servants.

Coming out of the front door, he saw a stable boy holding his animal by the mounting block, but his attention was taken by Creevy signalling to him, clearly a plea for attention. Given

252

the man was standing over some ornately trimmed yew topiary, Henry assumed it was that he wished to talk about, so he decided to give the gardener a minute or two. He did, after all, care for the first impression given to a visitor approaching the house and the formal parterre was an important part of that.

'What can I do for you, Creevy?' he asked, once the man's hat had been removed.

'There's som'at I reckon you might like to know, your honour.' The look of mystification had Creevy blurt out what it was. 'Upton has taken to walking some of his horses down by the lake of a morning, regular like, if different animals.'

'I cannot see that makes—'

Henry stopped, looking right into the old man's watery eyes, slightly thrown by the look the gardener sent to right and left, as if, absurdly, he did not want to be seen talking to his employer. It was that look which nailed it, but he was not going to ask if Upton met anyone on those walks. Creevy was not to be alerted to family affairs, but it was obvious what he was driving at.

'I'm obliged to you,' was delivered with a look that told him he was to say no more.

'Allas look out for you, Mr Henry, you bein' the kind gent you are.'

It would have shocked no one who knew him that Henry Tulkington took that at face value; he saw himself as a benevolent master.

'Garden is looking splendid. A testament to your care.'

With Creevy's hat already in his hand, an obsequious touch of the forelock was required, even if it was delivered to his master's retreating back. Henry could read into what he had been told everything that was implied. No one ever walked the horses in the woods around the lake, even if it was not expressly forbidden. Ergo, if he was doing so, it must be for a reason. Another problem to be dealt with, but finding what it entailed would have to wait. He mounted and, as soon as he was in the saddle, he kicked his mount into motion.

'Smooth it were,' was Hawker's report. 'Which is a relief, after what Spafford and his lot got up to last time.'

What had been a smiling face clouded; Hawker was still smarting from having part of the previous cargo pinched from under his very nose, on the same strand of pebbles he had visited the night before. It had sent him into the passion that had ended in him collaring Spafford junior, hauled out of a gin shop and very publicly dragged along the main road of the town to the slaughterhouse.

'Speaking of which?'

'Couldn't risk any trouble with a cargo comin' in, so I's sat on matters regarding Brazier. But I can tell you, it's festerin' and, for my money, the longer that goes on the better.'

'Holding them all here has a risk, John. It can't be kept a secret forever.'

'With respect, I don't reckon anyone to take me on and another day won't hurt. I'll get out and about once I know all's well at the bay. A little bit of coin spent on porter and gin for the right folk and they'll be champing to string the bugger up.'

'Which must be prevented.' Seeing a look bordering on disappointment, Tulkington was quick to add an admonishment. 'He might be a sod and one I would welcome gone permanently, but he is still a post captain in the King's Navy. A man like that is too elevated to be strung up by a baying mob, without which we will suffer serious repercussions. Understand that those responsible for order hereabouts will stand for much and look the other way, but not that.'

The expression on Tulkington's face left no doubt about his sentiments, nor were they a mystery. For all his power locally, it rested on certain norms that must not be breached. It was axiomatic that those who turned a blind eye must not be given cause to look in order to protect their own position.

'Out of Deal will serve, though a few heavy bruises won't go amiss.'

'Those I will see to personally,' came with a growl, which was a mistake; the rebuke was swift, with no concession to his pride, already a touch dented.

'I've told you, John, stay out of it!'

It hurt to reply in a voice, which, to him, sounded weak and submissive. 'Course, Mr Tulkington, I was meaning, I will see the right folk know what to do.'

'And what not to do, which is to go too far. Now, the manifest.'

The document was handed over to be perused, but he did not produce from his pocket the matching list, one of two documents, which had been couriered down weeks past by Dirley. The two would not match exactly, given that goods coming from various regions of France could not be guaranteed to arrive in a given time.

That country was cursed with any number of internal borders, with each region seeking to levy a transit tax on anything going to a neighbour and beyond. Quite apart from legal delays, a lot of inter-province smuggling went on, which also had an impact. There was no cause for concern if some things were late, as long as they came over the Channel eventually, so the books in Dirley's safe balanced over something like a twelvemonth.

'You don't want to see Spafford, then?'

'I will spare myself that.'

'He keeps asking about his boy.'

'Who is safe from everything but his own bad habits.' Catching the look of enquiry, Tulkington went on, 'Tell him nothing. The less he knows, the better.'

Me too, by the sound of it, Hawker assumed.

Sarah Lovell had not been fooled by Henry's unruffled response; she had known him too long and too well and had been prepared for a blast of invectiveness. When it didn't come, it naturally set her to thinking. It could not be anything to do with her feelings – her nephew was indifferent to those, and not only hers.

A woman who rarely sat down for long, she went to the drawing room and took up a chair in front of the unnecessary fire, one lit to keep the master happy, looking into it as if seeking a solution. Something had changed in their relationship, just as it had between her and Elisabeth, though in that case it had done so for the worse.

It was slow to surface, but come it did, and the notion of an alteration vis-à-vis Henry warmed her more than the blazing logs. But what animated it? Was it need or fear? The need to control and watch Elisabeth, or a dread that she might turn against him and act as a witness for her niece, one so potent the marriage could be annulled? As well as warmth, there was a delicious feeling of power, one she had not felt since lording it within Canterbury society.

'To be enjoyed as long as it lasts.'

'Sorry, Mrs Lovell.'

Spinning round, she saw an under footman with a scuttle of logs. Thinking the room empty, he had entered without knocking, which got him an immediate rebuke, more harsh than necessary due to her being surprised as well. The decision she made then was one to make her blood course, an exercise of what she saw as her new power, though few would have rated it worth the description.

'No more wood in here, it makes too much mess. Coal from now on.'

That acknowledged, she went up to knock on Elisabeth's door. As soon as it opened she said, with a sweet smile, seen by the recipient as deeply insincere, 'You say you wish to visit the Colpoys again?'

'I do.'

'Then send a note over this morning, asking if you can call this afternoon.'

'Henry has given permission?'

'No, Elisabeth,' was delivered firmly. 'I have decided it should be allowed. I take it you will be going out for your usual walk?'

'I will.'

'I would find it obliging if you would find me and tell me first.'

* * *

Daisy Trotter was sat on the long pebble strand of Sandwich Flats looking at the twin luggers owned by Dan Spafford, pulled high up the beach and well out of the water so even the highest tide would not trouble them. He was wondering what to do, if anything, about them. Would a sum of money get Dan free and would selling the boats meet the purpose? Would that be approved, given they were his sole way of making a crust?

Daisy had never realised before how much he depended on Dan. It came as a jolt to realise how the way he had seen their relationship was the complete opposite of the truth. His old friend flattered him by letting him think, for old time's sake, his advice was not only important, it was welcomed, heeded and needed. In truth, Dan disposed and he obeyed – perhaps a decent payment for the saving of, if not his life, then . . . ?

The large and hairy bugger had had an eye for handsome young Dan and would not leave him be. It had taken time before the matter could be sorted, with both unsuspecting what was coming. The sodomite had cornered Dan on deck during a dark and cloudy night, with a bit of sea running off the Skagerrak. Hidden by the man's bulk and pleading to be spared what was being suggested, Dan had not even known his assailant had been knifed. He might have guessed by the time the third strike went in.

Daisy's victim had turned to deal with him, screaming blue murder. Quick as a flash, on spotting Daisy and the slight gleam of his blade, Dan had whipped a marlinspike out of the rack by the falls and thumped the sod over the crown with all his young lad's strength. Stunned, Daisy got his blade into the ribcage, seeking the heart. Dan never knew if he found it, only that the bugger crumpled to the deck.

How they found the strength to lift his dead weight and tip him over the side was as much a mystery. The blood was there for all to see come morning, while all knew one of their number was missing and what he was like. If they had an inkling of who had done the dirty, no one let on. It was logged as a mystery and one soon forgotten once the deck had been sanded and swabbed.

They'd been like two peas in a pod ever since and, if Dan knew what Daisy secretly longed for and never dared say out loud, he kept his own counsel. Now was just like being on that dark and rolling deck again. The man he loved was in danger and it was down to him to sort it.

Betsey was still wondering, as she walked, about that exchange with her aunt. No one could accuse Sarah Lovell of being meek, but for her to imply, and she had, that she was acting without Henry's approval, or perhaps even his knowledge, came as something of a shock. Having gnawed on it for a while, Betsey reckoned it an aberration; there was no way she would defy her nephew. The thought evaporated as she spied Upton leading another horse, this time a big bay stallion.

'Mr Upton, do we have another sick animal?'

'No, ma'am,' came with a meaningful look. 'This one's fully fit and being taken down for stud duty. Just thought I'd come this path, then make my way round to the north gate for a bit of a change. I hope you don't mind.'

'If you're going that way, it would please me to accompany you. I too could use a change of scenery.'

As they began to walk, their heads either side of the equine head, Upton posed a question. It was pronounced in a manner that told Betsey he had worked himself up to it, so strangled was his voice.

'If I was to say the servants are all in a lather about what's been goin' on, would you mind it?'

'The servants?' Betsey asked cautiously.

'Not all, I admit,' Upton gabbled, 'but to include them who's been here a long time, those who knew you as a . . .'

The inability to finish prompted a rare smile from Betsey, as well as a question. 'Knew me as something of a handful?'

'Never that, miss – sorry – ma'am. We can't help feeling you'se troubled, not that we can do much about it, easing matters, like.'

What to say? It sounded too outlandish in her head, never mind spoken out loud, the stuff of silly romances in which a hero rescues a damsel in distress from an evil baron. She didn't want to explain in detail, it was too diminishing, but nor, if the head groom was to be relied upon, could she let such an opportunity pass.

'All I will say, Mr Upton, is that I am denied the liberty to depart Cottington Court as and when I please.'

'And that you would wish for?'

The stallion was slightly startled by a pair of pigeons noisily exiting a full-leaf tree, which had it throw its head in the air, with Upton pulling hard on the bridle. His face was briefly visible and on it she observed a look of genuine concern, one which decided Betsey to take the plunge.

'What I require is the liberty to leave this house and grounds and never return, on foot if I must, but . . .'

He had to know what she was suggesting; not only that he let her out through the north gate, but that he provide a horse as well. The stallion's head had been lowered again, so it was impossible to read Upton's expression as he replied.

'To be thought on, Mrs . . .'

'Langridge, Mr Upton. And if you hear me referred to by any other name, give it no credence. On this occasion, I think I have walked with you far enough. Perhaps another day.'

'I recall you used to be fond of dropping into the stables from time to time. Might be a notion you should go back to doing that.'

'Walked an' talked, Mr Creevy,' the young lad said, he having been sent to follow Upton at a distance. Ten years old, he was sprightly, freckled and missing his front teeth, bonded to Cottington to learn the gardening trade. 'Each side of the horse too.'

'You weren't spotted?'

That got a furious shake of the head. 'Take a sharp eye to catch me.'

'Well, keep it to yourself. A loose word will see you out the gate with a bruised arse.'

'Wouldn't say the story, Grady,' Upton intoned, his face sad. 'Seemed to me like she was shamed by it.'

'Since you've no idea of what happened, how could you know that?'

'A feeling. Might be she'll open up if we talk a few more times. I think she trusts me.' Grady started to wheeze, looking to deliver humorous riposte on being trusted, but Upton cut off his sally. 'Stow it.'

'It's you who might be stowing it if Tulkington finds out. I told you to have a care.'

'I ain't daft, Grady, an' that's another one that don't need your humour. I will not walk as often as I've been doin' of late, in case som'at is suspected. You know what a nose the master has.'

'Make a good truffle hound, he would.'

'Best not give him owt to sniff at then?'

'You're the one doing that, friend.' Grady tapped his head. 'I ain't as short on a shilling as you.'

'Have a care your Christian charity don't show.'

Betsey, with no one to talk to, was thinking on the same subject, alternating between the fear of a trap, then castigating herself for thinking that of a man who had always been kind to her. Had he got the drift? If she was to get away, he would have to unlock the gate and let her out on a horse, which would require a saddle. A reasonably competent rider, Betsey had no notion to go bareback over ploughed fields and pasture, with fences and hedges to jump if there was a pursuit.

There were side-saddles in the stables but how could one be taken to where it needed to be without exciting comment? Sarah Lovell didn't ride and was, in any case, in terror of horses, so that left only her. Walking a horse was one thing, doing so with one saddled up would look bizarre. The first thing to do was visit the stables as invited, to see how the land lay and how long, in terms of time, she might have to wait.

The knock at the door interrupted her thoughts and she went to open it to find her aunt there. 'A note came back from Annabel, I hope you do not object to my reading it?'

Betsey was suddenly full of fear. What would Annabel say if she thought she was replying to her? Might she mention the note to Edward? Her heart was in her mouth until Sarah Lavell said, 'She is happy to receive us at three of the clock.' The brow furrowed. 'Odd she refers to the fact of my coming too. That you never mentioned.'

Nor will I mention, Betsey thought, that you read my note to Annabel without asking, so the reply was larded with sarcasm. 'I daresay she knows I never go anywhere without first begging you to accompany me.'

That was taken badly. 'Have a care, Elisabeth. Do not tempt me to replicate your brother's ways of behaving.'

CHAPTER TWENTY-ONE

Having checked his goods were as near as they should be to what was expected, and a note made of discrepancies, Henry Tulkington could make his way back to Deal and the Lodge in which he was a Master Mason. It was here that the important people and decision-makers of the town and surroundings gathered to celebrate their craft. Magistrates, men of business, the owners of large farms or sailing ships, plus the numerous chandlers who supplied them.

The vicars and deacons of the local churches were attendees, also those of the brotherhood merely passing through, at temporary anchor in the Downs. Likewise, many of the naval and marine officers stationed in Deal at any one time would attach themselves as affiliated members. So would the Trinity House pilots, who saw ships down the Thames and back up again.

It was in these rooms that various appointments were made. Who should hold the various plums in the gift of the Deal community, such as a harbour master, for a place lacking a harbour. The duty involved seeing to the orderly berthing of ships and to extract the fees due for the right to anchor, a portion of the revenue retained by the office holder.

The beach within the boundaries of Deal was no free for all either; if you wished to haul up a lugger, hoy or fishing boat on to the shingle, you had to pay a fee to the Beach Comptroller. He, not wanting to spend his life chasing his dues, tended to let them out in blocks for others to exploit. Likewise, he would issue a licence to the wherries – small boats, which transported passengers to and from their ships

That the brotherhood looked after each other's interests was a given, but there would be no shame shown for that being so: it was seen as the natural order of things. The world required to be ruled by people of substance, with a stake in the maintenance of the law of the land. Mayhem would ensue if the lower orders were granted any powers.

To those who might complain of their vice-like grip on local affairs, they would counter with their record on charitable giving. Money was raised by Lodge members for the care of foundlings, as well as women widowed by the loss of their man between the shore and the Goodwins, a not uncommon occurrence. It was within these walls the collection had been made which part compensated the beach community for the loss of their boats due to Billy Pitt's arson.

Henry had been inducted as a young man and was now a person of real standing, easily a match for his father. Likewise, his Uncle Dirley was a brother who had risen high in the Grand Lodge, where he mixed with the male offspring of King George, as well as a very large number of members of the House of Peers. It was said as many decisions of importance were made there as in Westminster.

In the Deal Lodge, Henry would meet with those who could, if they chose, cause him difficulties. Not that such things were allowed to fester; as soon as any problem surfaced, it would be smoothed over, either by support for a cherished place or project, a gift of some very superior contraband and, in one or two cases, a downright bribe. It was also the case that no brother was required to pay John Hawker anything other than their taxes.

'Admiral Braddock, I find you in good spirits, I hope?'

Henry was sitting at a table with a coffee pot, and seeing Braddock making to join him, he signalled for another cup.

'Tolerable, Tulkington, tolerable. Missed you at my soirée yesterday.'

'I was sadly away on business. I take it Mr Pitt attended an event in his honour?'

'He did,' came with a glum expression, as the admiral watching his coffee being poured.

'Can I assume, from your look, he gave you the usual lecture?'

'Nail on the head, Tulkington. Why am I not out catching smugglers, the booby? He's had it from me, as well as my predecessor, that it's not a task for the navy. I'm damned if I know why he still bothers asking. If he wants us to chase contraband, he must get a bill to do it through Parliament, as well as a vote for the funds for an expanded role.'

'Ah, Parliament, of which he's supposedly the master.'

The ruddy sailor's face took on a sly look. 'But he ain't, is he, much as he would have it otherwise?'

Henry Tulkington wanted to gainsay the sentiment, for if governance was a bear pit in which action was ever stymied, Pitt had fared better than most, after the near ruinous expenditure brought on by Lord North's handling of the American war. The public debt was down and still falling, even if he had bought in several sinecures, posts drawing an income for no work, which he saw as inimical to the public good.

'Elizabeth Carter was there,' Braddock added. 'The eternal spinster. Too clever by half, that woman.'

'I didn't know she was back from town,' was said with more interest than was truly felt, which allowed him to ask another question. 'What about that captain who's taken Quebec House? Name escapes me.'

'Brazier?'

'That's the fellow. It's being said he's a friend of Pitt.'

'Not if what I saw of them is true. Observed them talking and, I'd say, there was little love lost. Brazier looked as if he was giving Pitt a piece of his mind.'

'Strange cove, nevertheless, wouldn't you say?'

That got a chortle. 'If you'd ever been in the navy, Tulkington, you'd scarce say that. We have some ripe specimens in our cabins. But Brazier has got some baggage.'

'Really! More coffee?'

Braddock was very eager to tell Henry that which he already knew about Brazier's relations with Prince William, albeit he was short on details of what had brought on the court martial.

'Found for the premier and went on to reprimand Sailor Bill, who is, by all accounts, a fellow with a foul temper.'

'A royal prerogative.'

'Not one he'd exercise if he was under my command,' Braddock huffed.

That was taken with a large pinch of salt. Tulkington might know little of the navy, but he knew a lot about men like Braddock, for whom ambition topped all other considerations. This would make him putty in Prince William's hands as he grovelled for royal favour. If he detested Brazier, it did no harm to note he was not of that ilk.

'He's got another bit of bother on his plate,' came with the smug air of a fellow knowing he possessed inside knowledge. The querying look from Tulkington had the admiral shuffle his backside forward on the chair, so he was closer, which allowed him to drop his voice. 'Some malarkey in the West Indies, it's rumoured. His commanding officer pegged out in questionable circumstances, I'm told.'

'Pegged out?'

'Found the deep six, or was despatched there in short order. Next thing you know, Brazier's swimming in gold.'

'Are you saying the two are connected?'

Braddock threw himself back into the chair, this time with an enigmatic and superior smile. 'Depends if you believe in coincidence.'

The man Henry had come to meet appeared over Braddock's shoulder – he waved to indicate recognition and that he would be with him shortly – while Henry was wondering how he could probe further without revealing how well he knew of Brazier and his past.

'It's all rumour, mind, Tulkington, nothing definite.'

'Still, an interesting tale. Is what is implied being investigated?'

'Not as far as I know.' The face closed up and Braddock looked angry. 'But then, what the devil do I know, stuck in this godforsaken—' He stopped himself from cursing Deal as his personal backwater, sitting where he was and with whom. What he said next was to cover for a degree of embarrassment. 'I'll let you know if I hear any more.'

'Please do, Admiral Braddock,' Henry said, standing up. 'One thing, what was this flag officer's name?'

'Hassall. Never liked the fellow myself. Too much given to showing off.'

'If you'll forgive me, I've arranged to meet someone.'

That someone was a fellow Master Mason called Tobias Sowerby. He owned and ran a comprehensive business, transporting goods around the locality by horse-drawn vans: further afield it was by barge. People moving between Deal, Sandwich and the surrounding parishes needed his services to carry their chattels, while the local tradesfolk, not willing to bear the expense of their own conveyances, plus a carter and possibly two, often hired Sowerby to move sale goods.

There was a bit of a frisson to this meeting. Henry, having lost, he later established, a cartload of tea to Dan Spafford, sought to mitigate the damage by billing Sowerby and demanding recompense. He reasoned it was from his man the stuff had been stolen. The demand had been refused, with the arch observation that if Henry Tulkington wanted goods distributed, he might have to do it himself, unless he wished to insure them.

'I hope you're not still smarting from our last encounter, Tobias?'

'Why would I?' was an obvious lie. 'The matter was settled.'

Henry smiled and laid an affectionate hand on Sowerby's shoulder. 'And if I admit I was in the wrong' – that caused a deep intake of breath: Henry Tulkington was not a man much given to apology – 'I was in a bit of a passion, as you would be to see your possessions filched. I spoke in haste and I now regret it.'

Sowerby had his own problem: this man was his best customer by a county mile, while it mattered not to him the nature of the goods he was being asked to carry. Indeed, it allowed him to charge a premium, the basis of the demand for recompense, one which had permitted him to undercut his rivals on normal commerce and drive several out of business.

'I came today with an offer to meet you halfway, Henry.'

'Why, that's noble, Tobias.'

'So the matter is now settled?'

'It was settled in my mind, before I ever got home. But I will recall your kindness should I ever be tempted to let my temper get the better of me again.'

Henry, all bonhomie, handed over the details of what required to be delivered within horse carriage distance, some to private addresses, mostly to various coaching inns, where those doing the buying would bring their carriages to meet the Sowerby vans. In addition came Dirley's list of what was required to be despatched by barge, a regular run to a warehouse at Chelsea Harbour.

If he was smiling and calm, it was all outward show; behind that facade he was seething. Sowerby meeting him halfway did not fit the bill, he should have coughed up the lot. Henry was as aware as the man himself how he used the profits from moving contraband to grow his enterprise. The swine should have been grateful to him for his prosperity and taken a chance to show it in silver.

One day, Sowerby would end up like others, bleeding and battered, dumped in a muddy ditch, getting what he deserved from John Hawker. How he wished it could be him handing out the deserved retribution and he conjured up the scene in his head. The confrontation, the denials, the blows delivered, the pleas for mercy, utterly ignored as a hard boot finished Sowerby off. It could not be, he had to hold back from that: his responsibilities prevented Henry from proving to those who crossed him the price they would pay for their stupidity.

But he truly wished to be the deliverer of punishment. It was a point often made to Hawker, if few other people, a notion the man scoffed at. For all his power, Hawker knew Tulkington was a weed who would as like faint at the sight of blood.

As he rode home, Henry's temper seemed to increase, until he was loudly denouncing various souls, going all the way back to his childhood. Those who had taken advantage of his inability to grow – at aged thirteen he had still looked like a child. The same people then guyed him for gaining inches by the week, until he towered over people he'd previously been obliged to look up at. If he gained height, it had not been matched by bulk, which left him still the victim.

No one humbugged a Tulkington – not his fellow pupils at school, the likes of Roger Colpoys or his sister and her friends, with their insults they thought to disguise as witty sallies, which was doubly frustrating for he could not touch them. There were others who had been shown the error of their opposition. Sowerby surely deserved to be next.

But not yet: he was needed. Henry, as he passed through Upper Deal, had calmed somewhat, moving on to turn over in his mind not only Sowerby getting his just deserts but how he might be financially ruined as well. It was a sad conclusion, by the time he reached his gate, that he needed the man too much to do that which he wished.

He would have to stick with him. The only other option was to take over the organisation of transport himself, which flew in the face of how Dirley and his father had arranged his inheritance. But he must find a way to send him a message and remind him who held the whip hand.

He could recall, although he was not far beyond being breeched, a time when Sowerby was no more than one man driving a dilapidated cart, with a patched canopy and drawn by a near knackered horse, too old for the plough. He had risen from near beggary to the ability to more than hold his head up in the Lodge. But his elevation had come from the Tulkingtons on certain conditions.

All transport charges were settled in cash, John Hawker advised not to look too closely when tax gathering, part of the arrangement being that he kept no records of their transactions. Therein lay the purpose of the premium payment, to shield the name of Tulkington from his activities.

Edward Brazier knew he was engaged upon something that had more hope attached to it than any possible chance of a positive outcome. Joe had gone through his possessions to dig out from under a mass of other objects his telescope. This, from a vantage point of a dipping incline, some five hundred yards distant, was now trained on the Colpoys' house, while his protection was dotted around behind him, to make sure he was not disturbed.

The building was typical of the area, four-square and red-brick, quartered with regulation windows of large sashes and small panes, added to enough chimneys to rate it substantial. It was set in a dip and well away from the barns, with haystacks in between. There was a water tower on the highest nearby point, speaking of no need for the courtyard well, which alone denoted prosperity. No formal gardens fronted Home Farm, as at Cottington Court. It was a beach shingle driveway, with chickens darting around pecking for food.

Having been there for some time, he had seen a trio of carrot-topped children, trailed by excited dogs, go about their morning tasks, collecting eggs from the hutches into which the fowl retreated at nightfall, turning over the filth of the pigsty and taking indoors a milk churn brought to the house from the cowshed. In both build and such duties, it reminded Brazier of his own childhood home in Hampshire, bringing to mind the smell of freshly baked bread. That always managed to give his maternal grandfather indigestion, which had him drink near-boiling water to relieve it. His father was often away at sea, but when he was home Brazier felt complete.

As a ship's surgeon he dealt with the common ailments of tars and was circumspect in description, so it had been a few years of ignorance for son Edward before he witnessed, at too close a hand, what those ailments were. Sailors were permanently costive from too restricted a diet, which required extraction by a long probing spoon dipped in oil.

Delirium tremens brought on by an excess of harboured rum rations, too swiftly consumed, or a long period of drunkenness ashore – and that usually meant the pox as well, which brought out mercury and the terrifying probe. Worst of all were the results of a severe flogging for some heinous crime; a mincemeat back added to the luminosity of battered flesh, running with blood, fresh enough to glint in the morning light.

When Roger Colpoys emerged, it was obvious he was the master of Home Farm. It lay in the overbearing way he waved his riding crop, added to the adopted spread-feet stance of impatience, when whatever unheard instructions he issued took too long to be obeyed. Brazier could see, but not hear him, shouting at his children and that pleased him, though he had no idea why. They did their best to ignore their irate sire even when he was remonstrating them from the elevation of the mounting block. Eventually he had his horse brought out, got astride it and, with the gate opened in readiness, rode off at a fast canter. And then there was nothing.

Home Farm fell, as it would, into its daily routine: servants going about their duties, piles of stinking hay being forked out of the stables onto carts, to join the collected dung being taken to the fields as fertiliser. The arrival of a dog cart set his blood running, until it disgorged an elderly, stooped cove, carrying books.

If Dutchy, Peddler and Cocky could not see as clearly as their captain, it took no great wit to comprehend little of interest was going on and time was flying by. Peddler was moaning about being hungry, for the sun had peaked, which got a scoff from his mates for his rumbling gut.

'Happen they'll hear that belly rumblin' doon the hoose, Dutchy, what d'ye reckon?'

'They will if you fart, you Scots git,' the victim of this jibe growled.

'Fool's errand this one,' Peddler insisted. 'By my reckonin', the Turk can't go near the place.'

'What tell't ye that?' asked Cocky.

'If he could, we would have knocked at the door right off, as sweet as kiss my hand, to be shown in to a farmhouse breakfast.'

'Some folk,' Cocky cawed, 'the sensible ones, dream about wimen. Wi' you it's eggs and smoked ham.'

'Lasts longer as pleasure, Cocky, old mate. Fill a sack, instead of drainin' it.'

'Coach comin', lads.'

Dutchy's warning had all three sink into the tall meadow grass, left with the sound of clopping hooves, as a Berlin approached the gate of Home Farm, that opened by a lad rushing to the duty. Even at a distance, once the step had been lowered, the trio could see two women alight. Only Edward Brazier, using his telescope, could put names to the figures.

He felt a near physical pain to see Betsey, replaced by a flash of anger as he identified the inevitable aunt. A swift shift showed Annabel Colpoys in the doorway, a gesture of welcome very obvious. Words were being exchanged and he could not hear them. Would the Colpoys woman convey back to Betsey his determination to rescue her? If not, what could he do?

Brazier needed no secret gate to gain access to Cottington Court. A man who could climb a hundred feet of rigging in a howling gale would not be troubled by a mere brick wall. But the obstacle was not made of stone. He needed to know that Betsey would be waiting, of which he was reasonably sure. If

Betsey was a regular visitor to Home Farm, and she had been there a day or two before, would this be the best place from which to snatch her to safety? These thoughts occupied him as the three women disappeared indoors.

But about what were they speaking? With Sarah Lovell present, he doubted it would be about him, unless it was deeply unflattering. Now they were out of sight, he could allow his thinking free rein, even if, in doing so, he visited upon himself the maximum degree of discomfort. To add to that and complicate any half-formed plans, he saw the two coachmen from Cottington take up station without the gate, one with a fowling piece very prominently displayed. Precautions were being taken, a notion no doubt emanating from Betsey's brother.

CHAPTER TWENTY-TWO

The previous meeting with Annabel Colpoys had been bizarre: this one was even more so. At least Roger, with his forced cheerfulness, was absent, but two of this trio of women were engaged in a strained conversation, with only Sarah Lovell seemingly impervious to the atmosphere. In some ways she was acting as if a different person, less self-contained, talking, indeed quietly boasting, about her life prior coming to live at Cottington Court.

Annabel did not know her as well as Betsey; her aunt was not a regular visitor to Home Farm, in truth no visitor at all, unless part of a general social gathering, so Annabel had to be less aware of the change in her behaviour. While seemingly listening in rapt attention to the level of the Lovell couple's social pre-eminence, the two friends were trying to communicate, by look and slight gestures, an almost impossible message to convey.

'I think it is fair to reflect that our opinion mattered,' was imparted with smug satisfaction. 'Mr Lovell was admired for his sage commercial advice, while I know that my good opinion, on the behaviour of the society to which we were part . . .'

'Surely you mean the society of which you were leader, Aunt Sarah?' Betsey interrupted.

There followed a remarkably quick transformation in expressions; first the self-righteous look disappeared, to be replaced, for no more than a split second, by the pinched appearance of someone who knew she was being challenged. But that evaporated just as swiftly, to be replaced with a condescending smile.

'One does not like to boast, Elisabeth, but you are, of course, correct. My opinion was canvassed by many on the merits, or otherwise, of any proposed action, which might even have marginally detracted from the accepted norms. Standards had to be maintained, for if they are not, what ensues?'

'You are so right, Mrs Lovell,' Annabel interjected, clearly seeking to strike a middle way, but managing to get in a barb as well, given she was looking at Betsey. 'The behaviour of some people beggars belief.'

Sarah Lovell had no choice but to agree, but her niece had some hope she might be drawn to reflecting on her own actions. In the very short silence that followed, Betsey and Annabel exchanged another look, which had within it the slightest nod, an attempt to pass the message that the note had been delivered. The response was so vague, Annabel had no idea if her friend had got it.

Betsey's mind was operating on two levels, the first obvious. But she was also wondering if she should burst this bubble of self-aggrandisement in which her aunt was indulging, for she knew it to be gross exaggeration. There was a temptation to ask her where said Mr Lovell, that paragon of advice on money matters, was now. It had ended up with both of them living off Tulkington charity.

How much other people knew about her misfortunes was moot. She never openly discussed it, even within her adopted home and it was not even extensively aired by the family. This was not from a feeling of disgrace, but from an assurance that it was no one else's business. Samuel Lovell had upped and left without explanation and it seemed crass to over-enquire. Thus, the surprise was total when Sarah Lovell addressed the point directly, quite forgetting some of the things she had just said.

'I cannot tell you how badly my husband took it to find that people in whom he placed absolute trust were so dishonest in the most egregious way. He was brought low by trust, Mrs Colpoys.' The look aimed at Betsey was flinty in its defiance. It seemed to say, check me if you dare! 'But he is an astute man of affairs and is, I am sure, working to repair both his reputation and our position in society.'

He had been gone for years! Being well raised, she did battle with the desire to tell the truth, but what won over all was the need to keep this woman onside. To challenge this utter farrago of an explanation for being deserted by her husband would be futile. Likewise, undermining her claim to social prominence. Nothing Betsey had heard in the years since her aunt had shared Cottington led her to suspect there was even a sliver of truth in any of her assertions.

It was not hard to see through what was being implied: that Samuel Lovell, through shame at his position, had gone off, in secret and without explanation, to repair his fortune and would return in triumph, when that happy estate had been achieved, to reconnect with the woman he loved and had so disappointed.

'Men do too often suffer from feelings of shame.'

Annabel said this with a sad face, leaving Betsey wondering if she was talking about Roger. Sarah Lovell was looking at her in a funny way, which hinted at the notion her wholly imagined, sainted Samuel, was being made to sound vapid, but there was added a soothing addendum.

'And the pity is, they will not share the burden, for, despite their common opinion, we women are stronger than they by some margin.'

'How very right you are, Mrs Colpoys,' was the firm agreement, from an enthused Aunt Sarah. 'They are frailer than they know.'

'Some men are, of course, strong on the course they have set, and I'm sure your husband will be that.'

If Sarah Lovell preened in agreement and was so busy feeling vindicated, she failed to notice the last remark was aimed directly at her niece, who got the message clearly: Annabel was telling her Edward Brazier would not waver. She was thus happy when her aunt declared they should be going.

'I would wish to be allowed to call again, Mrs Colpoys,' Sarah Lovell said, when she was back in her cloak, which got an odd look from her hostess. 'In the company of Elisabeth, of course. I know how close you are to each other.'

'You are most welcome to call, as is Betsey, although I would wish for some prior warning. With three children to see to, I must be sure I can afford you proper attention.'

'I think you will find, Mrs Colpoys, that when it comes to

the proper exercise of good manners, there are few who can surpass me.'

It was as well she turned away then to take her gloves from the waiting servant, which allowed her to miss the look of fury on Annabel's face, quickly masked as she addressed Betsey, moving to embrace her.

'You know you are always welcome.'

'Perhaps you could call on us, Annabel, and bring the children over to play in the woods and around the lake, which we used to do ourselves.'

Just about to agree, the response was dampened. 'Yes, Elisabeth, we must enquire of Henry if that would be appropriate.'

'Gone? Gone where?'

'I believe it was to visit Home Farm, sir,' Grady responded, ignoring the glare that went with the question. As usual he kept his eyes from contact, aiming them just above his master's head.

'Again?' was larded with suspicion. 'And who came up with that notion?'

That was not an enquiry to which it would be wise to respond so Grady did not. He waited for what was to follow, but that merely turned out as a demand to tell him when they returned.

'I will be in my study. Fetch me some coffee.'

On the way there, and once settled at his desk, Henry sought to deduce if there had been anything in Upton's expression to arouse suspicion. The fact that he had, once dismounted, pushed aside the boy sent to bring in his horse, and instead led his own mount into the stables, was singular. He rarely visited the stables or the stud farm, having little interest in matters equine, outside the value gained from the sales.

With what Creevy had told him, added to a memory of his sister's love of riding as well as looking after horses, there were good grounds to be suspicious. Elisabeth had spent much time in the stables and, as a young woman, insisted on grooming her own animals and even, on occasion, mucking out their stalls.

He could well recall the obnoxious stink of horse piss and damp straw that attended her when she came in from carrying out such menial talks. Also a memory was her being distraught when they died, or fell so ill they had to be put out of their misery. It was an attraction he had never understood: a horse was a means of conveyance, nothing else.

Which took his mind back to Upton. Was there a difference in his attitude, enough to warrant a feeling of disquiet? And then there had been that damned blacksmith banging away at horseshoes to kill any chance of subtle enquiries. He could not put a finger on anything specific, other than a vague suspicion. More pressing was the fact of that second visit to the Colpoys, which could only have been sanctioned by his aunt, and that was troubling. A week ago, she would not have dared act in such a fashion without consulting him first.

The knock brought him coffee and biscuits, plus the news that he was being called upon by the Reverend Joshua Moyle, which, initially unwelcome, quickly came to be seen as the very opposite: a distraction. After a trying day in which he had travelled far and encountered some success, as well as one intractable problem, the thought of sharing a glass or two with Moyle, whose antics always amused him, appealed.

There would be no challenge in it, apart from the effort to avoid going glass for glass with the divine, for Joshua Moyle was a toper of quite exceptional ability. His faith was the opposite, skin-deep and wholly to do with self-interest. He would act – and had – in whatever capacity Henry Tulkington wanted in order to keep his living. It was probably the only sentiment wholly shared by his long-suffering wife. Few dispensers of such offices would employ Moyle, while the Church probably reckoned him an embarrassment.

'Best fetch the brandy, Grady, and some wine for me.'

It was rare to see Moyle sober; even in such a state he looked far from the priest he should be. His clothing tended to the unkempt, his waistcoat a repository for much of the snuff that missed his nostrils. The face was cratered with veins and the hair was wild, grey and unruly. That admitted, he was generally a cheerful soul, but not this day. Having greeted Henry in serious mien, he sat down heavily and addressed him with gravity.

'Had the oddest enquiry today, from the diocese.'

'On what?'

That got Henry a jaundiced look, as if to say there was only one matter that was germane. 'About the wedding.'

Any response had to wait 'til Grady had knocked, come in and placed the drinks ordered on the desk. Eyeing the bottle of brandy, Moyle surprised both when he said in a serious tone, 'Best stick to coffee for now.'

'That will be all, Grady.' Door closed, Henry enquired, 'What kind of query?'

'Was it properly done?'

'And your response?'

'Unequivocally yes, but why was the question being posed?'

'You might know that better than I.'

'It wouldn't have been asked, had there not been someone babbling. I haven't had a visit from the bishop's chaplain since I took up my post here. But there he was, yesterday, looking through the register and asking about the weddings I've conducted.'

'Of which there are not many, Moyle.'

There was a pointed reference in that; anyone of social standing locally would not use Cottington for the ceremony, they would apply to St Leonard's in Upper Deal and, in the odd exception, to St George's. The Tulkingtons themselves rarely visited, only attending at Christmas, Easter and the various festivals like the Harvest, all occasions that brought to the pews the estate workers. Henry was obliged to attend as lord of the manor.

'Why was he asking, though?'

'What did he say, apart from looking at the register?'

'That it might be time I paid a visit to the Bishop, who, it was pointed out, I had never paid my respects to since his appointment.'

'A short trip to Dover will do you no harm,' Henry said in a jocular way.

'It's not amusing. The ceremony I carried out was—'

The jocose manner evaporated in an instant, as Henry barked, 'Correct in every way, Moyle.'

The rheumy eyes watered slightly, a sure sign of self-pity. 'If you insist on it being so.'

'Which I do. Now for the sake of the Lord, if not the Bishop in Canterbury, have some brandy, lest I think there's been a second coming.'

'If it's referred up to the Archbishop, well, what then?'

Moyle threw up his hands at such a prospect. The supreme head of the Anglican Church was not a man he ever wished to meet. Henry forbore to say the chances were slight from a divine who spent most of his time living in Lambeth Palace, so as to be close to both government and royalty. Because of his near permanent absence, the incumbent in Dover was given oversight of the Canterbury diocese.

Henry poured a brandy and took it to Moyle, holding it close enough under his nose to allow the fumes to rise. The man was in a faraway mood, no doubt imagining all sorts of ecclesiastical difficulties. His hand took the goblet absent-mindedly and the act of putting to his lips followed in the same manner.

'We must hold steady, Moyle,' Henry said.

'Aye,' came with a blast of bottled-up air.

It occurred to Henry, watching him, that there was a danger of him admitting the truth of Elisabeth's wedding. It was as likely to come from drunkenness as from guilty sobriety, which was a worry to add to the several he already had. The knock at the door brought Grady again.

'Mrs Lovell and your sister have returned, sir.'

'Do you not mean, Grady,' came the icy response, 'Mrs Lovell and Mrs Spafford?'

The whole contents of Moyle's brandy glass disappeared down his throat.

* * *

'Henry, if she is left to mope around the house she will do something dangerous to test your constraints.' Sarah Lovell put down her soup spoon and spoke with real emphasis. 'Let me take her to meet her friends and acquaintances, which will help to lance her frustrations. Elisabeth needs time.'

Henry, looking into his own bowl, wanted to respond by saying she needed the whip and always had, but that was held back. He was seeking to adjust to his aunt's very obvious and new-found air of confidence. Previously, she had ever been careful to avoid direct eye contact; now she was looking at him in a manner very close to being a test. Yet he could hardly argue against her point regarding time being a healer, one he himself had cogitated upon.

'Perhaps Elisabeth and I should speak to each other directly.'

'I doubt she would readily agree.'

'Then I look to you to persuade her,' he snarled.

Again, there was the difference: instead of being cowed by his blast of frustration she held his gaze, as if to say to him, such a request is mine to accede to or deny.

'I have things to convey to her, which I think might mitigate her hostility.'

They had to wait while servants came to remove the soup plates and put before them the broiled chicken, potatoes and vegetables that had been ordered for dinner. Then Grady had to pour the right wine for that course before withdrawing, having ensured all was well.

'Those things are?'

'Certain facts I have come across, Aunt Sarah, which may temper this mad passion for that damned sailor.'

'Henry!'

He did apologise for his language, but it was perfunctory: a man had a right to blaspheme in his own house. 'Let me just say, Brazier is not the paragon Elisabeth sees him to be.'

'He is ten times the man you will ever be, Henry.'

That came from the doorway, in which Betsey stood, her face a mask of fury. If she thought it would throw her brother, she was mistaken. He produced one of those humourless smiles she so detested.

'I wonder if you will hold to that when he's being taken up the Newgate steps, to have a rope put round his neck. Or will you choose, unlike myself, to bear witness to the justified demise of a convicted murderer?'

It was Henry's turn to be thrown as Betsey let forth with a laugh. 'I never had you down for a fool, Henry. A misery, yes—'

'Close the damned door!' A shocked Sarah Lovell put her napkin to her mouth, though whether it was brought on by blasphemy or noise was unknowable. 'Are we to have our conversations held in the hearing of the servants?'

'Why hide from them what they already know, Brother, and have done since you were first able to talk? Your servants despise you as much as I now do. To think I recommended so recently that you should seek a wife. God forbid such a fate should befall one of my sex.'

'Perhaps I should bring Spafford back to Cottington and lock you both in a room. Would you be so spirited then, I wonder?'

'If you do, I should send for an undertaker, for one of us will not emerge alive.'

With that the door was slammed, with Sarah Lovell opining

in a soft and very disapproving voice, 'Henry, such references are untoward.'

The day had started well and gone to the bad. First his frustration at not being able to extract proper redress from Sowerby, then coming home to his suspicions of Upton and getting nowhere. The annoyance of finding both his sister and aunt out of the house without this permission rankled. Finally came Moyle and his fear of the damned bishop. Put together it was enough to make his blood boil. It certainly had an effect on his response to being checked on the matter of carnality.

'Aunt Sarah, it has never been my way to tell you to shut up, although it is often warranted, but I do so now. Either stick to eating your dinner, or go and leave me in peace.'

Henry was never to know that in her new-found confidence she addressed him as she would her absent husband, just as she would never acknowledge the possibility that her constant carping, which had been bad before he lost all their money but had made her a termagant afterwards, might be what had driven him away.

'I will leave you, Henry. But in peace? That, I doubt you deserve.'

CHAPTER TWENTY-THREE

If there had been little wisdom in observing Home Farm, there was possibly even less in what Brazier did when the coach had departed. Dutchy, who had him in view, saw him rise up and head down the hill, there being little doubt where he was headed, which had him call to the others.

'We're under way, lads, and, I reckon, heading for stormy waters.'

'Well, leastways, I won't be seasick,' Pedder complained. 'There be owt in my gut to puke up.'

He was at the gate by the time they were halfway down the hill, with Dutchy calling a halt. 'We can see from here if there be trouble.'

The dogs alerted the occupants of the farm to Brazier's presence, rushing to bark through the bars of the gate with more excitement than threat. Of the few people around there was one elderly fellow, with a long pipe in his mouth, who saw it as his duty to come and enquire of his business. As he was approaching, Brazier caught sight of a trio of young faces, full of curiosity, at an upstairs window.

'I would like to see Mrs Colpoys.'

'And who should I say is a'calling sir?'

'Just tell her it's a naval officer. She will require no more. And also tell her I will not depart until we have spoken.'

The old fellow blinked and his jaw started working as he sought to make sense of the reply by chewing. But whether it eluded him, or fired his imagination, he did as he was bid and went to the front door of the house, a servant answering his knock. It made Brazier curious as to why they had not responded before. They must have heard the dogs, now wagging their tails and competing for affection.

It was several minutes before Annabel Colpoys came to the door to look out at him, but she failed to move from there or indicate that he should enter, her confusion obvious. Tempted to shout and reassure her, he stopped himself; that would probably drive her back indoors. Finally, she must have decided having him in the house was more discreet than any public exchange, so she told the servant to fetch him in.

Brazier was struck again by a touch of nostalgia on entry, for if the exterior of the farm and house evoked memories, so did the interior. There was none of the finery of Cottington: this was a working, occupied household and if the furniture was of decent quality, it showed it had been subjected to human usage. It felt like home.

'I promise not to stay long.'

'You'd better not, for my husband will be home shortly and he is prone to the horsewhip if aroused.'

It would not serve to say he would be prone to a ducking or a clout with a club if he tried, so he acknowledged the right. He

290

was, after all, a strange man, by his hearth, with his wife when he was absent. People had been shot for less.

'I saw your visitors come and go.'

'I guessed as much, otherwise you would not be here.'

'I need to know—'

She cut across him. 'Betsey has been told of the delivery.'

'And?'

'And what?' came querulously. 'I suppose you wish to know if there was a response. Well, let me tell you, even to allude to you with Betsey's aunt present was impossible. I am sure I managed to convey to her that you are not downhearted.'

'Hardly true,' he said softly.

'You know what I mean. That you are determined to save her. How that is to be achieved, I do not know and neither do I want to know. Now, you have come for that which you required. Oblige me by departing.'

'I want—'

'Captain Brazier, I have already told you I am not prepared to be your messenger.'

'Then be Betsey's. All I ask is that you find out if she is willing to be rescued from Cottington Court. By the fact she has an armed escort, I suspect it cannot be done elsewhere without great risk.'

'Armed escort?'

Which meant she had not seen them; explained, it did nothing to cheer her mood. 'This will end badly.'

'It depends on for whom. Find out if she's willing and leave the rest to me. That's all I ask.'

'In itself, it is a great deal.'

'If I were to call again in a couple of days . . .'

'No.'

'Because it might embarrass you with your husband?'

'Are you witless? You have already embarrassed me with my husband. Do you not think he will hear of the calling of a stranger, one I invited into his house? He will be told of it as soon as he returns and, if not by one of the farm hands, then by a servant.'

'Or perhaps your children, whom I saw at their window.' She slowly shook her head. 'Surely you can explain?'

'You do not know my Roger.'

'I can stay and do so, if you wish.'

That got a small, breathy laugh. 'Go, please. I doubt I will be able to deliver your message, but I will try for the sake of my dear friend.'

'And how will I know the answer?'

'You must leave me to find a way to solve that. But oblige me by never calling at Home Farm again. I want that as a promise, for I believe you to be a man of your word.'

'You have it, and thank you. How much better it would have been if we'd become acquainted at a wedding.'

Once he had gone, Annabel sat and pondered for an age; that was until the children, free of any lessons, their afternoon session having ended, created too much noise to easily think. Oddly, it was that which provided the possible solution. Sarah Lovell had as good as invited her and them over to play in the woods. What better place to find out what she needed to know?

The next problem was how to deal with her husband, who

came barrelling in, riding crop waving, to demand why she was receiving strangers in the house. 'Don't you mean strange men, Roger?'

That calm enquiry threw him; he was all set for meek explanation. Her soft tone he found harder to deal with than noisy defiance. 'It's damned unbecoming. What happens if it gets talked about?'

'The person most likely to talk about it is you.' Seeing him about to explode, she did finally shout. 'Do you think so lowly of me that you would harbour doubts about my virtue, or allow anyone to impugn it? Perhaps Henry Tulkington will be able to say to you what he likes, and you will meekly accept it.'

'I'm damned if I know what you mean.'

Her voice dropped, but now it held a note of sadness. 'Don't you, Roger?'

'I've a damn good notion to let you feel this crop.'

'Do so, Husband, if it serves to make you feel like a man.' He had it up in the air ready to strike, seemingly oblivious to the three young and alarmed faces just outside the door. 'But that would be better served by taking it to the man just mentioned. The pity is, you don't dare.'

'I—'

'I know, Roger. I want to ask you to tell me how I should feel about it. If you will not defend yourself, will you do that for me or the children?' She had stopped him, it was in his eyes, slowly more obvious as the crop dropped to his side. 'Let me tell you what he has done to his own sister.'

'I won't hear a word against the fellow,' were words lacking in force.

293

'You will, and from me. Now pour yourself your dose of claret, which I suspect acts as a balm to your conscience, while I see the children fed.'

When she came back, having given the orders for the children's meal, she saw him standing over the unlit fireplace. There was a glass of claret on the mantle, seemingly untouched, and by his posture it appeared all the passion, which was his normal mode of behaviour, had gone out of him. Annabel closed the door and, if he heard her, he did not turn round, so she told him about Betsey, in a low voice and without passion. She named Edward Brazier, the man her friend had wanted to wed, as the caller. It was only when she voiced her intention to help reverse matters that he reacted.

'I forbid it, Annabel.'

'Which means for the first time in our lives together, I will have to defy you.'

'You can't fight Tulkington.'

'You may not be able to, but I intend to try. What happened between him and you?'

'Don't tell me you did not guess.' She waited, hoping for more, but not sure it would come. 'He set his brutes upon me, not that it was ever admitted by him. I met him afterwards and it was as if he had no knowledge. But the words used by those beating me with clubs left me in no doubt of the consequences of defiance. So I dropped the boundary suit.'

'You could have fought on, I would have supported you.'

'Then you might have ended up a widow and my children would have been without a father.'

'You believe that?'

'After what you have just told me, I would be surprised if you do not.' He turned round finally, showing eyes reddened by now-dried tears. 'Tulkington controls everything around these parts. I made discreet enquiries about having him taken up for what was done to me. It is at such times you find out who your friends are. No one was prepared to lift a finger.'

'So you will appease him.'

'As I must, until those mites sitting eating are old enough to take over from me. Then perhaps . . .'

Annabel walked over and kissed him gently on the cheek, then took his glass from the mantle and put it in his hand. 'Drink it, Roger, and bellow, or our mites will wonder if you have been struck down.'

Upton was a poor reader of signs. It never occurred to him that Henry Tulkington, bringing his own mount into the stable the day before, signified anything. So when he said he was going to make a visit to the stud, taking the north gate key and one of the spare coach horses with him, and sure Miss Elisabeth would be out on her usual mid-morning walk, he saw matters as progressing nicely.

Creevy, alerted to keep an eye out, was outside his master's study window, and informed him as soon as he saw the route Upton was taking. For all his desire for subterfuge, Henry was not one to go out in his indoor clothing; he required a cloak, a hat plus a muffler. Given there was no call for a coach or a horse it engendered curiosity in Grady, then, when he thought about it, a degree of alarm. Added to that was the knowledge that if it did point to trouble, he could do nothing to aid his friend. So he busied himself with the tasks that filled his day, all done, on this occasion, with a silent prayer.

The path Henry was on was not unfamiliar, it was just not one he took much pleasure in. He rarely walked anywhere by habit, which, to his way of thinking, was just another fundamental difference between him and his sister. There had been some rain overnight, so the ground was soft enough to show the odd hoof print and these he followed. Instead of taking him to the lake as he had thought, they went in the direction of the north gate.

He finally spied Upton, not far from where he reckoned the gate to be. Or, to be more precise, he saw the horse he thought was normally hitched to his carriage visible through the trees. Its moving head drew his eye as it cropped the grass. Upton came into view with a slight sideways shift, and there too was Elisabeth, deep in conversation, but very frustratingly, much too far away to overhear.

Not being a natural country fellow, Henry felt it would not do to seek to get closer. Then something occurred which rendered it unnecessary. Upton was holding up a key, one large enough to be seen at a distance, and it took no great imagination to work out what it might fit. Shoulder against an oak, he watched them talk, saw the key being waved, in another part of his mind recalling that these two had always had a connection, one he was sure went beyond mere respect.

Not trusting servants was not just a habit of his; it was a common topic when he met with others, not least their stupidity in the acts they expected to get away with. Was Upton plotting to help Elisabeth escape? He could very easily see the way it would be done. Nor was there any doubt as to where she would go. The groom would suspect, since he never visited the stables or the stud, he would not know a horse was gone. With the gate padlock intact, he might not even suspect the means.

Having seen everything he thought he needed, Henry crept back until he was sure he was well out of sight, then strode out for home. He must be back indoors before Elisabeth returned, which made him stop. What if she was planning to leave this very minute? Thinking hard, he concluded not; what he had observed indicated they had been plotting some future event. Back indoors, disrobed and in front of the fire in his study, he could warm his hands and consider how to handle matters.

Upton had to go, but how to effect it? Would he seek to follow Elisabeth again, either the next day or one thereafter? The thought of catching them in the act provided a delicious frisson of excitement, but that soon subsided; Henry chuckled at his own silent pun, regarding shutting stable doors after his sister had bolted, but there was a serious side to that, which meant waiting was risky.

Should he dismiss Upton with Elisabeth looking on, as a signal her hopes were ever destined to be dashed? Or just leave her to find out, which would have its own pleasures, albeit he would not witness her despair.

'If it were to be done, it were best done quickly,' he said to himself, vaguely trying and failing to recall if that was a Shakespearean tag, when it was time to go in search of Creevy.

'I need to know when a certain party is seen returning. Come to my study window and knock once more.'

'Got it clear, your honour.'

He waited impatiently until the gardener finally appeared and a knock was all he got. Elisabeth was already in and back to her room before Upton appeared, leading the horse he had taken out. The shock came when it was led into the stables, for Henry Tulkington was waiting for him, looking grim. Beside him stood the most senior of his boys, who could not look him in the eye.

'Mister Tulkington, sir, two visits to your stables in two days. I's honoured.'

'Honour,' Henry said, seeming to roll the word around in his mouth. 'Not, I think, given the circumstances, a word that is appropriate.'

Upton was thinking, but not about what he feared might be coming. It was the cook on whom he had been sweet for such a long time. He could almost feel her lips, the stolen kisses and the promise of so much more, the thought bringing a lump to his throat. This he fought to control; he was not going to break down in front of this man.

'I know you are conspiring with my sister. I saw you this very morning. You have in your possession a certain key, the one that lets you out to the paddocks.' A hand was held out and, once the object was fetched from his pocket, it was snatched from his hand. 'I suspect, on the coming visit, you plan to use this to let my sister exit alongside you, to perhaps take out a horse already placed in the paddocks.'

'I admit to talking with Miss Elisabeth on her walks, but it be because I've known her for years and I see her as lonely.'

'That, Upton, is not your place.'

'Didn't reckon it forbidden,' came out with a hint of defiance.

'How dare you assume what is permitted and what is not? That is for me to decide, as it is I who employ – and those I do, Upton, must have my complete trust. That you have forfeited, so pack a sack with your possessions. I want you out of Cottington Court as soon as that is done!'

Henry drove home the disgrace by handing the key he was holding, which for many years had been Upton's to care for, to the lad who would succeed him. He, embarrassed, required a nod to accept it.

'Your things.'

In his upstairs cubbyhole, as he shoved his possessions into a sack, Upton was left to ruminate on how little he had accumulated in his years of service. A set of slightly better clothes for the annual celebrations, which took him to church. A few knick-knacks he had fashioned in his spare time, and a pair of good boots he got as a gift from the saddle maker for putting business his way. There was a set of kitchen implements provided by the visiting blacksmith, which were, one day, going to be put to furnishing the kitchen he and the cook had dreamt of. They were too heavy to carry and would have to be left.

From behind a loose and removed brick he took a small leather pouch, a very limited stash accumulated over the years, mostly gifts from visiting gentry for care of their horses. It was money that would be going, one day, to pay for a wedding and the entertainment after. What did it matter now? That dream was shattered.

Back down from the loft, sack slung over his shoulder, all that was needed to set him on his way was a hand gesture from Tulkington, pointing towards the main gate. There were to be no farewells, none of the senior servants dared to show sympathy and watch him depart; to do so would anger their master. Even Tanner, well away from the house, had a care to keep his nod of farewell discreet.

Outside the gate, thanking God he had not been searched, he turned for Deal, feeling in his pocket the second key, made as a copy by the blacksmith, the one he had shown to Miss Elisabeth to compare with the original that very morning. He had wanted to give it to her, but she suggested it should stay with him until it was to be used, worried that whatever precautions they took, he would be accused of providing her with aid when she was found to be missing.

'Do you think it has not been observed, you taking the path to the lake when I'm out walking? What happens if my brother questions everybody, which he will surely do? Will they risk their place to lie to him about that? You need to be solid in your explanations, for it would grieve me that you should suffer. If the worst happens, I must send you to where you will find shelter.'

He was to make for a place called Quebec House, but that would have to wait 'til the morrow. For tonight, he must find a place to lay his head.

CHAPTER TWENTY-FOUR

Edward Brazier, as he walked through the town the following morning, was too preoccupied to notice anything unusual. Had he been more aware, he would have sensed every eye seemed to be upon him, people peering at him as if seeking something internal, rather than the fact of a naval officer merely making his way to wherever he was going. Perhaps his lack of awareness lay in the fact that he was accustomed to attention of that sort.

Aboard ship, when the captain was pacing the quarterdeck with anything in the nature of action being imminent, he became the subject of excessive scrutiny and for a very good reason. From him would flow whatever followed, and seeking to guess what that might be was the common purpose of everyone from the waisters to the premier.

Dutchy Holland, following a few paces behind, and Brazier's sole escort on this morning, had a sharper antennae, so sensed something amiss. Because no one was looking at him, he could see the way they were eyeing Brazier, to the point, in one or two cases, of stopping, once he had passed them by, to take in his back.

The tasks of this morning were first, to drop by the office of Saoirse Riorden's lawyer and pay his rent, and to then go on and settle the various bills being run up to keep Quebec House going; food and fuel, plus deliveries of wine. This could have been entrusted to Joe Lascelles, but Brazier saw it as occupying him when he was in limbo.

Some twenty yards behind him and Dutchy, the grubby youngster trailing them was part of the scenery and no cause for comment. It would be his task to tell John Hawker where Brazier had gone and who, if anyone, he visited. Having been out and around the town the previous night, disbursing liberally in the article of bought ale, Hawker knew the cursing and coupling of Brazier and Pitt was coming to a satisfying head. This night, and after he had settled his own bill, he would ensure it caught light. First, he had to make sure the other part of the intention knew what was required of him, unable to avoid alluding to the reward Tulkington had offered.

'You would never have got such an arrangement from me, Spafford. I would have tied you to the tiller of your lugger in deep water then knocked out the bilge planking.'

Spafford, his ruddy face part hidden by days of growth, managed a grin and a shake of his shackles. 'Can't wait to tell Tulkington you think he's gone soft.'

'He knows my thinkin',' Hawker growled, 'so don't you go bothering.'

'Sold any poor bugger to the Revenue today?'

That had Hawker ball a fist, but it stayed by his side as a still-grinning Spafford drove home what was, in truth, a guess. It was based on a number of inexplicable happenings over many years about which, locked up here, he'd had time to recall and wonder about. Beach folk being nabbed at the same time as there were indications a Tulkington's cargo was coming in.

It had clearly never occurred to Hawker that his way of playing both ends against the middle was not as clandestine as he supposed and he was thrown off balance. Spafford drove the point home.

'Offer up a sprat to save Tulkington's mackerel is it? Happen there will be a temptation to dob me in, once I'm back at the trade.'

'Why bother,' was unconvincing and told Spafford he had hit a nerve.

'Tell that streak of piss you work for, if he tries that on me, every ear in Deal will know how many suffer, with his blessing, to keep him safe. An' you'll never get out of Deal alive.'

'Who's goin' to believe the likes of Dan Spafford?' came with a manufactured sneer.

'The same fools who will fall for a fancy tale about some sailor cove being hand in glove with Billy Pitt. Who is he, anyway, and what's he done to get Tulkington so het up?'

'None of your concern. Just do as you're bid when darkness falls, then get back to grubbing for a crust. First, you've got to talk to your men and tell them what's been arranged.'

'They don't know yet?' Hawker just shook his head. 'Need to tell 'em what's been agreed too.'

'Up to you, Spafford. I'll have jugs of ale and some gin fetched in to get them in the right mood.'

'What a caring soul you are.'

* * *

Betsey, out on her walk, as was normal, wondered where Upton had got to. This was to be the morning in which he would let her out of the gate, using the key he had contrived to have made, and immediately return to the stables to cover his back. A horse she could manage easily had been left in the paddock beforehand, for the notion of fetching along a saddle was too obvious.

'Best I leave the real key behind, Miss Elisabeth – forgetful, like.' Upton had said this with the air of a man pleased at his cunning. 'You must take the one I will use with you. Then, once you're out, I can go back to the stables and slap my head for the booby I am for leaving without the key. Any suspicions an' you'll be far gone.'

All she could do was make for the spot where the plot had been hatched and wait with mounting frustration mixed with anxiety, aware of time going by and the need not to be away from the house longer than was normal. With a sinking feeling, she finally began to retrace her steps, as usual, when she entered the formal garden, taking a doffed cap and a greeting from Creevy.

She was sorely tempted to cross to the opposite gate, which led to the stables. That had to be resisted, so she went to and opened the front door to find Henry in the hallway. Both his presence and the look on his face, a superior air, led her to suspect her plan had been thwarted, not that she let on in any way; she just tried to ignore him.

Grady appeared, as he always did, to take her cloak, his long face a mask devoid of emotion. If something had happened to Upton, he would know about it and, if he had never been as open as the groom, she was sure he felt sympathy for her. But there was no chance of showing any with his master standing close by; he was not going to let on by even a gesture.

'That will be all, Grady,' Henry said, which had the servant depart with more than normal haste. As Betsey moved towards the staircase, her brother sought to block her way 'Much as you may not wish it, Elisabeth, you and I are going to have to talk.'

'We have nothing to discuss.'

'Yes we do, not least how unsuitable was your choice of prospective husband.' That required another sideways shuffle to block her attempt to progress. 'I have learnt things about him that entirely vindicate my initial reservations. Call it intuition.'

Betsey actually laughed, a little forced and louder than she felt it warranted, but enough to have the effect required. Henry hated to be laughed at more than anything, a fact she had known from a very early age. It was a pleasure to see colour come to his pallid face, a sure sign of anger, proved by his grating tone.

'It had been imparted to me that he may well have committed murder.'

'Then I am not the only one to think you stupid.'

'Practice of your wit will not alter the facts.'

'Facts? What you surely mean is your imaginings, or the bile someone has been pouring into your only-too-ready-to-listen ear. Now you will oblige me by standing aside and allowing me the stairs.'

'So who killed Admiral Hassall?' Henry asked, expecting her to be shocked.

'A snake killed him, one of your venomous kindred spirits.'

'You knew of this?'

'Not that it's any of your concern, Henry, but I knew of a great deal of idle gossip, most of it generated by jealousy at Edward's good fortune. To that was added a strong dislike in the planter community for a man who put his duty before the notion of popularity. Now, do I have to push you aside or will you get out of the way?'

'My God, you need to be tamed.'

'I need to be free, Brother, and that I will have.'

She slipped by him and took the first riser, glad her back was to Henry when he said, in a voice of studied calm, 'Not with the help of Upton, you won't. That I can assure you.'

It was necessary to turn and look confused, difficult with a heart racing from disappointment. 'Upton. What about him?'

It was Henry's turn to produce forced laughter, very obviously, given there was no humour in it at all. But as he made for his study, he was meditating on the aforementioned taming to a conclusion that there was one way it might be achieved.

Not normally a man to be troubled by gossip, Daisy Trotter could scarce avoid taking an interest in what was being whispered and, in some cases, openly espoused about dealing with Brazier. For some, there was only one way to deal with spies, and even excisemen too keen on their task. It had been sorted before and it could be again.

Everyone in Deal knew this referred to the burying of a Revenue officer, one who had been so bold as to take up residence in one of the alleys leading to Middle Street, this so he could keep an eye out for the running of contraband. He had been assiduous in his application too, calling in his mates from

Dover to raid houses and search cellars and attics and knock for concealed spaces; in both he had enjoyed too much success.

The way the authorities dealt with goods found in cellars, the favourite hiding place, was to fill them with beach shingle, so they could never be used again. The method by which the community reacted, and it was few who ever did so, was to visit the same fate of the overactive sod – no one was going to finger them.

When he disappeared, there was a frantic search to find him, run by Revenue men from all over the county. Someone must have passed over a whisper, for suddenly every shingle-filled cellar in Deal was being emptied. They found him in one, located in a street running from Beach Street to Middle Street. This housed the most prosperous farrier in Deal and was generally named after that enterprise.

He had been interred under tons of pebbles and with not a mark on him to say how he expired, before or after. The horror soon spread that he had been buried alive as a message to the Revenue to stay out of the town. Should he care? Daisy didn't know; certainly he could see a reason not to, given the way he had been treated in the card room of the Old Playhouse. Yet it kept nagging him; when it came to taking on Tulkington and possibly getting Dan free, he was bereft of help. Brazier did not represent much of a chance to gain any, but there was none other possible.

This left him dithering for near the whole of the day, at one moment determining to issue a proper warning, at others, with the sneering face of Brazier recalled, a determination to leave the bugger and the tars protecting him, too few in number to take on a Deal mob fired up with drink, to stew in their own juice. All he could do was keep an eye on the slaughterhouse and hope something would turn up.

Saoirse Riorden had a feeling something was looming: she had well-honed feelers for any trouble brewing in the town, a necessity given her location on the Lower Valley Road. If there were a riot – and if such things were infrequent, they were not unknown – she knew her business lay on the main thoroughfare for protest. She needed to be sure that, as any mayhem went by, none of it got onto her premises. Being the tax gatherer's time to visit, she sought to quiz John Hawker.

'You sniffing sommat that's eluded me, Miss Riorden. And not much gets by John Hawker.'

'I would appreciate a warning if there is.'

'Do no harm,' he lied. 'If I pick up owt on my travels, I'll send a message.'

'Good of you,' Saoirse replied.

She was wondering why he was being so accommodating, a feeling that persisted after he had departed. That was not the Hawker way, which did nothing to quieten her concerns. Had he been open, Hawker would have told her she was too friendly with certain people to be trusted with what was coming, not least Vincent Flaherty and, in some way, Brazier himself. And who was the true owner of the place about to be attacked?

It was no secret she was his landlady, nor when he had been subjected to a beating, where he had been looked after. The doctor who bandaged him was not discreet and neither did he hold back on where the treatment he had administered was given. There was more than a hint that Saoirse Riorden, noted for her immunity to male attentions, might have taken more than a shine to him.

She, too, had errands to run connected with her business: food to order, a mass of materials to pay for, already delivered, which allowed her to drop hints with the various purveyors of services. But she was either talking to the wrong people, or those who had a sniff but were too unsure to let on.

In blissful ignorance of that which was brewing, Edward Brazier was being entertained by his near neighbour, Miss Elizabeth Carter, not on his own, it had to be said. Yet he was well aware of being in the company of a group of some dozen people whose erudition vastly outstripped his own. It was for once a relief that they showed a degree of interest in his career and how he had come about his rank.

'For Admiral Braddock vouchsafed to me, Captain Brazier, it did not come from the possession of interest.'

There had to be one or two of the assembly who were singularly lacking that in its true form. But they would not dare to check the famous bluestocking, for Elizabeth Carter was a person to hold her own in any gathering; in her own house she reigned supreme.

'I am told it is the bane of the service, sir: the promotion to post rank of the undeserving, for the mere quality of their connections. Do you agree?'

'I would rate it imperfect, Miss Carter, yet I have met good officers who have come up in that fashion, as well as those who, as the expression goes, came to the navy through the hawsehole. We have competent admirals who started out as ship's boys.'

'I have never heard the words competent and admiral in the

same sentence,' she replied, with an arch expression and a bit of furious fan waving, which denoted it as a sally. It turned to a smile when laughter ensued, along with calls of, 'Very droll, very droll indeed, Lizzie.'

Brazier was obliged to give a brief outline of his career, how he had come to the navy through his father's service as a ship's surgeon, added to the good offices of a serving captain who esteemed him. There were years of very little happening, several sojourns ashore on half-pay too.

'And there was, it has to be said, very little in the way of action until I sailed to the Cape of Good Hope under Commodore Johnstone.'

'Braddock was with you, he told me.'

'He was captain of one of the seventy-fours.'

Brazier went on to describe the part-failure at the Cape, redeemed by the destruction of a dozen Dutch merchantmen, then the success at Ceylon, which saw him get his step.

'And then the West Indies, Captain?'

'Dull service, Miss Carter,' was his quick response. It was a place to which he did not want to go. 'Repetitive in the extreme.'

There was a glint in her eye, which told Brazier she knew more than she was saying, which made him wonder if Braddock had been subjected to some untoward gossip through the naval grapevine. Then, of course, she had just come down from London, and moved in elevated circles when there. Who knew who was saying what? It was with gratitude he heard her address another guest to enquire on a new translation of Ovid, a subject on which he could happily stay silent.

* * *

The noise of children at Cottington Court was so unusual it brought almost all the servants out to have a look at an apparition only the oldest of them could recall. And in the Colpoys trio, they had noisemakers of quite exceptional ability, able to render their presence known within seconds of them alighting from the coach. Even within his study at the rear of the house, Henry picked up a bit of their squealing and was obliged to come out to investigate.

'What is going on?'

This was addressed to his aunt, standing at the bottom of the stairs. 'Visitors for Elisabeth, Henry. And, before you enquire, it was at my invitation.'

The look past him could only mean his sister was coming down the stairs and, with Grady standing within easy hearing distance, it was no place for remonstrating, though it could not just be allowed to pass.

'I would have been obliged if I had been asked.'

'Why trouble you, nephew?' Sarah Lovell replied, with the tiniest over-the-shoulder flick of the eyes. 'You are so busy. Anyway, it's Annabel Colpoys, Elisabeth's best friend and her children. We thought to take them down to the lake and perhaps they could even fish.'

Henry spun enough to glare at Betsey, for if he felt he had enough cause already to hate her, to that was added even more as he recalled that location and the number of times he had been used there, when home from school, as a verbal punchbag for their childish games.

'Make sure none of them drown,' was said in such a fashion that the sentiment was questionable.

'Grady, our outdoor clothing if you please. And could you ask Cook to make some of her delicious shortbread for the Colpoys children? I'm sure they will devour it. They can eat in the kitchen. We adults will take tea in the drawing room at four of the clock. Please send someone to fetch us at the appropriate time.'

If Henry did not hear it all, what he did pick up was enough to cause a slammed door, which produced from his aunt a smile and a remark.

'Must be the wind.'

CHAPTER TWENTY-FIVE

Had there ever been such a fractured conversation? Betsey wondered if it was actually possible to make full sense of any message delivered or information exchanged, one or two words at a time. Yet that was the purpose, while throughout she had to formulate a reply and articulate the difficulties that must be faced. She was made aware Edward had visited Annabel, though little of what they might have talked about could be properly imparted. It was as much by look as speech that her good friend let her know she was aware of her true situation.

After the loss of Upton and that plan being destroyed, Betsey knew she was under observation wherever she went, even within the grounds of Cottington. Annabel must have seen the way the coachmen were armed, for when that was whispered over carrot-coloured hair and a fishing rod, there was no shocked reaction.

It was necessary to keep a constant watch on Sarah Lovell who, if she could help it, was never far away from Betsey. The only method of detachment was provided by the children, with their natural needs and ability to get into situations requiring adult intervention, which included the two boys fighting. With no experience of such creatures, she was too slow to react. Betsey was no better served in that regard, but youth allowed for swift movement.

Edmund, the eldest boy, was bossy, indeed cocky, and sure he could look after himself. Roger Junior wanted so much to be older and sought to do as well, if not better than his brother, in all the activities: tree climbing, stone skimming and rod casting. Both were miniature versions of their father, while Hermione, the youngest, was a sweet child who took after her mother and was quite content making daisy chains or knotting long pieces of grass.

The conclusion to, 'Tell him to find a way,' had to wait until Roger got stuck up a tree, with, thankfully, Aunt Sarah too afraid to help in getting him down in case he dropped upon her.

'He needs a sign,' Annabel hissed.

'Not possible,' Betsey gasped, as heavy-boned Roger landed in her arms.

When the servant arrived to say tea would soon be served, the pair had done better than they knew. Obliged on the way back to stop communicating in anything other than banalities, both could assess what had been established. Since no fixed arrangement could be made with Edward, Betsey would have to be ready to decamp at a moment's notice and with nothing in the way of possessions. If it was fraught with the potential to go wrong that just had to be accepted; desperate times required desperate actions.

Vital to Betsey was his obvious willingness to make whatever effort it took to get her free. Against that she was frustrated, as she had been at Home Farm, at not being able to talk properly to Annabel, to tell her about the hell she was going through, Henry's behaviour and, most of all, how close she had come to getting away.

And here, as they walked, was her Aunt Sarah, burbling on about days spent in the Blean Woods around Canterbury, picking wild flowers and sometimes, in the right season, mushrooms. In her story, every day was sunny, all the people accompanying her and her dear Samuel clever and amusing.

'What an idyll, my dears, I cannot tell you,' she trilled, this while Betsey stopped herself from pointing out she had been doing nothing else for a good twenty minutes. 'I shall ask Henry to join us for tea.'

'Aunt Sarah—'

That stopped the trilling and reminiscing. Sarah Lovell went right back to the way she had been in Jamaica and since, looking censorious. 'I have had recent disagreements with your brother, my dear, but on one thing I cannot gainsay him. Nothing will be achieved if you don't talk to each other!'

Annabel aimed a swift eye movement in her direction, making it plain there was a flaw in this logic. Sarah Lovell responded in a low voice so as not to be overheard, which was unnecessary given Edmund was being roundly chastised for punching young Roger so hard he had started to cry.

'Annabel being present will prevent the raising of anything intimate, or likely to bring on dispute. But it will also serve to provide the kind of gentle conversation during which, you might find, it is not impossible to communicate. He will need to be as polite and constrained as you.'

The problem came in Henry's downright refusal to comply with the request, which obliged his aunt to explain to her guest that his affairs were so complex he was mired in paperwork. The expression on Annabel's face was unobserved, but it told Betsey her friend thought Henry was mired in something, and paper was not it.

The children, full of fresh milk and covered in crumbs from shortbread, were obliged to say how much they had enjoyed themselves and Betsey reckoned it was part truth – no adults would have been better – but it was enough to have her aunt say they must come again, which was a positive.

She was more guarded and tactical when asked about the day, saying, instead of outright repudiation, that she found the children exhausting. Aunt Sarah, who'd had little real contact with them, pronounced herself enchanted with their vital spirit. The result was achieved; it would not have done for Betsey to have shown any enthusiasm of a kind that might cause suspicion as to her motives.

She could retire to her room and work out a way to get either a message or a signal to Edward, saying to come and get her as soon as he thought the situation propitious. And then she was afforded time to reflect on the way much of the day's activities had seemed so normal, in contrast to the reality.

Annabel had been wonderful, never once putting a foot wrong. The danger lay in what she knew but must never allude to, even obliquely, and that had been carried off with aplomb. In addition, Betsey decided, for all she had harboured previous reservation about children, and the Colpoys' brood in particular, it was possibly a thing to hanker after in an imagined and happy future.

* * *

'Someone to see you, your honour,' said Joe Lascelles, as Brazier came through the front door, his hat taken.

'Again? I seem to be becoming popular.'

'Easy error to make,' Joe sniffed, before grinning and indicating the drawing room.

The man within, not one in his first youth, who shot to his feet on entry was no more comfortable in these surroundings than Daisy Trotter had been in the card room. That was a recollection that reminded Brazier he had behaved badly and unnecessarily so. With that thought in mind, it was a moment before he enquired as to the nature of the fellow's business.

'I was sent here by Miss Elisabeth, sir.'

His heart was very suddenly in his mouth. 'Mrs Langridge, you mean?'

'If she can still be styled that, after recent happenings.'

'She has sent you with a message?'

'Not quite, sir.'

The fellow was clearly nervous, and being towered over by a saturnine and hard-faced naval officer who looked set to board an enemy deck was not going to help. 'Please sit down again, as will I. And I have yet to enquire your name.'

'Upton, sir, head groom at Cottington Court, 'til yesterday.'

'What happened yesterday?'

'Mr Tulkington showed me the gate.'

'I sense you have a tale to tell me. Have you been offered refreshment?'

'Your servant was kind enough to do so, but . . .'

'Then allow me to get you something. Beer and a sandwich, perhaps.'

Joe was ordered to fetch a tankard from the nearby King's Head tavern, while Cocky was tasked to knock up some bread and cheese, as Brazier extracted from Upton the tale he wanted to tell in the time he wanted to tell it, which began with his service to Mr Henry's father as a stable lad. There was surely something he would come to, words Brazier was eager to hear, but this Upton would not be pushed. He wanted to be understood and it was possible to be thankful for naval service and command, for that had given Brazier much experience in dealing with such men. Not all tars were of the garrulous type and Upton was certainly slow to relate his story, not aided by simultaneously eating and drinking.

'Worked my way up over the years,' he munched, 'only to be shown the gate like some kind of beggar.'

'The reason?' was asked with some suppressed exasperation.

'Sought to aid Miss Elisabeth . . . call her that, sir, cause I've known her since she was born, an' I have to say she was a delight as a growing girl, for she loved a horse, as I do. Have to take to the animals, given the position. If you find them awkward, it will never serve.'

'Quite.'

'Not like Mr Henry, not horses for him or dogs. I am takin' it you know sommat of her situation?'

'You set out to help her?' was asked with some relief, but there was no need to answer the question Upton posed. A nod sufficed.

'Escape, sir. Plan was to get her out through the north gate, but we must have been seen plotting, for Mr Henry was awaiting when I came back from talking with Miss Elisabeth and there was never a chance to lay out an excuse.'

'Did she give you a message for me?'

'Never had the chance.'

'Then I'm curious as to what brought you to my door?'

'Her instruction. That if anything went awry and I suffered, I was to come here. Go to Quebec House, she told me, an' if I had trouble a'finding it—'

'You're here now,' was designed to stop another litany.

'Am I to throw myself on your charity, your honour?'

'I daresay Betsey would want it, so that is how it will be. But I had hoped for some words for me personally.'

'Might be in possession of sommat better.'

'Which is?'

The tankard was laid aside and his sack of possessions pulled to sit between his feet. A rummage produced that which he was seeking and, as it came out, it produced in Brazier only confusion.

'Key, your honour, opens the padlock on the north gate.'

'From which side?'

Upton had not thought of that for his face showed concern. 'Inside.'

Brazier stood to take it from his hand, feeling the weight and pondering. 'You will berth here, Mr Upton. One of my men will show you where you will sleep.'

John Hawker's intentions were not without risk. He had to take away early, from the slaughterhouse, enough of his men to overcome Brazier and his support, without leaving so few that it hindered keeping a firm grip on Spafford and his lot. That would be difficult, given they would be assembled to be the lead element of the mob.

That was a task his employer would have wanted him to undertake himself, to get things moving before fading out of view, but he could not be in two places at once. Not for the first time, he was glad of the distance from Cottington to Deal – not, in truth, great, but enough to deter Henry Tulkington from being a constant presence.

The latest information he had from one of his scouts was that Brazier had returned home from visiting a neighbour and he and his men were within Quebec House, seemingly settled, so it was possible to time how matters would be handled. As soon as twilight was well advanced, he could move to take his revenge, surprise being his advantage.

'We go in through the window and quick, in case the door has a chain. The noise will alert the street, but we must not care for that. I have my pistol, which I will use if we are threatened by one holding the same, but I want it to be clubs and a proper thrashin' for all, no exceptions. Timed right, we'll have done the necessary and be on our way afore the crowd gets close.'

'Don't we get to take part in the torchin', John?' asked Marker, one of his most trusted men.

'You might, I best not.'

'Face too well known?'

He was not going to say what he had been ordered to do.

'You have the right of it there. Now you lot spread out and see if we can put some fire into a few beach folk bellies. Get them proper fired up and willing to burn the bastard out, but listen out for the bells of St George's, an' when they strike seven, I want them setting a light to torches and you back here.'

* * *

As usual, when the day's work drew to a close for those who worked the beach, it was time to claim your spot in your favourite drinking den, to swap ale and a tale with your mates. The women who vended fish had been ensconced for hours, having packed up their stalls much earlier, salting what fish they had failed to sell and dropping both crabs and lobsters into creels, left far enough out from the beach to be underwater for the night.

When it came to raging against perceived injustice, no one could hold a candle to the Deal fishwife and they were just as partisan on behalf of their menfolk, fathers, husbands and sons. Many of those subsisted in a meagre existence, but for the occasional run across the Channel. It was a fair bet they knew the names of the fellows who had done for and buried that too-nosy exciseman, but it would never pass their lips, barring a whisper in the ear of one known to be safe.

The other thing in which they could match their men was in consumption of drink, gin being their favoured tipple. Having had a couple of hours' head start, they were ripe for stirring up by the likes of Marker, especially since he was willing to stand a flask or two. By the time the menfolk joined them, the fuse had been well and truly lit for activity instead of talk. Brazier being chastised had gone from if to when, the only pity being they could not get Billy Pitt at the same time.

Dan Spafford was rubbing chafed and sore wrists, which had been in shackles for days now. He had no difficulty in doing what was being asked of him; getting free was the most important thing. He needed to earn, so he needed to smuggle, and then there was his boy. There was no way to get Harry free of Tulkington if he was chained up or, if Hawker got his way, rooming with Davy Jones in his locker.

Finally rejoining his men, he was glad to see the relief on their faces, for him being free meant they were too and it did not have to be said. Most were convinced they had been for slaughter and the pork barrel, so it was not a surprise that one or two had a tear, thinking they had avoided such a fate. The first thing he did was ask how the hell they had come to be here in the first place, listening with increasing gloom as he heard what had happened while he was locked in Tulkington's cellar, which included being told about another party of hard-looking souls getting involved, one of whom had a pistol pointed at Tulkington's head, with no other explanation provided.

With so many seeking to explain, what they sought to describe was garbled and unclear. That it was beyond odd just had to be accepted. More important was what was to be done now, the tale of which produced some very glum faces, a sentiment he shared but which had to be put aside.

'You will know it don't sit well with me to do Tulkington's bidding, but do it we will, for once it's over we can get back to our own hearth.'

'Will Daisy be there?' asked Dolphin Morgan, called that because he was reckoned to be as dense as the wood of the beach berthing posts.

'Since I has been as locked away as you have, an' he ain't here, I don't know how you reckon me to answer that.'

'Just wondering. If he weren't with you and he weren't with us . . .'

322

'It could mean he's free.'

'Or pegged it.'

'Remind me, when I'm low, to ask you to cheer me up. Now, listen hard you all, this is what we're set to do.'

On a warm evening with twilight coming – there was a southerly wind blowing up from Spain – and a gut replete with gin as reward, Hawker's watching urchin, sitting with his back to the Navy Yard wall, nodded off. So he did not see the five souls exit Quebec House, making their way to the corner, turning down towards the Lower Valley Road. Left behind, by agreement, was the former head groom, who was not much of a drinking man and was also so happy to have a room to sleep in.

It was as if he feared to go through the front door, lest he never get back in again. Upton felt he might have landed on his feet, for the man Miss Elisabeth had sent him to was going to talk to another, called Flaherty, who had a set of paddocks and stables, about giving him a place.

Part of the reason for going out was so they could talk without Upton being given a chance to overhear their discussion. What to do with the acquired key, which Brazier had in his pocket?' The card room was out for them as a group, but the main tavern area was quiet, it being early for the kind of clientele who favoured the Old Playhouse.

As soon as they were sat round a table with drinks in front, it was Peddler who said what was at the back of more than one mind, if not Brazier's. Was it not a bit too convenient, the key turning up as it had, with a fellow not one of them knew, apart from what he himself had related?

'Sorry, Capt'n, wishing for him to be an honest fellow don't make it so.'

'Good way to catch us, knowing how we'll get in?' Dutchy added, emboldened by what Peddler had said.

'We don't have to get in that way,' Brazier insisted. 'Walls like that will not stop us using grappling irons.'

'But the getting out,' Dutchy added. 'Can't see your lady hauling herself up a rope like a boarder.'

Peddler wasn't finished. 'Caught in the act of abductin'. Must be a tariff in irons for that.'

'She would save us from that,' Joe said.

'I don't think it's a trap,' Brazier insisted, partly in desperation. 'But if you fear to go along . . .'

'Now that, Capt'n,' protested an offended Cocky Logan, 'is no fair.'

Dutchy made a strong point. 'We got out last time, Capt'n, by the skin of our teeth. Without we had that Hawker sod as hostage we would have been done for.'

'Joe, your opinion?'

'If I smell a rat, Capt'n, I am minded to set it a trap.'

It was a discussion that went round in circles for an age as the light outside faded towards night, with the bells of St George's Church ringing the quarter, half and the hour. In Quebec House, having spent the previous night under a hedge, Upton was happy to lay down and sleep.

CHAPTER TWENTY-SIX

Perhaps if the night had been cold, or the wind had been coming in from the north-east, the one generally icy and feared locally for its ability to drag ships from their anchors, the riot John Hawker was seeking to create would have fizzled out like a damp squib. But the southerly was warm enough to add need to a thirst, while being outdoors – even as night fell – seemed the right and comfortable place to be.

Dan Spafford had led his men out of the slaughterhouse, to take up station halfway between the town and Sandown Castle. He was watching for the first sign of congregating, easy to spot, as folk would do so under the flaring exterior torches of the numerous taverns that lined Beach Street. There was barely a corner, or indeed a row of houses, which lacked a place to drink, while some boasted more than one.

Within them were not only locals, but sailors having a run ashore from their merchant ships, added to some just paid off and spending heavily, as newly ashore tars always did. If they were not concerned by the notion of anybody seeking to control smuggling, they were of a breed ever ready for disturbance, and which port that took place in made no difference.

Thus, when the grumbling became louder, they were quick to pick up on the mood and see sport in it. Not content to merely watch, they began to egg on the local malcontents, calling their intentions feeble, which was not an affront to be borne. The first angry group began to form outside the Albion, a favourite watering hole for the Deal fishwives. That was soon joined by others, the flaring of smaller individual torches the signal for the Spafford gang to move.

Closer to the town centre, word began to spread of trouble brewing, which had Garlick, in double-quick time, getting up and fitting the stout wooden storm shutters on the windows of the Three Kings. He was not alone: there were other hostelries that were not mere drinking dens, and these too had well-worn drills to protect themselves – normally from a raging sea bursting over the beach, but also irate humans when the need arose.

At the Navy Yard, the officer on duty got wind of trouble and roused out everyone under his command who could wield a marlinspike. He doubled the marine guard on the gate and ensured those needed to back up that position were close enough to do so, and quickly. There was no requirement to protect anything other than that which was navy: the town could burn and the service would stay where it was.

Yet, when Admiral Braddock was informed of what was afoot, he had a quartet of marines, with instructions to shoot their weapons if necessary, despatched to the roadway leading to Miss Carter's house opposite the yard, to ensure protection for her property. Saoirse Riorden got the news fairly quickly and was thus able to alert the pair of stout and ferocious-looking doormen who manned the entrance. They were told to be extra vigilant but, if it looked too hard to contain, they were to shut the thick double doors and bolt them, locking everyone inside.

She then went to tell those already present. Brazier spotted her as she came through the door, but it was some time before she got to his table, nodding to the quartet with him whom she had met once before.

'I have come to tell you there's trouble brewing.'

'Story o' his life, lady,' said Cocky.

'What kind of trouble?' Brazier asked.

'Could be we're in for a bit of a riot and don't you be asking me the cause.'

'You know everything that's going on in the town, or so I'm told.'

'That will be Vincent indulging in flattery.'

He couldn't resist it. 'Flattery from a Flaherty.'

'That's not the best witticism you ever produced, even if it has your lads smiling. I'll be thinking you tars are light in the article of drollery.'

'There has to be a reason,' Brazier insisted, as the smiles disappeared.

'Sure, did you not hear? I don't know. Had a feeling there was something brewing this day, but what it's about?' She shrugged and tightened her lips. 'Anyway, it's not come our way yet. But if it does and it looks bad, I'll be locking and barring the door, so if you're planning to leave, now's as good a time as any.'

A look around the table established they were happy where they were and, with a wry smile and pat to Brazier's shoulder, she moved on.

'She's a fine lookin' woman,' Peddler said, to general agreement. 'Has a soft spot for you, Capt'n.'

Brazier held up the key, which had been in his hand so long the metal was now warm, before challenging the amused looks he was getting from round the table. 'Let's stick to the business at hand, shall we?'

Basil the Bulgar's Molly-house emptied quickly, the customers dispersing when told something was brewing. It was too often a handy target for those who saw its purpose as devilish or unclean. Daisy Trotter was one of those who had no desire to be caught inside but, out in the fresh air, he felt safe enough to wander up to Beach Street, to see how things were progressing. He took the view that, although a disturbance was brewing, it had yet to get beyond the point of being stationary and the shouting of grievances. Still, knowing the intended destination, he was again assailed by the same quandary. Should he go to Quebec House and warn Brazier, or let him suffer for his arrogance?

John Hawker was approaching that very address as Daisy pondered, glad to see the shutters open and a lantern light within. A peer through the low window showed the front parlour was empty, so he raised an arm to call forward his men, all of whom were in possession of long and sturdy clubs. The crash as the first of those broke glass was enough to wake the dead, the splintering of wood from the frames holding the small panes less obvious.

Enough of the thin strips of wood were shattered to allow the rest to be displaced by boots, so in less than half a minute, Hawker's brutes had pushed their way inside, to be followed by John Hawker, with his primed and loaded pistol. There was no need for him to issue any orders now, his men knew what to do: clobber the tars as hard as they liked but not Brazier. The man bent on revenge wanted him at his feet and begging to avoid his just deserts.

Stood in the parlour waiting, the sound of rushing feet and shouting was evident, but Hawker was not hearing conflict. He had no doubt that Brazier and the men he employed were hard bargains themselves, and would put up a fight even against clubs, but that meant screaming and shouting. It was even more troubling when the house fell silent, to soon resound with the thud of boots moving downstairs at a steady pace.

'No sign, John,' Marker said as he entered the parlour, having hesitated briefly in the face of a pointed pistol. 'They're not here.'

The other men had trooped in behind to crowd the doorway, one admitting he had found one cove on the top floor, not one of those they were seeking, but had given him a good clubbing anyway.

'Out,' Hawker barked, wondering how he had not been informed. What he then said, in a bitter voice, made little sense to those who heard it. 'By the blood of Christ, I'll have those little buggers pay for this.'

They exited to a deserted street; if any of the neighbours had been disturbed, and they must have been, they were not going to come out of their front doors to investigate what sounded like violence. So they would not have seen the dark-clad figures moving swiftly if noiselessly toward the town centre. It was quite some time before, after a long period of silence, one ventured out to look at the smashed window frame and then decide it was none of his concern.

Dan Spafford had moved, seeking to mingle with the knots of those whining for retribution outside the taverns. His shouts that it was time for action got many a cheer. This alerted those ahead that things were warming up and made them ready to be receptive to joining an increasingly numerous crowd. Spafford, torch in hand, was to the fore, to be spotted by Daisy Trotter who, heart pounding and tears forming, rushed to meet him, yelling his name.

'You're free, Dan.' The cries of greeting from the others he ignored, getting alongside his friend, hooking an arm and matching his pace, unable to make sense of what he had just become part of and having to shout to make himself heard. 'How has this come about?'

'Tulkington's price, Daisy. We've got to burn out some poor bastard who's got the wrong side of him. That done, we're free.'

'Of the name of Brazier?' Daisy gasped.

'How in God's name do you know that?'

Daisy had been in a quandary before. It was ten times that now and required some very quick calculations. This was made harder by Dan pushing into a crowd outside the Three Compasses, urging them to action and he was not alone. Those already with him, and that excluded his own men, were doing their own encouraging. The crowd were fully up for pandemonium now. Spafford was visibly surprised to have

Daisy grab his arm and haul him back with more strength than he was supposed to possess.

'You've got to put a stopper on this, Dan.'

'What the hell are you on about?'

The thought of seeking to explain in this situation seemed impossible, but he had to try. 'Take my word, it's the wrong way to go. Doing Tulkington's bidding will be damaging our own.'

'But, Daisy—'

'No fuckin' buts, Dan. You'se got to trust me.'

The look of utter confusion on Dan Spafford's face did not provide one ounce of encouragement, as Daisy screamed at him, quite prepared to exaggerate, even to lie.

'Brazier is more friend to us than enemy. He came close to shooting Tulkington the night we was rumbled. He hates the bastard and will side with us against him.'

'Tulkington's goin' to let us carry on in the trade with no interference, Daisy.'

'Then ask yourself why he's paying that as a price.'

'Dan, what do you want to do, the crowd's moving on?' demanded Dolphin Morgan.

That got a confused look, for Dan Spafford had no idea. It was Daisy who spoke, his face a picture of despair as he looked at the now-surging mob. And his voice matched the look.

'There's no controlling it now.'

'We's got to get to the front and start the torchin', that's the arrangement.'

'No, Dan,' Daisy insisted, for the first time not needing to shout, given the noise of the throng was receding. 'We have to get back to Worth and see how we's to proceed.'

'Got to say no to that, Daisy, Tulkington's got my boy.' Dan's shout came as he started running, calling on his lads to follow, which left Daisy standing alone, silently cursing Harry Spafford's hold on his pa.

It took effort to push back to the front of the crowd, but Dan Spafford did not lack for muscle or the odd fist if some sod would not quickly clear a path. The stream of human anger swept past the Three Kings, where Garlick and some of his guests were watching from the open first-floor window, only to come to a halt at the sight of four redcoats and raised muskets.

'This way.'

Dan Spafford, having resumed the leadership, slipped down a narrow alley, one of the dozens that connected to Middle Street, with everyone following. The noise, which had been loud on Beach Street, hit a level many times that in the confined space between two sets of high buildings and barely diminished when they poured into Middle Street, the confining lack of space turning the whole into a seething liquid mass.

Now they were shouting the name of Brazier, and in there was many a loud curse aimed at Billy Pitt. Those within the houses along the route heard it and, even if it made no sense, they trembled, praying to be spared whatever was about to occur. This applied especially to those who were neighbours to Quebec House who, if they dared look out onto their street, were presented with a sea of heads, flaring torches and bellowing imprecations.

It was talked of in the aftermath. Maybe if the window had not already been smashed, the torch would not have been thrown through it. It was never to be established who the culprit was, while even such an excitable mob was wont to hesitate when it came to the actual carrying out of that which they had been encouraging each other to do. But once one went through, others followed.

The drapes took light quickly, to be followed by the furnishings. The crowd had to ease back as the flames took hold, for fear it might singe them. That retreat went further as the glass burst outwards on the first floor, soon followed by lively streaks of red and orange. Quebec House was now well and truly alight and it was soon remarked that no one had come rushing out of the front door, in order to save themselves.

Murmurs grew and spread; the place had to be empty. The purpose of the night had not been met. The person they had lined up for a sound beating was not there to suffer. That, combined with the enormity of what they were gazing upon, had those to the rear begin to slip away, lest there was a price to be paid for this so-called merriment.

There were bells ringing too as the volunteers who manned the Deal fire engine, paid for and maintained by monies raised by the Tulkington family, responded to the call telling them their services were required. At the same time, word was spreading to those not involved, leading to alarmed and head-shaking denunciations about the endemic stupidity of the lower orders.

The news was relayed to Saoirse, known to many as the owner of Quebec House. She passed it on to Brazier's table, which would have had them rushing out of the front door and heading for Middle Street if she had not stopped them, with an argument hard to dispute, even as she herself donned a cloak.

'It has to be you they're after, not the house.'

'Tulkington,' Brazier spat.

'More likely Hawker,' came from Dutchy.

'Stay here,' Saoirse insisted. 'You can't face a mob, even armed, and certainly not in that uniform.'

'And you can?'

'Edward, no one has me marked.'

'She's right, Capt'n,' Peddler said, which got a murmur of agreement from Cocky and Joe.

'I will send for you, as soon as it's safe to do so.'

Then she was gone, leaving a quartet to wonder at what they would find when they did get sent for, which had Brazier cry, 'Upton!'

Any restraint evaporated and he was first out the door, his sword hauled out and pointed ahead of him, ready to skewer anyone who got in his way. Behind him, three cutlasses were also shaped for the taking of blood, only Joe Lascelles reduced to bunched fists. They came upon the rear of a multitude breaking up, partly because the man who had led and encouraged them had disappeared and was, unknown to all, heading for the marshes that ran to the north of Deal.

Bellowing got Brazier through, for no one wanted to take on the wild eyes or the blade, while behind him his men were swinging right and left looking for flesh. The flames were now shooting out of the roof, while in front of the house the firemen were furiously working their hand pump to send what looked like a feeble stream of water up the exterior walls.

Having got too close, Brazier had to fall back in the face of the searing heat, only vaguely aware of a line of the more responsible citizens, forming up to pass a line of buckets all the way from the foreshore. Unseen and only revealed later, there was another group at the rear of the properties trying to damp the flames from there. A second engine came trundling into the street from the Navy Yard, manned by sailors, while behind them their mates paid out a rolled canvas hose to suck water from a well. By the time they had that operating, he found himself standing alongside Saoirse.

'Play on the neighbouring houses,' Brazier yelled, saying words that he knew might upset her. 'Try to keep it from spreading to them for the main one is beyond saving.'

'What folly caused this?' she said, in a tearful tone.

'Hatred was the cause, Saoirse, and I am sorry to be the reason for it.'

The crowd, or at least those who had not got away from potential trouble, had retreated to form blocking lines of bodies. Mixed in with them were the residents of this part of the street, very likely some from the buildings the firefighters were now trying to preserve. It took no great wisdom or knowledge of fires to see that Quebec House was truly beyond saving, for what had been a searing conflagration was now morphing into a great plume of smoke.

'Dutchy, see if you can find Upton anywhere.'

'Don't want to leave you unprotected, Capt'n.'

It was in a voice cracked from smoke inhalation that he replied. 'I doubt those who truly want to do me harm have stayed around. Cowardice will see them long gone.'

He was there all night and able, in the morning, to gingerly enter the ground floor. There were no others, the ones above having crashed down to form a pile of hot wood under a roof open to a sky beginning to lighten. In amongst that, and only found when everything had been drenched in water, they found a body, charred and reduced to the dimensions of a child.

It did no good to say to Edward Brazier he was not responsible. He knew he was.

CHAPTER TWENTY-SEVEN

It was a sombre breakfast that was taken in the Old Playhouse, following the discovery of Upton's remains, for it could be no one else. It did mean that whoever had set light to Quebec House was guilty of murder, not, given the size of the crowd who had been outside at the time, that anyone was likely to be brought to book. The names not mentioned, because they would set everyone's teeth on edge, were those of Tulkington and Hawker who, it was suspected, had to be the authors of the whole event.

It would not have cheered them to know that Hawker, too, was fuming. The first reason was very obvious: he had failed to get his revenge. But second was the written instruction from Henry Tulkington, delivered by some stable boy, ordering him to travel to Chatham and bring back to Cottington Court Harry Spafford, no explanation as to why being given. If he was unaware of every detail, Hawker was burdened by a feeling his employer had not handled recent matters very well. From being a man in iron control, he seemed to have moved to where he was seeking to cover one error with another, and now they had piled upon each other.

Spafford and his thieving gang should have been disposed of, that being the only way to ensure a finish. If that threatened to raise problems, well, they seemed to have more now. Refusing to have Brazier as a brother-in-law, he could see, but wedding his sister to drunken and whoring Harry Spafford as a solution he could not fathom. Prior to departure, he collared a couple of the street ragamuffins, a pair sound asleep, the others being too numerous and fleet of foot to be caught, and gave them several hard blows round the head, as well as a promise, if they wanted for gin, to find a new chump to provide it.

Next came a bit of a tour of various taverns, seeking to ensure his name was not linked to the fire at Quebec House and in this he was satisfied. The fact of a body being found bothered him, but only in the event it was the wrong one. No one even hinted at him as responsible, but there were plenty willing to tell him who had been outside while the fire raged.

Hawker was tickled, if not surprised, by the general caginess of those he queried, most reluctant to admit they had been party to the riot at all. But the one name that did crop up suggested a notion. Could he put the blame for the whole thing, not least that dead body, on to the head of Dan Spafford? This might, at least, get shot of him, which would serve, for without their leader his gang was useless. But a care surfaced at the same time: the sod knew too much about the Tulkington operations and what he got up to with the Revenue to be threatened with a rope.

Perhaps matters would settle in the time he was away. Brazier and his lot were homeless and his hopes on Tulkington's sister were dashed, so he might well move away. Spafford, if not at the bottom of the sea, was back to where he had been previously – small-scale smuggling – thus not really a problem. John Hawker was fairly relaxed as he got one of the vans that ran regularly to Sandwich, where he would pick up a coach that would pass through Chatham.

Hawker was not alone in reviewing recent events, though he would have been obliged to admit a real difference in conclusion. Henry Tulkington, who would have denied he was feeling sorry for himself, was yet reflecting that fate had dealt him a very difficult hand, and in a very short space of time. The coincidence of his problem with Brazier, simultaneously compounded with Spafford's thieving, had obliged him to juggle where he would have preferred to carefully manage. Now he had a feeling his actions to resolve these problems, in which he had lacked both alternatives and room for manoeuvre, were bringing disapproval in too many quarters.

He would have to check his Uncle's Dirley's attempts to intrude in Elisabeth's affairs, which, if it promised to be unpleasant, provided an opportunity for which he had been only vaguely aware he had been waiting. The balance of their relationship needed to be set beyond peradventure. The days of him as the novice were long gone. He was fully his father's heir, the man in control, and Dirley was there to do his bidding.

His aunt would have to be put back in her dependency box; her behaviour these last few days had been impossible. Worse still, he had been obliged to acquiesce in the acts she had initiated without even a pretence at consultation. Either she would have to conform to his way of doing things, or he would condemn her to the poorhouse.

Then there was his sister, who needed to be forced to accept the present dispensation. He knew her to be wilful, but she must come to realise his resolve was stronger. For too long Elisabeth had thought she could act as she wished, thought she could condescend to him, even make him the butt of her and her companions' jokes. Having Spafford here as a threat would help to rein her in. And if she refused, well he was her husband.

Was Hawker still as reliable as he had been in the past? Recently he had taken to questioning his instructions, instead of merely obeying them, putting forward opinions of how to resolve matters that were beyond his responsibilities. The man thought he could not sense his frustration; Hawker should surely have realised by now that his employer had a feline's sense for dissent. It would require to be carefully handled, but Hawker needed to be reminded, quite forcibly, of his place.

Spafford he would keep an eye on and, provided he did not overreach himself, and stayed well away from the Tulkington operations, he presented no real threat. There was a certain degree of advantage in his trying to compete, albeit in a very small way. Better that the Excise had more than one possible target and he constituted one, a sacrifice if it were needed. As for others, like the opportunists of Deal Beach, John Hawker would encourage where it suited and betray them when it was expedient.

A bell was rung to alert Grady that it was time to come and shave him. As he lay back and allowed the razor to go where the man ministering to him felt it necessary, he could reflect that at least, in the department of menial service, in the dismissal of Upton, he had asserted his absolute authority. It was in the nature of servants to get ideas above their station, just as it was a requirement of those who engaged such people to occasionally remind them of their dependence.

Had he been able to see into Grady's mind, he might not have been so sure of himself.

'Jesus, I'm not offering you my bed, Edward, but a place to lay your head.'

Slightly shocked at the openness of her allusion, while also being obliged to put aside the stimulating thought of what that might bring, Brazier had the tricky task of being grateful, while determinedly refusing. How could he say that a single night spent here, one in which he'd had no choice being near unable to walk, had very nearly ruptured his relationship with Betsey?

He had been obliged to lie to her to cover for it. The Old Playhouse was not a place she had ever visited, but that did not mean she had no opinion of what went on within its walls, in truth a lot less than the more pious citizens of the area supposed. It was bent more towards entertainment than carnality, for there were no attractive young girls pretending to be hostesses while touting for later custom.

Yet, in its main rooms, it was a place where a visiting sailor might entertain a woman, one who felt herself too cultured for the more raucous venues or a common tavern. That did not mean said tar was not expecting reward for his attentions and disbursements, while it was certain a fair few succeeded. So it was perceived as not much above a whorehouse. For the likes of a man connected to Betsey Langridge, to cross such a threshold was to enter the Devil's lair. Lord knows what she would think if he took up residence!

'I have to see to my men as well, Saoirse, and I still need them with me at all times. So I will ask Admiral Braddock for temporary accommodation, until I can find another house to rent.'

'You'll struggle there, Edward. Anyone letting to you will reckon their property soon to be torched. You might say you and Pitt being hand in glove is nonsense. There are eejits here about who are convinced it's a fact.'

'He did try to engage me on the very purpose they suspect.' That got a reaction – wide-open eyes and clear shock. 'I refused.'

'And how in the name of Old Nick were you supposed to go about that?'

'Pitt got from Garlick—'

'Loose mouth that he is,' she said, butting in.

'—that I was involved with the Tulkingtons.'

'So he suspects them?'

'The very opposite, Saoirse. He was at pains to tell me how honest and diligent Henry Tulkington is as his damned tax gatherer. Every penny raised paid in and never a query on his accounts.'

'So how were you supposed to help?'

'The connection to Betsey would have put me in the top social layers in this part of Kent. Pitt is convinced smuggling's being done on an industrial scale . . .'

'He's not wrong there.'

'. . . and it's being run by someone of deep pockets and real brains. It is not being carried out on such a level by those whose boats he torched. He suspects one man or a cabal of wealthy individuals are financing and overseeing the trade, well connected to the local magistrates who might, themselves, be deeply involved. He wanted me to spy on Betsey's friends, to see if I could turn up anything useful.'

'But now you know, so why not tell him?'

'I rate you clever enough to work that out yourself.'

If she thought on it not much time went by and what she said in response came out in a way to make him curious, it being half-amused, but also longing. 'Sure, a smitten heart overcomes so much.'

'Now, I must go to see Braddock. And then, me and mine must trawl what emporiums there are in Deal, for clothing and everything else. All we possessed went up in those flames.'

'Best watch out for Hawker.'

'Wrong, Saoirse,' Brazier replied, with some vehemence, as he picked up his sword. 'He best watch out for me.'

'Of course, Brazier,' Braddock huffed. 'Circumstances call for a bit of charity. But I'll have to list you as supernumerary to the muster.'

His visitor knew what that meant. 'I will meet the bill sir, of course, just as I do so for the stabling.'

'Pity about Quebec House and pity the owner. She has not only to rebuild it, but to compensate her neighbours, I hear, for damage to their property. Miss Riorden, or is it Mrs? No one is quite sure. Fine lookin' woman, be a surprise if no one had bedded her.'

'I'm sure you mean got her to the altar, sir.'

'Obviously,' came a blustering response; he hadn't meant that at all.

Brazier declined to say that the cost of rebuilding, as well as any other bills, he had promised to meet. This was another connection to the Old Playhouse, and to Saoirse as well, which must be kept from public knowledge.

'We have a guest suite here in Admiralty House, Brazier, which you may use.' The ruddy round face looked gloomy. 'Not likely anyone will come down from the board to want to use it.'

'Obviously, sir, if they do . . .'

'Backwater, Brazier,' was stated with more animation, 'without there's a war with France. I've said it before and, by damn, I will say it again. You'll dine with me tonight, of course?'

'You're too kind, sir.'

Braddock took that, not as the platitude it was, but, by his expression, as the unvarnished truth.

There was a great deal that needed to be purchased; not even Brazier's sextant had survived the inferno in a fit state to be used. Also gone were some irreplaceable personal possessions, like his mother's locket, which had within miniatures of her and his father. Luckily there were portraits, stored back in Hampshire, which he had hoped would have ended up in a home shared with Betsey.

A new sextant could wait 'til he had a ship, but he required new uniforms, one second-hand and showing it, as a working kit, another ordered brand new to replace the much-singed coat and breeches he was wearing. Added to that was a buff coat of the kind favoured by merchant captains and a tricorne hat to go with it. There were stockings, smalls, shirts and even hair queues to buy as well as all things needed for personal care for both himself and his own crewmen. The hardest to find was spare shoes.

He took one detour, his back and his purchases fully covered, to the graveyard behind St George's Church, looking for a plaque in the enclosing brick wall dedicated to Stephen Langridge, Betsey's late husband. There was slight guilt in that he had not bothered before, as he reprised her description of him, which he could not but admit was the polar opposite of his own.

Fair-haired and gentle Brazier was not, and nor was he her cherished childhood sweetheart. Langridge had succumbed to the endemic fevers of the Sugar Islands, he had not. Was it possible she could love two so very different men? This had him reflecting there was no certainty in such an emotion, only the hope that it was the case.

'What's that he's lookin' at?' asked Cocky.

Dutchy, in receipt of the question, just shrugged. 'No idea.'

'Have you a notion of what's goin' to happen now?'

'Why don't you ask him yourself, Peddler?'

'You are in better than Cocky and me. I doubt even Joe here gets to know as much about what's on the Turk's mind as you.'

Joe Lascelles produced one of those white-teeth smiles that lit up his dark-skinned face and nodded. 'Don't tell me much.'

'Spare a penny, guv'nor.'

The youngster had emerged from behind a gravestone to beg, the first thing obvious that he had been crying at some time. There were clean streaks on his otherwise filthy face and a trace of blood, which had crusted the bottom of his nose. A second dwarf edged out from the headstone to be visible, he showing a mass of bruises on his face.

'Who has been troubling you, lad?' asked Dutchy, who, with nippers of his own, was of a more charitable bent than the others. Also, with that warm and rolling West Country accent, he did not sound threatening.

'Nobody,' was the automatic reply from the first one, but his battered mate was less reticent. 'Fell afoul of John Hawker, we did.'

'That sod again,' Peddler swore as streaky-face berated his mate to 'Shut your gob'.

'Sling yer hook,' Cocky snapped. 'The pair o' ye. Ah'm no payin' fer your gin. Gawd, ye stink of it.'

'Promise not to dog you, if you'll go to a sixpence.'

Dutchy put a hand on Cocky's chest to stop him swearing at them. 'What'd you mean by that, lad?'

'Don't tell him,' spat streaky-face.

'Hawker paid us to watch where you was goin' an' we did.'

'And you told him.'

'Promised a flask we were, an' he was as good as his word, 'ceptin' Danny, who was to look out for you last night. Fell asleep an' he came lookin' for him this mornin'. Couldn't catch him, though, but he nabbed us asleep. Hawker don't know that bout Danny, mind, so don't you go letting on.'

'Capt'n,' Dutchy called, 'best you come over here.'

The thought obviously did not go down well with these two urchins and they looked to sidle off. Dutchy grabbed them both by their rags, telling Joe to catch hold too. Brazier sauntered over, to cast a jaundiced eye at these two brats, as Dutchy said, 'Now tell him what you just told me. And I will reckon it to be worth a shilling.'

All five were back at the Navy Yard long before dinner, no more needing to be said than that which had made up their conversation on the way from the graveyard. It was agreed they had been lucky, for there was no doubt if they'd been in the house it would have led to serious injuries and possibly a lot worse. Any residual doubt about who had set the mob on them, and there wasn't much, disappeared.

Now, with a quartet sat on some bollards, looking out at HMS *Bellerophon* and the people working on her deck and rigging, it was no great stretch to conclude Tulkington and Hawker were unlikely to let matters rest. The next question to arise was obvious: what to do about the ongoing threat?

Brazier had stayed standing; familiarity with these men was fine in private, but here where they could be seen, a post captain did not sit jawing with common seamen. Now he began to pace about.

'I'm not minded to run away.'

'Never thought you would be.'

Peddler said it; all by their expressions established they agreed.

'This is a private quarrel, lads. To do with my own hopes, not yours.'

'Was,' Dutchy growled. 'Not much like to forgive some bugger who would see me dead, Capt'n.'

Brazier had no need to explain, but he did so anyway. The

whole thing had arisen because of his pursuit of Betsey and, if they had been recruited to join him for protection, he had not known the true extent of what they would face.

'So it's my fight, not yours.'

'Is that no the same as private quarrel?' Cocky looked to the others for agreement, quickly forthcoming, to then turn back to Brazier with a querying expression. 'No like you tae repeat yerself, sir.'

'So we agree: the chances of their having failed means them trying again.'

'Certain,' Joe Lascelles said. 'An' if it were me I'd be looking to kill now, not maim.' That came with a throat-slitting hand gesture. 'Safer that way.'

'So it's run or fight, but I can't ask you to take part if it's the latter. My only aim is to get my lady out of Cottington Court. That done, I have nothing else to seek and not revenge.'

'Where you go, your honour, we go. Right lads?'

'Spot on, Dutchy,' said Peddler Palmer.

'Nae bother,' came from Cocky. Joe just smiled.

'So what now?' Dutchy asked.

'Eat, then I think I've got to try and find that Daisy Trotter.'

Cocky put a hand to his hip to make a teapot arm. 'Ye ken where to look.'

'I'll settle for leaving a message. The other thing is where to get hold of some muskets. It can't be in Deal, if we're being watched.'

'Looks like we're in for a serious fight.'

'Maybe you're right, Dutchy, and it's one I can't lose, though I'm hoping a threat will suffice. Now, let's go to dinner.'

For him, that was in the main dining room of Admiralty House, where he would mingle with the officers based in Deal and be queried about his past exploits. Dutchy, Cocky, Joe and Peddler messed in a hall at the kind of tables they were accustomed to, and were soon swapping tales with men who, like them, had been at sea for years, a few now too old for that kind of service.

CHAPTER TWENTY-EIGHT

The obvious place to buy weapons was Dover; every port in the land had a gun shop, but those that harboured a lot of merchant vessels, who required them for protection from piracy, would be the busiest. The notion of borrowing them from the Navy Yard had been mooted but dismissed; there was no way of knowing what was going to happen. The knowledge that Brazier and his men had such weapons, rarely used on land, by anyone other than the military, would be like a pointed finger at them being the culprits.

Even purchasing in Dover required time to get there and a degree of subterfuge, added to a cock and bull story about a ship on the way down from London, first tested in a chandler's emporium buying rope and grappling irons. This invented ship would be picking them up for a scientific expedition to the South Seas, 'they' being Brazier and Dutchy, though false names were used.

Gun oil was purchased too and material for swabbing the weapons, bought in at the next stop and with the same tale. Not that it seemed the gun shop owner was that bothered; a dry stick of a fellow with a face that reminded Brazier of a day-old cadaver, he was more interested in getting a good price.

He would tell his friends that evening about the two boobies he'd had in his works, who had paid way over the odds for weapons, four fifty-six-inch Brown Bess muskets, which he had bought from the local Fencibles.

'Barrels so worn they're as big as a cow's arse. Doubt the balls they purchased also will come close to a fit. A lot to steer clear of, I say. Good powder they got, mind, Faversham's best.'

The four men who would use them had fired muskets before, but not of that length. The sea service version, much shorter to avoid snagging the rigging in a fight, was also easier to load, the ram being shorter. But it was not a favoured weapon whatever its size. A musket handed out before a battle was never likely to have anything approaching accuracy over fifty yards, and sometimes a lot less than that.

The marines had the most effective weapons, for they cast their own lead balls to fit a barrel they would keep for years, replacing the stock if that got worn. Thus, their balls came out of the muzzle straight, which gave them some hope of hitting a target. An ill-fitting ball, being loose, would not only lack velocity, it could go anywhere.

They had to be sneaked in and out of the Navy Yard the next day, wrapped in canvas to conceal them from prying eyes, then taken to the woods near the village of Ringwould where, in the trees, the sounds of shots could be people hunting rabbits. Then it was load, ram, prime and fire several times until his quartet could be sure of letting fly with them as a group, if not being sure to hit anything. He would be wanting them to frighten anyway, not maim.

It was an accident that, in cleaning the barrels, first with water and then with gun oil, necessary after the day's practice, they were caught doing so by the Yard's master-at-arms. He was on his rounds as the man responsible for ensuring the tallow wads, which would be needed at night, were fit to last. He came into the barracks in which they'd been accommodated, empty during the day as the personnel who used it went about their tasks. Quite rightly, he asked what they were about.

'Captain's keen on hunting rabbits.'

That sounded as feeble to Dutchy as it did to the man on the receiving end, judging by the look he produced. But these four were not on the muster, so he was obliged to accept what they said, though he did mention it to the officer of the watch, not that he seemed overly concerned. Tempted to tell the master-at-arms there might be things he would not want to hear about Captain Edward Brazier, he decided to keep his peace. It would never do to denigrate a fellow officer with one of petty rank.

Brazier had ridden out to Cottington, though going nowhere near the front gate. He had no need to be told where was north and that was the one he wished to examine. He took his rented mare, Bonnie, past the stud paddocks, having trouble keeping her head in the direction he wanted as she sought to show off to the other horses. It was tail out like a stiff pennant and her stepping high and boastful. Curiosity brought those inside the fences to look, smell and whinny.

Upton had told him the gate was kept locked unless in use, when it was opened on the inside and locked with the same padlock and chain on the outside. In his buff-coloured coat and his hat pulled low, he rode along the high brick wall, thinking how helpful it would have been to see over. But he had been inside Cottington before and so he had some idea of what they would face, mostly woodland.

Grappling irons would be used to get over and undo the padlock, the gate left open for a quick exit, with Joe Lascelles the man to close and lock it once the others and their mounts came through. He being no man for a horse, and damn near impossible to see at night in dark clothing, he would make his way back to Deal on foot. His orders were to go to the Three Kings, where a room would be booked for Betsey, not that her name would be used.

There had to be more than one key to that padlock, and means – a ladder perhaps – to get from inside to out. But the period to fetch it and get the gate open again must be measured in a good part of an hour, plenty of time for the main party to get well away. All that was needed was a mount for Betsey, and that came from Vincent Flaherty, a pony she had hired before and was fond of.

'Now, why would you be wantin' Canasta?'

'Am I required to say?'

'I suppose not, Edward, as long as you pay.'

'I'll be stabling him at the Navy Yard for a few days.'

'Right. When Saoirse asks where he is, I'll say you've got him.' Seeing the look of enquiry, he added, 'Did you not know, since you've taken Bonnie, it's her favourite?'

'No.'

A recollection came then of his first days in Deal, when he

had rented Bonnie from Flaherty. He had met him later in the Lower Valley Road and Vincent, a friendly sort with an easy manner, had taken him to the Old Playhouse for the first time. That led to an introduction to Saoirse, while Brazier had been able to observe how enamoured of her Vincent was. He was a man clever enough to do addition.

'Vincent, I would not want my having this pony broadcast.'

'Lips sealed, Edward,' was not wholly convincing, but that could just be his way of ever being jocose.

Back at the Navy Yard, he told his lads. 'All we need now is a night with a bit of moon.'

'Not full, Capt'n.'

'No, a half or less will do.'

Too much was like daylight, none at all and it would be too dark to see anything. And there was one more string he might be able to add to his bow, but that had yet to materialise.

'Why have we brought that wretch back, Henry? I am doing my very best to get Elisabeth to accept her situation, and you throw this in her face. All my efforts will be undone when she finds out.'

'I have my reasons, Aunt Sarah, and I do not see the need to explain them to you.' Seeing her puff up to respond, he raised his voice. 'And, I will add, you have tested my patience quite enough these last few days and I will not have it so again. I would remind you that you depend on my charity. Don't give me grounds to withdraw it.'

Sarah Lovell exited with as much dignity as she could muster, her back so stiff it was designed to send a message to her nephew she was unbowed. It was not replicated in her face, which registered her lately found position of advantage was no more; she was back to being merely useful.

Henry was left working out how to play the game he had decided upon, namely that he would use Spafford to threaten Elisabeth. Misbehave and he would allow the scrub to ravish her, as was his conjugal right. She might fight, but she was a woman and, if Spafford was a weakling, he was also proven randy.

Kept here and denied his daily diet of whores, to then be offered a delicious flower like his sister, whom even Henry acknowledged as physically beautiful, and the man would be like a slavering wolf. Fight she might, but succumb she would in an imagined scenario that occasioned him some quite pleasant discomfort.

He was tempted to encourage it anyway, just for the pleasure to be had from her distress, a payback for years of ridicule. But that was to sacrifice an advantage, which would be foolish. But she must be told what she risked and he must be primed. On the night, should it come about, a drop of brandy and an offer of her body would surely do the trick.

With Hawker back he would go and see him on the morrow, to remind him of who deferred to whom. Elisabeth could keep her door locked for one more day and she would, for their aunt was bound to tell her who was a few doors away.

Daisy Trotter was not one to enter Deal on a regular basis, but when he did, Basil's Molly-house was his port of call, a place where he knew everybody and, given they were like souls, was never thought different for his tastes. He always hoped for a few ships fresh in, and some of the younger crew members having a run ashore, looking for the right company, willing to part with a bit of coin for congress. When he was passed the message that a certain naval captain, no name given, though everyone knew it, wanted him to call at the Navy Yard, he was a bit more than thrown.

'Lucky you, Daisy,' squealed Basil the Bulgar, truly born in Dover, with a loose-waved wrist that did nothing to enhance his fat-lipped, round and rouged old face. 'If you can bed that one, you'll be in paradise.'

'Not the type for me, Basil. Too hairy. Now I need someone to write a note for me.'

Out at Worth, Dan Spafford might be planning a run, and short of coin it would have to involve some thieving, but he only had half his mind on it what with fretting about Harry. Was he at Cottington or not and, if yes, could he be got out without them having a repeat of what had gone before?

Daisy, fed up with the same litany, had not just let Dan rant on. He said it to him plain that the boy was not worth a bit of his spit, which had seen Daisy taken by the throat and half-pushed up a wall, until he was struggling for breath. In all the years he and Dan had berthed together, there had never been a hand laid on him, and they'd had disputes, some shouted ones. But his lifetime shipmate could not take the criticism of Harry and now they didn't talk at all. Daisy was lucky to get a glare.

If Brazier wanted a meet, and it would have to be here, there might be something in it to make things good again, but he knew he would have to have a care. Any notion he might have known about what was coming to Quebec House, though he had never thought murder was part of it, would have to be avoided.

Brazier was dining with the officers when the note was delivered, listening to a marine captain drone on about his proficiency with the violin, which made it a doubly good reason to make his excuses and leave. As was ever the case, as soon as he went through the door, he became the main subject of conversation, generally held to be an odd cove. And, of course, since he was absent, they could probe each other for any fresh gossip on the cloud he was rumoured to be under.

'If the fellows he has with him are anything like a clue, he's more than strange. The Lord only knows what they're planning to do with a set of army muskets.' A babble of queries meant that had to be explained; the master-at-arms had come across them cleaning their weapons, which left the speaker with a quandary. 'Do you think I should tell Admiral Braddock?'

'Best to cover your back, I say,' opined the boring violinist.

'There must be somewhere else we can talk, Trotter. This place feels as though the walls have ears.'

'No need to be uncomfortable, Capt'n,' came with a knowing smile. 'You're safe here.'

What Basil called his 'palace of delight' was far from full, yet felt cramped. This was just as well: crowded, the brick walls ran with human perspiration. Daisy was not to be moved: he felt safe here, but he did ask Basil if he could use his upstairs bedroom, a place so garishly decorated it looked like a seraglio.

That was just as much a curiosity as down below, with so many people being obvious about what was usually hidden. It wasn't that Brazier had never encountered such a thing before. It existed in a small way in the service and not always just on the lower deck. But the imperative for officers was to turn a blind eye, as long as it was not thrown in their face. The efficient working of the ship was paramount.

'Is young Spafford at Cottington?' Brazier asked.

'Don't know, and it's driving my Dan to a frazzle wondering.'

'What would your Dan say, assuming he is there, if I offered to get him free?'

'He'd bite your hand off. But why would you?'

'He has something I want.' That really pricked his interest. 'I'm going to tell you a tale you'll scarce believe, and I want you to know it's one I want kept discreet. Tell no one you don't have to, on pain of meeting my sword.'

The knife was out in a flash, a long thin silver blade, which had Brazier move back in haste. 'Don't reckon me easy quarry. Yours wouldn't be the first gut I've filleted. Now tell me your tale, an' I'll decide if it goes any further.'

This Trotter was very different from the one he had met previously, but that did not alter the fact of what he wanted done. So he told him of what he'd missed that night he'd lain doggo in the grass, which was a way of also telling him why Brazier had been there. The shock was total.

'Harry, wed to a Tulkington?'

'To spite me, yes. But it was forced upon her and needs to be annulled. I will undertake to get Harry free from Cottington. In turn he will swear, on oath, that the woman

358

to whom he was wed was coerced and probably drugged. He will swear this was done at the behest of her brother and that the ceremony was a farce carried out by an ill-named reverend called Moyle.'

'So you can wed her yourself?' A nod. 'You'll be goin' there to snatch her away, then?'

'I will, and as soon as I have the right kind of moon. So there's no time for any to and fro. Put it to Spafford and get me his promise that I will get what I want. Then he can have what he wants.'

Daisy dropped his head so as not to meet Brazier's eye. He was thinking, and the blessing was that the man with him reckoned him to be doing just that. But the purpose was different. Harry would never pass up being married to a rich beauty, no matter what his pa tried to get him to do. But if he could take to Dan the news of what was being offered, happen they could get back on good terms.

'I need to know how you're going to do what you say.'

'I take it my word will not suffice?'

'T'other way round, would it then?'

So that had to be imparted, for Daisy had the right of it. He told him of how they had got the key and what had happened to the bearer, at which point Daisy had to again drop his head. Brazier explained he would once more put a pistol to Tulkington until Betsey was brought out. If Harry Spafford was there, he would be brought out as well, willing or not.

'I am taking my men in, armed with enough threat to subdue. No one is going to get hurt . . .'

'Not even Tulkington?'

Brazier shook his head. 'Tempted as I am. But I need an answer and quick.'

That took some thought. 'I'll try to come back here tomorrow evening, if not the night after.'

'Fine. I will have someone keep watch for you.'

'One thing?'

'Which is?'

'You don't seem to care much about what Tulkington does for his wealth?'

'It's none of my business, so if you're one of those people who thinks I'm in league with William Pitt, you're mistaken. I have only one interest where he is concerned and that is to take his sister away from him.'

'Won't have it, Captain Brazier. If anyone's goin' to get Harry free, it has to be Dan hisself. What he's sayin' is he will come along . . .'

'Alone?'

'Never in life. It will be all.'

'It's not needed. All we're going to face is Tulkington and his servants, and they're not fighters, barring a couple of coachmen, perhaps. We'll be in and out in a blink.'

'An' what if he don't just want Harry? The way Tulkington treated him needs paying back.'

'He's said that?'

When Daisy nodded, Brazier was forced to think. Did it really make that much difference? If Dan Spafford wanted to revenge himself on Henry Tulkington, what was it to him, as long as he got what he needed from his son?'

'Will I get Harry's sworn testimony?'

'Dan will lock him up 'til he agrees. Harry, with no drink for a week, would sign away the Crown Jewels.'

'Very well. Tell me how to get to where you reside and I will tell you what time we will come.'

CHAPTER TWENTY-NINE

The first night Harry Spafford was back in Cottington Court was the time at which Betsey determined to arm herself. There were guns in the house, left over from her father's time, he, unlike Henry, being a keen hunter of woodcock and pheasants. She had no idea where they were stored and, even more tellingly, no notion of how to load them, always assuming she could also find the shot.

During the day she was careful to avoid any meeting with him, in this aided by her aunt. He was not one to rise early, indeed the morning seemed alien to his nature, so she could undertake her walks and be back and out of sight before he called for sustenance. All her meals she took in her room and, like her food, the means to carry out a daily toilette came from the servants fetching hot water. Refuge was found in reading, Sarah Lovell fetching the means to do so from the library.

The mood swings of this purveyor were a mystery and would remain so, given enquiry was clearly not welcome. So ebullient and confident for a few days, her aunt seemed to have shrunk back into submissiveness with the arrival of Spafford. She had, though, managed to convey, albeit elliptically, that he was present as a threat to ensure her compliance with her brother's wishes, one that had no need to be elaborated upon.

A knife was the only viable option and it was necessary to wait until the entire house was asleep before attempting to secure one. On a cloudy night the house was in near-Stygian darkness, so only long familiarity with both the layout and the furnishings allowed her to make her way down the stairs and through to the kitchen. Even there, it was only memory from long ago that served her needs.

As a child she had often come here for food and milk, but not as an adult. So it took, through touch alone, a long time to find the wooden block in which the sharpest utensils were stored, and that could not be achieved without some noise. Every incident of bumping into or knocking something had her freeze, heart thumping, listening for a reaction. Even when she found the block, it was a case of feeling for the kind of pointed implement that would serve to stab.

One located – and it came close, when she felt it, to cutting her own flesh – it was just as difficult to leave as it had been to come. She was feeling her way along the large table on which food was prepared and at which the staff ate, when the door to Grady's pantry opened. The lantern he was holding illuminated the room, leaving her standing stock-still, knife in hand and, Betsey was sure, easily visible.

Nothing was said, they merely looked at each other, until Grady's eyes dropped a fraction, obviously to what was in her hand, which, on its blade, was reflecting the light. About to speak, Betsey could not find the words she wanted to say. How could she explain to him the purpose of such a weapon? It turned out to be unnecessary. Silently, Grady nodded and shut his door, which told her he understood and probably approved.

Back in her room, and that took just as long to get to as it had going to the kitchen, Betsey sat on her bed by dim candlelight. She began trembling, in sharp contrast to the steadiness she had shown when setting out. Finally, that subsided enough for her to undertake the next step, which was to hide it where none of the servants who cleaned the room could find it.

She was not to know that, come morning, when the cook noticed one of her knives was missing, Grady told her she was not to mention it to anyone and especially not to the master. Thus the house went through its own daily rhythms without disturbance, Betsey with her toilette, her tray of food and her walk, knowing she was being trailed.

Henry had his usual shave from Grady, followed by breakfast in the company of his aunt, she no longer as talkative and certainly not as assertive as of late. After some time in his study, he went off in the coach to whatever business he was dealing with that day, so it would have been hard for anyone to know there was any difference to any other.

And then Harry Spafford woke from his slumbers and began to demand the kind of endless attention that set everyone's nerves on edge. On hearing his shouts through her locked door – he was not content to summon with a bell – Betsey found it hard to concentrate on the book she was reading and had to constantly feel for the knife, which would spend its nights under her pillow and its days close to her hand.

* * *

Henry came away from his meeting with John Hawker sure he had got the point across, without causing too much damage to the man's self-esteem. He could not help but silently reprise the words he had used to examine them for any possible hurt, and was satisfied there could be none. For once, there was no turned back and hand warming at the stove; it was direct contact, eye to eye, as much for Hawker's sake as to gauge his reactions.

'If there are things I don't tell you, John, it is because you do not need to know. It is not that I don't trust you, it is that I have no need to explain. If I did not tell you what transpired from my first meeting with Spafford, it was because I was unsure of how matters would play out.'

An expressionless face could be taken in various ways and Hawker wore one. Was it stony anger or cold calculation, listening and assessing? Only one conclusion was possible: he was not going to give anything away and that was not something to be concerned about.

'You disagreed with me about how to deal with Spafford and that I cannot have. It is not a lack of respect for you, but the need for there to be one controlling head running things. It cannot be done by debate, as I'm sure you understand.' That got a jerk of the head, more than a nod. 'Good. Now let us carry on as we should to mutual profit.'

Henry had sent his carriage ahead to wait at the Lodge and, unusually for him, he was to be seen walking through the town, where he acknowledged the nods of acquaintances and studiously ignored those from folk barely known to him who would, if he engaged with them, be either pleading for something or merely grovellingly obsequious. There were many too cautious to even make eye contact and that was pleasant to a man who cared as much to be feared as respected.

'Mr Cremins, I find you well?'

A carter in a small way, indeed a small man with cropped hair and worn features, Cremins was surprised to see in his yard a man like Tulkington. He was of the kind who barely stooped to even nod from within his coach. That induced a sort of half-bow, half-crouch as he sought to demonstrate his deference.

'Is trade good?' Henry continued.

'Passable, your honour, no more. If I may make so bold, some folk are hard to match in prices charged for carting.'

'Quite. Would it be of interest to you if I was to put a bit of trade your way, shifting my farming produce, perhaps?'

'Why, sir, I'd be more than grateful.'

'I trust the price would be competitive?' Cremins knew Sowerby transported the Tulkington goods and, Henry thought, also knew what they consisted of, though he would never let on. 'If that was so, it might lead to more business.'

'If I was to match your present tariff, Mr Tulkington, would that serve?'

'Mr Cremins, how could it not be? I will be in touch when we are ready to shift crops, you have my word on it.'

As he left he made a mental note to tell John Hawker that Cremins was to be left alone from now on. He would no longer be required to pay so that his business ran smoothly and free from trouble. Sowerby would soon hear of what was coming and it would be of interest to see how he reacted. Whatever, it would send the required message: the family that raised you to prosperity can just as easily bring you down.

Two days of cloudy weather, the result of a brisk westerly wind, occasioned deep frustration for Edward Brazier. With communication thought to be unwise, it could only be hoped what had been arranged with Trotter would hold. The others, more stoical, seemed to be less troubled, which he put down to their being the kind of seamen for whom decisions, outside their daily tasks, were made for them. Inactivity, which made him nearly physically itch, was taken as normal.

He had another dinner with Braddock, though it was relieved by the presence of others, one of the main topics of conversation the news from France of the travails of King Louis, as he tried to deal with the bankruptcy of the country. While all welcomed the French having troubles, there was yet a lingering professional disquiet. It was a country that could scarce go to war in its present state, which meant a lack of opportunity for those eating at Braddock's board.

Another cloudy night was spent at the Old Playhouse drinking with Flaherty, though in a more abstemious fashion than previously, occasionally joined by Saoirse, with Brazier watching the pair carefully to see if they were harbouring information he did not wish them to share. It was on his way back to the Navy Yard that he felt the change in the wind, the westerly swinging round to, he hoped, the north-east, which would bring clear skies and with it a half-moon.

Having gone to bed hopeful, he awoke to a sunny morning and the sure knowledge that if it held, he would be going to rescue Betsey tonight.

Total avoidance proved impossible and, unusually, Spafford had risen early enough to catch Betsey on the stairs as she came back from her walk. Unknown to her his consumption of drink had been severely curtailed by her brother, which rendered his morning head much clearer.

He was standing on the landing, an infuriatingly superior smile on his face, while he looked like he was not going to budge to let her pass. The knife, which went where she went, was wrapped in a muffler she had declined, over the last couple of days, to let Grady take with her cloak. Sarah Lovell, having seen to her return, was still in the hallway when the first words were exchanged and, on hearing them, she hurried to fetch her nephew.

'Get out of my way.'

'Is that the right manner in which to address your husband?'

'You are no more my husband than that newel post by which you're standing.'

'Do you not miss what you had with your Stephen?' When she looked angry, he added, still smiling, 'Henry told me all about him. Sounds rather pathetic to me, so happen I could bring to you that which he would have struggled to provide. In my company your screams would wake the house.'

The knife came out to be pointed at him. 'It will be your screams, Spafford, for your spilt guts, if you come anywhere near me. Now let me pass, so I can go to my room, unless that is what you wish for now.'

'Elisabeth.'

Henry's voice did not cause her to turn round. Her more pressing enemy was still before her and it was he who spoke, his tone jocular. 'She's threatening to stab me, Henry. I must say you have found me the most spirited wife. Bending her to my will should be a pleasure, my body even more so.'

'Go to your room, Harry.'

'Ah, my silken prison.'

'Do it,' was sharply delivered, not there to brook an argument. Spafford pulled a face and did as he was bid. As Betsey made to move, Henry spoke again. 'I think that knife be best handed over to me, Elisabeth.'

She spun round and glared at him, a look that encompassed Sarah Lovell who stood alongside him. 'Come close and it will be you who feels it.'

'I don't doubt you mean that, and I fear your dear aunt would not be safe from your ravings. So I will send a couple of people from the stables to take it off you. I doubt you'll stab a servant, you're too fond of the breed. If they fail to do so, they will pay the price of dismissal.'

'You bastard,' got Lovell hands to the Lovell lips in shock. On Henry, it had little effect.

'A category not unknown in our family, but I am not one of them. I am master in this house and, for you, controller of your fate. The knife?'

It was thrown at his feet, while she turned and fled to her room to lock the door, throw herself on her bed and break down in tears. In the hall, Henry picked up the blade and gave it to his aunt.

'This can go back to where it belongs. And perhaps Cook should be told to lock it away. Now, oblige me by telling Grady I want my coach ready in half an hour.'

The journey into Deal left plenty of time to reflect on all the matters concerning him, not least his sister's behaviour. Was it grounds to reckon her deranged and was that a solution to keeping her under control? He was on his way to a Lodge dinner and medical coves would be there too: one, indeed, had supplied him the drug used to subdue Elisabeth on her wedding night, never asking a question as to what it was to be used for.

He would consult with the fellow and, if it seemed favourable, it might be best acted upon. What to do then about Spafford was a problem of a different nature, but he was sure a solution could be contrived.

Brazier had the horses out of the stables and lined up ready to depart when Admiral Braddock appeared from Admiralty House, which had his inferior officer wave to prevent Dutchy and the others emerging carrying the muskets; even if they were wrapped in canvas, their shape would give them away.

'Off somewhere, Brazier?'

'A little jaunt with my old crew, sir,' was the forced reply of a mind scrabbling for an excuse, the one which emerged sounding feeble. 'If it takes me far enough, I may call upon Sir Eustace.'

'Long way to Pollock's, is it not?'

'We would rest the night there, sir, as I have done before.'

'Well, give him my best wishes if you do.'

With that, Braddock bustled off towards the Lodge and the dinner he was looking forward to attending, one in which the talk would not be exclusively nautical. Behind him, Brazier signalled to wait until he disappeared, before calling the lads out. Dutchy had a long length of rope coiled round his body, while Cocky had the grappling iron, the canvas-wrapped muskets being lashed on to the saddlery.

Peddler was his usual unhappy soul when it came to riding and Joe, who was a bit scared of horses, was told to mount Canasta, which Brazier would lead. On the way back, now the plan had changed, he would double up with Dutchy.

Sure that Braddock was well gone, they passed through the Navy Yard gate with a nod to the ex-tar in charge. By the time they passed Sandown Castle and hit the northern marshland, which would take them to Sandwich Flats, Admiral Braddock was on his second glass of wine. He was also deep in conversation with Henry Tulkington, wondering why the fellow kept looking over his shoulder, as if seeking out someone else, until he put it down to a less-than-polite habit.

'Rum business that riot the other day, Tulkington. Had to deploy some marines to make sure they never came near the Yard. You're lucky to live well away from such things.'

'That Brazier fellow was burnt out, I gather.'

'He was, and a body found in the embers.'

'I heard. All on the rumour of a connection to our First Lord of the Treasury.'

'Balderdash, as I keep telling anyone who will listen. Had to put him up at Admiralty House, so I'm seeing a bit more of him than I would strictly welcome.'

'Any more on that West Indies business you were telling me about?'

'No. Stuff and nonsense, probably. That said, he is an odd cove. Keeps men with him who were on his ship, which must be costing him a pretty penny. Loyal they are, too, though only the Lord knows why he's provided them with muskets. Some nonsense about hunting rabbits, one of my officers told me.'

The sudden pallor on Henry's face Braddock put down to genuine surprise.

'Saw him going off as I came here, his men as well, I should guess, given he had all their mounts out and saddled.'

'Hunting rabbits?' was not really a question.

'Damn silly weapon for it,' Braddock snorted. 'Hitting a barn door is trouble enough with a Brown Bess, never mind a scurrying rabbit.'

A voice from the dining room announced that dinner was about to be served and would the gentlemen take their seats, Braddock turning to look at the sound of the voice. When he spun round again to say it might well be an idea to get a refill before going in, it was to find Henry Tulkington gone.

The two lounging men, having a bit of a snooze inside his coach got a shock to hear him yelling, even more at the rush he was in. 'Get me to the slaughterhouse, now!'

The Lower Valley Road, which they took, was the usual mix-up of carts refusing to give way to each other and not fussy about which side they occupied. This made it a journey that had Henry thumping the opposite seat in frustration. On arrival, he leapt out and headed straight for John Hawker's upstairs office, to discover it empty.

Once back on ground level, it was 'Find him', to whoever was about, his coachmen included, which sent half a dozen people to scour Deal to locate him and, when he was found, to get him to hurry back to the slaughterhouse.

'Every man you can spare, John, to Cottington. And make sure they are armed.'

CHAPTER THIRTY

Brazier did not take to Dan Spafford on first acquaintance. Mind, he had still to warm to Daisy Trotter, so, when it looked as though they were going to discuss his business in front of their men, and that would include Betsey, he laid down an immediate objection.

'Another room.'

'What you frightened of?' Spafford demanded.

'Loose talk.'

Spafford shrugged and led the way to the room in which he had had occasion to lock up his son, not that such information was vouchsafed to him. That left Dutchy, Cocky, Joe and Peddler sharing less than pleasant glances with the Spafford gang.

'I take it Trotter has told you what has happened to your boy?'

'Fallen on his feet, by the sound of it. Mind, I expect the Tulkington bitch is too refined for his tastes.'

'I wouldn't go callin' her a bitch, Dan.'

'Why not?' he grunted.

'Because I might just put a ball in your skull,' Brazier spat. 'That is why.'

Spafford squared his shoulders as if ready for a fight. 'Never met a woman who was owt else.'

'Looking at you, I can see why.'

'Stop it, both of you,' Daisy pleaded. 'Think on the purpose.'

It took a few moments of mutual glaring before Brazier spoke, his voice tight.

'As I told Daisy, I want to get my lady out and away. Then you can walk through the open gate, but not before.'

'You comes it high and mighty, matey.'

Brazier realised he had a problem and it was in that remark that his son had fallen on his feet. It was a stupid slip of the tongue because it implied he was thinking about money, Betsey's money. He might not stick to the agreed bargain, as related by Trotter, because legally it belonged to Harry.

He had to keep a straight face as he gnawed on this, wondering if he would have to kidnap that sod to get what he wanted. Whatever he decided, this was not the place to make it happen. There had always been a risk he was delivering himself into the hands of some very unsavoury people, but the die had been cast and it was go forward or abort. Even that would be hard, given the numbers in this house, four times his own. They could just take the key Daisy knew he possessed.

'I struck a bargain, which I will stick to. All I ask is that you do likewise. Am I right to assume there will be no one guarding Cottington Court?'

'Never is, normally, though he arms his coachmen. Tulkington keeps the likes of Hawker away from the house. Feart of the connection becoming too well known. Pure as snow is Henry Tulkington, and beyond the reach of the law.'

'He was there the last time you tried to rescue Harry.'

'Happen he was forewarned.'

'Or clever enough to anticipate what you would do, once he had him.'

'Same thing. But he won't keep them around. Sets tongues waggin' that does.'

'Well, it should be safe enough tonight. But I ask again, will you stick with things as they have been arranged?'

That got a shrug. 'Why would I not? As long as I get my Harry and a bite at Tulkington, I will rest content.'

'What do you have in mind for him?'

'D'you care?'

It would not suit to have him murdered, that Brazier knew. He was too well known and seen as a pillar of the community. His death would not go unpunished and who knew how many would get caught up in that? But there was little point in saying so; it was not in his hands.

'No, I don't. You have weapons?'

Brazier meant his gang; Spafford had two pistols in his belt, one of which he patted. 'Primed and loaded. My lads have muskets.'

He pulled out his watch from his waistcoat. 'Time to go, then. The house should be well asleep by the time we get there.'

They could have taken the Canterbury Road part way, but Spafford said that was unwise, which left them following footpaths strange to the Brazier contingent. This killed off an idea he had to open a gap between them, for him to be there in time to get Betsey out of the house and on her way. Ideally and originally, he wanted to pass Spafford on the way out of Cottington and be well gone before anything else happened.

The notion of snatching Harry had to be abandoned. It would lead to a firefight and Betsey could be with him. If he couldn't get old man Spafford to stick to the deal, surely Betsey's own testament would be enough to ensure her assets were rendered untouchable? She didn't need them, anyway; he had more than enough for them both.

It was eerie riding along, with Bonnie picking her own route bar the odd tug on the bridle, the landscape around them bathed in a not very bright silvery glow of a half-moon and starlight. It had turned cold as the warmth of the day rose into the clear night sky. There was the occasional mumble from behind him and, once or twice, a curse as one of Spafford's men tripped on a hummock of grass or a tree root.

There was also the feeling of being cut off from reality, one often experienced at sea, where you could sail for weeks and not sight either land or another sail. That was rendered different by the odd hooting owl and, once they got closer to Cottington and Moyle's church, the swish of bats missing their heads by a fraction. Then the brick wall loomed up, black and forbidding, to be followed until they came to the north gate.

As they dismounted, Joe took the reins to hold the horses steady, while the weapons were untied and made ready for use. Dutchy uncoiled his rope, even in near darkness having no difficulty lashing it to the grappling iron.

It was then tossed skywards to grip on the top of the wall with a metallic clang that sounded as if it could be heard a mile away. Tugged until it dug into the brickwork Cocky, the most nimble of the four, took it from his mate and pulled himself up, 'til he could lean out and jam his feet on the wall.

Then it was an upwards walk until he got a leg over the top, the grappling iron being detached and reversed. Soon even Cocky's outline was gone as he slipped down the inside. Brazier was close enough to the high wooden gates to hear the movement of the chain as he sought the padlock itself, then the slot for the key.

There was an extended rattle as the chain was pulled out and seconds later one of the double doors opened. About to tell Spafford to wait, Brazier was nearly bowled over as the whole of his gang, their leader at the head, ran through the opening, leaving Brazier and his men to follow. There was no shouting, but a lot of cursing, to no purpose.

'Let's move. I don't want them getting to the house before us.'

He did not want to contemplate what might be the level of betrayal that had suddenly occurred. What if Spafford got to Betsey first, and took her as well as his son? What would he do then?

There was a pathway and Brazier could vaguely pick out the figures in front of him, they being in no rush. He, ahead of the others, had just caught up with the last of them, entering a sort of clearing in which the sky and stars were visible, when they were suddenly surrounded by lights, lanterns unshaded, with others holding either a pistol or a musket. Then came an unmistakable voice, speaking as if he was simultaneously laughing.

'Well, well. I seem to have caught a shoal, not just a few tiddlers as I expected. Harry, would you believe it? Your pa has come to try and rescue you again, which, I must say, I did not expect. And I'm sure I spy a certain fellow who is, along with those he pays, fond of 'hunting rabbits when not in pursuit of wealthy widows.'

'How in Christ's name—?'

Spafford was cut off before he could finish the question, not that he was left in want of an answer. Tulkington moved out to be visible, John Hawker beside him, both with cocked pistols.

'When are you going to learn that nothing happens in Deal of which I do not know?'

'Give me my Harry and this ends, Tulkington.'

'Have you asked yourself if he wants to be rescued? I assume you, Brazier, have not come on his behalf?'

'Your sister is a tool in a sham marriage, which I intend to expose.'

'What a fine pair of fools you are.'

That was an accusation that hit home to Brazier; whichever way he turned this sod seemed to be able to humbug him. Right now, he was wondering if a surrender of their weapons would suffice to get him and his men out unharmed. There was no point in continuing.

'Harry, boy,' Spafford pleaded. 'Come away with me. We'll leave peaceful and this bugger won't dare shoot.'

'Tempted as I am,' Tulkington said, 'the amount of explanation for so many dead bodies would be tedious. You're right, you may all leave in peace, without your weapons, of course.'

He paused before turning his gaze on Brazier.

'I wrote to tell you to get out of Deal, but you ignored it. If a warning, followed by a narrow escape from Quebec House, does not suffice I may have to resort to other measures. My sister is not for you and never will be, so get away from this part of the world.'

There was little point in saying if he had written a warning, it had not been received, and right now, it seemed Tulkington might be speaking the truth about Betsey, however hard it was to bear.

'But you, Spafford, if you ever smuggle so much as a bag of tea, I will crush you. We had a bargain, you broke it.'

'What say you, boy?'

Harry walked out into the pool of light, a sneer on his face. 'What, leave here?'

'Come home.'

'You call that hovel "home"? I reckon you can leave peaceful all right, but it will not be with me. Tell him, Henry. I could have walked out of here any time I wished. I ain't here 'cause I'm being held, I'm here of my own free will and happy so.'

'We're blood, Harry,' his father pleaded, the choking sounds of tears obvious. 'You're all I got.'

'More's the pity, if it be true. You don't see hate when it's staring you right in the face, but I hate you. It's my fond hope I never clap eyes on you again.'

With everyone looking at Dan Spafford, crestfallen and seeming to shrink as these words hit home, Daisy Trotter moved so quickly it took everyone by surprise. The fact that he had snatched one of Spafford's pistols from his belt, as well as cocked it, only became obvious when it was up and aimed, the trigger pulled when he was close to Harry Spafford.

'An end to this, you ungrateful little shit.'

The crash of the shot stunned everyone, but not as much as the hole that appeared in the centre of Harry's forehead. His eyes opened in shock before he began to crumple, his father pulling out his second pistol, surely with the aim of killing Daisy.

It was the wrong thing to do. Hawker grabbed Tulkington to drag him away, as near two dozen weapons spoke at once, which drowned out Daisy telling Dan he loved him.

Spafford went down before he could exact revenge, but Trotter took a number of balls anyway. It hardly needed Dutchy to grab and pull at Brazier, he knew it was time to run. The blow in his shoulder as he left the clearing was like being hit by a hammer, making him stagger forward, only held up by the strength of his old coxswain.

There was no time to register he had taken a wound, they had to get mounted and away, as behind them, those who had discharged their weapons were now seeking to club each other with the stocks to the sound of screaming imprecations. But some must be reloading and, when that was complete, they would not hesitate to shoot. Even a blind discharge could kill.

They made the gate with Brazier staggering but mumbling, 'Did any of you fire?'

A negative chorus greeted that. Brazier was glad all replied, despite knowing he was badly wounded enough to slow them down. Even fighting for breath, he gave clear orders.

'Get mounted and get away. Leave the muskets and I'll make sure you're not pursued.'

'Never, Capt'n.'

It took every ounce of effort he possessed to scream at them, 'That's an order, Holland. Damn you, obey it.'

'Gotta refuse,' Peddler shouted back.

'I won't be able to ride, you can. The shooting has begun and it won't stop.'

'Wrong way round, your honour,' Joe Lascelles cried out. 'Dutchy, Cocky, get him mounted.'

Brazier, despite his feeble protests, was grabbed and lifted, his cries of pain ignored. They got him in the saddle and put the reins in his hands, even if he was laying over Bonnie's neck and they hung loose. Peddler smacked her rump and set her in motion which, in a slight panic, became a very fast trot.

There was no direction and, if asked, Edward Brazier would never have been able to say how long he managed to stay mounted and where his horse took him. He became delirious, talking to himself about things that made no sense. Eventually he slid out of the saddle, one hand still gripping the reins, to roll onto his back and look up at the stars, cursing all and everything. He had fought many a battle; how could it come to this, to die in a field and not at sea?

As he lay there he heard gurgling water, a soothing sound that was close enough to wind-driven waves. With that in his ears he closed his eyes to slide into oblivion.

DAVID DONACHIE was born in Edinburgh in 1944. He has always had an abiding interest in the naval history of the eighteenth and nineteenth centuries as well as the Roman Republic, and under the pen-name Jack Ludlow has published a number of historical adventure novels. David lives in Deal with his partner, the novelist Sarah Grazebrook.